She was approaching the nerve wracking part for mos standing on the precipice. Th loosened by her feet, as it slid over the edge. Grinning with anticipation she pulled her longest rope over her shoulder, getting ready for the long decent to the ruins far below. Leaning out with her arms spread wide in a gentle dive, she let gravity have its way with her.

When she approached the bottom of her decent, she carefully slowed and directed the angle of her fall by kicking off of passing buildings. In this way, she carefully steered her descent into the carpet of skyscrapers littering the cavern's floor far below. She kicked another building, to correct the angle of her decent as the rope hissed hotly through her gloves. Her brake kicked up a racket in response to the abuse, as she kicked and pivoted in her controlled dive towards the ruins.

She landed with a spin and a jingle. The gear on her tool belt rattling together pleasantly, as it fanned from her hips as she spun. Having braked only at the last possible moment, she ate up her extra momentum by spinning in place. Touching down only lightly in the dust. Still holding tightly to the rope she'd ridden down, Ashley leaned back twirling. She watched as the long spiral of rope curled back to the surface far above her with a smile.

Ashley enjoyed spending the day exploring the wreckage of the sunken city. She spent a pleasant and productive morning salvaging treasures for the future, from the ruins of the past.

Even deeper still, memory stirred. A semi-conscious thought slithering to the surface of millennial slumber, long disturbed by epic dreams. Memories of times lost in the ancient past. Their recollection reawakened depths of loss, long ago released into forgetfulness. The half healed scars of time, pulled away once more by the half-conscious recollection of long past events. The memories sparking pain better left to the depths of time. Shifting again in an attempt to return to blissful slumber, the semi-conscious thoughts faded once more. Into endless epic dreams.

# Dragon Dreams

## A New Beginning

By Chandelle Hazen

Dedicated to the future generations of Earth.

May they have a healthy planet to live on.

# Prologue

When a large chunk of Greenland and most of Antarctica crumbled and melted with shocking speed, not only did the oceans rise but the chaos ensuing from the massive influx of cold fresh water, spurred the birth of natural disasters worldwide. The storms, tsunamis and hurricanes generated by the turbulent temperatures of the rising waters, devastated our species and our world, in what could only be called, an apocalypse.

Florida, San Francisco, most of New York, London, and the Netherlands were all wiped out in the course of forty-eight hours. Japan, Beijing, Shanghai, Calcutta, and Bangladesh, were swamped by massive tsunamis, hurricanes and unprecedented flooding. It all happened in such a short space of time that there was very little time to react. Only two days after the first announcements that Antarctica and the Northern Ice sheet were becoming increasingly unstable, hundreds of millions of people had lost their lives.

It was not unwarranted however, we had warning. Years of scientists saying that we had to change the way we lived. Yet, here it was, an abrupt end to our carefree civilization and the beginning of a new struggle. Just to survive here on earth.

In countries where they had systems of mass transit, such as buses, trains and airplanes, many were saved. Although as there had been so little time, only the first wave of evacuees were able to reach their destinations safely. The government officials and FEMA, together with the hastily assembled CCC or Climate Change Committee, had decided that the children came first. They were the future of the country. If our people were to survive, then the children had to survive.

So it was on their orders, that all of the children of coastal towns were taken from their parents and put on buses, trains and flown on planes as far inland as could be managed. All in the midst of innumerable and increasingly devastating, natural disasters.

As far as anyone knows, all who were left behind perished in the onslaught. For the storms did not pass, they came rolling in day after day, only increasing in ferocity. One another, with no moment of respite, no sign of relief. As the planet thrashed about, in what we

7

could only pray, were not her death throws.

The seas rising turbulently, the skies dark and thunderous, there seemed to be no end in sight to the disturbing changes in our atmosphere. The Midwest was tormented by twisters larger and more numerous than ever before and the coasts were swamped by tsunami after drenching tsunami. While the children of our country and the political leaders that had also fled to safe haven, could do nothing but huddle together in fear. Hoping against hope, to survive.

FEMA had provided what supplies they could to the shelters where the children had been sent, but each lay amongst teeming masses of other crying children. With each one of them asking plaintively for their parents, and wondering aloud when they could go home. Finally, after a seemingly indefinite time, the weather began to settle.

At first, everyone was relieved that the storms had finally abated, leaving a deathly stillness in their place. Anything was better than the incessant bombardment of ferocious weather, or so they thought at the time. As they finally emerged from their now cramped and stuffy shelters, they found the world that they had known, to have been completely transformed.

The land had been ravaged by rain and wind, and large areas were now scared by the passage of tornadoes. The abundant fields they had driven through to get here were now shallow muddy pools. While the roads that had led them to the shelter, had been torn up chunk by chunk, where tornados had crossed their paths.

"Oh my God..." The FEMA members murmured to themselves. No one had ever expected the devastation, to be so complete.

Once the adults gathered their senses, they met to discuss the situation. They decided that their only option was to try to get the kids to the nearest city. There, they would hopefully be able to contact their superiors for further support and instructions. Many of the buses had been damaged however, and a few were missing altogether. Presumably they had been taken off by the tornadoes heavy winds. So they crammed all the kids onto the remaining buses, with many left standing in the isles.

The children were stunned and exhausted by the course of events. Dispirited and overwhelmed by the devastation of their surroundings, they simply did as they were told. As the buses began their treacherous trek over broken roads, the children alternately cried to themselves and did their best to comfort one another.

The sight that greeted them when they finally reached the sought after city, was not a pretty one. It seemed that no building had been spared damage from the blasting winds, and as they drove further into the city, they found no signs of life there to greet them.

"It looks like a war zone..." Chuck said quietly to the woman driving his bus.

"Shhh... don't say things like that in front of them..." Her eyes darted towards the children not far behind them, some of whom were still crying. Many had fallen asleep on the long and arduous trek. Chuck covered his mouth with his hand and nodded, his eyes lingering on the sad crew of kids that they had saved.

*'Why?'* He wondered to himself. *'What did we save them for, if everything else has been destroyed?'*

"Look for a radio tower," Sherrie said sharply. "If there's any chance that we can get in touch with headquarters, then that will be our best bet." She looked herself as well, hoping to see a sign or a tower. Any indication of a communications station. Looking back Chuck saw the other buses were following their slow progress down abandoned roads, apparently as out of ideas as they were.

"If there's anyone left there to get in contact with." Chuck muttered to himself. Sherrie glared at him, so he shut his mouth. He still thought that it was unlikely that headquarters had fared any better than anywhere else they'd seen.

He did start to look though, keeping an eye out for a radio or television station, and eventually he was the one to spot it.

———

"Over there! To your left." A once brightly lit neon sign, now simply the cracked and hanging logo of a television station, was a few blocks up on their left. As the buses parked one by one, the adults gathered once more, to quietly discuss their options.

"It's going to be hard to move all of them at once, and it's going to be hard to keep them together." Chuck mentioned. He said that he didn't think that it was a good idea to take all the kids in with them, since they didn't know if there was going to be enough power to get a signal.

"Well we're not leaving them here alone! Besides, I don't think that any of them want to be alone right now. They'll stay together, that won't be a problem." Sherrie raised her voice as she turned to address the kids.

"OK, you guys, we're all gonna go into this television station. I need you all to stay together, and I need you all to stay calm and quiet. We're gonna try to get in contact with our supervisors so we can decide where to go next, all right?" She smiled as she said it, trying to project an aura of calm authority.

"What about my parents?" One little girl asked. "Can we call them too? H-How will they know where to find me, if we go in there? What if they go looking for me at the shelter?" She looked really concerned, and there were many smudges on her cheeks from tears.

"We'll find out as much as we can, about all of your parents, once we get in touch with headquarters. If anyone will know where they are and how they are, it will be FEMA." Again she tried to project a confidence, which she just didn't feel.

It was unlikely that any of their parents had survived, if the state of the city around them was any indication. Besides which she was pretty sure that power was down nationwide. She was hoping however, that there would be a backup generator somewhere in the building, or anything else that they might get to power a communication device. Anything would be better than nothing right now, and she was sorely aware of how few the rations were that they had left.

None of the other children argued, it seemed that they just didn't have the energy. After his initial comment Chuck just shrugged, seeming rather despondent himself. She sent him over to the other buses to let the other FEMA members know the tentative plan, while she orchestrated the careful disembarking of the overcrowded bus. She counted heads as they went by her, so that she would have a better idea of how far their rations would stretch and asked everyone to find a partner.

"Please hold hands at all times, it will make it a lot easier for us all to stay together that way." She scooted over to the other FEMA members and asked them to do the same, first counting heads and then assigning pairs.

As they filed inside, she took one last look around the ruined city. If there was anyone left alive here, they would no doubt come when they heard the generator kick on. She only prayed that whoever might be left here would not be too crazed with hunger and fear. She felt very protective of these kids.

They did find a backup generator in the basement. They had filed everyone through the building until they found a room large enough to accommodate them all. She asked Patty and Doug to hunt down food if there was any, and asked the others if any of them had any experience with electronics.

"What kind of experience are you looking for?" Ted asked her shyly.

"We need to know what the generator is hooked up to, so that we know whether it will work for what we need or not. We don't have much fuel to run the generator for long, and I'm nervous about the sound as well. So I'd like to make sure that it's worth it when we turn it on, if you know what I mean." She was hoping that she wouldn't have to explain.

She didn't want to be the only FEMA member there who was nervous about meeting up with more people who might need help. On the other hand, she had been at enough disaster relief sites to have seen the desperation people felt, when their accustomed surroundings were destroyed. As well as the sometimes unpredictable behavior that such desperation brought out in people.

"What do you mean?" Heather asked, "I don't get it. Are you just concerned about the lack of fuel?" She obviously sensed that there was more to the statement then that, but just as obviously, did not understand the implications. Sherrie sighed, but as she took a breath to respond, Jacob spoke up in her place.

"She means that the sound will attract any nearby survivors." He left it at that a moment, obviously waiting to see if Heather made the connection for herself.

"Isn't that a good thing? Shouldn't we be trying to find and help other survivors?" She seemed genuinely puzzled, and a little offended to have had to say it. That was just the reaction that Sherrie had not wanted directed at her. She was very grateful that Jacob had taken the lead in explaining this. She was already getting tired of acting the part of the leader, and she was glad to share the burden.

"While that's technically true," he said with a sigh, "we're in a very precarious position here. We have a whole lot of kids that have been entrusted to us and not enough food or water to keep them. On top of that, anyone who is still alive in this city has already been scrounging for weeks, battling ferocious weather and probably fighting with the other survivors here for food and resources as well.

They may not be all that friendly towards us for coming into town with more mouths to feed." He sighed again; it was obviously hard for him to say it.

It was against all of their nature to fear their fellow people; after all they were members of FEMA. It was each and every one of their jobs to care for those in need, and most of them had gotten into it because they liked to help people.

"Right now, keeping these kids safe needs to be our top priority. Even if it means protecting them from other people." Jacob said, and as he met her eye Sherrie smiled as reassuringly as she could. Heather looked very thoughtful, but she didn't say anything else, just nodded when Sherrie asked if she would help go look for food.

While the kids were occupied eating food raided from the vending machines the members had found, the FEMA crew cobbled together a radio and set it up just outside the room with the generator, to try to make contact. Eventually they did get a hold of a government official, who let them know the awful news.

That there were devastatingly few survivors.

# 1

Deep beneath the heat twisted concrete streets of Newcity, Ashley carefully worked her way forward. Testing her footing and checking each handhold before trusting her weight to it, as she climbed ever deeper beneath the broken surface far above. Secure in her next step, she reached back to tug her rope for a little slack. Its long stretch whispered along the rough maze of cracks stretching out behind her, slithering into its new position as she pulled.

Confident now that she had enough slack to move forward, she made her way one step at a time, through the vast network of crazed rock. Already far beneath the city itself, she planned to go deeper still. After spelunking her way through the broken subsurface of Newcity's bedrock, she would repel into the collapsed buildings far below.

In the devastating earthquakes that followed the ferocious storms of the initial climate shift ten years ago, the entire northwest section of the city had suddenly collapsed. Without warning, it had fallen into a cavern in the bedrock the city was built upon. As the surface buckled and crumbled under the force of the quake. The unexpected collapse of this area took with it several city blocks.

Which ten years later, was now a veritable treasure trove of salvageable hardware, for anyone willing to make the effort. She was not the only one who mined the abandoned ruins far above her for useful objects. That abandoned outer ring of Newcity, now known as the outskirts, since they surrounded the city's currently active center. The area she was heading for today however, was almost untouched by other salvagers. It was inaccessible, in a way that the rest of the abandoned outskirts of Newcity were not.

She stepped over cracks, hopping or climbing when she had to. She spat out the grit that fouled her mouth, as she worked her way relentlessly forward. She knew the way, and she was almost to her final point of decent. She had come this way any number of times over the years. Ever since Old Tom had offered her his hand drawn maps of the cracks. He had explained just what it took to descend to the remains of the sunken city. She licked the dusty sweat from her lips. The day was uncomfortably warm already, even though the sun had only just risen. She continued to make her way closer to the edge of the gaping maw ahead.

As she scrambled through the ravaged edge at the lip of the cavern left by the city's collapse, still far above the sunken ruins below, she allowed one corner of her mind to wander. Wondering where her friend Jen was today. This was the part of the climb, threading through the cracks, which Jen had really balked at. Even before Ashley had mentioned the occasional remains she came across in her excursions to the sunken suburb, Jen had shaken her head at the cracks.

Ashley knew she was taking a risk. She would have no options if there were another earthquake while she was here, but she'd been lucky so far. As had Old Tom before her. So she did it despite the danger. She enjoyed the opportunity to follow his old routs, now that he was no longer able to make the climb.

She lamented silently the lack of communication these days though, wanting to talk to her friend. She remembered back before the climate shifted ten years ago, how her mom's cell phone had made things like getting together or checking in so easy. She sighed, at her inevitable thoughts. That was then, things had changed. Even once the survivors of the devastation, had gathered the resources to reestablish communications, first locally and then globally, the ever increasing solar storms had made all of their efforts moot. The vicious electromagnetic storms knocked out system after system, as survivors worldwide tried to reestablish functional use of their old electrical grids.

The solar flares however, increased not only in frequency but in ferocity, making even the most basic of infrastructure impossible to maintain. The lawmakers of Newcity had made the decision that such complicated communications systems would be limited to the use of the lawmakers themselves and their enforcers, since it took so many resources to maintain them.

Leaving peons like herself, having to run around like a headless chicken just to get together with a friend. She sighed again, reliving her frustration at missing Jen again yesterday. She had really hoped to connect with her. She was brought fully back to the moment though, by her drop off point coming into view ahead. She was finally approaching the edge.

This would be the most nerve wracking part for most people.

She loved it. Standing on the precipice, the trickling sound of tiny bits of rubble slipped over the edge, loosened by her feet. Her eye was drawn not to the rugged landscape of the broken city far below, but to the ragged expanse of the craters edge beyond the gap. It was so far across; she couldn't even make out the details of the other side's debris strewn rim.

Grinning with anticipation, she pulled her longest rope over her shoulder. She got things ready for her decent to the ruins far below. Once prepared she leaned out beyond the edge with her arms spread wide in a gentle dive and let gravity have its way with her. As she eventually applied her brake, in short bursts, to eat up her extra momentum, she paused to get her bearings and check the time.

Slowing to a stop she set the break on the rope, dangling. Her weight was held firmly by the harness around her hips, still far above the crumpled skyscrapers. She checked the buildings below her against Old Tom's map, and dug out her pocket watch. It was a beautiful antique. Salvaged from the ruins below by Old Tom himself, it was solid and heavy in her hand. Flipping it open she saw that it was still early. She would have hours to explore down here, before she'd have to head back to work.

She had left at first light, to ensure she would have the time to make it worth the trip. She didn't work until mid-afternoon today. So she had decided to get some spelunking in this morning, before she had to stand still for hours. Eyeing the remains of the sunken city below her, she chose a spot to land and released the break. She carefully controlled her fall, kicking off of passing buildings to correct the direction of her decent. While the rope hissed hotly through her gloves. Her brake kicked up a racket in response to the abuse as she kicked and pivoted in her controlled fall, to the street she'd chosen as her starting point.

She landed with a spin and a jingle. The gear on her tool belt rattling together pleasantly as it fanned from her hips. Having braked only at the last possible moment, she ate up her extra momentum by spinning in place. Touching down only lightly in the dust, she still held tightly to the rope she'd ridden down. Leaning back, she twirled watching as the long spiral of rope curled back to the surface far above her. She was so grateful for Old Tom's guidance, or she would never have made it down here. She had no idea where he had gotten all his climbing gear but the ropes alone were priceless.

She grinned, relishing in the glory of being outside and free to move around as much as she wanted. She couldn't wait to see what this new area she'd chosen to explore had to offer. Loosening her rope and removing her harness she tied the rope off to a twisted spike of rebar protruding from a crumbling chunk of cement. It was just one of many, a piece of one of the buildings that had not survived the sudden drop intact.

More than half of the buildings had collapsed into rubble either on the way down or upon impacting with the cavern floor hundreds of meters below. Some of them however, mainly the tallest most closely knit buildings had supported one another in their fall. Though now cracked and crazed with faults, the walls remained relatively upright. The dark broken windows looked like many unseeing eyes in the lifeless towers. The buildings still stood though, leaning drunkenly against one another like old comrades.

Smiling at her own analogy, Ashley set out. She had chosen a new direction to explore today. She focused in this first pass on the doorways of any standing buildings, dismantling their hardware. Porch lights, doorknobs, hinges, frames. Anything she could easily remove intact she did, making tidy little piles of her spoils beside each door.

This was an exploratory mission. She was exploring an area that neither she, nor Old Tom had looked through before, so she was simply marking her trail. She would find her way back to her rope by collecting the best of what she'd found at each site, until her pack was full. She would come back to collect the rest on another day.

She could trade all of these things to Old Tom for trade goods or to the hardware store if she needed City Credits. All unnecessary combustion had been made illegal several years ago, due to its harm on the atmosphere. So cast metal had become exceedingly precious. Since there were now no forges to make more.

Whistling to herself, her tools tinkling together with every step, Ashley explored deeper into this unknown area of the sunken city. Scrambling over rubble, exploring and dismantling as she went, she spent a pleasant and productive morning salvaging treasures for the future, from the ruins of the past.

———

Even deeper still, far below the surface of the world; deep inside the protective planetary crust of the molten fire within, memory stirred. A semi-conscious thought slithering to the surface of millennial slumber, long disturbed by epic dreams. Memories of times lost so far in the ancient past that their very recollection reawakened the depths of loss, long released into forgetfulness.

Writhing in an agony of remembrance, in the face of those freshly opened wounds of the heart. The half healed scars of forgetfulness, pulled away once more by half-conscious recollection of long past events. Pains better left to the depths of time. Shifting again in an attempt to return to blissful slumber, the semi-conscious thoughts faded once more, into endless epic dreams.

———

Ashley thought back to the tremors she had felt while at work this afternoon. She reflected on the timing of the earthquakes. Tremulous as they'd been, if they had come this morning while she'd been threading through the cracks on her way to the drop off point. Well, things could have gone very differently. Sighing to put it out of her mind, she set her dishes in the sink. It had been a very long day. After spelunking the sunken city this morning, she had spent several hours haggling and trading her finds, with Old Tom. She had almost stayed there too long. She enjoyed hanging out at his pawn shop so much, that she was almost late for work.

Stretching her arms out wide, Ashley yawned. Her shoulders and legs ached from the long climb back to the surface, but it was a good ache. It let her know she was alive. Shaking her head, she tried to bring herself back to the moment. Taking notice of her digital gallon counter she saw there was 4.6 remaining. There was less than half of her daily allotment left and it was only sunset. She had no idea how people managed without one. It had been well worth the effort to make it. There was no way to pace your water usage without knowing how much water you used at a time. She wondered idly if she should do her dishes yet.

Having just finished a homegrown salad, freshly picked from her balcony garden, she decided not to wash up yet. Instead, she snagged her sketch pad and a precious sliver of charcoal. Drawing pad in hand, she settled herself on her little balcony overlooking the street four stories below. The other refurbished tenements across the way, didn't leave much breathing space but that's just how it was here in the heart of Newcity.

It was equally crowded amongst the pots she sat between. Since the balcony itself was such a tiny space to begin with. She had left herself a little niche amongst the plants however, were she could sit to eat or draw. As she settled herself gingerly onto the cushion she kept there, the green beans on their trellis brushed her arm in a soft caress. She smiled at the touch and picked a bean. She munched its juicy sweetness quietly, as she let her gaze shift out over the city.

People were just turning their lights on, as the sky to the east darkened. She loved this time of night. If she let her eyes tear up a bit and squinted through her lashes, she could imagine that the twinkling lights were stars. She missed the stars. She had often stared into their depths, with her parents as a child. They would lie on the beach in front of their house and count them as they fell. It was a pity the stars could no longer be seen, through the omnipresent cloud cover. The twinkling lights were beautiful to her, despite the sounds and smells of too many people crammed into too small of a space. She leaned heavily against the tomato pot, taping one finger on her empty page.

'*What should I work on?*' She wondered to herself.

There were some projects that she'd half thought up, including one for Jen's next birthday but that didn't feel right. So instead she shut her eyes and blanked her mind, hoping for a glimmer of inspiration.

Eyes flashed into her mind. Big, beautiful, glowing eyes. She kept her own eyes tightly shut, as she listened to her coal scratching along the page. She mentally explored the edges of the face. She could almost see and felt her drawing hand mirroring her inner explorations.

It was a strange face, angular, and spiky. She wondered for a moment if it was some kind of animal. She couldn't really see it all at once. It was as though she held a lantern in the dark and as she moved it around the face; she could see only a small piece illuminated at a time. As she came back to the eyes she tried hard to distinguish their color, but they shifted and changed in the light, pink one moment, blue or green the next.

She tried to get a little closer, hoping to distinguish it further with the light of her mind. As she mentally approached however, the eyes turned to look at her, rather than through her. Her breath caught at the intelligence and sorrow that she saw there. It startled her into opening her own eyes and losing the connection.

"Damn it Ashley!" She muttered quietly to herself.

That had been very different from the sorts of things she usually found in her meditations. Never before had she felt that the image she was exploring in her consciousness, was also conscious of her, or had it respond to her mental movements that way. For long minutes she sat there, eyes closed, with her mind blank but for her residual frustration. She was hoping to miraculously recapture the image, or reconnect with the curious creature. But there was nothing to be found, save the darkness of her mind.

Sighing she gave up for now, moving on to a different visualization technique. Focusing on one tiny spot in her mind, she opened it, letting a little glittering light in. Then she moved to another and another, painting her mind until she had reached the limit for what could fit in her imagination at once. She mentally stepped back to admire her handiwork. The glittering night's sky she'd carefully crafted filled her mind, and her breath caught at the beauty. She felt herself smiling and feeling a bit fanciful after her experience with that interesting face, she included a bright shooting star.

She let it sail gently across her minds sky, landing ever so softly in the water illuminated by its sudden light. The fallen star's glow diffused slowly, fading into a cerulean smudge in the otherwise black water of her inner sea. She imagined the sound of the ocean waves breaking gently upon the shore. She imagined that she heard the roar of the wind in her ears, as she allowed her feet to touch down on the illusory sand. The shore was glittering silver, when she finally tore her gaze, from the beauty of the stars. She decided to sit there at the water's edge a while. She paddled her feet in the gently lapping waves, which were warm, like it had been in the summer when she was a girl. That was when she had still been able to live by the sea. When her parents had still been alive and no one knew yet, what disasters were to come.

The stray thought broke her visualization. The beautiful image of stars and sea shattered, leaving her mind in lonely darkness once again. Her eyes were damp as she opened them to the true darkness of the night. The sun's light having finished fading while she was lost in her own thoughts. She squinted to make the lights of her neighbors seem as stars again, but she had lost her ability to enjoy it.

Instead she was haunted by the memories of her mother,

sobbing her goodbyes. While her father had ran along the train tracks, yelling.

"We'll come find you! I love you! We love you!!"

That had been the last time she had seen them. As Ashley and the other children of her seaside home were born away from everyone they knew. Away from all that she had ever known. Just before the water had come and washed it all away.

It was too much. Her breath shuddered with suppressed sorrow. She had trouble shaking the grief this time. She physically shook her head, taking a deep breath and holding it. After a few moments her heart began to calm, and she let the breath out again slowly. She wiped at her eyes and lifted her chin, determined not to spend the whole night in this fowl funk.

She smacked her own cheek lightly, to bring herself back to the present and spoke aloud to herself.

"Alright Ashley! Let's get those dishes done."

She was definitely not going to eat again now. Her stomach was a hard little knot of unshed tears. She was afraid that if she started crying, she wouldn't stop. As she went inside, she absentmindedly set her sketch pad on the table, trying again to regain control of her emotions. Bustling over to the sink, she turned on the light as she went. The dim illumination only pushed back the darkness a little within her tiny studio apartment. The low energy bulbs that the lawmakers supplied could not compare to the incandescence or fluorescent bulbs of her childhood. Although any light was better than no light, she supposed.

As she filled her little tub for washing, she watched her gallon counter to make sure that she used no more than half a gallon to wash with. That way she would still have enough to rinse with. She added a little of her homemade soap to the water swishing it with her fingers to make if bubble. With her mind rather blessedly blank, she began the mundane task of washing each dish. She set each one in the other half of the sink to await the rinse, and when she was done she used the water to wash out the sink and to wipe down the counters as well.

She looked around and didn't see anything else that needed to be cleaned. So she took the little tub into the bathroom and added it to the flush tank. She had long since disconnected the automatic fill for the toilet tank. That way she could control how much water it used, instead of just leaving it up to the design of the machine.

Having been designed before the climate shifted, it took several gallons to fill the flush tank. Which were several gallons more than she was willing to spare, from her ten gallons a day allotment. She'd have four gallons left once she finished the dishes. Once she had set aside her gallon to bath with and a half gallon for drinking till morning, she might still be able to skim a little off for her emergency water jugs.

She had collected herself a small army of jugs, in which she put any water she had left from her ration each day. Those ten gallons a day was all you got, regardless of how much or how little you'd used the day before. So she saw no reason to waste what was hers by right. If she had any left each day, she stored it in her little apartment with her. Just in case.

Once the dishes were all rinsed and set in the rack to dry, she took her little rinse tub out to her potted plants and carefully shared the remaining water amongst them. She concentrated on the plants that she knew needed it most. The tomatoes and the green beans both got some, since they were making fruit, and her lettuce and her other greens got a little as well.

She scraped away the thin layer of homemade mulch, which she dried and shredded by hand from any fallen leaves her plants dropped and stuck her finger into each pot to see who was the driest. Those were the ones that got what was left, before she went back in and set the little tub in the dish rack to dry.

Having long forgotten about her sketch, she was thoroughly exhausted by the fight with her emotions. So Ashley decided to go to bed early. She drew her rationed water, setting aside some for drinking and elected to skip her bath. She put the remaining three and half gallons into one of her jugs, which was now almost full.

She tightened the cap and with her gallon counter on the tap now glowing a bright red zero behind her, she turned off the light, flopping onto the futon on her belly. She took a deep breath and closed her eyes. She was already feeling lightheaded and still on the verge of tears. So she repainted the inner image of her night's sky in her mind once more. As she fell asleep, she felt as though she was falling slowly, ever deeper, into space.

When she dreamed however, she dreamed of the eyes. She

dreamed of those glittering glowing, rainbow eyes, watching her.

———————

Matt had awoken from another strange dream of fire.

*'Or was it molten rock?'* He'd been talking to someone but it had sounded like singing or humming. Unlike any words he'd ever heard awake. He had been happy, he'd felt loved. He'd felt like he had been with his family. The barren dusty room he saw as he opened his eyes, reminded him of how untrue that was. He was alone. He had always been alone. Sighing, he rolled himself out of bed.

Michael looked up from his work when he heard the bell ring, but seeing it was only Matt and not an actual customer, he bent his head back to his task. Matt was used to his friend ignoring him in favor of his projects. So he idly wandered the shop, admiring the different instruments displayed there. He knew that Michael would say hi once he'd reached a place in his work where he could easily stop.

As Matt wandered the isles of his friend's store he let his eyes wander unfocused across the various books, instruments, strings. He admired rows of picks, pre-climate shift catalogs and other music related gear. He stopped to admire a particularly beautiful guitar on the rack, shining in the stores coveted full spectrum lights. This guitar was the one that Michael had finished most recently. He picked it up and strummed it experimentally, the sound resonated to his very core. He sighed with a smile.

*'What a great sound.'* He thought, as he started to set it back where he'd gotten it from. To his delight Michael spoke up from behind the counter.

"Feel free if you'd like to play, it won't distract me." Michael hadn't even looked up from his carving, but he was obviously aware of every movement that Matt had made. "You know I'd actually love to hear you play that one. She's a beauty and I'm the only one who's played her so far. At least that I've heard." He continued working, his head bent over the neck of the violin he was working on. He was intently focused but not distant.

Matt picked the guitar up again, cradling it against him. She sure felt sweet in his arms. Her finish was soft and smooth under his gently exploring fingers. He decided to take Michael up on his offer. It wasn't often that he had the opportunity to play such a beautifully crafted instrument. He carefully made his way to the back, where Michael was working, and sat gingerly on one of the empty stools. He held his hand across the strings to keep them silenced, as he thought about what to play. He went through several ideas, Pearl Jam, Rolling Stones, the Beatles, but finally settled on an old Jeff Buckley song that he wasn't sure Michael had heard before.

He was hoping to entertain him as well as surprise him, since Michael had let him play the guitar. He hummed the vocal melody under his breath as he played, keening quietly to himself on the high notes. When he took a moment to peak, he saw Michael was nodding his head to the tune as he carved, with a very pleased smile on his face. When he came to the end of the song and the cords slowed and drew into silence he sat quietly, letting the last hum of the song vibrate through him before he opened his eyes with a sigh.

"That was fantastic Matt," Michael said quietly. He always spoke quietly it seemed, as though he was shy or something. Matt supposed that maybe Michael was shy, with other people. Although they had known each other for so long he wasn't shy at all with Matt himself. He thought of Michael like a brother, he'd known him for so long. In fact, meeting Michael at the shelter was one of Matt's earliest memories.

"Do you know that one?" Matt asked. He was really hoping for a no. It was always a treat to be able to introduce Michael to a new song. He seemed to know them all, even the oldest of the oldies that Matt had sought out at the library. Matt had spent years now trying to surprise him. Matt wanted to make Michael feel that same thrill that Matt had felt, when Michael had first played for him all those years ago.

Michael had somehow managed to keep hold of his violin, even through the chaos of the shift. When he had played it for Matt, in their room together at the orphanage Matt had never heard music performed live before. At least that he could remember and it was one of his best memories from their years there together. Staying up late, listening to Michael play the violin or the guitar once he got one. The guitar had been a gift from a kind man who had heard of Michael's playing and wanted to encourage him. The music had seemed like magic to Matt then. It was long before Michael had offered to teach Matt himself how to play.

He waited expectantly now, watching Michael's face for his

reaction, bent as it was over his carving. He knew the answer before Michael spoke though. The look on his face answered as clearly as words. Michael looked up from his work with a rueful smile.

"Sorry, but yeah." He smiled, knowing full well that Matt was trying to impress him. It had been a running joke between them, ever since they left the orphanage. Matt would spend hours at the library looking up old music, trying desperately to find another fantastic old song that no one played anymore. Hoping to find something new to Michael, but it was very rare indeed that he had done so.

"Jeff Buckley, right?" He chuckled at the look on Matt's face. "Did you check out his dad too while you were there?" He laughed out loud as Matt's jaw dropped his irritation palpable.

"Tim Buckley had some really amazing stuff too, not quite as moody though..." Michael smiled down at his carving as though not really seeing it. Instead probably relishing the look on my face, Matt thought with a frown. "You should check him out some time." Michael said it casually but his grin was real.

"Is there anything you don't damn well know about music?" Matt asked in aggravation. He asked that a lot and Michael's answer was always the same.

"Of course there is!" Michael seemed almost angry about it. "There will always be more to learn and even more, that I just can't remember!" He growled, seemingly angry at himself this time. Matt grimaced, chagrined. He had known the answer before he asked but he always asked it anyway. It was just so frustrating sometimes. It always seemed that no matter how much he studied or how hard he worked, Michael always knew more than he did. He sighed to himself. '*And he always would,*' he realized. He grinned as the thought though.

'*That's what keeps me going. That's what keeps me studying, and struggling, and practicing. The thought that someday, I'll be able to surprise him. In fact...*' As the thought struck him, he quickly turned his head to hide his smile.

"Oh yeah? Well how about this one!" He strummed the guitar once, checking its tuning more out of nerves than any need to make sure it was tuned. He hadn't shared this song with anyone yet but if he was going to play it for anyone, it might as well be Michael.

He took a deep breath and started tapping a time with his toe.

He kept his eyes shut tight. He was afraid that seeing any kind of reaction on Michael's face might make him loose his nerve. So he began to play the slow soft introduction to the song he had been working on for months. He couldn't help it; the song demanded the counter melody so he crooned it softly. Wordlessly singing, quietly enough that he knew his song wouldn't leave the shop. He definitely wasn't ready to share it with strangers just yet. He needed to see what Michael thought first but he didn't want him to know it was an original, yet.

He could tell by the lack of scraping sounds, that Michael had actually stopped working and was paying very close attention. Matt tried not to think about that and instead immersed himself fully in the song, letting the images and colors brought up by the sounds, roll through his mind. It was as though he was swimming through another world. One that he had created, in his dreams.

A world of beauty and color and light. A world of wonder and friendship and flight. His hands easily played the chords he'd put together, almost of their own accord. He had played it so many times now; that the song came effortlessly to him. The melody followed the humming of the song he had heard in his dream. It described wordlessly, the fiery worlds in which he swam and flew when he was sleeping at night.

As the song slowly drew to a close, just as in the beginning the notes came few and far between. The resonance was as much a part of the song as the notes themselves. As he came fully back to his body he realized to his horror, that just like when he'd played it at home, his face was wet with tears. The song had brought with it a wonder and a sorrow that he could not escape. As the last note grew silent and the resonance slowly stilled, he sniffed, running the back of his hand across his cheeks. He was embarrassed, but there was nothing he could do about it now.

This was one of the reasons, that he'd been so hesitant, to share this song with anyone. He had been trying for weeks now, to play it through without crying but he invariably lost himself in the song and when he was done, his face was wet every time. He cleared his throat roughly and coughed a few times trying to gather the nerve to open his eyes. To face the judgment of the one person in his life that really mattered to him. He heard Michael sigh, cough and wipe his face.

That startled Matt into opening his eyes and he found that

Michael too had tears on his cheeks. Matt was really surprised. He had rarely seen Michael cry, in all the many years they had known each other. It was even more rare that he would cry over music, but there was no mistaking it. Michael was rubbing his eyes and clearing his throat just like Matt was. When their eyes finally met, he looked just as sheepish about it as Matt felt.

"I've, uhm..." Michael cleared his throat and tried again. "I've, uh, never heard that one." He looked very somber. When Matt met his eyes, they seemed haunted or shadowed with memory. Just like Matt himself felt, whenever he played that song. Or had those dreams. "I really liked it though. No I loved it!" He corrected himself. "Who is it by? Where did it come from?" He ran one hand across his face, his wood gouge hanging forgotten in the other.

"It seems vaguely familiar somehow." He muttered. "Like something, I've heard in my dreams." He trailed off, staring into space. He just looked puzzled but Matt was startled by his last comment. He stared hard at him until Michael noticed his gaze.

"What is it? What's wrong?" Matt could hear the concern in Michael's voice. It gave him a pang of emotion, realizing just how much Michael cared about him.

"So who wrote it? I want to know if I've heard it before. Tell me! Come on, the suspense is killing me!" He was trying to lighten the mood, Matt realized. He smiled.

"I did." Matt said slowly. "I, uh, I heard it in a dream…" Their eyes met, as the significance of the statement sunk in. They stared at one another in surprised silence.

Later that night, not long before dawn, Matt trudged slowly back towards his apartment. His head hanging with fatigue, his groceries swinging heavily from his fist. Work had been dead slow tonight. No one had come in at all on his shift and he'd finished stocking up instant breakfasts and canned foods far too quickly. He made it through his entire shift without seeing a single customer.

He was able to spend almost half an hour repacking. Unwrapping boxes and cans from the cases they came in, and reorganizing them for individual sale. There was so little required to run the little convenience store though, that he had soon seen to all of his duties. He had even swept up a bit, just to kill some time. All of his duties that is, except to simply be present, all night. There to ring someone up, just in case anyone came in. It was a boring job even when he'd been working days and had gotten to deal with customers. There were still far too few to fill the day, even then. So he spent a lot of time hunched over the music magazines that he bought from Michael.

It was especially long and boring on the night shift. Even with his new magazine to keep him company. He had soon found his attention wandering and his eyes drooping stubbornly. Although he'd really done his best to stay alert throughout his shift he had still managed to fall asleep out of sheer boredom, sitting upright no less.

He'd come awake with a start, at the sound of the bell on the door. Although it was only the person on the next shift, much to his chagrin. He'd quickly bought himself a bag full of food. Choosing mostly instant breakfasts and open and eat soups, before heading home himself. He didn't recall any dreams from his nap at work but the curious thought brought him back to Michael's comment last night, about Matt's dream song.

*'What did Michael mean? When he said that he'd heard that song in his dreams too?'* He wondered as he walked head low, contemplating his thoughts. *'Is that even possible? Can people share dreams?'*

He wasn't sure what to think. Part of him was deeply relieved. He had been half fearful of mentioning his dreams to Michael, because he thought he might be a little crazy.

*'I mean really.'* He thought, shaking his head cynically. He imagined himself saying, "So I've been dreaming about flying through fire every night, sometimes I even swim through it!" He shook his head at the only possible reaction to such a story. The brilliant green of the clouds above caught his attention for a moment. The turquoise glow of the sky contrasted sharply with the orange light of the energy efficient streetlamps lighting his way. Turning his attention inward once more he continued his thoughts.

*'Hmm, I think I may have been the one that was doing the singing too. So if Michael had heard it that would argue that we really are actually sharing the same dream. We're not just having similar dreams. We're actually sharing our dreams, and not just once or twice, but every night!'*

He chuckled to himself, shaking his head at how crazy it sounded, even though it was true.

*'No, I was sure that he'd think I was nuts if I mentioned it. I mean, flying through fire every night? Dreaming of another world? But to hear that he's having*

*similar dreams, well...*' He let the thought trail off unfinished. Somehow though, he felt reassured of his sanity, none the less.

# 2

Jen was nursing her shot of rice wine moonshine in the farthest corner of the Underground that she could crawl into. Her head was still splitting from her over indulgences the night before. So since, as everybody knew, the best cure for that was more of the same. Here she was in the early afternoon, nursing her second shot of the day to try to cure yesterday's ills, when a stranger entered the Underground. So called because it operated illegally on the edge of the Outskirts, as they called the abandoned buildings left empty and derelict surrounding Newcity proper. The young stranger was dirty, dusty and dressed entirely in leather.

*'Those must be disgusting in this heat.'* She thought. *'Why would anyone wear such thick clothes this time of year?'* She shook her head at his foolishness but was immediately sorry that she had. She caught her breath as the pounding in her head increased. Sipping her drink and shading her eyes to try to ease the pounding in her head, she missed seeing his next movements. Once her head had calmed down enough that she felt it safe to uncover her eyes again, she saw that he was deep in earnest conversation with the bartender.

After a moment the bartender nodded and waving the young man behind the bar with him, they disappeared together through a door behind the bar. She dismissed them from her thoughts, although she eyed what was left of her shot warily, wondering just how long the barkeep was likely to be gone. As often seemed to happen though, her very desire not run out, made her sip at it all the faster. So no sooner had the barkeep returned, then she had finished her shot off and needed another.

She stood slowly so as not to upset her head. She waited a moment, clinging to the table trying to get her bearings, through the fog of pain between her eyes. It was then that she realized that wherever the men had gone to through that door, only the barkeep had returned. As she made her way to the bar for a refill the question tickled at her sore and sodden mind. As she slid her glass across to the bartender and he silently filled it with more of the same, she couldn't help letting the question slip out.

"Was that fellow a friend of yours Jack? I haven't seen him around before. He was kind of cute." She said, as an excuse to have brought him up. She smiled a little and rubbed her blurry eyes. She hoped that she wasn't going to offend him by talking about something privet but she'd had to ask. Jack just slid her shot glass back across the bar to her though, full this time. He nodded when she met his eyes. By that she took it to mean that it was supposed to seem that the young man had vanished. In fact by his silence, she took it to mean, that the young man had never even been here at all.

Taking a sip of her rice wine, she nodded to acknowledge his silence.

"I see. Good drink." She smiled at him and was happy to see him grin back at her. Lifting her small glass, she made her way back to her small corner table and sat again with her back pressed to the wall. She hoped that the fact that he'd returned her smile meant that she hadn't pissed him off with her question. His silence made it clear however, that she shouldn't ask again.

Unfortunately that only made her even more curious about the young man and where he had gone. Deciding it was helping to distract her from the headache, she allowed her imagination to dwell on the possible answers to the quandary.

She came up with many imaginative ways he could have escaped, via trapdoors or magic portals, each theory less likely than the last. Yet somehow, it wasn't until she was riding her bike back towards her apartment, that the wind of her passage seemed to clear the cobwebs from her mind and she finally put two and two together.

She thought again about his dirty clothes and their secretiveness, as well as the fact that he didn't want to be seen leaving the bar. It all meant that he was probably one of the Nomads or Traders that supplied the bar with the alcohol and tobacco for sale.

Of course he'd be secretive. Since it was all illegal. And of course he'd be dirty, if he'd just come in out of the wastes. Feeling quite clever for having thought the mystery through, she dismissed it from her mind. Rising on her pedals she hurried home, so she could lie in a puddle of drunken bliss, until it was time for work.

———

Turning away from the back door of the Underground, Jimi wheeled his motorcycle around silently in place. His now empty side car made the maneuver far more difficult then it needed to be in the narrow alley. His father was a half-step behind him, with his own bike. Now they would head back out to where they had stashed the rest of the trade goods, in an empty building on the outskirts.

It was too risky to use the bike engines this close to the city. At best they could get their bikes confiscated, since all combustion engines where long since illegal within the city limits. So they always conducted their deliveries in stages. First they moved everything to one of their bases. They had several bases out on the edge of the old city, now commonly known as the Outskirts.

The Outskirts were where the crumbling, long abandoned buildings brushed up against the desert wastelands surrounding the reanimated corpse of the inner city herself. Those wretched wastelands were all that was left of what had once been rich agricultural fields. Or so he'd been told. Now that they had delivered the last of the moonshine and cigarettes to the bar, it was time to begin delivering the other packaged food they'd managed to scavenge this trip. His people searched for any canned or stored food in the ruins of other now long dead Cities.

For the next stage in their deliveries, they had to enter Newcity proper. They came to here to trade with grocery store clerks and restaurant owners, so they had to stash their motorcycles when they went back to their base. They smacked the worst of the desert dust from each other and began loading the bicycle trailer and the hand pull cart with cases of canned goods and other non-perishable food. They had scavenged as much as they could from the other, no longer operational cities en-route to this one bringing what food supplies they could.

Jimi reflected on the state of the world and how it had come to be this way for a moment but only for a moment. Then he was far too busy trying to keep the pull cart balanced and to keep himself moving forward. As he followed his dad out on the long trek, into the working heart of Newcity.

———

Ashley shifted her left foot as surreptitiously as possible, trying to ease a cramp in her calf without moving. She wasn't allowed to move of course, not right now, not at all. She breathed slowly and deeply. She was using the mediation techniques she'd learned from tapes she looked up at the library to keep herself relaxed. Using them she was able to keep her muscles loose, even in her current climactic pose.

That was the secret to her work, keeping her body relaxed, even in often uncomfortable positions. Doing so helped to mitigate the muscle fatigue she otherwise earned, in her long stints of holding awkward poses.

She currently stood before one of the sculpture classes. Her head held high, chin thrust out confrontationally, her arm held high as though flaunting a sword that was not there. Since the sword in her sheath, was far too heavy for her to pose holding, no matter how much Schrödinger might have wanted her to. She had managed to hold the sword up, for the length of time it took the students to put in their rough sketches, but then she had begged mercy. The sword was far too heavy to hold at arm's length indefinitely.

Schrödinger finally relented and allowed her to sheath her sword after the break. He agreed that she could simply hold the pose. Although not before a thorough rant about Joan 'De Arc and her heroic soul, expounding eloquently on why he had chosen her as today's theme. Just holding her hand up in this way was hard enough though. Ashley's arm was already numb, with random pins and needles and she knew from experience that it was going to be throbbing when she was finally allowed to rest. Work was work however, and this was why she was here today after all.

Sweat trickled down her neck. It tickled its way down over her bare shoulder and beneath the mock breastplate she was wearing. Schrödinger must have gotten it from the theater department. She closed her eyes for a moment to better appreciate of the feel of the cool metal where it pressed against her in the heat of the day.

The feathers on the helmet tucked beneath her other arm tickled a little. They had seen better days and this wasn't one of them. The poor abused ostrich plumes would be further greased and matted by the end of her stint here, since she couldn't help the sweat that she was getting on them. Not without changing her pose, which she could not do. She knew from her experience on the other side of the pencil, that the slightest changes in expression or even a deep breath could change crucial shadows. Like the muscles of her neck, or of her exposed shoulders.

As an artist herself, she understood firsthand the frustration of having a model move at just the wrong moment. Which made her very patient and diligent, when she was modeling herself. The scratching of the students pencils and chalk on their paper or whiteboard and her own heartbeat, were loud in her ears as her unconscious mind strained to be free of this room. Her thoughts were straining, reaching hard to hear something beyond these four walls. Still though, she heard nothing. Schrödinger himself was here now, nodding over a book in one corner, while the students worked. Although earlier he had been chatting with someone in the hall.

She shifted again, ever so slightly. She tried to be subtle in her movements. For although she might be patient, her body had opinions of its own. Which were, that it was hot, tired and ready to be done. Drawing in a deep breath, she again concentrated on relaxing as many muscles as the pose allowed. It brought her some relief, but she would still be very glad when this class was done for the day and she could move freely again. Closing her eyes she invoked patience and allowed her mind to drift for a while.

When she finally got off work, Ashley went to the Library on her way home, as usual. She spent a lot of time at the library. She often researched agriculture and sustainability, and she was always looking for something new to inspire her artwork as well. As she perused the video section, hoping for just that, she noticed the section on climate change. She had always avoided it. She was afraid that it would lead to her losing control at the library and crying her head off in public, but she was in a strange mood today.

She'd been brooding a lot lately, and she wasn't sure why. Taking a steadying breath, she approached the climate change section of the video isle with trepidation. For some reason she felt drawn to it today. She decided that maybe she would just read the back of a couple of them, that shouldn't be too bad. So she picked up one after another, gazing at the backs of them, and then returning them to the shelves.

She couldn't actually bring herself to read them thoroughly, but she skimmed them enough to get the idea, before returning them to their respective spots. Most of what she saw here were documentaries that had been roughly put together after the fact. Pieced together in the last ten years, as survivors tried to figure out just what had gone wrong. There was nothing new there. She'd already read many of the books handwritten on the subject. However she had read them in the privacy of her apartment, where she could scream and cry or rail against the unfairness of it all, without disturbing anyone. This time however a very different title caught her eye. It was the Unfortunate Truth.

*'What a strange title.'* She thought. *'Who would refer to such a worldwide tragedy by such a seemingly benign name?'* It offended her as much as it intrigued her, so she picked it up to see if it explained. Glancing at the back of it, one thing in particular stood out to her immediately. Down in the right hand corner, next to the minute amount and the rating was the year it was produced.

*'2006? That must be wrong.'* She decided to read the back of this one more thoroughly then she had the others. Several things caught her attention this time. First was that this film had been put together by one of America's former Vice Presidents. As well as that it was a documentary on climate change that was put together before 2006. The second to last line in the description seemed to repeat itself in her mind. "We must act now to save the earth."

*'Could it really be?'* She wondered. *'Did people really know that long ago that this was going to happen? Then why?!?'* She thought to herself. *'If they knew then, and they had the wherewithal to change things, why had they let this happen?'* She felt tears of frustration threatening already, but she decided to go ahead and watch it anyway. She had to know just what information they'd had. What had their Vice President had to say way back then, and could it have helped to avert the global catastrophe that had so affected her life.

She was still hesitant to commit to watching it, while there were other people lingering in the library though, so she carried it with her while she pretended to peruse other sections. She noted that there were only a couple of people left, as it was getting late. Most folks had already gone home for dinner. She did notice a couple of what looked like University students working together and there was a young man who was listening to music in the audio section. He was nodding his head to the music, obviously really enjoying himself. When she skirted around him, she noticed that his eyes were shut and he seemed completely oblivious to his surroundings. She sighed to herself, she was just stalling now and she knew it.

She slowly approached the library's help desk and when the women came over to assist her, she had to clear her throat twice to ask for a key to a viewing room. She didn't have a way to watch the movie at her apartment.

She lived as frugally as she could, and so she was very familiar with the machinery available at the library, for viewing films or listening to music. The librarian clucked her tongue disapprovingly as she checked the time till closing, as compared to the run time on the video. As she handed it back, she mentioned that if Ashley got it started now, she should have a little less than half an hour to spare. The librarian finally agreed and gave her a key to viewing room three.

Ashley walked slowly down the hall. She knew that she should be hurrying but it was as though her feet were dragging of their own accord. When she reached viewing room three she saw that it was right across from the bathrooms, and decided to duck in and snag some toilet paper. If this went the way she thought it might, she would need to use it as tissue. She just hoped that she could calm down enough after watching the film, to thank the librarian and leave without making a scene.

*'Why am I even doing this?'* She asked herself. *'Why torture myself? It's not going to change anything. What's done is done and no amount of films or books is ever going to take things back to the way they were.'* These thoughts may have stopped her mind but her hands put the film in the player and she slowly sat down, as it rolled through the introductions.

———

Jimi and his dad wheeled their empty carts back to their base in the Outskirts just as the sun was disappearing. They had made all their trades successfully today and they'd be heading out in the morning. They shared some simple rations and water, before laying down to rest. Jimi's thoughts wouldn't still however, as he lay on the heat soaked concrete. The floor was as hot as it was hard, and the dust tickled his nose. Its dust driven tickle only exacerbating his wakefulness.

It had been a long day, and he found his restless mind reviewing it. They had spent the last few days going from store to store, accepting oil or water in trade for canned goods and preserved foods. They supplied the restaurants and the little grocery stores that still spotted the city. They traded nuts and bolts, screws and nails to the little hardware store and there were other scraps and parts that they wagged down to Old Tom at the Salvage yard. There they traded for credit with Tom himself rather than City Credits, which was the way most other businesses worked. The only City Credits exchanged at Old Tom's happened in the pawnshop. He paid city tax on that much of the exchanges he made, but just in the pawnshop. In the yard people traded him wares for wares, in the form of credit with Tom himself. Those credits could be spent on anything in the yard. Old Tom used that system of personal credit for the junk half of his junkyard, making most of his transactions and trades under the table. As far as Jimi could tell, he only paid tax on the City Credits that changed hands in the pawnshop part of his salvage yard.

The pawnshop itself was a rambling shambled affair, cobbled together from the largest pieces of scrap that had made their way to Old Tom's over the years. It was made of a variety of substances from cardboard to sheet metal. All overlapping at unpredictable angles and none quite matched. The front part, the more secure section, was set up as the pawnshops office.

This was where he kept what he deemed most valuable. While the rest of the rambling structure doubled as his living space. Jimi thought the pawnshop area that he'd been in so far was dark and cramped and dirty. It was overcrowded with the scraps of things that Old Tom deemed valuable. He wondered about the rest of Old Tom's house sometimes, though. He'd seen hints and glimpses through the randomly shaped and placed windows, which led him to think it might be altogether different inside.

Sighing heavily Jimi rolled over again, hoping to finally clear his rambling mind and sleep. The air in the still room was stifling hot and he wasn't tired yet, because it was only sunset. Tomorrow was going to be a long day though. They would be heading back towards base camp, since they had finished their deliveries and trades here in Newcity. That meant another long haul, to try to make as much distance as they could before the heat of the dawn.

They would be miles from here by the time the sun rose. So somehow he had to force himself to sleep. Something about the very heat of the air however, its weight in his lungs, had him feeling peculiar. *As he dropped into edgy, heady dreams, he took flight. Into a world of fire and of light.*

# 3

Matt was really rocking out. He was listening to some crazy smooth jazz from the mid 1970's that he'd stumbled across, when someone tapped hard on his shoulder, startling him. Jumping a little in his chair he pulled the headphones down to his shoulders. Looking around quickly, his eyes met the irritated eyes of the librarian.

"Oops, am I late again?" He asked her sheepishly. He tried a smile, hoping to charm his way back into her good graces. She knew him well. He was here every free day that he had. Even so he often stayed too late, listening to music until he lost track of time.

"Yes, you are." She said sarcastically. He could tell by the way the corner of her mouth twitched however that his smile had done the trick. He could see that she wasn't really angry at him anymore. "The library closed ten minutes ago. I've finished all that I need to. It's time for me to go home. So pack 'em up, and head 'em out." She said, motioning the way he had seen cowboys shoo cattle, in the movies.

He laughed at her attempt at a southern drawl and gathered his things. As he stood up however the headphones still around his neck jerked him back towards the player like a leash. This time she was the one that laughed, long and hard.

Flushing at his own awkwardness, he gingerly removed the headphones and placed them back on the desk. He grabbed his bag and they started to head towards the door, when she stopped suddenly.

He looked at her questioningly, afraid that he'd done something wrong. She had her hand pressed to her forehead like she'd just slapped herself and she was muttering under her breath.

"That girl! That damn girl! I knew that she'd be too long! I almost forgot her in here!" She turned on her heel and hurried back towards her desk, fumbling to turn the overhead lights back on.

"Who?" Matt asked, thoroughly confused.

"A girl was watching a film in room three. It should have been over half an hour ago. I don't know what she could be doing in there! Maybe she's taking notes or something." She muttered the last comment under her breath, as though trying to sooth herself. As she got the lights back on, Matt had a sudden thought.

"Why don't I go let her know that its time?" He suggested, trying to sound sincere, as though he just wanted to help. Which was partly true, but also he really had to pee and he wasn't looking forward to the bicycle ride home with a full bladder.

Before she could respond, he took the initiative. Dropping his bag on her desk, he sprinted across the library towards the hall that led to both the viewing rooms, and the restrooms. He decided that he couldn't hold it a moment longer. So to compromise, he tapped on the door to viewing room three and ducked into the restroom. He hoped that whoever was in there had just gotten distracted with something and that his knock might make her notice the time.

———

Ashley had cried herself into a stupor. She sat with her head on her folded arms. A distant part of her was aware that the movie had been over for a long time, since she could hear the menu soundtrack repeating itself. She could hardly hear it over her own angry thoughts though.

*'How could they?'* She took a deep breath and held it, hoping to cure her hiccups. She always wound up with hiccups when she cried hard. The toilet paper roll she had snagged from the bathroom was half gone and she was surrounded by piles of used tissue. She vaguely realized she had better clean up before the librarian saw the mess. She couldn't seem to break out of the cycle of thoughts that the film and all its slides and statistics had left her with though.

*'They knew! They knew all that time! Since the 1970's he said! They understood the danger, they knew exactly what they were doing to the planet, and they just kept doing it anyway!'* She hit the table with her fist hoping to help bring her thoughts back to the moment.

She was having an even harder time calming down then she thought she would. She couldn't break out of the reverie into which she'd sunk, once she had finally stopped crying. She was angry. She was really angry. She fostered the anger, actually. For it helped to blot out the pain. The footage he'd shown of the flood victims hit so close to home that her heart hurt just having seen it. If she let her mind wander for even a moment, she saw again the floating body of a drowned man.

It could have been her father, her mother, or any of those left behind when the train had evacuated her and the other children to safety, but not their parents. So instead she fostered the anger. To distract herself, she allowed herself to rage at the fact that *they* had let this happen. That they'd ignored all the warnings and just kept on with business as usual, right up until the bitter end.

She lifted her head groggily; it felt stiff and full from tears. She stared at the repeating menu without really seeing it and finally sighed.

'*I'd better get moving, the librarian is gonna be pissed.*' Just as she had the thought, someone tapped on the door. Startled she almost jumped out of her skin.

"Just a minute!" She called out, as she hastily gathering up tissues, trying in vain to hide them all in her pockets. The door wasn't locked. So she was surprised that the woman did not just come right in. She was grateful however, to have the moment to gather her trash and wipe her face once more. As she was taking the film from the player, the door finally opened behind her. She was surprised to see not the librarian but the young man who she'd seen listening to music earlier.

"Um, I'm sorry to bother you but the librarian wants to go home. She sent me to let you know that it's time." He smiled a little as he said it to try to reassure her, she thought. "Actually it's half an hour past." He grinned, scratching his head rather sheepishly. "We were all running a bit late tonight." He looked away then, as though to allow her time to gather herself. She was grateful for his thoughtfulness, even trying to take the blame on himself.

"No, no I'm sorry." She said, smiling back to try to hide the fact that she'd been sobbing and out of control a few moments before. "I kind of, lost track of time…" She let her sentence trail off and looked away. She decided he could think whatever he wanted about what had caused her to get so distracted. She gathered her things and headed towards the door.

"So what film were you watching?" He asked as they walked down the hall. "I'm just curious." He seemed to be trying to make light conversation but she didn't feel up to talking about it. So she just handed him the film and let him read the back himself. He read its description while they slowly made their way back to the librarian. Ashley was glad that he didn't seem to be in a hurry. For some reason just being around another person, was helping her to feel more in control of herself. Less like she was going to fly to pieces at any moment.

"Wow." He said, handing the film back to her. "That's heavy stuff." He sounded so serious that she looked more closely at him out of the corner of her eye. He was quite handsome in his own way she noticed. She wondered if he was one of the other orphans from the coast too. He certainly was the right age, from what she could tell.

"What's your name?" She asked him suddenly. She realized now that she'd seen him here a lot, usually listening to music or in the music books section. "I don't mean to pry." She said quickly. "I just, I think that we both spend a lot of time here. You seem familiar." She felt herself blushing and she ducked to hide it. She fiddled a little with the film in her hands and cleared her throat as he answered.

"My name is Matt." He smiled at her as he said it. Her breath caught at the brilliance of his smile. It made him seem to glow it was so radiant. "What's your name?" He seemed to honestly want to know, rather than just being polite, and she blushed a little harder at that warmth in his eyes.

"Um, it's Ashley." She said looking down again. She was painfully aware that she could not stop blushing.

*'What's wrong with me?'* She wondered, biting her lip. She wasn't normally so shy with people, even handsome men. Maybe it was just that she'd been crying and she was emotionally raw right now. That must be it, she decided. She probably needed to eat too, to ground herself again. She sighed as they came abreast of the librarian's desk, where the librarian sat trying to read a book. Ashley could tell that she was impatient though and she wanted to apologize.

"I'm so sorry that I was in there so long." She said, as she set the film onto the desk. "I'm afraid that I lost track of time. I didn't mean to be a pain." She said it quietly but she meant every word. The librarian's eyes softened, as Ashley met her gaze.

"It's all right dear. I'm just glad I remembered you were in there! I almost locked you in!" She smiled as she said it but Ashley could tell that she was telling the truth. It gave her a bit of a start to realize that she almost spent the night in the library with no supper. All that, just because she was crying her head off, instead of watching the clock. She took another deep breath. The librarian turned off the lights and the three of them went out the main doors together, into the dim orange glow of the streetlamps outside.

As the librarian was locking the door behind them, Ashley looked around for her bike. She was still trying to come fully back to the present and for a moment she had a hard time getting her bearings. Matt headed off to the left with assurance, so she just trailed in his wake, assuming that he was probably riding a bike too. Cars were few and far between anymore, unlike when her parents were still alive. Since the ban on all unnecessary combustion such conveniences had long gone by the wayside.

"Goodnight you two!" The librarian called out behind them. She seemed to be in a very good mood now that she was on her way home.

"Good night!" Ashley called back to her, as the librarian began her walk home. Ashley wondered if she lived really close or if she just preferred to walk. She shrugged to herself at her own curiosity. She reached the bike rack just as Matt was pulling his loose. She struggled a moment to free her bike and he was already straddling his, when she looked up again. She was a little surprised that he was still there, although she was also grateful for the company. She wasn't looking forward to going home to her empty apartment tonight. She normally enjoyed the solitude, but tonight she was afraid of her own thoughts.

"Um, well goodni-," She began, but he cut her off.

"Do you want to get dinner somewhere?" He smiled again as her jaw dropped. He hurried on before she could respond. "I was just thinking that it's getting really late. I don't know about you, but I'm starving." He seemed to be casual enough about it. He was rolling back and forth on his bike while he spoke. As though her answer didn't really matter to him, but he thought he'd ask. "I know a great little spot that's not far from here. It's just a little late to get cooking, you know?" He was very persuasive. So although she didn't normally like to spend her credit allotment on anything but necessities, she was really hungry and she was even hungrier for company.

"All right." She said quietly. She noticed that he stopped rolling his bike as soon as she spoke and she smiled a little. Apparently he wasn't quite as casual as he wanted to appear. "Where did you have in mind?" She was really curious. She hardly ever ate out unless Jen dragged her, so she didn't know many places.

*'Knowing a good place to eat this close to the library could come in very handy in the future.'* She rationalized to herself. *'If I like it I can always take Jen.'* She decided that she was going to try whatever she wanted, and screw counting credits.

For once she wouldn't worry about how many she spent.

"Great!" He said with a grin. As he let his excitement show, she was really flattered. "Do you like ethnic food? It's a fantastic place, and it's not far from here. I've known them for years and their really good people. I don't eat out often, but when I do I try to give my credits to them." He winked as he said it and his smile was broad and warm. She felt as though it warmed her from the inside out as she smiled back. She didn't think that she had ever had ethnic food, whatever that was. She was so hungry though, that she didn't care what she ate.

"I don't think I've had it before, but I'm game to try." Was all she said out loud. His excitement was catching and she was starting to feel it too. She wondered just what this food was like, that he was so happy to get to eat it.

'Or perhaps.' She wondered. 'Is he just happy to be eating with me?' She made herself cut that train of thought short. She didn't want to get ahead of herself. They had literally just met after all.

"Follow me! It's just a few blocks from here." He spun his bike around and she followed him down the street, riding just a few feet behind him. She made sure to ride just off to one side of him, so that she wouldn't crash into him if he stopped suddenly. They passed the street that she usually took to get home.

As she looked down the long dark street, barely illuminated by the low energy streetlights as it was, she was very happy to have a distraction form the dark night. She had not been looking forward to the sad memories that filled her mind at home alone on nights like this. All the visualization exercises in the world couldn't erase the memories that clung to her. All she could hope to do was paint over them for a moment or two, with something else that she might be able to enjoy. This was a really nice distraction.

————

Matt couldn't believe his luck. His heart had almost stopped when she agreed to go to dinner with him. He'd had no idea when the librarian said that some girl had been watching a film, that it might be her. He had first noticed her a couple years ago, as she sat reading in the library.

'Ashley.' He reminded himself with relish. She was right, when she had said that they both spent a lot of time there. She was always there, it seemed. Whenever he came in to look something up, or to listen to music, it seemed that she was always there. She was usually in non-fiction he'd noticed. He often saw her in the agriculture section or the human sciences. As exemplified by the film she'd been watching tonight.

'*Whew.*' He thought. '*What a heavy film for a climate shift survivor to watch.*' At least, he assumed from her teary reaction to the film and her relative age that she was another of the many orphans of the climate shift. Her eyes had still been puffy from tears, when he'd come to the door, to let her know it was time to go. He'd been a little shocked at how ragged she looked, until he saw what film she'd been watching.

'*She's a lot braver then I am.*' He thought solemnly. He didn't even remember the shift or anything from his life before it actually. Still, he didn't go around prodding old wounds by reading or watching films about it. Sometimes he was grateful for his lack of memory. Since it made it so much easier for him to simply accept the way things were now as being normal. Rather than trying to live in the past. He sighed to himself at the thought.

'*That's only half true and you know it.*' He did wish that he could remember his parents. He had no idea of who they were or who he had been before he was injured in the evacuation. He didn't even know how that had happened. He just woke up one day at around ten, or so they had guessed. He had awakened to a splitting headache, with a huge lump on his head and a FEMA member hovering protectively over him.

'*Anyhow.*' He thought pointedly at himself. '*No use dwelling on the past. Especially not tonight. Instead...*' He grinned, glancing back at Ashley, where she was following along behind him. '*Dinner.*' They were almost to their destination. It was just around the corner and since Ashley too looked like she was brooding on dark thoughts, he decided to let her know.

"We're almost there." He called out to her over his shoulder. "Food is just around the bend!" He smiled again and she laughed. Then soon enough, they were there.

"The shop is too small to have their own bike rack. So I usually just stuff mine in the alley." He showed her what he meant and she followed suit. He flushed a little nervously as she brushed by him to push her bike into the narrow space. He decided to hold his breath a minute and try to act normal. She had just met him after all. Even if he had been admiring her for years, she didn't know that. He didn't want to scare her off.

"Shall we?" He said as casually as he could. He ducked his head as he gestured, to hide his flushed face. He hoped that if she noticed his red cheeks that she'd put it down to the bike ride.

"Why, thank you." She smiled warmly at him as she sauntered past. She was definitely getting her spark back now that she was away from the library. He thought that she seemed to be getting more comfortable with him. He made himself hold his breath again, as he tried to keep from getting overly excited about that as they stepped inside.

She gasped in delight, looking around at the dimly lit room. He'd forgotten how it looked if you weren't used to it. He took a moment to admire the beautifully embroidered tapestries. Thai dancers were depicted with gold embellishments. Together with the many other accents they had placed about the little room, it seemed very festive indeed.

He smiled, remembering when as a child he had asked them where they had gotten them all. They had looked at him like he was stupid. "Well, they're ours of course. We brought them from home!"

He'd had no idea, at the tender age of around fourteen, where their home had been. Let alone, of the years of travel that they had endured, on their post-shift journey here from Thailand. As a kid, he'd had no idea of where they were talking about. Nor had he any idea that global communications had finally been haltingly restored for a few years, before the increasingly ferocious solar flares knocked out any electronic systems that people tried to reestablish.

It wasn't until years later, that Sam had confessed their story to him. He had explained that after losing their only son in the tsunamis caused by the climate shift, they had left Thailand on foot. They had hiked out through Korea in the hopes of starting a new life together. Even after Sam had explained their story, Matt had still not known what they meant.

Even once Sam explained that they'd sailed from Korea in the hopes of making it to Hawaii to find Nat's sister, Matt had not really understood. Unfortunately they had wound up missing the Islands.

After a seemingly indefinite time stuck in the doldrums, they had finally washed up on the newly risen western coast of pre-shift America instead. Matt had looked it all up at the library, trying to figure out where they were talking about. Geography classes at the orphanage had been somewhat hazy, since the oceans had risen to their new heights.

A loud grumbling from Ashley's stomach answered quickly by his own brought his attention back to the situation at hand. He smiled down at her, as Sam let himself through the kitchen curtain at the sound of the bell on the door.

# 4

Ashley instantly fell in love with the beautiful furnishings of the little restaurant. She had never seen such beautiful tapestries in her life! There were statues and bright silk flowers everywhere she looked. There were so many colors and gold embellishments on everything, that she felt for a moment that she were entering a little palace. A palace that smelled divine. Her stomach rumbled embarrassingly at the smell and she put a hand to her belly trying to quiet it.

"Matt! Long time no see!" A man called out to him with a smile. He had come out from behind a split curtain; in answer to the little bell they had set jingling. "Hey Nat! Matt's here! Whip up something good!" He winked at Matt smiling as he got closer, just as his wife called from the back kitchen.

"It's all good and don't you forget it either!" She poked her head out the door to smile at Matt. "Who's your pretty friend Matt? I haven't seen her here before." She smiled warmly as Ashley blushed. Chuckling to herself she pushed her way past the curtain and back into the kitchen. "You want sate'?" She called over her shoulder to Matt as she disappeared.

"Yes please! Some summer rolls too!" He turned to Ashley, suddenly looking concerned. "Do you eat meat? Do you like salad? Or noodles? Or soup?" He seemed very concerned and she wondered what it was that he had ordered. She usually did not eat meat of any kind, but right now she was so hungry, that she thought she could eat anything.

"I'll eat whatever you suggest. Since I don't know what's what here." She smiled shyly. He grinned at her, and he turned back to his friend to rattle off another order of who knows what. She was just thrilled that they seemed to have the place to themselves. While it seemed absolutely incredible, that food was already being prepared for them, before they had even found their seats. She had never expected such personal service, and could not have anticipated having no wait at all.

"Come, come!" The man said gesturing as he led them towards a table for two at the back of the restaurant. It was nestled into a corner. It was quite cozy once they were settled there. Matt let her have the seat towards the back. She was glad, as it gave her a good angle to continue admiring the wall hangings and other decorations around them. As they sat, the man grabbed Matt by the shoulders giving him a squeeze. His smile said more than words, about his affection for Matt.

"You should come by more, you know. It's been too long." He squeezed Matt's shoulders again. Matt reaching up, patting Sam's hand on his shoulder in response to his affectionate squeeze, he smiled up at the older man.

"You know how it is Sam, my credits get less every year, or so it seems! I do miss you and Nat, but I don't want to just stop by just to bother you two." Sam scoffed at his answer, shoving his shoulder lightly.

"You know that's no excuse! You can eat here anytime, credits or no! We'll just make you wash dishes." He winked at Ashley as he said that last, and Matt laughed. Sam turned to yell over his shoulder to his wife. He was starting to ask where their food was, just as she came through the curtain with her hands full of trays. Sam shut his mouth just as quickly as he'd opened it, but it was too late.

"You know it would be much faster if you'd help me Samyan! I can't cook and serve food at the same time! You take this tray and I'll go stir the soup! And you leave these kids alone! They didn't come in here to see you!" She winked at Ashley again as she set several dishes between her and Matt on the table. She also laid out an empty plate for each of them, and Ashley wondered why. Then grabbing her husband by the arm, she dragged him forcibly back through the curtain. Samyan smiled once more at Ashley, as he disappeared and she couldn't help but laugh.

"They really love you." She said as she watched Matt pull apart some chopsticks and rub them together. She tried to copy him, rather clumsily. She had seen chopsticks in movies but she had never had the chance to try them. She hoped that she didn't embarrass herself.

As though he had read her mind Matt demonstrated the mechanism a couple of times for her. He corrected her fingers on the sticks a few times, until she could almost move one. She laughed, but she was really starting to wonder if she was actually going to be able to get food to her mouth this way.

Matt set his sticks down on his plate with a chuckle and lifted one of the little rolls the lady had brought with his fingers. Ashley was so grateful, hungry as she was, that she followed suit without hesitation.

"This is finger food. So it's a good place to start." He said as he took a bite and then spooned some sauce from the little dish on the table into the opening. She copied him and as she took her second bite of the somewhat bland little roll this time it burst with flavor! This time instead of just tasting the roll itself, her mouth was overwhelmed with sweet and spice like she'd never had before.

"Oh my God!" She choked out around the food. She chewed, swallowed and tried again. "That's amazing! Is it all this good?" She spooned more sauce into her roll and devoured it with clear appreciation. Matt laughed at her obvious delight. Nodding around another mouthful, he chewed his own bite of tasty little roll. He too ate as fast as his hands and mouth would let him. "What is this called again?" She asked as she reached for another. She was really glad that Nat had brought two for each of them. There was no way that one would have been enough for her.

"Itss…" He chewed and swallowed and tried again with a grin. "It's called a summer roll. Not to be confused with a spring roll. Although, those are good too." He watched as she devoured the last of her roll, pouring the remaining sauce onto her last bite. He laughed a little at her enthusiasm over the food.

"What's the difference?" She asked, as she hungrily looked for what was next.

"Spring rolls are fried, and they tend to have more meat in them then summer rolls. The sauce is just as good on them though, if you're in the mood for something warmer." He looked up then as Sam and Nat came out again this time carrying a dish each.

They set down a big bowl of soup and a large plate of noodles. With yet another friendly wink, Sam set a fork by each of their plates, while his wife set down little bowls and spoons. She couldn't help but laugh at his demeanor. She was grateful that he'd taken pity on her but it made her more determined than ever to learn to use the sticks. Later, once she was fed.

Ashley looked from the soup to the noodles, as Nat and Sam retreated behind their curtain again. Both dishes had been set in the middle of the table, evenly between her and Matt. She wasn't sure what was hers, so she waited for him to take the lead. He apparently noticed her confusion and reached over to pick up one of the wriggly things on a stick. They had been brought along with the summer rolls.

She noticed with delight that this too had come with a sauce. She copied him, holding it on the end its stick over her empty plate, the way he did. He grabbed his fork and pulled the yellow chunks off the stick with it, sliding it onto his plate.

She tried again to copy him but somehow she must have pushed too hard. Instead the stick broke and half her food and her fork as well, went flying across the table with a clatter. She was horrified. Matt just laughed though and grabbing her fork, he handed it back to her with a smile.

"It takes a lot of practice." He reassured her. "I've been coming here most of my life, and believe me, I've thrown my fair share across the table! I think its tradition." She was still embarrassed but she was grateful that he'd made light of it. She was self-conscious about wasting it though. So she grabbed it off the table and managed to get it off the stick this time. Chuckling he spooned some of the sauce onto his own and ate a bite with his fork.

When she copied him, taste again exploded onto her tongue. She'd never had anything like it. It was rich and creamy but light and sweet all at once.

"Is it peanuts?" She asked him, around another bite of the delicious combination of flavors. She couldn't get enough. When she'd finished what was on her plate, she was so glad that there was another one waiting for her.

"It is." He answered, with a nod, even while he ate just as hungrily as she did. "It's called chicken sate'. It's got curry and coconut milk, and then the sauce is made from peanuts. It's pretty magical, I don't know how she turns peanuts into that, but I'm glad she knows how!" He chuckled again as they both finished their food and looked around for more. He seemed to sense her confusion about what was what and where to start next. He answered her without her having to ask.

"They taught me when I first came here, that if you're with other people it's best to go family style." He saw the lack of understanding on her face and dished some noodles and rice onto her plate as he continued. "Basically, you share." He smiled and dished noodles and rice onto his plate as well.

Seeing that they each had their own little bowl for the big pot of soup, it all clicked into place.

"Oh! I get it!" She exclaimed in delight. She was excited that she'd get to try everything. That way she would know what she might want to get next time, if she came back. She grabbed his bowl and served him some soup, the way he'd served her the noodles. Then she filled her own bowl as well. She decided to taste it, before she got sucked into noodles and rice. Once again she was completely blown away by the incredible blend of flavors.

*'Sweet, sour, spicy and creamy. All at once!'* She thought to herself, closing her eyes to savor it. She was used to mainly home grown salads. With only an occasional outing to a coffee shop with her friend Jen. She was not at all prepared for such rich flavors. When she opened her eyes she found that Matt was smiling at her over his bowl. He was obviously watching her enjoy the soup. She felt her face heat up again at the warmth in his smile. She buried her face in the tiny bowl of soup to hide her confusion.

"What is this called? It's delicious!" She was honestly curious, but she also wanted to distract him from looking at her like that. She wasn't sure if she should be feeling so strongly about someone that she'd only met an hour ago. To her relief he looked down as he answered.

"It's called Tom Kha Gai." He smiled again at the confusion that spread across her face at the unfamiliar words. "Nat told me it means something like Chicken soup with milk, meaning coconut milk." He filled his bowl again as he said it. As she drained her little bowl as well, he took it gingerly from her hand, his fingers brushing against hers. The tiny touch sent little shivers up her arm, raising gooseflesh on the back of her neck.

She swallowed, trying hard not to show how much that small touch had affected her. When he handed her bowl back, his hand lingered in hers just a moment longer then it really needed to. His hand was very warm from the heat of the soup. Her cheeks were hot and she tried to hide behind the tiny bowl until they cooled again.

Smiling, he ate in silence for a while. He was obviously enjoying the food and she tried to keep her thoughts centered on how delicious everything was. She was grateful to have gotten to try such amazing cuisine so unexpectedly. She experimented with the noodles and found that they were just as delicious as everything else. When she finally tried it, she found that the rice was a nice way to transition her taste buds from one thing to another. When she realized that she was starting to get really full, she set her bowl down with a sigh.

Looking around she realized that there was very little left.

"I can't believe how much we ate!" She said, quite startled by it. She normally did not eat very much. The food here had been so delicious though and so unusual, that she had eaten until she couldn't possibly eat another bite. Matt laughed out loud. He seemed to laugh a lot.

"I can." He said. "I always eat so much I can barely walk my bike home. It must be because it's so good!" He said it loud enough for Nat to hear in the kitchen Ashley realized, and she smiled at his cunning. As if that was some secret signal, Nat and Sam came bustling out of the curtained doorway, their smiles beaming. Matt smiled at them. "You did it again Nat." He said with mock sternness.

"What? What's wrong?" Nat asked him, confused. Apparently she had not picked up on the humor in his voice.

"You've outdone yourself! You made everything so good, that I ate till I burst! I don't think I can get home in this condition. Do you think I could just sleep here?" He pretended like he was going to fall asleep where he sat, pretending to tip over in his seat.

Laughing she smacked his shoulder playfully.

"You." Was all she said, but Ashley could see how much she'd appreciated the compliment.

"Thank you so much." Ashley piped up. "I've never had anything like this before! It was so good that I think you've inspired a whole new combination of flavors for me! I can't wait to try it at home!" She really meant it. As Nat looked her in the eye, she could obviously see that and burst into a huge smile.

"You're welcome back anytime, dear! We're always here, and any friend of Matt's is always welcome at our table." She smiled and patted Ashley on the hand, in a very motherly way.

The gesture was so sweet and familiar, that Ashley felt tears dampen her eyes. She had actually managed to forget, in her enjoyment of the meal, just how close to the surface they were tonight. She smiled trying to hide her reaction. Luckily Nat had already turned towards Matt to talk to him. Samyan however was watching her over Nat's shoulder. As their eyes met, he nodded a little and smiled as though to reassure her. She tried to smile back but she looked away quickly. She took a deep breath, afraid that his kindness would bring even more tears to her eyes.

Nat was berating Matt for not visiting more. Ashley focused on it as a pleasant distraction from her feelings.

"We haven't seen you in almost six months! Look at you!" She pinched his arm by way of example. "You're skin and bones. The both of you!" She winked over her shoulder at Ashley as she said that last. Ashley took a closer look at Matt across the table. Although it was true that he was thin, she wouldn't say he was skin and bones. She hid a grin at how motherly Nat was towards him.

"If I don't start seeing you at least once a week, then I'm gonna come looking for you!" She continued. "Don't think I don't know where you are! I know you spend all your time at that library! It's only just down the street! You'd better start stopping by on your way home. Weather you eat here or not, I just want to see you!"

Ashley couldn't help it, she laughed out loud at the look on Matt's face. He seemed somewhere between bemused humor and feeling rather put upon by her demands. She hoped that Nat wouldn't be offended. She really hadn't meant to laugh out loud, but the look on his face was so worried she couldn't help it. Luckily Samyan chuckled behind her and called his wife to heel.

"Come on Nataya, be patient with the boy. He's grown into a young man while we weren't looking, and young men have busy lives!" He put one hand on her shoulder in a loving gesture, squeezing her a little. Ashley suddenly realized that Nat actually had a hint of tears in her eyes. Nat nodded though and let her husband turn her back towards the kitchen.

"I will come see you more, Nat!" Matt called to her reassuringly. "I promise." She nodded but continued back into the kitchen, seemingly overcome with emotion. A few moments later Samyan reappeared with their bill in hand. They hadn't even had to ask. He had also brought a couple of little paper to go containers. He set the bill down and deftly fit the remainder of their meal into the little box. He poured the last of the soup into another little container with a lid. While he did so Matt picked up the bill and looked it over.

"Sam, you forgot something. This is only half of what we ordered." He handed him the bill looking concerned but Samyan just waved it away.

"Don't worry about it, it was our treat. We were just glad to see you again. We're especially glad to see you so happy." He smiled rather sadly at Matt. Ashley could feel the tension of unspoken words between them. She wondered what it was that was going unsaid. They both seemed to feel it. Having seen the tears in Nat's eyes, she decided to ask Matt once they left the restaurant. She hoped that she wouldn't be prying. Matt handed Sam his credits card and Sam went back behind the curtain with the bill before Ashley could react. She protested to Matt, trying to hand him her own card to pay for her half but he wouldn't take it.

"Don't worry about it." He said quietly. "They paid for your half." He winked at her, obviously trying to recapture the jovial spirit they had shared during dinner. "Besides," Matt said. "Maybe you'll come again with me sometime? You can pay your half then, if you really want to."

He smiled as he said it. Ashley wondered if he'd really let her or if he was just trying to get her to eat with him again. She decided that it didn't really matter. She'd had a wonderful time, and she would definitely like to eat here again. In fact she'd already been thinking of bringing Jen here sometime.

"All right." She sighed as she put her card away. "Sounds like a plan." She said grinning at him. The light that jumped into his eyes as she agreed, reminded her of the way he'd been looking at her earlier. She felt a little shiver run though her. She took a deep breath and just enjoyed the sensation this time, instead of trying so hard to suppress it. It ran the length of her body, from her head to her toes.

"Are you cold?" He asked, apparently thinking that she was shivering. She decided that was a good excuse for the movement. Since she didn't want to have to explain it, she simply said yes.

"Would you like some warm tea before we go?" Although she thought he was very thoughtful, since she was only pretending to be cold, she politely declined. When Sam brought his card back, Matt thanked him again and as they stood to go he gave Sam a big hug.

"Goodnight Samyan." He said solemnly. "Please give Nataya a big hug for me too, won't you?" Sam smiled at him and said that he would. Turning to Ashley, he held out his hand for her to shake. She took it gingerly and he pulled her into a hug as well.

"You have a good night young lady." He said to her shoulder. "Maybe when you come back, I'll even find out the name for your beautiful face." He smiled as he pulled away. His accent made the phrase sound almost lyrical. She smiled back. Taking his hands in both of hers, she held them.

"My name is Ashley. It was lovely to meet you and your wife both. Thank you both so much, for everything." He grinned at her. Pulling one hand free, he nudged Matt in the ribs with his elbow.

"She's a cutie, you should keep her." He said in a mock whisper and with a wink. He smiled at them both and trotted off to rejoin his wife in the kitchen. Ashley couldn't help the smile that lit her face. When she looked over to Matt though, she found he was beet red. As she looked closer, he seemed to be holding his breath. She laughed out loud and asked him playfully.

"Are you alright?" He nodded, apparently still not willing to breathe. She laughed again.

'God it feels good to laugh.' She thought. 'I can't remember the last time that I laughed this much!' She smiled at him and on a whim, she hooked her arm in his and steered him towards the door.

She leaned into his arm as they left the restaurant. She couldn't believe how good it felt. She had to let go, to pull her bike from the alley. By the time she had it loose and upright once more, he seemed to have regained his composer. Although, she noticed, he was still pretty pink around the ears.

She thought it was ironic how he had seemed so confidant at first. Yet now, he was as awkward as a boy. It was sweet, she decided. She straddled her bike, sticking the leftovers in her basket and waited while he got his own bike out of the narrow alley. This time, it was she that rolled back and forth a little impatiently, although mostly out of excitement.

———

Jen was on her way home from the bar. Weaving slightly, she walked her bike through the shadows of the outskirts on her way back towards the inner city. She was thinking back on the overly aggressive guy that had driven her out of the bar. He'd stank of booze and wouldn't stop leaning over her seat at the bar trying to insert himself into her conversation with Jack.

She'd drunk enough that she was no longer feeling aggressive herself or she might have picked a fight with him over it. Instead she thought of the half bottle she still had at home and excused herself quietly. She noticed with a disgusted shake of her wobbling head, that he had just moved on to do the same to the next woman at the bar. Who had also shrank away from his foul breath and called for her tab. Jen chuckled to herself.

'*Some guys just never learn to read signals.*' She shook her head in disgust and had to pause a moment. She leaned on her bike, as her vision spun in response.

She decided she'd better not shake her head again. Instead, she went back to the careful task of walking her bike from shadow to shadow, along the long desolate street. She clung to the shadows intentionally, so as not to attract attention. Not that there was anyone there to see her, but it was a well-worn habit of hers. She always snuck through the outskirts rather than riding openly. Especially on nights like tonight, when she'd been drinking or had liquor in her pack.

The last thing she needed after all was to attract the unwanted attention of the enforcers. Since she knew if they ever caught her going to or from the Outskirts this late at night, they would search her for sure. From her case of cigarettes, to the flask in her back pocket, she didn't need that kind of attention. Even the antique lighter Old Tom had given her for her birthday, was totally taboo as far as the lawmakers and the enforcers were concerned. She shuddered a little at the thought and slunk further into the shadows.

Slowly making her way towards the city proper, she could see the dim glow of the streetlights just a few blocks ahead. This was the most risky area. Since the edges of Newcity were patrolled much more regularly then the Outskirts were. Once she cleared the crossing and was fully in the light of the streetlamps she'd be able to ride again. Once there she would use her blatancy as the key to diverting suspicion. For now however, she slunk. She moved slower and slower as she neared the final block between herself and the comparatively well-lit streets of Newcity proper.

Slowing her progress to a crawl, she strained her ears for any sound in the streets around her. They were mostly deserted this time of night but for the enforcers on patrol. She listened and listened and finally in the distance she identified the matched thumps of two sets of feet. They were marching together in time. The enforcers.

Now she really strained her ears but it wasn't long before it was clear, that they were moving away. She let out her breath in a sigh of relief. It was always safest to cross right behind a patrol. They had the curious habit of assuming the areas they had already checked were secure, and would move on without a second thought.

Then again, they were really out here to prevent robberies and depravity. They didn't seem to focus on squelching the few citizens who resisted the restrictions the lawmakers had imposed, for the greater good. Although that would not keep them from searching or detaining anyone they deemed suspicious. Nor from enforcing any other law they observed being broken. They had curious blind spots however, which Jen had come to think might be intentional.

Like the Outskirts, for instance. It was rare indeed that she'd seen them out there, except for a few carefully scheduled patrols. It seemed that perhaps the lawmakers were more understanding of the position their populace was in, then their laws tended to imply. There were the Traders, for example. She had never heard of the enforcers breaking their supply line or of them harassing the Traders in any other way. Although now that she thought about it, they were ridiculously easy to identify. Dirty and dressed in their filthy leathers and all.

'*Hmm...*' She tapped her chin thoughtfully with one finger, thinking about that. After checking thoroughly to see that she still had the street to herself, she led her bike carefully into the light of the streetlight, even as she finished the thought.

*'I wonder. Is it because we're so dependent on them for the supplies they bring in? Are we really that dependent here?'* She wondered. Thinking about the garden that Sister Mary grew on the lot of the orphanage, and how she grew so much that she was even able to supply the boy's orphanage with fresh veggies for their meals as well. '*Are we?*'

She thought about her own diet now that she lived alone. Now that she was away from the orphanage and their home grown produce, she didn't eat that well. She thought about the pre-shift packaged foods that she lived off most of the time. She practically lived on instant breakfasts, which she used to supplement her drinking binges, since they were cheap and plentiful at the convenience store lately.

"It's all packaged, isn't it?" She asked herself out loud. "All of it. Does that mean that the Traders bring in all of it? Do the Traders actually feed most of the City with their trade goods? Maybe that's why the lawmakers look the other way about the booze they traffic in, as well? I wonder…"

She straddled her bike once more. She was confident now that she was in the city proper, that she could talk herself out of any trouble she might run into. Should she encounter any enforcers on her way home from here, she had her story all prepared.

She'd thought it out already, about why she'd broken curfew and about her sick friend that she'd had to tend late into the night. She'd made this story up years ago, just in case she was ever stopped. Whether it was just dumb luck or the confidence of being prepared she didn't know but she had never been stopped. So she'd never had to use it. Somehow, she always made it home unscathed.

---

Dinner had been wonderful. Ashley was full and happy. Although she still wanted to know what there was between Matt and the owners of the little restaurant. She wanted to know what made them love him so much. As he straddled his bike beside her, she wondered if he would mind her asking. She thought maybe she should wait for a better time. Then her curiosity got the better of her and she decided to feel him out about it.

"So, they seem to love you an awful lot." She waited for a response, and saw that he actually seemed to relax a bit. He seemed glad for the change of subject. "Nat almost seems to think of you as a son." She said it with a smile. She meant it half-jokingly but he nodded his face very serious.

"She's very like a mom to me. Since I don't remember my own." He said it very quietly. "She and Samyan lost their own son, in the series of tsunamis that swept Thailand during the shift." He paused to look at Ashley from the corner of his eye. He seemed to be waiting to see what her response was. She was very solemn. She had not expected such a sad story.

'*Although what did I expect?*' She wondered. She remembered now, that he'd mentioned over dinner, that they were refugees. She hadn't thought beyond that at the time.

"I first met them when I was around fourteen or so. It was around four years after the evacuation at least. I'm not really sure how old I am." He was speaking very quietly now. So she rolled her bike closer to hear better. She wondered what he meant. How could he not know his own age? She didn't want to interrupt though, so she just listened.

"When I first met them, they had just arrived here. I just happened into the restaurant. I was just a kid, wandering around, exploring. I had no idea how serious a situation they had just come from." He sighed and taking a deep breath, he continued.

"I don't really remember the shift, or the evacuation. I just remember waking up in the shelter with Sherrie watching over me and a pounding headache. I can't remember anything before that either. It's all just blank, until that day."

He paused, as he waited for her to respond. She didn't know what to say though, so she didn't say anything. She just rolled her bike close enough to put her hand on his, where he held his handlebar. He smiled at her sadly and continued.

"When I first met Nat I was such a goofball." He said ruefully. "Since I didn't have any memories of the disaster I was just, well. A normal kid, I guess. I've never known any world but this one. So I think that to her, I seemed just like a regular kid from before the shift. I guess I must have reminded her of her son. I think that's why she adopted me immediately. She started feeding me and hugging me, and threatening to put some meat on my bones! Which she definitely did!"

He laughed, trying to lighten the mood. To Ashley's ears it sounded hollow though. Despite what he had said about this being the only world he'd known, she could tell that it was hard for him. Not knowing. She could only imagine what it would be like. For him to not know his parents at all. To not know where he had come from. She at least had those happy memories from the years before the disaster. They were a crutch she could to fall back on. She knew who she had been born from and that they had loved her. She realized that was what she would miss most, if it were ever taken away from her. Her knowledge of their love. She tightened her hand reassuringly on his.

"Even if you can't remember them Matt, I know that your parents loved you. Even as Nat and Sam love you now. Because you deserve it! And as much as you may have needed their affection as a child, they needed to be able to give it. It was a blessing for all of you, really." She looked into his eyes and saw the tears welling there. He looked up to hold them back. Taking a deep breath, he tried to keep them contained but she leaned across their bikes and hugged him.

He tried to fight his feelings. He took a deep breath but the tears kept coming. He cried quietly into her shoulder for a time. His breath was shuddered and sporadic, as he fought for control. She rocked him gently, rubbing his back as he cried; like she remembered her mom doing for her. Her mom had always been there to comfort her. Whenever she'd had a nightmare or scraped her knee. She felt tears pricking at her own eyes, thinking of her mother. She let them come. They had all suffered a lot. Everyone had, more than anyone deserved.

Somehow she felt that sharing those few tears with him had lightened the burden of grief. Although she had carried it all these years. Somehow that handful of tears eased it even more, than the torrent of tears she'd shed that afternoon.

*'It must be because we're crying together.'* She thought. She held him a little tighter. Their bikes balanced awkwardly between them, as his arms tightened around her as well. It felt incredible to cry in someone's arms, instead of crying all alone. She couldn't remember the last time that she was held as she cried. It must have been back at the orphanage but she couldn't recall it. They stayed that way for a long time, even long after they had both run out of tears.

Ashley finally realized that she was shivering and that her legs were starting to go numb. Her circulation had been cut off from being pressed into her bicycle seat. Reluctantly she loosened her grip and she felt him follow suit. She slowly leaned back, her hands sliding down to his arms. She felt him run a hand over her hair. It was such a familiar gesture that it made her tingles come back and she took a deep breath. Before she could say anything though, he spoke up.

"Thank you, Ashley." He said it very quietly. She looked up, meeting his eyes. They had gone dark with emotion. "Thank you for what you said. And, thank you for, well. For letting me cry. I guess. I didn't realize how much it would help." He seemed genuinely surprised, as well as a little embarrassed. "I feel, lighter, somehow." He seemed puzzled by it, but she knew exactly what he meant. It was just how she was feeling too. She nodded.

"I know what you mean." She said slowly. "I feel the same way." Since he had been so open with her, she decided that she would try to be as honest with him as well. Even if it was awkward.

"I can't remember the last time someone held me while I cried." She said quietly. "It's like those couple of tears, were worth a bucketful of the tears I've cried alone." She couldn't think of a better way to say it. "I'm sure that someone must have held me at the orphanage. Since I cried all the time once I realized that my parents were, never going to come."

She swallowed hard, feeling the tears threaten again. Once I realized that everyone that we had left behind that day was dead. Somehow no matter how much I cried, it didn't really help. The tension was still there, still the same. Still just as painful."

"I know exactly what you mean." He said it softly. She could feel his eyes on her face. After a moment she lifted her gaze to meet his. She saw that he was actually smiling a little. Again it amazed her. It seemed like he was always smiling, or laughing. That was so rare these days. Everyone seemed to be struggling and hard pressed. Fighting for water, food or health. Yet here was Matt, smiling at it all. She smiled back at him as wholeheartedly as she could manage.

He cupped her chin in his hand, tilting her face up. For a moment, she thought that he was going to kiss her. Her heart beat fast, at the thought. Instead he leaned forward and touched his forehead to hers very gently. She closed her eyes, leaning into the soft touch. She found that to her surprise, she actually did want him to kiss her. Although she barely knew him. His voice startled her out of her thoughts.

"We're the same, you know. You and I." He smiled into her startled eyes, from only inches away. "Yet we're also, different." He stroked her cheek softly with his thumb. His touch was so gentle that it set her shivering again. He started to pull away, to put his weight back on his bike

Quickly, before she could change her mind, she darted forward. She kissed him lightly on the cheek. Then she backed up and settled onto her bike. She looked down, embarrassed, her cheeks hot. When she looked up at him again however, she found that he was smiling broadly. His eyes were warm on hers and she could feel heat coursing through her whole body now, not just her face. She was no longer feeling the cold.

"G-Goodnight." She said softly, thinking it was best to quit while she was ahead. "Thank you, for inviting me to dinner. It was lovely." He grinned back at her.

"Not as lovely as the company." She felt herself blush even harder and he chuckled. "I guess I'll see you at the library sometime then?" He smiled at her but rolled his bicycle back, giving them both more space. The distance made it easier for her to gather herself once more and she nodded.

"Yeah, I guess. I know where to find you after all." She smiled as he looked a little puzzled. "You're usually listening to music, aren't you?" His eyes widened in surprise. She grinned at him this time. His smile was slower this time but it reached and warmed his eyes.

"Yep." He nodded, seemingly amused. "You've got me pegged." He spread his fingers out against his handlebars pretending to be embarrassed but she could tell he didn't mean it. "So I guess that it's time to head home." He gestured back in the direction of the library. She took that to mean that he lived somewhere beyond it.

"Yeah, me too." She said and lifting her feet she began rolling gently in that direction. "My street is just up here a ways." She said over her shoulder rolling past him slowly. He followed suit, the two of them rolling slowly together in silence for a while. When they came abreast of her street she put her feet down to stop. He swung his bike around to face her again.

"Well, this is my street." She blushed. It was so hard to say goodbye to him. Yet she knew that it was getting really late. A thought struck her and she cursed out load.

"What?" He seemed a bit shocked, and worried. He backed his bike off a bit, as though he thought he had offended her.

"Oh, it's nothing. I just, well." She grumbled. "It's just that I'd meant to keep my chopsticks!" He laughed out loud. He seemed relieved that it was something so trivial. "It's not funny!" She said trying hard not to laugh herself. "I wanted to practice with them at home. I really want to learn how!" She couldn't help it, his laughter was contagious and a smile tugged at her lips. "Don't laugh at me!" She demanded playfully.

"Don't worry. I'll bring you some." He smiled as he said it but he had stopped laughing. Now she couldn't help but laugh. While she was laughing he rolled forward and quicker then she could react to plant a kiss on her cheek. She caught her breath in surprise. She found herself partly excited and partly disappointed that he'd only kissed her cheek.

"Goodnight, Ashley." He said with another of his slow smiles. "Sleep well." With that he spun his bike around to pedal back towards the library, picking up speed as he went. She didn't move for a long time. She just watched him scoot off, until he turned out of sight. He was several blocks away when he finally turned but she thought that he looked back and waved. In the dim light of the streetlights it was hard to tell though.

She took a deep breath and held it a minute. She rubbed at her cheek where he'd kissed her, then rubbed at her lips where she'd kissed him. Sighing heavily, she turned her own bike around and rolled slowly home. It was late and she did her best to be quiet as she entered the building, so as not to wake her neighbors. When she got home, she stored her extra water and put the leftovers from dinner in her tiny energy efficient fridge. Then, worn out, she all but fell into bed.

Once she was safely tucked into bed, she lay in the dark of her apartment. The faint light from the streetlamps outside made playful shadows on the ceiling above her bed, as it shined through the plants on her balcony. Her snap peas were moving in the rising heat radiating from the concrete far below. It almost looked as though the shadows were dancing with each other.

She was enjoying the playful shadows but she wasn't really focused on them. Instead her mind replayed it all. Meeting Matt at the library. She thought back on his incredible smile and the warmth in his eyes, as well as their conversation after dinner. She finally settled on the memory of how it had felt to hold him as he cried and how it had felt to be held in return.

She sighed heavily turning onto her side, trying to make herself sleep. Although she tried to blank her mind, it kept coming stubbornly back to her kissing his cheek and him kissing hers. She buried a grin into her pillow. As sleep finally came for her, she didn't even realize that for the first time in a long time, she hadn't had a single painful thought of the past.

# 5

Matt awoke excited and invigorated. He took a quick spit bath while he slurped down some instant breakfast and was out the door as soon as he was decently dressed. He couldn't wait to talk to Michael, or to see Ashley again if he could. He wondered if she would be at the library today, or if maybe he should play it cool and wait until tomorrow to go. He didn't want to scare her off after all.

The thought of her possibly waiting at the library or looking for him made up his mind for him though. No matter what, he didn't want to disappoint her. So he'd go. Even if it meant listening to the same song over and over, he would go. He grinned to himself at the thought of seeing her and took the stairs two at a time. He planned to head straight for the music shop.

---

Michael was having a rough morning. The peg he had been working on for his now almost complete violin had split at the last moment forcing him to scrap it and start over. He was picking through the wood scraps to start another, when Matt came in whistling a tune. He didn't recognize the song. The look on Matt's face said something great had happened though, and Michael sighed.

He wasn't sure he had the energy right now for a happy Matt. He spun like a top when he was really happy. While it was nice to be around from a little distance, Michael preferred to move a little slower than that himself. He decided to just come out and ask in order to get it over with. The sooner he knew what was going on, the sooner he could get back to his carving.

"So what's up with you? You're looking awfully sunny today." He said it a little grumpily. He was holding what he thought was going to be the perfect piece of wood in his hand and he glared at it.

'*You'd better not crack.*' He thought at it. Setting it on his workbench by his tools, he turned his full attention to his friend.

Michael raised an eyebrow as Matt just grinned at him. He was hoping to incite a comment, in answer to his question. Instead of answering though Matt spun on his heal. He turned a full 180 and then plopped onto the stool across from him. Michael couldn't help but smile.

'*Just like a top.*' He thought, laughing under his breath.

Now that Michael had turned away from the frustration of his project, Matt's good mood was catching. Michael was actually starting to get excited to hear what had his friend so happy.

"So? Are you gonna tell me or are you just gonna sit there grinning like an idiot all day?" He prodded. He was a little impatient with Matt's unusual quiet. Michael gestured a little with his hand in what he hoped was an, out with it already, kind of way. Matt sighed happily and finally opened his mouth to explain.

"Do you remember that girl I had told you about? The one at the library? That I thought was so pretty?" He had a ridiculously dreamy look on his face and Michael was glad he was sitting still and not walking around; he was worried that Matt might walk right into a lamp post or something.

"Uh, sure." Michael said, thinking back. He did vaguely remember Matt going on about some girl a while back but he hadn't really paid much attention at the time. He'd figured then that if anything ever came of it, he'd find out. Apparently he had been right. "So, what? You found out you checked the same book out or something?" He asked sarcastically, hoping to spur the story from Matt without a lot of preamble. It worked.

"No!" Matt seemed impatient for a moment but apparently you couldn't keep him down today. A moment later his smile was back, big as ever. "We went to dinner last night, at Sam's!" Now that really was news to Michael. He didn't think that Matt had ever actually dated anyone. At least that he knew of and he was pretty sure that he would know if anyone would. He wondered what had prompted this. He raised an eyebrow questioningly, hoping to entice more information. Once again, it worked. They had been friends a long time and they knew each other very well. The way that Matt had bustled in here first thing, it was obvious that he was dying to talk about it.

"Well it turns out that her name is Ashley. She and I were the last ones at the Library last night. I won't go into too much detail but we ended up connecting. I asked her out to dinner, and she went!" He was obviously ecstatic. So much so, that he didn't realize that he was repeating himself.

"Yeah, you said that already." Michael muttered, but he was

smiling. It was good to see Matt so happy. Not that he was a melancholy person or anything but it had been rare that Michael had seen him practically bouncing off the walls this way. It was usually over music, not girls. He'd get excited at having found a new song or on the rare occasion that he had managed to find a song that Michael himself didn't know yet.

Although he was a friendly guy, Matt rarely let people in past the surface. That was probably the reason that he'd never really dated anyone. To see him so excited about a girl and to hear that apparently she was interested in him as well, was really something of a phenomenon. Not that Michael himself was a lady's man or anything.

He had dated a few girls and he'd found that most girls were just too shallow to be of much interest to him. He was much more passionate about his music and his instruments than he had ever managed to be about them. One by one, they had fallen away. Which he had found he was alright with, in the end.

"She had never had Thai food before. So the whole evening was a blast! Watching her try everything was so much fun! Oh, and the look on her face when she tried the soup! Hah!" Matt continued with a grin, bringing Michael back to the moment. He tried to look interested. Which he was but he'd been momentarily distracted by his thoughts. He didn't want to hurt Matt's feelings. This was obviously a very big deal to him.

"We even sat outside the restaurant for what felt like hours afterward, talking about stuff." Matt flushed a little when he said it, Michael noticed. He sensed there was more to that part of the story then that but he decided not to pry.

"So are you going to see her again do you think?" Michael asked, even though he thought he already knew the answer. He didn't think that Matt would be so smitten if this were a onetime event.

"Oh definitely! Hopefully she'll be at the Library again today." He looked a little worried as he said it. So apparently he wasn't as sure as he had tried to sound. "We didn't really set a time or anything." He explained further. "We just agreed to see each other at the library." Michael noticed that he was fidgeting a lot, playing with his hands, like he didn't know what else to do with himself. Michael decided that maybe it was time for a little distraction. Reaching behind him, he grabbed his now almost complete violin by the neck and handed it silently to Matt. As Matt took it gingerly he caught his breath.

"This is beautiful Michael! I had no idea it would turn out so well! I mean, I guess I should have known." He gingerly turned a peg as though tuning an imaginary string. He slipped it expertly onto his shoulder and holding his chin where the chin rest would be, he closed his eyes and pretended to play. Michael watched him smiling. Matt had learned so much over the years. Michael remembered when he had first offered to teach Matt to play. Matt had actually burst into tears. He had been amazed that Michael thought that Matt could learn an instrument.

Now only a few years later, Matt could play every instrument that Michael himself had been able to teach him. Michael was only sorry that he couldn't teach Matt more. He had the feeling that Matt could learn anything.

*'If only more musicians had survived the shift.'* Michael thought sadly. He had the thought a lot. *'There is still so much that I just don't know. There are so many instruments that I can't make yet. And for all his knowledge, Greg only knows what he knows, as well.'*

He sighed aloud at the thought. He felt guilty for it. He was extremely grateful for Greg's generosity, which allowed him to live here and help Greg run the shop. As well as continuing his education in music and instrument production. Yet he wondered sometimes if he was limiting himself by staying here.

He had learned so much from Greg over the years but he had kind of reached the cap. He wondered if there might be other musicians and other luthiers out there, people that he didn't yet know about. There might be people who could teach him more. Those who could teach him how to make or play other instruments. Or songs that he had never heard sung.

Sighing again, he tried to shake off his reverie and come back to the moment. Looking up he found Matt deep into some silent song. His eyes closed in concentration, Matt played the unfinished violin as though he heard the notes, without even the strings to play them.

Michael watched his movements closely, trying to identify the piece. He kept his eyes on Matt's fingering, mentally noting each chord, until he had a complete phrase. With a mischievous grin Michael picked up his own violin, complete with strings and bow and began to match Matt's movements, note for note.

Matt's eyes popped open briefly, as the first sweet note struck the air but he quickly closed them again so as not to lose his place. As they played together, one instrument full voiced one silent, Michael marveled at it all once again. At the gift of their friendship. The amazing ability's that Matt had musically and at the pure chance of their meeting. He marveled once more at the slim chances of them having been shuffled onto the same bus and then off to the same shelter when all hell broke loose in the world.

Michael almost missed a note as he realized with a shock, that without the devastation of the shift, he and Matt may never have met. He closed his eyes in an attempt to concentrate more thoroughly on the music. The thought stayed with him as he played, though. Of the irony of it all. The thought, that without losing everything, he would never have gained that which was most important to him now. His best friend.

As the song slowly drew to a close and he finished the last refrain, he opened his eyes to see Matt still mimicking his fingering perfectly. Right down to vibrating his imaginary strings to give the last notes their traditional haunting chill. Michael was smiling broadly as he lowered his bow. When Matt opened his eyes at last, he smiled at Michael just as wide, before gently setting the unfinished violin in his lap.

"Well. Thank you for breaking her in." Michael said quietly and he meant it. "I feel truly blessed. What a lovely first piece for her to play, strings or no." He winked and they laughed out loud at their own foolishness.

———

Ashley woke late, stretching in the sun that was spilling in her balcony door and across her little futon. She rolled over onto her stomach yawning to look out at the new day. She hardly ever slept this late, but then she usually went to bed early too. She smiled as the memories of last night and the reason for her late night seeped into her sleepy mind.

Closing her eyes she brought up a mental image of Matt, sitting across from her. His smile lighting up the room. She sighed and buried her face into her pillow, smothering another grin.

'What to do? What to do!' She thought to herself, amused. She didn't want to seem overly eager and just race off to the library like a schoolgirl. She did want to see him again however. She decided that the best thing would be to take things slow. She would have breakfast and organize herself. Then she'd go to the library when she was darn well ready.

Rolling back over, she levered herself up. She was reminded by how sticky she felt, that she had skipped her bath two days in a row now. Making a face at herself, she got up and mindlessly filled her little wash tub at the sink. She scrubbed her teeth clean with as little water as she could. She realized that she had forgotten to do that last night as well. Still half asleep she swept into her little bathroom with her little tub of water, her washcloths and her tiny bar of handmade soap.

Not long later she came out, shivering, but clean. She had forgotten to warm the water first and so she'd had a very cold spit bath, but she was certainly awake now! She took her wash cloths, one for soaping and one for rinsing out and hung them on her balcony rail to dry. She needed to go to the laundromat again soon. They were looking a little worse for wear and they were her last even close to clean pair.

Deciding to pick herself some breakfast while she was out there, she hummed to herself as she searched for anything that might be ready. She found full sized snap peas, green beans, and some other crisp sweet goodies, which were her favorite breakfast. When she came up a little shorter than usual, it occurred to her that she could add them to her leftovers from last night. She had slept so long it would be lunch time soon anyway, so she might as well eat brunch instead.

She drank as much water as she could before she began breakfast, just in case she forgot to drink while she was out and about. She had a quart jar she drank from and she tried to drink 3-4 every day. She always felt better when she started the day off well hydrated. When she got the leftovers out of her tiny refrigeration unit, she could smell it as soon as she opened the door. Her mouth began watering and she smiled remembering just how delicious everything had been. She thought back on how kind Nat and Sam had been as well.

She hummed to herself, as she warmed the soup up on her little single element stove. She had made sure all her lights were off first. She always unplugged her little fridge as well so she wouldn't blow the circuit. It was a long way to the basement, if she overdrew her power and had to reset the breaker.

'*Better safe than sorry.*' She thought to herself, as she nibbled on snap peas and stirred the soup. It smelled divine. Her tummy rumbled a bit despite the peas and beans she snacked on. Once she had brought it to a simmer, she set it aside in a bowl to cool down and dumped the leftover noodles and rice in the same little pot. She added just a trickle of water to it and put a lid on, carefully lifting the pot and shaking it every once in a while to keep it from sticking.

After only a few moments, she decided it was probably good, and dumping it onto a plate. She snagged her bowl of soup with her empty hand and took them both to her crowded little dining table. She gingerly pushed her sketchpad over with her plate, sighing at the piles of paints and pastels covering the rest of the table. She ate on the little corner that she had shoved clear.

She found that she was really hungry. It was so delicious that she had eaten most of the noodles and rice before she even remembered the soup. As she reached for the soup, her eyes fell upon the top image of her sketch pad. It was unfamiliar to her. Curious, she sipped her soup and set it to one side. Picking up the book, she took a better look at it. As she deciphered the strokes and movements of the coal, she suddenly recognized the face that she had drawn during one of her last visualizations.

She had forgotten it completely until now. As she stared again into the coal black eyes of her sketch, she remembered how they had looked at her, as if it were a conscious being. As though it knew that she was there. She shook her head, as a shiver passed down her back. Setting the sketchpad down again, she continued with her meal. It wasn't that the eyes had been menacing in any way, but she had certainly never had a visualization of hers consciously react to her before. Not without her intentionally visualizing it doing so, anyway. She felt a little uneasy about it but she decided that it really had nothing to do with today. She should try to stay focused on the now.

As she finished her meal and set all the dishes in the sink, she thought again about going to the library. She looked at the angle of the light to see what time it was and found that it was still only just past noon. So she decided instead, to see if she could find Jen first. She wanted to tell her about the little restaurant, and even more about having met Matt. She tried hard to think like her friend, as she let herself out of her apartment.

'*Where would she be right now?*' She decided to try Jen's workplace and favorite coffee house. It was one that had a little hidden balcony in the back, where people could hide to smoke their cigarettes in peace. Since all unnecessary combustibles were illegal now, because of their impact on the atmosphere. These little dens had begun to appear, about five years after the abolition began.

Jen had even told her there were hidden bars here in the city but Ashley had made her stop. She didn't want to know. She was already torn enough that her best friend in the world would do things that she knew contributed to the environmental problems they were all suffering from. Ashley really didn't like to be reminded of it. It hurt her feelings when Jen seemed to brag about it.

Somehow, Ashley loved her anyway though. They had been friends so long now that their friendship seemed to transcend their differences. They had first gotten to know each other at the girl's orphanage, where they had both grown up. Even though Jen had been a refugee from the northeast and Ashley had been a refugee from the southwest, somehow they had seemed to be inexplicably drawn together. It was as though it was simply meant to be.

Ashley tried to shrug off her thoughts. As she reached the bottom floor of her building she pulled her bike from the rack and she made her way outside. Quickly she rode off, heading for the coffee shop.

# 6

Jen woke slowly. She stretched against the bed, not enjoying the lingering ache between her brows from last night's overindulgence's. Groaning, she rubbed her eyes. Glancing at the clock she tried to make the blur settle into the numbers she knew it to be. Flipping over onto her stomach, she lifted herself to glare at the clock as she tried again to get the numbers to make sense. She thought perhaps the first number was a one. It didn't seem to be a very big blur.

"Close enough." She sighed to herself, dropping back onto the bed. If it was only one something, then she had plenty of time. She didn't have to work until after four. She wondered idly if she had any of last night's rice wine left. Before her stomach growled loudly enough to remind her that she hadn't eaten dinner.

Sighing again, Jen rolled herself out of bed. A yawn split her face and she grimaced at the grimy feel of her hair as she ran one hand through it.

"Yuck." She muttered to herself. Instead of getting dressed, she pulled her night shirt off and headed for the shower to wash her hair. When she emerged dripping, a short time later, she had run her water ration for the day dry. She felt much better then she had though, with clean hair. Her stomach again reminded her that she'd best eat something today or the hangovers would only get worse.

*'I wonder if I could drag Ashley out? She might want some lunch or something. I haven't seen her in over a week!'* She decided to head over to Ashley's apartment before she went to work. She was hoping that they could grab a bite together before she was swallowed up by the coffee shop she worked at for the day. So she went straight to Ashley's to look for her.

———

Ashley was thoroughly hot and frustrated. She had ridden all over town and had still been unable to find Jen anywhere. She had finally decided to give up and go home for a breather. She needed to drink some water and wanted to have a bit of lunch. As she was putting her bike in the rack, one of her older neighbors came down the stairs. Ashley nodded politely at her. She was still a little too irritated to be as friendly as she normally would have been. Rather than passing her by however, the woman startled her by exclaiming and grabbing Ashley's shoulder lightly.

"Ashley! My dear! I didn't know you were here!" The poor woman seemed upset about it and Ashley wondered why.

"Well, I actually wasn't here Mrs. Palmer. I just got in. What is it?" She asked. Her curiosity piqued despite the heat of the day.

"Oh! Well, it's just that, a friend of yours just left! She stopped by not too long ago and when I saw her in the hall. But I told her that I didn't think that you were home. She just left a little while ago. I am so sorry!" She looked truly chagrined. Which Ashley found rather silly, since she truly hadn't been here at the time. She kicked herself mentally for riding all over town, when Jen had been here at her apartment looking for her.

"Don't worry Mrs. Palmer. I really wasn't here until this moment. So you weren't wrong in saying I was gone. I know that you were only trying to help." She made herself smile, hoping that it didn't seem stiff with frustration. "Did she happen to mention where she was heading next?" She hoped against hope that maybe Jen had mentioned it in passing. The shake of Mrs. Palmer's head answered her before the words were out of her mouth, though.

"No my dear, I'm afraid that she did not. She just thanked me for my help. Lot of help I was! She scooted off as quick as she came. I am so sorry." She seemed truly distraught over it and Ashley wanted to reassure her. After all, it truly wasn't Mrs. Palmer's fault that Ashley had been out.

"It's alright Mrs. Palmer. We'll connect when we're supposed to." She smiled, patting her shoulder reassuringly. "I'm grateful that you were looking out for me. I'm glad that you spoke to my friend at all! Truly, I appreciate it." She meant it as she said it and Mrs. Palmer seemed to feel it. She finally relaxed and gave Ashley a small smile.

"Well, all right then dear. If you're sure it's alright. I just feel so bad for butting in. She may well have waited if I hadn't." She still looked a bit concerned but was obviously trying to look happy for Ashley's sake.

Ashley smiled for real this time. She was touched and amused at the sweet old woman's concern for her. So she tried to reassure her again.

"Don't you think it Mrs. Palmer. If I know Mz. Jenever Jones and

I do, she'd never have waited around anyway. That's just not how she is. She's far too impatient for that." She winked at Mrs. Palmer trying to coax another smile out of her, to help her relax. It seemed to work. Ashley startled a smile from the poor old woman. She squeezed Mrs. Palmer's shoulder reassuringly and ducked around her. As she started up the steps behind her, Ashley said over her shoulder.

"Thank you again, for looking out for me Mrs. Palmer." She said it with a smile. "I need to get some water now though. I've been riding all morning. You make sure to keep hydrated in this heat too, alright?" Mrs. Palmer nodded, as Ashley continued up the stairs to her apartment.

Ashley was still irritated that she'd missed her friend. She'd been really looking forward to talking to her about Matt, but she'd meant what she'd said to Mrs. Palmer as well. She was sure that they would get together whenever it was truly meant to be. Shrugging to herself, Ashley decided to let it go and to get on with her day. As she let herself into her apartment however, she saw a slip of paper flutter to the floor.

*'It must have been shoved into the door jam.'* She thought, bending to pick it up. As she unfolded it and began to read, she recognized Jen's familiar handwriting immediately.

"I missed you! Where the hell are you?!? I wanna see you! Let's do lunch." Ashley laughed out loud at the squiggly little smiley face at the end of the note and all the exclamation marks too. It was just so Jen. She sighed as she shut the door behind her. It made her miss her friend even more. They tried to get together at least once or twice a week. It had been their habit ever since they had left the orphanage. Without a consistent way of finding each other though, it was up to chance when they were actually able to meet.

She set the note on the counter as she filled her drinking jar. The tap water came straight from the aquifer beneath the city. That water source was why Newcity had been selected for the new metropolitan center after the shift. The water was delicious. She was so thirsty from riding around in the heat of the day, that she drank it dry in moments. Taking a deep breath she smiled to herself.

The cool water helped her to feel more like herself again. Feeling much less grumpy, she decided to refill her jar and go pick some lunch. So setting down her newly refilled water jar, she set it on the counter and got out a big bowl. She went out onto her porch and began checking her plants, to see what was ready to eat today.

She decided to start with her lettuces. She took only the outermost leaves, from the largest plants so as not to damage them. Once she was done, she moved on to her tiered rows of root vegetables next. Their container was an old magazine rack. She had brought it home from the outskirts on her bike trailer and converted it into a planter.

She picked a few of the tender young beet greens and proceeded on down the row. She made her way around the tiny balcony, doing the same kind of careful pruning. She took only the outermost leaves, so as not to hurt the plants themselves, in her gentle harvesting. As she passed over the poisonous leaves of the potato plants, she descended hungrily on her arugula patch. She popped one in her mouth and the sweet and spicy leaf made her stomach rumble. Stuffing a few more leaves in her mouth, she relished the sweet and spicy flavor of them, as she added more of them to her quickly filling bowl. Turning around she looked back towards the door. Surveying her garden from the end of the little balcony, a glimpse of bright color among the bushes caught her eye.

'Really?' She thought with delight, as she hurried to her tomato plants. She had been patiently waiting for what seemed like months now, for her tomatoes to fill out and ripen. As she gently pushed the branches aside, the smell of the plants teased her hungry nose. She was ecstatic to find that one was finally ripe. She tested it, squeezing gently. She found that it had just the perfect amount of give; not too hard, not too soft. With a happy sigh, she plucked it from the vine and dropped it into her now complete lunch bowl.

Beginning to turn away, she saw another hint of red among the leaves. Gently prying back the branches, she found that she had several more that looked about ready. She decided to save them, since she still needed enough for dinner tonight.

She snagged some peas on her way back in however, since the poor vine was almost overwrought with them. Since she hadn't eaten in the night before they had grown like mad in the heat of the day. Settling herself onto her little cushion, she nestled amongst the plants and decided to just eat out here.

She hungrily chomped the tomato. She ate it whole. Enjoying it a bite as a time. She hung her head over the bowl, so as not to lose any of its precious juice.

As she finished devouring her delicious lunch, one fresh picked leaf at a time, she licked the last of the tomatoes juices from her sticky fingers. She realized that she'd better go in and wash her hands, before she went to the library, since she didn't want to get any of the books sticky. Thinking of the library, she realized that while she had decided to go, she really didn't have anything she needed to look up. She set her bowl in the sink and washed her hands.

She wanted to have something to look up, though. After all, if Matt wasn't there, she didn't want to just sit around feeling like an idiot with nothing to do. It was ironic, since normally she could entertain herself for hours at the library.

The possibility of seeing Matt again, was so distracting though, that she couldn't think of a single thing to do there today. As her eyes darted nervously around her apartment they landed on the edge of her sketchpad. It was still sitting on her little table, almost lost amongst her many art supplies. She wandered over to it, looking down at her most recent sketch. She picked it up to get a better look.

'Hmm...' She thought to herself. *'I wonder if this is a real animal. Maybe I can find a picture of it at the library?'* The creature intrigued her, since it had seemed to come out of nowhere. Having appeared in her mind, as it had. It had reacted to her as though it were independently alive, aware. She really wanted to know if it was some kind of creature she hadn't seen before.

*'Maybe it's the long dead spirit of some animal? Perhaps I stumbled across its ghost, while it was wandering the earth, looking for its body?'* She pondered the idea for a moment, and then gave up with a shrug.

Setting it back on the table again, having committed it to memory, she decided she'd ask the librarian. It was an angular face, with spikes and horns. It almost looked like some kind of lizard. It was unlike any lizard she'd ever seen pictures of though. There was something about it that tickled at the back of her memory. For some reason, she thought of Jen when she looked at it. The face was broader and the eyes larger, then any lizard she could think of. She was looking forward to asking the librarian when she got there; maybe she could get a push in the right direction.

Looking out at the angle of the sun, she decided that she'd stalled long enough. It was time to head to the library, if she was actually going to go. Slipping her jar of water into a bag, she stuffed her little purse in with it, so she'd have her library card. Suddenly excited, she took the stairs two at a time in her rush to go get her bike.

---

Jen sighed to herself, as she pushed open the door to the Dragonfly Café. The beautiful tinkling of the chimes on the door simply sounded like work to her. She had ridden straight to Ashley's when she got up, only to be told that she'd been gone all day. Her neighbor hadn't had any idea where she'd gone, so Jen hadn't known where else to look. She'd been by the Library and ridden out to see Old Tom. She had even gone over to the College, as a last resort. She had tried the little coffee shop they sometimes went to together. Which was where she had been hoping to take Ashley today.

By that point she was out of ideas and out of patience, so she went ahead and bought herself a sandwich at the coffee shop and left. She wanted a cigarette and a drink with her late breakfast. So unless she went back to the privacy of her apartment, there weren't too many places where she could openly smoke. So here she was, at work, almost two hours early. Which she hoped would be long enough for her to enjoy her sandwich and her cigarette, before she had to clock on. Amber looked up from the magazine she was reading but didn't close it since she saw it was only Jen coming in.

"Ashley came by a while ago. She was looking for you." She said casually, as she returned to her reading. "You know you're shift isn't for another couple of hours right?"

Jen growled an inarticulate exclamation of irritation as she stomped inside, trying to express her frustration. The dragonfly décor was as lovely as ever, but it did nothing to lighten her mood. With a sigh, she decided she'd try not to take her mood out on her friend. Instead she explained to Amber why she was so mad.

"I was out in the heat looking for her while she was here looking for me! Now I hardly have time to have breakfast before work, let alone trying to figure out where to look for her next." Jen heaved a sigh again, pouting. She poured herself a glass of water, hoping to sooth her feelings. The community water pitcher on the counter was just one of the reasons that she loved working here. The cool water on her parched throat felt lovely, and she took a deep breath when she was done. She reminded herself that she would see her friend whenever the moment was right, or so Ashley was always telling her.

Smiling, she turned to Amber to ask about getting a smoothie to go with her half a sandwich. Accepting it when it was done, she smiled her thanks to Amber and retreated with her spoils to the farthest corner of the covered porch outside.

Amber went back to her magazine as Jen was settling herself onto her seat. Jen could still see her through the window, though it was covered in dead vines. Most of the wall between them was equally enshrouded, but she knew from experience that it was easier to see out then in. So she smiled and waved just in case her friend was looking and tried to be nonchalant about tipping her flask into the smoothie to give it a little kick.

She opened her notebook to scrawl her thoughts down, as she tried to settle her mind. While she munched her sandwich and sipped at her spiked smoothie. The addition of a little liquor to her drink was thankfully beginning to ease her habitual headache. Flipping it open to a blank page, she contemplated the encouragingly empty lines, as her hands absentmindedly fumbled for a cigarette.

Taking a drag, she blew the smoke out in a cloud that hung before her. It glittered in the shafts of light, cut up by the stark bodies of the dead vines over the glass above. The vines both smothered and protected the house in the Outskirts that the Café was hidden in. The vines helped to hide the flare of matches and distorted the smoke of the illegal combustibles encouraged here.

From the outside, the Dragonfly Café was a half-hidden ruin covered in dead vines. It was just on the edge of the outskirts, in an abandoned residential area. Inside though, if you knew to look for it, was a cozy and functional little smoke friendly coffee shop. With its attached covered and enclosed porch set with tables and chairs. The walls were decorated with artwork. Customers were encouraged to sit out here with their purchases and have a smoke at the same time, safely away from the prying eyes of the enforcers. Jen loved it here, when she was in a good mood. The endless artwork on the walls, many of them depictions of dragonflies in all colors and shades were very inspiring. Looking up, she admired a mosaic dragonfly fit onto the slim wall between windows to her right. It was made from all sorts of found objects, some metal and iridescent strips and even a few pieces of what appeared to be seashells.

To her left she admired the waterfall mural on the thin strip of wall by the door. It filled the corner between the door to the Café and the far wall of windows, which looked out on the neighboring houses through the mass of vines. Looking down at her notebook, she found she had sketched it unconsciously. There was a rough if rather un-proportional dragonfly and a few streaming lines and a ruffle that could have been a waterfall. Since she'd scribbled them right in the middle of her previously blank page, she wrote a note beside it that said, paint your room!

'*Really.*' She thought with a smile. '*There's no reason why my apartment couldn't be this inviting. That is one of the things that I like most about the Café after all.*' She realized that was why she always felt welcome here. It was inviting and she felt accepted. They even had some of Ashley's art on the walls. And some of the jewelry they had made, when she was into that, was still for sale in the gift shop.

She had many fond memories of Ashley coming to visit her here, when Jen was the only one on and business was slow. She smiled thinking of some of the fun that they'd had experimenting. Making muffins and things from recipes Ashley had found at the library. They had even sold the results at the Café when they turned out well. Such experiments turning out well were mainly thanks to Ashley's influence, more often than not.

She remembered when she had been in her jewelry making phase. Jen had been really hung up over a guy at the time. Ashley had showed up day after day beads in hand, to sit and make jewelry with her. It had really helped to pass the long slow hours of her shift. It helped the days pass and it gave her something pleasant to think about. It was so much better then dwelling on heartache, as she likely would have if Ashley had not decided to come by.

Jen sighed. Her turn of thoughts had only worked to emphasize her frustration at having missed her friend again today. She had ridden all over town, checking Ashley's apartment, the library and had even gone down to Old Tom's but even he had said he hadn't seen her. He asked if maybe she was working. Jen had smacked herself for not having thought of it sooner and scooted over to the college to see if anyone knew Ashley's schedule or if she might be working. When she had got there though, she was told that Ashley was off for the day, since no art classes needed her.

By then Jen was tired and demoralized. So she had decided to give up and come to the Café so she could unwind a little before she clocked on. She really loved the little bohemian café. She blew out the last drag of her cigarette debating having another and deciding against it. Instead she finished her smoothie, looking around as she again admired the murals on the walls. She really enjoyed her time here.

'*Although.*' She thought to herself, looking in to check the time on the clock above Amber's head. '*There is something about being on the clock, which definitely makes it less fun to be here.*' Seeing that she had half an hour till she clocked on, she sighed again. That wasn't enough time to go anywhere else. She noticed that Amber was frowning with impatience. She kept checking her antique watch, a gift Jen had gotten her at Old Tom's, and she was obviously quite unhappy with the slow pace of the passage of time.

Sighing again, Jen took a last gurgling sip of smoothie and finding her hand empty when she automatically tried to bite her long ago eaten sandwich, she laughed at herself and gathered her things. Snubbing out the end of her cigarette, she brought the dirty ashtray with her to save herself a trip and turned to Amber as she came through the door.

"Go ahead and clock off. I'm already here so I might as well take over, eh?" She smiled crookedly at Amber, who let out a whoop of joy and took off to get her things.

'*I might as well. Besides, this way if she thinks of it, Ashley should know just where to find me.*'

# 7

Matt had spent much longer then he had meant to at the shop with Michael. They had gotten to talking about music. It was an endless subject for the two of them. Then Michael had wanted to play a new song for Matt on the violin. It was a new one that Michael had been trying to learn. It had been so beautiful, that Matt had insisted on Michael teaching it to him.

They had spent most of the afternoon, passing Michael's violin back and forth, as Matt mastered verse after verse of the new song. His fingers hurt from cording on the tiny neck of the instrument, but the melody hung in his mind like a new friend. He knew it was worth every finger cramp and every mistake he had made, just to learn a new song.

He felt tired but invigorated. As he straddled his bike to head for the library, he just hoped that he hadn't missed Ashley while he was caught up in the moment talking music with Michael. He'd feel really bad, if she'd been there waiting for him all day while he was enjoying himself learning a new song.

In fact, he hoped that she was there at all. They hadn't set a date after all. Neither of them had mentioned meeting today or anything, and he was starting to be sorry that he hadn't. At the time though, he'd been too tired to think of it. Not to mention too giddy from her kissing his cheek, to really think straight about anything.

He grinned to himself thinking of it, standing on his pedals for the hill. Although his smile faded as he remembered Michael's parting comment. As he had one foot out the door Michael had stopped him to say, by the way your breath stinks.

It had pissed him off, at first. After a moment's thought though, he realized that Michael was right. Matt had totally forgotten to brush his teeth the night before and he had been in too much a hurry to do it this morning. He only hoped that somehow Ashley wouldn't notice.

'*I'll just have to keep my distance.*' He decided with a sigh as he rode into sight of the library. As he turned to the right of the courtyard heading for the bike rack, he saw to his delight that Ashley was just heading towards the library doors herself. She must have just put her bike in the rack as well.

He couldn't help himself; he called out to her since he was so excited to see her again.

"Hey, Ashley!" He could feel a grin splitting his face, but he couldn't seem to stop it. Although, as she turned around in surprise, he realized that he really didn't know what else to say.

———————

Ashley swung around in surprise, as someone called out her name. Just in time to see Matt burst into a huge grin. She smiled back and waved, feeling a little embarrassed. She felt like she'd been caught with her hand in the cookie jar or something.

*'It's a public place.'* She reminded herself. *'I could be here to look something up. I didn't necessarily come just to see him.'* She felt herself blushing though and she knew it wasn't true.

"Hi there." She said, trying to sound casual as he rode up to her, instead of over to the bike rack. She could feel her cheeks burning and she smiled nervously. She regretted now that she had kissed his cheek last night. The moment loomed large in her mind and she tried to suppress it, so that he wouldn't catch the stray thought.

"How are you?" He asked her, as he pulled his bike up alongside her and stopped. She was relieved to see that he looked nervous too.

"I'm fine." She said with a smile. She took heart in his nervousness. For some reason, it made her feel more confident. "Should we go in?" She asked, gesturing towards the library door, pretending for a moment that she had something to do in there. He looked confused for a minute, then he began to blush and looked down.

"Uh, actually. I, uh, don't have anything I need to do at the library today." He said under his breath. He was obviously embarrassed. "But if you do, I can wait!" He assured her quickly. "I was just hoping to see you here, to be honest." He smiled at her, obviously a little unsure of her reaction to that but she smiled.

"Actually, I don't really need to go either." She said it quietly as well. Despite his admitting it first, she was still embarrassed to say it out loud. There was an awkward pause as they both looked at each other and then around. Obviously, neither of them knew just what to say. She opened her mouth to say something and he had started to speak as well. Their words tumbled over each other's in an awkward jumble and they both laughed nervously. She decided to try again.

"Do you want to go do something?" She wasn't sure what though. She didn't really do much, outside of the library and work. She didn't really feel like she could afford to eat out again so soon, even if she hadn't had to pay for her share. She would feel very guilty if he tried to pay for her meal again. She wasn't sure that she just wanted to repeat what they had done last night, either. Even if it had been fun. Once again the moment that she'd kissed his cheek loomed large in her mind. She tried again to push it down. She tried to bury it under other thoughts, but she felt her cheeks flushing again. His next comment did seem to follow her thoughts.

"Well, did you want to get dinner again?" He seemed unsure of the idea as well, as though he sensed her hesitation. Perhaps he too wasn't sure about simply repeating the same thing as last night. She shrugged unsure of how to answer him for a moment, then a thought struck her. She wondered if it would be too forward to suggest. Yet she couldn't think of anything else, so she went ahead and asked him.

"Would you like to come over for dinner? Do you like salad?" She was blushing so hot that she felt sunburned. As she asked the question, his jaw dropped open in surprise. He blinked at her stupidly for a minute. She wondered if he was getting the wrong idea. She really just couldn't think of anything else to suggest. She spent so much time at home, that she really didn't know anywhere else in the city to just hang out. She was about to try to take back the suggestion, when he answered.

"I would love to! I mean, uh, I love salad!" He seemed to sense her hesitation though. "Are you sure though? Is that what you want to do? I don't want to eat all your food or anything." He said shyly. For some reason his hesitance bolstered her confidence. So she nodded, wondering what might be ready in her garden. She hoped she had enough for two out on her porch. Thinking it over she decided that she definitely did. Especially since she wasn't actually that hungry, having just eaten her late lunch. She had those other two tomatoes that were ready so...

*Why not?* She thought to herself, even as she reassured him.

"I can't think of anything else we could do really. Unless you have an idea? As long as you don't mind the mess. It's a quiet place that we could talk, you know?" He shook his head hard, when she mentioned the mess. She wondered for a moment, just what his apartment might look like. She found she was warming up to the idea. She'd never had anyone over other than Jen once in a while, but she was definitely comfortable at home.

"It would be nice. I'd like to show you my garden. Not many people have seen it." She said with a smile. His eyebrows rose in surprise and he sounded impressed as he asked about it.

"You have a garden? Do you have a yard? I've never seen a garden here in the city. I've only seen them in movies. What's it like? Is it big?" His eyes were a little wide. She thought he looked like a little kid, since he seemed so excited. She laughed as she walked back to her bike. He slowly rolled along beside her.

"No I don't have a yard, and it's definitely not big. I just grow a few veggies out on my balcony is all." She said humbly. She was now really excited to show him her plants. They were like friends to her. She was excited to be able to share them with someone besides Jen. She looked over as they got to the bike rack and found that he still looked impressed.

"On your balcony?" He asked incredulously, as she pulled her bike free and straddled it. "Are you serious? I had no idea you could even do that!" She couldn't help but grin at his surprised excitement. She found she was impatient to show it to him now, since he was so excited to see it. She loved her little balcony and all of her plants. It was her own little haven, from the dirty broken remains of the industrialized world that they lived in. Suddenly she couldn't wait to share it with him.

"Come on! We'll be there in just a minute. Follow me!" That last she called over her shoulder. Her excitement had her standing on her pedals, heading back the way she'd come. When she glanced over her shoulder to see if he was coming, she found that he was right behind her. His face was again split by a big goofy grin and she laughed as she turned back to watching where she was going.

———

Matt was ecstatic. First that she had come to the library, and secondly that she'd invited him over for dinner. He had been admiring Ashley from afar for so long that he had an inkling of what her interests were. Based on the sections of the library that he'd seen her in, he had a few guesses. He was really curious though, about who she was as a person. Even with all of that aside, he really couldn't wait to see her garden.

'*Wow.*' He thought to himself, as she glanced back to make sure he was following. She was riding fast, obviously just as excited as he was. '*A real garden! Here in the city!*' He could tell that she wanted to show him her garden, as much as he wanted to see it.

He hadn't been joking when he'd said that he had never seen one. At least not that he could recall. There was very little that grew here in the city at all. Between the heat storms in the summer and the ice storms in the winter, it was a very inhospitable place.

The humans here could take shelter in the underground bunkers, when the heat hit or the ice storms came. Any plants that had managed to root in the cracks of the crazed old concrete though, were quickly scorched to death or frozen solid depending on the season. He couldn't remember the last time that he'd even had fresh greens outside of Nat's place.

'*It must have been back at the orphanage.*' He thought to himself.

He wondered for a moment just where the orphanage had gotten their greens for salad. He had never really thought about it before. As he followed Ashley down the street to her apartment though, he found himself wondering just where they had gotten those fresh greens. He had never seen anything like them at the market where he got his own food. It was all packaged foods left over from before the shift that he sold there. In fact he couldn't think of when he'd seen anything like fresh produce since leaving the orphanage. Yet they had almost always had fresh salads with their bread at night and veggies in their soups, even in the winter.

He decided that it didn't matter now. He shook his head to try to bring himself back to the moment. He was really excited to be spending time with Ashley again. As well as to get to see her garden. He was excited that she wanted to share it with him. He couldn't wait to see just what she had going on out on this little balcony of hers. He was so lost in his thoughts that he almost ran into her, as she slowed her bike suddenly in front of him. She rolled her bike around so she could see him and smiled as she gestured to the building on their left.

"Here we are!" She announced. "And there's my little garden." She said, pointing up several stories, to a balcony overflowing with greenery. He felt his jaw drop in amazement. He had never expected it to have so many plants! The whole balcony was covered with leaves and vines. From here against the pallor of the crack crazed old building, it looked like an oasis in the desert.

"Are you serious!?!" He asked her incredulous. "You grew all that yourself?" He looked back to find her grinning from ear to ear, obviously understandably proud of her hidden grotto. She nodded and he asked her again. "Really? From seed?" He felt h his eyebrows crawl up into his hairline, as he looked up again in amazement. Even from the street four stories below, he could see just how lush and full the little space was with plants.

She nodded again and started in the direction of the front door of her building. He tore his eyes away from the plants long enough to try to get his bearings. He wanted to remember where she lived if he could and as he looked up and down the street; he realized that he knew exactly where they were. They were only a few blocks from Nat and Sam's restaurant. He had ridden by there any number of times. Yet somehow he had never noticed the little balcony above, with its overflow of lush greenery.

*'I must have been too busy watching where I was going. I wonder what else I've missed.'* He thought to himself. Hopping off his bike, he followed her inside. He carefully walked his bike through the door, as she had. He shut his eyes as they entered, trying to help his eyes to adjust to the dimly lit room at the bottom of the stairwell. When he opened his eyes again he could just make out Ashley as she shoved her bike into the rack under the stairs. He could dimly see her through the spots in his vision, left by the bright day they had left behind.

"It's this way." She said over her shoulder, as she started up the stairs, obviously too excited to wait. He quickly shoved his bike into the rack beside hers and followed her up the stairs to the third floor landing. When they reached her door, he noticed there were little paper flowers and a butterfly, that she had cut out and stuck to the door somehow. He smiled at the homey touch it gave the otherwise unremarkable door, deciding that it would make it much easier to remember which apartment was hers. Although he didn't think that he would forget. It was the first door as they came to her landing.

*'That makes sense.'* He thought. *'Since her balcony faces the street.'*

She smiled over her shoulder at him shyly, as she opened the door. As she entered, she gestured grandly, showing that he should follow her into the tiny room beyond.

"Sorry about the mess. I don't usually have anyone over. I didn't think that we would be coming here when I left or I would have straightened up a bit." She pulled the blanket straight on her little futon, which sat in the in the middle of the overcrowded room. As she said it, she kicked an extra pair of shoes under the bed as well, trying to make more space in the tiny studio. He looked around, completely taken in by the hominess of it all.

There were paintings on every wall, with stacks of other canvasses leaned up against the base of the walls as well. There were even more scattered onto every available surface, along with stacks of library books, paints and sketchpads. She had a few plants scattered in here too. One little plant on her tiny bookshelf and there was another on the counter by her sink. It was a far cry different from his own stark little room. Which contained only his bed, his guitar and a chest for his cloths. Most of which were actually on the floor at the moment, he thought with a little embarrassment. Her space was amazing to him.

"I didn't know that you were an artist." He said, as he admired the large painting on the wall opposite the front door. It was a beautiful if fuzzy garden scene, and though it was a little blurry, he could make out a pond amidst some kind of flowers. She looked up from straightening things, to see which painting he was looking at and she let out a little laugh.

"Oh, that one! That's not even an original concept. I copied an old classic for that one. My art teacher at the orphanage insisted that if we were going to paint, then we had to start by learning how other people had done it. That way, we would have a firm foundation once we began to develop our own styles. I think I was about fifteen when I painted that." She smiled fondly at it but he was amazed. He'd had no idea she had that kind of talent or that anyone did really. Letting his eyes run over the painting again, he relished in the movements of the colors. Admiring the way the textures seemed to mimic the movements of plants and water.

"That is amazing!" He said, smiling at her warmly. He was thoroughly impressed and he hadn't even seen the garden yet. She laughed again shrugging, trying to play it off as normal. He took the opportunity to look a little more closely at some of the other paintings leaning up against the walls. He saw portraits and swirling sky scenes. With quite a few paintings of the ocean, and those where just the ones that he could see from where he stood. There were obviously more hidden in the stacks behind them, that he couldn't see and he really wanted to look but he didn't want to push her.

He could tell that she was embarrassed and he remembered that she had said that no one ever came over. So he supposed that she was unused to getting compliments on her work. He decided to change the subject, to see if he could make her more comfortable.

"Do you want to show me the garden? I'd love to see it!" He let his enthusiasm show in his voice and it seemed to remind her of why they had come. She put down the stack of library books she had been fidgeting with and nodded with a smile.

"Yeah. That's a good idea."

As she led him towards the doorway to the little balcony, he ran his eyes along the spines of the books on her little bookshelf. He had to squeeze between it and the bed to get to the sliding door of the balcony. He saw a lot of books on agriculture, many on art and art history and others on subjects that he had never even heard of. He wondered if he would ever get the chance to read them. He decided not to dwell on the thought. He either would or he wouldn't.

She went out ahead of him, onto the balcony. As he stepped out onto the crowded little porch, he was blown away at the sheer number of plants out here. He couldn't even begin to count them all, and when he looked closer he saw that she even had two, three or four kinds growing in one pot sometimes. He had never heard of such a thing, so he decided to ask her about it.

"How come you've got them sharing pots? Is it just to save on space out here?" He supposed that was it. Since she definitely didn't have as much space as she had plants but when he looked over to her for an answer, she was shaking her head.

"No." She said. "Well, I mean, that's part of it but there's more to it than that." She brushed her hand gently across the leaves of one of her plants as she spoke, smiling at it like it was a friend. The smell of it wafted to him on the wind, it smelled like mint. "It's called companion planting. Each plant helps the others in some way."

She left it at that, as though she expected him to know what that meant. Since he didn't want to admit his ignorance he just nodded, feeling rather stupid.

"So I guess, are you hungry?" She asked, looking up as though suddenly remembering why they had come. He nodded even though he was too nervous to be hungry. He thought it would give them something to do other then make awkward conversation.

"Hmm." She looked around. "Let me go get a bowl."

She smiled as she slipped by him in the narrow space. There was very little room out here to maneuver and he had to grab hold of her elbows and carefully dance around the plants with his feet, in order for her to get back to the door. He wondered for a moment if he should follow her in but she was back again before he could decide. She handed him a bowl and had another in her hand, although he was far too self-conscious to harvest anything from her little garden. Instead he just held his bowl and watched. He saw her head for what he thought he recognized as several kinds of lettuce. They were growing all mixed together in a long tiered planter.

He wondered what the frilly leaves coming up between them were but he didn't ask. He watched closely but she didn't pick any of the frilly plants. As he watched she heaped the bowl she was holding with lettuce leaves of all varieties. He noticed that she always took the outer leaves. Again he wanted to ask her why but he was just too shy to admit how little he knew about plants.

When he was sure that the bowl couldn't possibly hold any more leaves, she turned and making her way carefully back towards him she held out her hand for his bowl. He handed it to her wondering if she was going to heap it just as high as her own. Instead she dumped half of what she'd gathered into it and turned back to her plants for more. He smiled with relief. He was glad that he only had to eat half that much, although she obviously wasn't done picking yet. As she started picking some spiky little leaves he didn't recognize he decided to go ahead and ask what they were. He was willing to eat whatever she gave him, but he was also hoping to start the conversation again. Asking about their salad seemed like something easy to talk about.

"What is that? I haven't seen it before." She glanced over her shoulder at him as he asked.

"It's arugula." She said, popping a leaf in her mouth she handing him one as well. He chewed it cautiously and to his pleasure found that it burst with flavor. It was sweet and spicy all at once. He had never imagined that such plain looking leaves could contain such potent flavors. It was delicious and set his stomach to growling.

'*Maybe I'm hungrier than I thought.*' He thought, a little embarrassed. She just smiled at him over her shoulder though and kept picking. She was going form pot to pot, gathering the outer leaves of her many plants.

"Do you like broccoli?" She asked him hesitating over a couple of plants growing next to the rail.

"Um, yeah. I think so." He said. He knew it sounded dumb, but he was also trying to be honest. He couldn't really remember what was what from when he'd had greens at the orphanage. They had never really mentioned the names of what they'd served. He had just been told to eat his veggies, and they had left it at that. He watched as she picked another couple of leaves from the plants in question before turning back towards him. She made her way over to stand directly before him and took half of the additional leaves she'd gathered from her bowl and tossed them into his. She just added them on top of the lettuce. She smiled at him and placing one spread had over the bowl she gave it a few expert tosses to mix the greens together.

He uncertainly tried to copy her. This time it was his turn to accidentally toss food everywhere however, as the leaves came up between his fingers. Cursing he bent to get them and they almost bumped heads, as she bent in the same moment. She laughed and steadied herself on his shoulder in the tiny space as she straightened up and let him pick up his own leaves. He gingerly picked them from between the leaves of the plants they had landed on. When he straightened again himself, he tried to smile his awkwardness away.

She laughed a little and stepping very close to him, she reached past him towards the vines on the rail that he'd noticed from below. He felt his cheeks heating, as she brushed against him trying to reach the vines. He leaned back, trying to give her more space. He wondered if maybe he should move.

"Am I in the way?" He asked her. He was unsure which direction to go, in order to get out of the way but pretty sure that he was in it.

She laughed and straightened up. She dropped a handful of green beans in his bowl and a few into her own as well.

"Don't worry about it. It's just that I've got it so crowded out here. It's not really designed for more than one person at a time." She smiled at him. They were standing very close together and he was conscious of how fast his heart was beating.

She seemed to sense his hesitance and she tried to reassure him.

"I really like being able to share this place with someone. It's usually just me and the plants." She smiled at him again, before turning away. Next she reached for some very large bushes, in very large pots growing up against the door. He didn't recognize them. As she began moving the branches though, reaching deep inside the plants he could smell tomatoes, and it again made his stomach growl. He put his free hand to his belly trying to quiet it. He was embarrassed that she'd obviously heard it, standing as close as they were.

"This is the last thing. I won't torture you anymore." She grinned over her shoulder and reaching back she dropped a large tomato into his bowl. "Alright. We can eat now." She said as she straitened dropping another tomato into her own bowl. She looked around then. She seemed to decide that there was definitely not enough room for them out here and she gestured towards the door. "I guess we should go in to eat. Since there are two of us today."

He took the hint and gingerly made his way inside. He wondered if that meant that she usually ate out here with the plants. Stepping inside, he moved away from the door, so that she could come in behind him. Once inside he had to stop to let his eyes adjust again. As his vision cleared and he looked around for a place to sit he realized that she must usually eat out there. Since the only table was covered in paintings, books, and art supplies.

She walked deftly towards the kitchen, obviously so comfortable in her space that she didn't need to wait for her eyes to adjust. She set her bowl down on the counter next to the sink. Almost as an afterthought, she opened a drawer to pull out a couple of forks. He made his way to the table to set his bowl down on the only clear surface. It was just big enough for one.

He thought that he should help and so he carefully stacked some of the library books to make some room there for her as well. When he picked up a sketch pad to move it, his eyes lighted on the image sketched there in coal. His breath caught in his throat and he couldn't help but stare. It was a face. An angular, horned face, with very large eyes. It seemed eerily familiar to him, raising a chill all over his body.

He felt the blood drain from his face and he felt a little woozy. Putting a hand on the table to steady himself, he studied the image, hoping to find the root of the familiarity. His dream song came to mind. The one that he'd played for Michael the other day. The one from his dreams. With a start, he realized that he had seen this face before, in his dreams.

"Ashley?" He looked up to find her watching him curiously.

"Where did this come from? Is this something that you've seen before?" He studied her expression, hoping to find an answer there, but all he saw was puzzlement. She shrugged and brought her own bowl over to the table, the forks in her other hand.

"I saw it in a vision." She said it so casually, he wondered if she had a lot of visions. She seemed to understand his confusion and she explained. "I do visualizations, when I need inspiration for art. A few days ago, that image surfaced in my mind during one of them. I'm not sure where it came from." She shrugged again and pulled a stool up for him. She pushed more of the things on the table over in order to make enough room for the two of them. Once she was seated however, she seemed to realize that he hadn't moved at all. She took a closer look at him.

"What is it? Does it bother you? Are you alright?" She sounded concerned, apparently having noticed how pale he was. She started to get up again and he shook his head.

"It's nothing." He said, setting the sketch down and taking the stool she had offered him. "It just seemed familiar to me for some reason." He tried to sound casual about it. He decided not to mention the dreams. Instead he accepted the fork that she offered him and dug into the salad with enthusiasm.

He decided to start with the tomato. He couldn't remember the last time that he'd had a fresh tomato. The flavor was incredible and the juice burst forth as he bit it. He laughed a little, as he tried to contain the spray of juices. She seemed to relax again as he ate with appreciation.

He saw her send one more glance at the sketchpad, before she delved into her own tomato. She had a similar problem with juices spraying onto her cheek. She laughed in embarrassment as she covered her mouth, trying to hide the mess. He felt himself finally relax completely. Whatever it was about that image that got his attention, he was sure that he would figure it out eventually. For now he wanted to enjoy their evening together, so he made an effort to concentrate on the meal and on appreciating her company.

———

Ashley sighed leaning heavily against the door having finally said goodbye to Matt. He had eventually admitted he needed to go or he would be late for work. She wondered what he did for work that he had to do it at night but she hadn't thought to ask. She'd had a good time talking with him and he had really seemed to enjoy seeing her garden. She wondered what it had been about her sketch that had made him go so pale though, so it was still on her mind. She went over to the table and lifting the pad. She looked closely at the drawing, wondering.

'*What is it about you, face?*' She asked it. She remembered how the eyes had seemed to look at her when she'd had her vision of it.

Shuddering a little, she wondered if Matt had seen the same thing in the sketch. That would certainly explain him going so pale when he stared at it. She sighed and set it down. There was really no way to know. It made her more determined than ever now to ask the librarian about it. She wanted to know just what this creature was that she had seen.

## 8

Matt and Ashley had agreed to meet at the library the next day. She had forgotten the sketch at home. She had been distracted by the prospect of seeing Matt again. So she decided to pick out some films that she wanted to show him while she waited instead. She chose mainly documentaries and histories. She added a few that were funny and a couple she'd found on music as well. When he arrived she planned to ask him to pick out something to watch today if he was up for it.

She had decided to ask him to go to Sam's with her too, once they were done at the Library. She wanted to make sure that he visited them. She had suggested that they begin making it a habit, to watch some films and go to Sam's. She wanted to encourage him to start seeing his friends more regularly. Ashley had become determined to take Jen there as soon as she could as well. She decided to write a note to Jen about it while she waited for Matt. That way she could leave it on Jen's door since they kept missing one another.

When Matt arrived, Ashley presented her choice of films for him to choose from. She showed him the whole documentary film section as well but he decided to choose from the ones she'd hand-picked. Possibly inspired by the visit to the garden, he chose The Sacred Life of Plants. As his second choice he chose, a Magnetic Storm. He said that while they both sounded interesting, he liked how different they were.

———————

As they settled in to watch the films he had chosen, Matt decided to ask Ashley about her job. She had mentioned over dinner yesterday that she had to work in the morning today, which was why they had met in the late afternoon. It had left him curious about just what she did.

"So you said you had to work today?" Matt asked over his shoulder as he put the disk in the player. "Just what do you do? I don't think I ever asked." She looked up from where she sat fiddling with the case of the other movie he had chosen.

"I'm a model." She answered. She glared at him when he snorted with surprised laughter. "What's so funny about it?"

"I'm sorry. It surprised me, that's all." He said, still smiling. "The only model's I've seen are girls holding guitars in old music magazines I've bought at Michael's shop." He was utterly confused by the term to be truthful. Michael had used it in reference to a few of the girls in the magazines and not in a flattering fashion.

Sighing, she gestured that he should sit down. She settled herself back in the chair to watch the film as it opened with a view of the ocean followed quickly by the sunrise.

"I meant that I'm an artist's model, idiot." She said, obviously still irritated with him for laughing. "Though mostly I sit for art classes for the college. I sit for portrait work, life drawing classes and sometimes for the sculptors."

"Oh." He still didn't really understand what she meant by sitting for classes. He was familiar with the college though, since Michael's patron worked there. So he assumed that she meant that she worked at the college. "Do you know Greg Brown? He teaches music." He said by way of explanation when she looked at him blankly. "He's about this tall." He said gesturing. "With light brown hair and a forgettable face." He smiled at his own description. It didn't sound like anyone recognizable, but suddenly her eyes lit up and she began nodding.

"I have met a man like that actually." She said nodding. "I did hear the students call him Mr. Brown now that I think about it. I didn't know he taught music though. He often stops in to visit Schrödinger when I'm there. I'm often in Schrödinger's classroom for his sculpture classes. I have to hold the same pose for days when they're first starting their sketches." She sighed a little. "I think their old cronies or something." She seemed thoughtful as she said as much, then asked him why. "How do you know him? Why did you wonder if I did?"

"Oh he's kind of Michael's adopted dad. He's the one that owns the music shop that Michael runs. I still need to get you over there to see it don't I?" He smiled, anticipating her reaction to the old fashioned store. With its smell of freshly cut wood from Michael's endless carving in the back. He just knew that she'd love the wall of Michael's finished instruments, proudly displayed under some technically illegal, though beautiful full spectrum lights. He really thought that she would love it.

"If Michael's dad is a teacher at the college, then why doesn't he go?" She asked him, when suddenly what had been quiet sounds gently accompanying the introduction to the film changed abruptly to roaring explosions of lava, interrupting her. Matt shook his head, answering her unfinished question anyway in between further blasts of lava.

"It's an old argument between them, believe me." He took her hand, grateful for the distraction from their earlier disagreement. "Michael just doesn't want to waste time, as he sees it. He says he'd rather spend his time making something real, with his own hands. Right here and now. Rather than sitting there listening to someone else repeat their opinion at him. He says he'd rather keep his own opinion."

Matt laughed, for he found that he rather agreed with his friend. Although he himself was not nearly so productive with his free time. The film had gotten going without them now, so when Ashley asked no further questions he kept quiet himself. He decided it wasn't worth battling the blaring music and crashing ocean waves to continue the conversation. Instead he turned his attention to the screen before them as it began to unravel the secret, of the sacred life of plants.

They watched in silence, as the narrator began to explain the interconnected web of life and how various spiritualists and scientist have proven its interconnectedness. About twenty minutes in, Ashley suddenly leaned over Matt to press the pause button, just in time to catch a glowing pink sunset on the screen.

———————

"Did you catch that? Wasn't that amazing?" Ashley smiled, inviting him to share in the revelation of what had just been said in the film. It went quick and she wanted to make sure that he heard it.

"You mean that thing about being one with all things? Is that what you mean? Did you see that waterfall? Everything is so green!" He was obviously enjoying the film but seemed a little puzzled by why she'd stopped it, so turning back to the player she backed it up just a minute to let him hear it again.

"They that see but one in the many teeming forms of Life in the universe. Unto them alone, belongs eternal truth." She quoted along with the film, to make sure he heard it. He raised his eyebrows and she sat down again, letting the film continue.

---

Not quite half an hour later it was Matt that paused the player. He turned to her in excitement.

"Alright, I heard it that time. He said that his tests have shown him that there is a profound consciousness or awareness that binds all things together. That it exists in even the tiniest of organisms, but what does that mean to us?" He seemed to be hoping she would spell it out for him. He seemed to be really trying hard to understand.

"All life in the universe is one, no matter how big or small. That's all he's trying to say. Weather it's animal or mineral or metal or plant, everything has a consciousness within it. Everything. We are all united, within that consciousness." She smiled, hoping that he had heard it that time. It could be very tricky, stretching the edges of the mind. Belief was a sticky thing, and it took practice to get comfortable with new edges of understanding.

She reached to turn the player back on but he intercepted her hand.

"Just a minute Ashley." He looked unwontedly serious and she paused, waiting for him to continue. "Do you think maybe that's why we dream? Do we, maybe tap into the experiences of other consciousness's when we dream? Or is that something else?" He eyed her very seriously, waiting to hear her response. She started to respond without thinking. That dreams were just a person rehashing their life but the memory of her own recent dreams intruded. They had been different for sure, and what she could remember of them was definitely not her rehashing anything she had ever experienced before. So instead she shook her head slowly, still trying to formulate an answer for him.

"I don't know Matt, I just don't know." She gave him an apologetic look but she certainly didn't want to say anything that would confuse him further. Taking that as a hint he pressed the player again and the film sailed on.

The scenes of radiant green foliage and lush forests, as well as his first real glimpse of what a real in the ground garden might look like, left him feeling sharply the lack he had never before known. It was unlike any film he'd ever seen. Ashley would probably call it artistic, with its dramatic music and inspiring nature scenes. He found it fascinating and strange by turns.

When the movie finally wound to a close, he shook himself and stood up stretching. He saw Ashley surreptitiously wiping her eyes and smiled to himself. It had been very touching and also convincing in its incredible arguments for the intelligence and cognition of plant life. He hesitated a moment, wondering what this meant about them picking their lunch in Ashley's little garden.

*'Does that mean that as we stood picking and grazing on her porch, the plants were screaming bloody murder? While we crunched and munched on green beans, lettuce and tomatoes, had the plants been crying out because we had torn their limbs off and eaten them?'* He shuddered. *'It's probably best not to think about that.'* He told himself. *'Not if I want to be hungry for dinner. Although actually, I am hungry. Hmm...'*

"Hey, Ashley!" He said as she stood, stretching as well. "Are you hungry yet? I'm starving. What do you think about getting some food?" She frowned but nodded.

"I am hungry but we have the room for a while longer yet and you had picked out another film. Are you burnt out? That one is a little slow I know. It was only an hour and a half long but it lasted a lifetime!" She smiled as she said it. She had obviously enjoyed the film despite her criticisms. He laughed in agreement. He checked the time on his watch. It was a beautiful antique that Ashley had given him when they met this morning. He had no idea where she had found one still working but the gift had touched him.

"Just as I thought, we have plenty of time if you're willing to wait for a bit. The other film is only an hour." She looked puzzled and he hurried to explain. "You can wait here and get the next movie cued up and I'll go get us some food to go from Nat and Sam's. We can eat and watch the next film at the same time! Like a picnic!" He was really excited. It sounded like fun, but Ashley was already shaking her head.

"Why not?" He asked, disappointed.

"The librarian. She doesn't let anyone eat or drink in here remember? It's a library rule, to protect the books." She sighed though, looking disappointed herself. He suspected she too, was getting really hungry.

"You just wait here. If I'm not back immediately, then I'll be back with food." He winked at her and took off before she could say anything. Once out of the viewing room he skipped until he came in sight of the end of the hall, then fell into a calm walk and approached the librarian's desk.

"Excuse me, Eloise?" He said, deciding to use her first name to open the bribe. "How are you feeling, can I get you anything? Are you thirsty? Hungry perhaps?" He smiled, waiting to see if she'd take the bait. He was being as obvious as possible since he'd noticed over the years that she responded well to sarcastic humor. Squinting suspiciously at him, she swallowed a little and he guessed that she was indeed thirsty, possibly hungry too.

"You see, I was thinking of going down the street to visit my godparents at their restaurant but Ashley really wants to watch another film. So I wondered if you're bribable?" He asked with an honest smile. "I'll buy you dinner! Anything you want, if you let us have a picnic in the movie room. I promise we won't make a mess or damage anything. I swear we won't even think of taking any books in there with us. So what do you think?" He tried to smile but it came out crooked. His confidence faltering in the face of her stoic and skeptical squint. He decided to try one last time before he gave it up as a lost cause and let the woman fetch herself some water to quench her thirst.

"I'll throw in an iced coffee!" He winked trying to entice her to take the offer. "They make a mean Thai iced tea too." With that last offer he was out of ideas. That was all he could think of that might tempt her. He thought he'd better start deciding whether he could sit through another movie without sustenance, when she seemed to bend a little.

"Coffee you say?" Eloise asked, suddenly perking up.

"Yep! Delicious sweet and creamy coffee and anything you want to eat! Just name it!" He said, ecstatic to have gotten a positive response at last. "They have soups, salads, finger foods, noodles, and meat dishes. What sounds good to you? Seriously my treat! Hand delivered." He winked again grinning, hoping to bring the deal to a close.

"Hmm, meat huh? Maybe some chicken, and noodles and salad and some finger foods." She gave him a challenging stare. "If I'm gonna take a bribe it had better be worth it." Then she unbent enough to smile a little and giggled.

"Are you sure you don't want soup too? Their soup is amazing!" He smiled remembering Ashley's first taste of that soup. He had loved the look of bliss on her face, but the librarian was already shaking her head.

"No, no soup, maybe in the winter but not right now. You bring me all the other things I listed and then we'll see where we stand, all right?" She smiled again, this time really broadly. He returned her smile with a little bow and pelted for the door before she could change her mind. He ran for his bicycle as fast as his feet could go. The sooner he could get there, the sooner he could get back.

When he walked into the little restaurant, the familiar tinkling of the bells on the door was like the sound of home. He was suddenly poignantly grateful that Ashley had insisted that he begin coming here more. She had been right. As Nat let herself through the kitchen curtain in response to the little bell, he saw her face light up with a smile. He pulled her into a hug and called his order loudly towards the kitchen for Samyan's sake.

"Two orders of everything and don't spare the love!" Laughing, Nat tried to pull free of his arms to go get started cooking but he held onto her stubbornly. He gave her a squeeze instead and she let him, still chuckling to herself.

———————

"How did you get her to let you do it?" Ashley asked in astonishment when he came in roughly half an hour later, his arms loaded with packages of food. Jumping up she helped him to get them all situated and began opening them up one by one to see what they were. He had gotten some of everything she liked, and she was obviously excited by what she found. He had even gotten a few things that she hadn't had before and he could see that she couldn't wait to try them. She mentioned that she was glad that she had already seen Magnetic Storm, the movie they were going to watch next, so she could concentrate on her food.

"I bribed her." He answered her question with a smile. "I bought her dinner too. Although I really underestimated trying to ride back with so much food! I was quite a sight I'm sure trying to balance it all and ride the bike uphill! I need to get a basket like yours." He had admired it a number of times but had yet to ask her where she'd gotten it.

"I'll get you one." She said nonchalantly. "They have them where I got your watch." She said it absently as she made herself a plate out of a container lid and began heaping goodies onto it for herself. He reminded himself that he too should eat while it was hot and that they had a film to watch but he couldn't help asking as he sat.

"Where did you get the watch? I had no idea things like this were still around, let alone functional." He had been meaning to ask her and was really interested to hear the answer, especially if the spot had other such enigmatic oddities as antique bicycle baskets.

"Oh, at the Salvage yard. Haven't you been out there before? Old Tom is an old friend of mine. We've been trading since I was a kid. Since Jen and I used to go treasure hunting all the time back then. You and I should go sometime too! I'm sure you'd be good at it. With your affinities you might even find musical instruments or something!" She seemed really excited both by the topic of conversation and the food, which she was devouring with enthusiasm as she spoke. She was somehow managing to eat between words or maybe speak between bites.

"Affinities? What do you mean by that?" He absentmindedly snagged a roll and started eating as she answered.

"Your affinity to something. Affinity means to like something, but it can also mean to be like something, do you understand? So if you think of people or objects or even places, as being individual and unique in their vibration, well... it's like the different strings on a guitar." She said, hitting on an analogy she seemed to think he would understand. "Each one is a string. They all resonate, but each one at a different frequency, a slightly different vibration. That's what creates a different sound or tone for each string, right? Now some of these frequencies are harmonious, and others create discord when they overlap, right?

Well, within this vibrational analogy, since like vibrations are harmonious it stands to reason that harmonious vibrations are drawn towards one another, while discordant vibrations repel one another. It's like magnets!" At his blank look at the word magnets, she shook her head. She seemed to be reminding herself that without his memories of grade school in the old world his knowledge of, for her even basic principles, was nonexistent. Shaking her head slightly she made an obvious effort to simplify it even further.

"So when we're out treasure hunting, we are each more likely to find things that are a vibrational match to us, then we are to find things that we would have discord with. I've even found that, when I concentrate on a specific item that I need, I almost always find it!"

She was very excited and practically bouncing in place while she spoke. She had stopped eating to explain this little tidbit but he saw that she had already made serious inroads into their meal while they were talking. He realized that he'd better get himself a plate made if he wanted any and smiled as he asked her further.

"So, Old Tom? The Salvage yard? It all sounds so exciting. I can't believe I've never heard of it before. It's here, in Newcity you say?" She nodded her mouth full. Rather than answering him further however, she concentrated on eating.

He had never realized how sheltered and ignorant he was, until he began hanging out with Ashley. She knew so many different types of things. Many completely unrelated to one another and he, well he had pretty much just focused on music. That had been enough for him, then. Now he could see how much more the world held. More of it becoming visible to him every day. He wondered if he could ever be content with so small a piece again, and wondering just how wide his scope might someday span.

With that rather daunting thought, he reached over and hit the play on the disk player. Snatching up what was left of the noodles he devoured them, alternating bites with some of the finger foods while the credits rolled for the next film. According to the back it was another documentary that had given warning signs of climate change, way back in the 21st century.

When the film was over they discussed it over the last of their meal. Matt finally asking the questions he had kept pent up while the film played through.

"What's a compass, exactly? And what year was this from? Does it say?" He snatched up the film cover to look for the date. "If it had been 70,080,000 years since the last shift in the molten core at that time, just how long has it been now? Or has it already shifted? I didn't even know the Earth had an iron core! Let alone that it was a sea of molten iron or that it had magnetic currents that could affect us here on the surface."

"What I want to know, is whether the aurora they speak of, is why the clouds glow different colors at night. Do you think?" Ashley asked excitedly instead of replying. "They mentioned how the aurora was visible only at the planets poles when this film was made. That being where the magnetosphere was weakest but now I think it's happening everywhere. Just like in their future demo of the time of shifting poles. You have seen the clouds glow sometimes, haven't you? At night? Sometimes their pink or green, yellow or white. Mostly they glow green though, in big patches. Haven't you ever seen it?" She asked, when he continued to look at her blankly.

"I guess, that I just never noticed. I don't look up much I suppose. I mean I walk home from work in the early morning all the time. So you'd think that I would have, but I'm not exactly paying attention to the sky, you know?" He scratched his head, embarrassed. Now that he was thinking of it though, he had noticed when the clouds were greenish a few times because it stood out against the orange of the streetlights. Somehow he had never thought to question why it was so before.

"So what's the significance of that then?" He asked her, feeling unpleasantly dense right at the moment. He was a little overfull with information, after watching two documentaries back to back. He couldn't help the yawn that escaped as Ashley answered his question.

"Well, if this film is right and if the lights we see in the sky really are the aurora then it's apparently happening everywhere because we're nowhere near the North Pole. So I guess that we're the grand kid's grandkids the film mentioned having to live without the protection of the magnetic field." She sighed seeing his continued confusion. "It could be partially responsible for our current climate crisis. The ice caps melting and the increasingly ferocious weather. All of it."

Matt shook his head. He had thought he understood the film but some essential element was eluding him. He decided it might be a good idea to watch this one again sometime. This time he'd keep the thought of its current relevance firmly in mind.

———

Over the next few weeks, they met at the library every chance they got. They watched movies together every day they could and Ashley sent Matt home with books that she thought might further deepen their conversations, which he seemed open to. Since the librarian was so into being bribed Ashley brought her a handmade cushion, and in exchange she was allowed to leave a few in the viewing room to soften the chairs. They ate together often, enjoying what Matt called their movie picnics.

They were both learning a lot from the films and their conversations got had gotten deeper and deeper. Delving into the origin of life, the concept of reality, and the nature of the world that they were currently faced with. Ashley was immensely grateful to have someone with whom to share her thoughts and feelings.

Jen had often let Ashley rant at her about these things, which had given some opportunity to vent but Matt asked intelligent questions that proved he was really interested in the conversation. He was always attentive and always listening. She found that when talking with him her ideas seemed to explore themselves, evolving naturally into more and more solid plans. Her dreams were becoming a reality that she dared to dream towards, just by virtue of exploring them together.

It was a co-evolution that was entirely new to her, but she relished the experience. Whatever they talked about together seemed to run away with itself, leaving them still talking hours later. It seemed the more they spoke and shared their dreams together the more their dreams flourished. She found them manifesting in small synchronistic ways, that nevertheless had a profound impact on them both.

These small synergistic events led them to movie after movie that spoke directly to their ongoing dialog. As well as leading them to occasional books. Just the right books. Books that Ashley had somehow never seen before would seem to pop off the shelf at her, answering yet more of their mutual questions.

She couldn't wait to tell Jen about him. She had stopped by the Café repeatedly and she had gone by Jen's apartment several times but somehow they kept missing each other. Yesterday she had found a note in her pocket that she'd written when she and Matt had first met. It was battered and worn but she had finally remembered to pin it to Jen's door this morning. She had gone by once more yet failed again, to catch her at home. The note had been simple. It just said, meet me at the library tomorrow around noon, let's do lunch! Ashley really hoped that Jen got it in time.

---

Jen was running late as usual but she was really excited. Ashley had left a note on her door saying to meet her at the Library and that they would do lunch. It was out of character for Ashley to suggest that they go out to eat and Jen wondered just what had occasioned the change. Jen arrived at the library, riding into the courtyard still standing on her pedals and breathing heavy. She was greeted by the sight of Ashley riding round and around the bike rack impatiently. She rode out around the pillar, into the courtyard and back again, round and around. Jen was halfway across the courtyard herself before she had her breath back enough to call out to her friend. Ashley looked up, and a huge grin split her face.

"You're here! Come on!" Ashley said in excitement. She spun her bike around, immediately heading back towards her own apartment at top speed. Or at least, that was where Jen thought she was going. A moment later however, they sped past Ashley's street and kept going. Now Jen was really intrigued. It was so unusual for Ashley to find a new restaurant on her own, since she didn't eat out very often. Ashley led her to a tiny doorway, showed her where to stash her bike and led her into a totally different world. Even the air had a sweat and sour tang to it. The gold gilt, silk flowers and paintings everywhere were really quite charming. Looking around, Jen could see why Ashley liked it.

Jen couldn't believe how good the food was when it came, or that she had never known this place was here. She would have thought that the smell alone would have drawn her in. The waitress, whom Jen assumed was very likely the owner, greeted Ashley by name. Her warm smile and her sideways hug showed how much she liked Ashley already. Which surprised Jen, since her friend was usually rather reserved with strangers. The friendliness with which Ashley greeted the woman, argued for a close friendship. True it had been a while since she and Ashley had seen each other but Jen wondered just what could have happened, to have changed her friend so much.

Once again surprising her, Ashley ordered food for them both, without reading the menu. When they were alone again, Jen quietly asked just that. In between loud exclamations of how excellent the food was which was an understatement really. Ashley very quietly told her about Matt. She explained that the restaurant's proprietors were also his adopted parents and she giggled, seeming a little embarrassed.

She and Jen oooed and ahhed loudly over the food again, to hide Ashley's nervous laughter. Jen asked her when she would get to meet the mystery man, but Ashley shook her head refusing to set a date. Although she did mention that Matt too had a friend that he wanted Ashley to meet. She mentioned how nervous she was to meet Matt's friend Michael. She explained that he was practically Matt's brother, in the same way that Jen was her own heartsister.

As the conversation wound down, Ashley described briefly an animal she was trying to identify. It was such a strange thing to say, that Jen questioned her more closely about it. Ashley described the reptilian, scaled face. She described it as horned and angular with quicksilver eyes that changed color from moment to moment. Jen snorted into her iced coffee. It was delicious even before the additional shot she'd slipped into it from her flask.

"It's a Dragon of course! What else could it be?" She ate the last bite of her meal and sipped her drink. She looked at Ashley's surprise with a jaundiced eye. "Really, Ashley. How many times did I make you watch sleeping beauty, huh? You know a Dragon when you see one don't you?"

"Of course!" Ashley exclaimed. "They even fly…" She continued, muttering to herself as Jen quirked an eyebrow at her questioningly. Ashley waved the silent question away though, and set to finishing her food.

As Jen rode her bike home she thought over their conversation. For although it had been great to see her friend, the whole luncheon left Jen feeling rather dissatisfied. She was glad that Ashley had found such an awesome sounding guy. On the other hand, she was more than a little frustrated with Ashley's shyness about letting her meet him.

She was also beginning to suspect that his presence might explain why she hadn't seen her friend in so long. She approached her apartment with a tiny box of leftovers in her basket. As she got ready for work that afternoon, she couldn't let go of her thoughts of Ashley and her worries about the meaning of this new man in her friend's life.

# 9

*Matt was hot. He was sweltering hot. As though he was in the center of a volcano but for some reason, he liked it. He stretched slowly, luxuriating in the heat. He felt every muscle pull taut, it felt wonderful. He rolled over onto his back. Looking up at the glittering stars above, they seemed so close that he could reach out and touch them. They were like glittering sparks, in the dark heavens above. The world around him glowed softly with a warm amber light. Again he felt that this was how things should be. It was how things had always been. How they always would be. There was nothing unusual in this, just the comfortable warm glow of molten fire...*

Matt woke with a start. He found to his discomfort that he truly was hot. He was burning up, and his bed was drenched with sweat. The sheet clung damply to his chest as he sat up. He fought to get his bearings, as he tried to sort dream from reality. He gazed about his small apartment blearily, trying to figure out why it was so hot in here. Twisting free of the sheets he stumbled to the window. Still half asleep, he opened it to try and let some heat out. The hot air hit him in the face, like a blast from a furnace. It almost knocked him over with its unexpected force. Slamming the window shut again, he was now fully awake.

"Oh, no." He said quietly to himself, as he realized that another heat storm was coming.

*'If it's this hot before dawn...'* He thought to himself with concern. He looked out at the barely pink sky to the east. *'It's gonna be a bad one.'*

He hurried to his sink to wash his sticky face. Splashing cold water down the back of his neck gave him a moment's relief from the encroaching heat. He had definitely made it worse by opening the window. He decided it was time to get everyone moving. If no one else in the building had noticed yet, some would no doubt be dead before they woke.

Throwing a change of clothes into a bag, he downed a glass of water. He glanced around, wiping his mouth as he tried to think of anything else he might need while at the shelter. He couldn't think of anything off hand. His thoughts were already beginning to blur from the effects of the heat. He realized that it didn't matter.

The only thing that mattered was getting everyone to the shelters, before the sun actually rose. He heard someone yelling in the hallway, as he stuffed his feet into his shoes and headed for the door. Apparently he wasn't the first one up, thank goodness. Someone knocked loud on his door just as he reached for the handle. Opening it, he looked for a moment into the shocked eyes of his neighbor Bob.

"Oh, you're awake!" Bob shook his head, recovering quickly considering the heat. It was probably making him as fuzzy headed as it was Matt.

"Good, help me. A heat storm's coming." Then he ran on to knock loudly on the next door shouting his warning. "Get out here, get dressed! We need to get to the shelter! Hurry!" He went from door to door with the same message, hoping to rouse everyone before he himself had to flee to the shelter.

"Bob!" Matt called down the hall to him. "Did you get downstairs yet?" Matt was trying hard to remember how many floors were in his building, through the growing heat haze in his mind. Bob didn't waste breath answering him aloud. Instead he just shook his head and continued down the hall. He ran on relentlessly, a man with a mission. Matt watched Bob a moment, as he ran to each door in turn, banging and calling out his warning to those within.

Shaking his head to clear it, Matt threw his bag over his shoulder and ran for the stairs. They didn't have much time. He took the stairs two at a time and hit the landing running. He knocked hard on the first door he came to and yelled through the door.

"Heat storm! Everybody out! Let's get down to the shelter! Hurry up! The sun is rising!"

He continued down the hall, banging on every door and yelling out his warning. He just hoped that those within were still aware enough to respond. By the time he reached the end of the hall, most of the doors he'd knocked on had been flung open by bleary eyed, panic stricken people.

"Hurry!" He yelled over his shoulder to them. "Get down to the shelter! Quick!" He sprinted again for the stairs and continued his rampage down the hallway of the floor below as well. Banging on doors and yelling his warning he ran on, although he felt himself dripping with sweat. The shirt he'd thrown on was plastered to his body with sweat and he was slipping and sliding around in his shoes.

"This one's gonna be bad…" He thought, as he finally made it to the bottom floor. He saw most of his neighbors, running in the direction of the nearest shelter. The street had filled with a gaggle of sleepy people. He watched as those from his building joined the throngs of others, who were also sprinting towards relative safety.

Glancing back at his building he sent up a little prayer that everyone had made it out alright. Turning in the direction of the shelter himself, a thought struck him. He worried suddenly if Ashley was awake yet. The heat increase was so gradual at first that many people slept through the initial stages of the heat storms. Those people simply never woke up. Their bodies gave out long before they could regain consciousness enough to try to get out of the immense heat. That was what made the storms so dangerous.

There was no lightning flashing, no loud winds to warn you. Just the insidious increase in temperature. Until it quietly reached temperatures so high that blood could no longer coagulate and motor functions gave out.

His vision was already getting blurry, but he could tell that the sun was about to come up. He took a step towards the shelter. Then indecisively took one back towards Ashley's apartment. In his current befuddled state, he couldn't decide what to do. With an anguished cry, he gave up and threw himself into a run towards her place.

He ran as fast as his faltering feet could carry him. *'There's another shelter near her building. If she's not there at her apartment, then I'll find her at the shelter. At least I'll know that she's safe.'* He thought, as he ran all the way there.

When he reached her building he took the stairs two at a time, hoping to goodness that she was already at the shelter. He only hoped that he would find her there soon and not pass out in the street himself, trying to get there.

When he got to her landing, he threw himself at her door. He pound on it hard, hoping not to get a response. If he left right away, he might still have time to reach the shelter. Instead however he heard a muffled response from inside, making his heart climbed into his throat. It had sounded like she had said, just a minute. He couldn't believe it, they didn't have a minute!

"Ashley!" He yelled at her door. "What the hell are you doing here? The sun's about to come up! We need to go, now!" He leaned against the door, gasping for breath. The sweat dripped off his chin in a steady stream. He swooned against the door, almost losing consciousness. He'd really pushed himself too hard, running in the heat like that.

"Matt?" He heard her say through the door he was leaning against. Just a moment before it opened out from under him. He fell, sprawled onto the floor of her apartment, suddenly too weak to catch himself. "What are you doing here?" She asked, leaning down to help him sit up. "Why aren't you at the shelter? The sun's about to come up! It's dangerous!" She seemed to be truly concerned but all he could do was stare at her. He wondered why she looked so much more together then he felt, when they were sitting in the same temperature.

"What do you mean, why aren't *I* at the shelter?" He demanded as she pulled his legs inside and shut the door. "Why aren't you at the shelter? I had a bad feeling about it, so I came to check on you. Now I'm glad I did! What the hell are you still doing here?" He was shocked as she turned away from him without answering, till he saw her turn around again with a glass of water. She shoved it into his hand, still without answering him. She ran again to the sink, where she wet a wash cloth. Kneeling beside him she began wiping his face to try to cool him down.

The sensation melted him. The cool rag on his hot skin was incredible. He couldn't believe how good it felt. As she stopped wiping his face so he could hungrily drink the water that she'd given him, he finally realized that he was surrounded on all sides by her plants. He blinked and looked around again but they were still there. For a moment he'd thought he was hallucinating.

She saw him looking around at them and it seemed to bring her back to the moment. Cursing she jumped up, throwing the washcloth at him. She ran out onto her little balcony and came back in again, with her arms loaded with even more plants.

"What the hell are you doing?" He asked her, completely dumbfounded. She just glared at him and setting the pots down very gently, she ran back out to get some more. "Ashley, if we don't get to the shelter soon were both gonna die!" He knew he wasn't exaggerating but he also wasn't sure that he had the strength left to stand, let alone run to the shelter. She ignored him however and continued bringing in her plants. She squished and stacked them onto every available surface that she could find.

He tried to stand to stop her, but his legs wouldn't support his weight. He sagged back to the floor in defeat.

'Yeah, definitely over did it with all the running.' He thought with a sigh.

He leaned against the big tomato pot he found himself beside. The pot was pleasantly cool against the heat of his body. He watched groggily as she drug a huge row of tiered plants in. It seemed magical, to his heat soaked mind that she could move so freely. Let alone have the strength to drag all this stuff around and somehow fit it into her tiny apartment.

That was apparently the last of the plants. She shut the balcony door and ran to the little closet by her bathroom. She began pulling out huge strips of something reflective. As he watched her move, she shimmered and sparkled with light reflected from the strips. The light dancing across her in his blurry vision.

He watched as she took it to the balcony door and somehow covered the glass with it, shiny side out. He was a little disappointed at the end of the light show. Even through the thick fuzz in his aching head though, he could feel the room cool down as soon as she blocked out the first rays of the rising sun.

When she was done, Ashley pulled the blinds shut and turned back towards him. She seemed to realize that he was fading by the concern in her expression. Things were starting to go dark and he was unable to stop himself from sliding down the tomato pot to the floor. Somehow he didn't have the energy to care. The last thing he saw was Ashley rushing over to him, as she tried to get him to sit up. He was vaguely aware of her slapping his face, as though from very far away. Then everything went black for good.

———

Jimi heard a distant whistle from behind him. Looking back, he saw his dad waving largely at him. Once his dad saw that he had Jimi's attention, he spun his bike around, heading back the way they had come. Back towards the mound a few miles behind them. Jimi cursed under his breath. There was no choice now, since there was clearly a storm over the city.

Jimi again raised his binoculars, looking out across the wastes at Newcity. It was still several miles away but he could see the flickering sparkles of intense heat. The city baked in the heat storm beneath the gently pinking sky of dawn. He could see the shimmer of heat waves rising off the concrete of what was left of the once dense metropolis. Trapped between the compact ceiling of ever present cloud cover above and the dense concrete and metal structure of the city below, the roving wall of superheated air, now hovered over the remains of the once urban sprawl.

The shimmering and sparkling heat waves looked like rain from here, but he knew better. Hurriedly he hopped onto his bike and tucked his binoculars back into his saddlebag. He gunned the engine and tore off towards the shelter of the hill. He should have plenty of time to make it. The heat storms tended to move pretty slowly. There was no reason to take a chance though, not on being cooked alive.

He pulled his bike up to the only mound in the otherwise flat and dusty plain. He walked his bike into the small maw of an opening in the little hillside. His dad was still in the waiting chamber. His dad's sidecar was packed and strapped high with the goods they'd brought to trade. So his bike was taking up most of the space in the tiny room.

"Storm's coming." His dad said, gesturing to the dog cowered by his side. "Bella told me." Jimi nodded confirming it.

"Yeah, I saw it. Looks like a hot one too." He parked his motorcycle next to his dad's. They had to work together to shut the door on their little hill before the storm came. "It's currently cooking the city. It looks like it's still at least an hour or two away unless it picks up speed." He grunted as he pushed and pulled beside his dad. Together they wrestled the huge sod and soil chunk that they used for a door on their little shelters, back into place.

"No reason to take a chance though." His dad said, grunting as they both grabbed the handles attached to the inner side of the sod, pulling it firmly into place. "I'm alright with dying, but I sure as hell don't want to cook."

He grinned at Jimi over his grossly accurate joke and they both laughed a little. Partly from relief, Jimi thought. He was grateful they had been so close to the shelter, when they realized that a storm was over the city. This way they had somewhere safe to wait, since they couldn't continue on just yet.

He sighed and leaned against the rough inner wall of their mound. He was very grateful not to live in that oven of a city right now.

*'All that cement! And glass and metal to reflect the heat even more! They must be crazy!'* He shook his head. He was very glad to have been born free to travel, instead of raised in a box like that.

"Common lad, let's get below." His dad gestured towards the tunnel leading down to the lower chamber. He noticed that the dog had already gone on ahead of them.

*'They're so much smarter than we are sometimes.'* He thought ironically as he and his father made their way down to the second chamber which was much deeper than the first.

"We'll wait a while yet to close the second door." He winked at Jimi and grinned again. "We don't want to avoid being cooked, only to suffocate when we run out of air, eh?" He laughed out loud at his own sick humor and Jimi couldn't help but smile. He knew his dad was right. He always was, but he sure liked to rub it in.

As he settled himself into the nice damp earth, Bella crawled her way over to him on her belly, obviously terrified. He pulled her into his lap and patted her shoulders hard to show her that it was alright. She whined and buried her snout under his knee.

"Don't worry girl, we're safe now. That storm ain't gonna get ya in here." He thumped her shoulders again affectionately. She shuddered again before finally relaxing into him. His dad settled himself onto the long chunk of earth that had been left as a makeshift couch and sighed. He tossed Jimi one of the salvaged food bars from the bag they kept in the shelters, for emergencies. Stretching out on the earthen couch, his dad leaned against the bag of them as a pillow. He could see that his dad had settled in to wait.

Jimi knew from experience that they would wait until they could just feel the heat rising to shut the inner door. In order to make their air supply last as long as possible. He patted the dog, to help pass the time and she snuggled into him. He smiled down at her, grateful for the companionship. He wasn't afraid of the storm. He knew that the earth above them would keep the heat out. Depending on how long the storm lasted however, running out of air was a very real possibility. The storms moved so slowly that they could bake a spot for days sometimes, before dissipating.

It was always possible that the storm wouldn't even reach them here though. It was very hard to predict which way it would go. It could even dissipate before it reached them. It all depended on how the air moved. He sighed. It was definitely boring though, having to wait it out to see. He opened the packaged food bar just for something to do, and nibbled on it. He made a face, it was far too sweet.

He took a long drink from his water skin and Bella sniffed at the bar. He broke a little piece off for her to try. She licked it and seemed to lose interest, much as he had. He wrapped the rest up and stuck it in his pocket for later. Since sweet or not, he'd eat it if he had to. He just hoped that they wouldn't be here that long. He had really been looking forward to going to the city this time. He always enjoyed their visits to the city. All the more because he knew he wouldn't have to stay. This time, he was really hoping go to the tiny restaurant they had found on their last trip.

They had brought a case of canned goods just for that restaurant, so he really hoped that they had some oil to trade. The cans had been heavy and awkward. His dad had grumbled a lot, about having to drag them so far across the wastes. The couple at the shop had been really clear though. They would trade for only certain things and said that if Jimi and his dad didn't have just the right thing, then they wouldn't take anything.

*'They even sent empty cans of what they wanted to make sure we brought the right thing.'* He thought to himself. *'They sure are lucky that we even found any. We had to go almost to the ocean to find a storehouse with this stuff in it.'* He wondered what it tasted like. This coco milk or whatever it was. The smells in that restaurant had made his mouth water but of course without any city credits, all they got for their trade was oil.

*'Which is what we really need anyway.'* He reminded himself. *'Without the oil we wouldn't get very far now would we?'* He lifted Bella's head gently from his lap so he could flop onto his back and straighten his legs. She resituated herself with a sigh upon his now flat lap, otherwise seeming unbothered by the movement. He imagined trying to push his motorbike across the wastes without fuel and made a face.

*'Wouldn't get very far at all.'* Sighing impatiently he rolled onto his side. The dog grumbled this time, as she lifted her head out of his way. He patted her head and she crawled over to lie beside him. He hugged her to his chest and felt her sigh heavily once more.

She was obviously still really nervous about the storm. He patted her shoulders and glared into the dark of their cave like little shelter. His eyes had long since adjusted to the darkness but there was still nothing to look at in here but dirt. He could dimly make out the lump of his dad upon the earthen couch. He wondered for a moment if his dad may have fallen asleep. He listened for a moment to his father's breathing and could tell that although it was slow and deep, his father was still conscious, listening. Waiting.

Jimi sighed again. He shifted around but didn't roll over again. He was impatient but he knew that there was nothing to be done about it now. He wished that he'd brought some kind of project to work on. He should have brought his stone carving kit. Of course they had no idea when they had left camp a few days ago, that the city would be under a heat storm when they arrived.

He wondered if the storm would even head their way, and how long they would have to wait until they checked the door. He tried to be patient, but he was much better suited to active work. To digging through abandoned buildings, then to sitting around waiting for something he couldn't affect.

That's why he was usually the lookout. Why he always rode point and why he'd jumped at the chance to join his dad at the scavenging and trading, when old Willie had decided to retire. Willie had decided to retire back to camp last season which had freed up the position for Jimi. Which had suited him perfectly, since he just couldn't stand being idle. Unfortunately that very decision had come between him and Sasha on his last trip back home to camp.

When he had finally returned to camp from their latest Trade trip he had headed for his girlfriend's tent, to let her know that he was home. He had knocked softly on the support beside her tent flap. However the greeting she gave him was not the warm one he had hoped for but an angry tirade.

He was summarily informed that she was over it! She said that she was tired of waiting for him to come back all the time. She had complained that he was gone more often than he was around. Questioning, just what she was getting out of the relationship?

He sighed, fidgeting in the dark. He found himself unable to curb the thoughts, although they still made him angry and uncomfortable.

"I'm with Jet now." She had said. "So you had better remember it! When you're around that is."

He had set out on his own the next day, ostensibly to go salvaging. Really he just needed to be alone with his thoughts. He took Bella with him, but his dad seemed to understand that he needed some time alone.

He'd done more soul searching then salvaging while he was out there on his own. He had eventually decided that he was probably better off. She was always really selfish anyway. She was probably sleeping with Jet already as well, given the way she'd been talking about him.

Even though he had decided that he was better off, the memory and her words still stung. He was lonely for more company then a dog could provide. He had often wondered since then, in the dark of the night, if there might actually be anyone out there that he could get along with. He thought about the irony of her argument. Saying that she didn't want to be with him because he was gone trading and scavenging all the time. Even though their people were completely dependent on the oil that he and the other scavengers salvaged and traded for. Their entire way of life relied heavily on what he and the others did out here every day!

"It's so dangerous! Climbing around those ruins that way! It's careless and I'm sick of worrying about you!" She had said.

"So I guess you'd rather not worry about me at all then, huh?" He'd countered, frustrated and hurt.

"Whew!" Throwing up her hands, she had turned on her heel and stalked off. At a loss for what else to do, he had turned and slowly gone back the way he had come.

With another sigh he forced his thought's to slow, then stop. He tried to clear his mind of all the worries and memories filling him. He closed his eyes and forced his breathing to be calm and slow. If he couldn't do anything else while they waited out the heat storm, maybe he could at least get some rest. He knew that the heat would wake him if the storm came near. The weight of Bella leaning against him was very soothing. Her breathing slowed to match his, and he slowly drifted off to sleep. Soon he was flying.

# 10

"Shit! Shit! Shit!" Ashley cussed, smacking Matt harder and harder without getting a response. He didn't even twitch at the impact. She could feel the heat radiating from him like an ember. He was hot under her hand, even through the saturated shirt where she held his shoulder.

*'He must have run all the way here!'* She thought desperately. *'I've got to get him cooled down quick or I'm gonna lose him!'* Her heart synched in her chest at the thought, but the panic gave her strength. Grabbing him beneath the arms, she hauled him one step at a time towards her little bathroom.

Once there, she pulled and shoved until she had his limp form crammed into the tiny shower stall. She was sweating buckets herself now. It was starting to get beyond merely hot. She had been running around since she first woke from the heat. Even before he came, she'd been trying to get all her plants inside and everything situated, in order to try to weather them through the storm.

She shoved the little plug into the drain hole in the shower and pulled the curtain shut on him. She reached in and turned the cold water on full, hoping that it still worked. She hadn't tried it since she moved in. She always took spit baths, with a wet wash cloth, to save water. The pipes gurgled and belched but after a moment the water did start to come. After checking to make sure that it was hitting him in the chest and not the face, she turned back to the rest of her apartment. Content that he was secured, Ashley ran to finish her other preparations, before it was too late. She shoved a towel under the door as hard as she could, feeling as she did so the heat that was seeping in from the hallway.

As she looked around to try to remember what was next, she swayed lightheaded. She caught herself on the edge of the counter and took a deep breath. She took another and another, trying to let the heat out through her lungs. That thought reminded her.

*'The little fridge.'* She turned into her tiny kitchen, where she unplugged the little fridge and hauled it with her into the bathroom.

She had planned to use it for the plants but right now, Matt was more important. Once she got him stabilized then she'd worry about the plants. She deposited it on the floor of her tiny bathroom, plugging it in quickly and went back out for more towels. She also grabbed the cup that he'd dropped when he collapsed. She needed to get him drinking once she had him conscious again.

She came back just as the water was overflowing the lip of her little shower stall, the half sized tub was only about six inches deep. Setting the fridge on the sink to keep it dry, she plugged it in. Then she reached past Matt, to turn the water off.

Taking a moment she mopped up the water spill with the towels she'd brought. Shutting the bathroom door, she shoved one of the towels beneath it as well, trying to isolate the little room. Then turning back to her little fridge, she propped the door open. Wrapping the damp towel around her shoulders, she stuck her face into the fridge and took a deep breath. It was lovely. It tasted like the first chill of fall. Matt groaned from the shower and it reminded her that she needed to help him.

Hurrying across the small room she moved carefully on the slick damp floor. Pulling the curtain aside she tried not to let out the cooler air from the cold water within.

He was stirring but didn't seem to be conscious yet. She knelt just outside the shower stall as he groaned again and she saw that he was shivering.

She sighed with relief that he was responsive again. Sticking her fingers in the water she almost shivered herself, it was really cold. It felt great though in the heat rising around them.

"Matt? Hey Matt?" She reached in and slapped his cheek again, more gently this time. "Are you with me Matt?" She was still feeling a bit groggy from the effects of the heat herself, so she decided to drink more water.

She drained glass after glass before filling it for him and then stepped into the shower with him. She slipped one foot between Matt and the wall and the other between his legs, which meant she still barley fit.

She'd crammed him in with his legs bent and he was leaning into the corner of the tiny stall. It felt great to have her feet in cold water and she sat gingerly on the little lip of the mini tub. Setting the full cup outside on the floor for the moment, she dipped the free towel into the water and wrapped it around his torso. He clung to it like a blanket and she tried again to get him conscious.

"Matt? Matt?" She shook his shoulders gently and slapped his cheek. He shook his head a few times but he managed to lift it to look at her. "Here, Matt, drink!" She said quickly, now that she had his attention. Snagging the glass from behind her, she shoved the full glass into his hand. He just held it, staring at her. Apparently he was not really awake yet.

Taking his hand in hers she lifted the glass to his lips and spilled a little on them to try and tempt him to drink. He licked his lips and that seemed to do it. His eyes focused on the cup and he drank it hungrily. He handed it back empty a moment later. She filled the cup again and again from the shower head, repeating the process. When she looked down at him around the spray water, she saw he had his face in its waterfall, obviously enjoying the feel of the cool water.

She smiled and wondered if he was recovered enough to talk yet. She handed him the cup once more and this time instead of drinking it, he pressed the cool glass to his forehead.

"Thank you." He said a moment later, eyes still shut tight. It seemed that he was trying to will the cool of the glass into his head. Ashley felt her own temperature stabilizing, now that she had her feet in the nice cold water. Dipping the washcloth, she washed her sweaty face and neck with it, savoring the rough coolness of it against her hot skin. Once she was done, she dipped it to wet it again. Pulling his hand with the glass from his forehead, she wiped his face with the cool cloth as well. He sighed and leaned into the touch of the cloth.

Deciding that wasn't quite enough she took off her towel and submerged it too into the water. Lifting it, she wrung it out only slightly and draped it over her shoulders again. When she was done she found him watching her, a slight smile on his face.

"What's so funny?" She asked, hoping to get him talking. If she could keep him conscious, she knew he'd probably be alright.

He chuckled self-deprecatingly as he answered her.

"Well." He said slowly, obviously still recovering from the heat exhaustion that had knocked him out. "I just think it's ironic. I came over here 'cause I was worried about you, yet you're the one who wound up saving me." He smiled at her. Reaching out, he gently took her hand from where she had been pressing her towel to herself; in an effort to transfer it's cool to her body.

"Thank you Ashley. I think you saved my life." She felt her cheeks grow hot, at the look he gave her.

'*Funny.*' She thought to herself. '*I didn't notice just how close together we are in here, until now. I was just worried about getting him cooled down.*' She swallowed and looking down, she said out loud.

"It's alright, what else could I do? Let you die in my living room?" She was trying to make a joke but it fell rather flat. They both knew how close he had come, to doing just that. She decided too late, that maybe it wasn't an appropriate joke. Uncomfortable, she changed the subject.

"Matt, I can't believe that you came all the way here, just to check on me. I mean, I'm grateful. I'm glad that you thought of me, but I don't want you getting hurt for my sake." She looked back up in time to see him grimace a bit.

"Yeah, well. I wasn't really thinking straight by that point." He grinned at her, chagrined. "I just couldn't handle the thought of being in the shelter over by my place. I'd have spent the whole time worrying about whether you'd made it or not. You know?" He looked sidelong at her through his lashes and she couldn't help but smile. "I obviously wasn't thinking straight!" He burst out suddenly, with a laugh. "I could have ridden my bike here in half the time, instead of running the whole way and almost killing myself!" His relieved laughter was infectious and she found herself giggling too.

She leaned heavily into the shower stall as she laughed, suddenly exhausted. Though even the thought of relaxing, made her realize that she should check on her plants. She had meant to water them all thoroughly before retreating to the bathroom. At least that had been the plan before Matt had shown up so unexpectedly. As she had the thought she also realized, that if she opened the bathroom door at this point, she'd let all the cooler air from the water out and they'd have to start all over again.

More than that, she realized, she was just too tired! She'd woken quite early from the increasing heat and she had been running ever since, trying to get all her plants inside. She couldn't help the yawn that crept from her mouth, so she covered it with her hand.

"Excuse me!" She said to Matt when she was done. "This heat is putting me to sleep too!" She smiled at him, trying to make a joke of it but he had straightened up looking around.

"Where are we, actually?" He asked suddenly glancing around, looking more alert by the moment. "Are we in your shower?" He was looking at the faucets and suddenly seemed to realize that he was up his waist in water. She laughed at the surprise on his face.

"Yep. Coolest place in the house!" She winked and he grinned back at her. He started to shift himself about.

"Here, I think I can move over so that you can fit too. You are still hot right?" He looked at her as though daring her to say otherwise. Which of course, she couldn't, despite all her best efforts it was still sweltering in here, and apparently getting hotter yet. She wondered how long the storm would last and whether it would break the record again. She really hoped not. The last record breaker had killed a number of people. Some had been older folks who succumbed to dehydration, some who didn't make it to the shelters before sun up and more yet who just never made it out of bed.

Nodding, she settled herself in beside him with a sigh. He put his legs together as she stepped out from between them and it gave her just enough room to sit in the water next to him. They sat with their legs bent and their feet in the water. Their hips and shoulders pressed together but at least they were both wet. The water was not as cold as it had been she noticed, but it still felt wonderful compared to the heat of the air. Sighing again she leaned her head against his shoulder. She was so very tired. She wondered if he would mind but even as she had that thought, he leaned his head softly against hers. She took the invitation and settled comfortably against him.

"Do you think it's safe to nap?" She asked sleepily.

"Safe from drowning? Or safe from heat?" He asked her.

She shrugged a little.

"Either I guess." She was fading. She'd been going strong since she woke up. It had been hours before dawn, and she had been hauling plants in and trying to arrange them to fit ever since. She was just about out of energy. She thought that maybe she should drink more water. It might help to revive her a little. She decided to say so.

"Here let's fill up again." She reached for the cup still in his hand and he drained it before handing it back to her. She took it with a smile and turned the shower on again. They both jumped a little at the cold of the water but it felt wonderful and she lifted the cup to fill it. She knew the tub was overflowing but she didn't have the energy to care. She drained the cup and refilled it several times more, before handing it back to him.

She did work the little plug loose though, while he filled the cup and drank his fill another three or four times and since she'd taken the plug out for now she just let the water run to cool the air. It really made a difference, she could feel herself perking up again as she cooled down. She decided she should drink more water too, when he handed the empty cup back to her.

"Thank you." She said automatically, as she accepted the glass.

"No, thank you! You're the one sharing all your precious water with me. I really do appreciate it Ashley." He smiled at her, as he said it and her cheeks grew warm. She offered him the cup again and when he shook his head, she turned the water off. She knew she was getting close to her limit and she really hoped that this storm didn't go on for too much longer. You never knew with heat storms, it depended on the way they moved. Sometimes they only stayed over the city for a few hours and sometimes they lasted for days.

Matt seemed to be thinking along the same lines, as he said.

"You know as cramped as it might be in this little stall, I'll bet we're a lot more comfortable then everyone crammed into the shelters right now. At least we have a lot of cold water to drink. Instead of drinking the tepid, emergency water, they keep down in the bunkers." She nodded.

"That's one of the reasons that I usually weather the storms out here. Although I was mainly worried about my plants." She sighed frowning, thinking about them, out in the other room. With no little fridge to help cool them, poor things. She really hoped that they would survive.

"Hmm." She looked at him and it seemed that he'd been about to say something and perhaps he'd thought better of it. She wondered what it was, but she decided not to ask.

"Where do you get the seeds from?" He asked suddenly. She was surprised that he would think to ask. No one else had ever asked her that, not even Jen. She smiled though, glad that he had asked. It was a valuable question.

"Well." She thought a moment and decided to begin at the beginning, since they were obviously going to be here for a while. "When I was little and we were all evacuated from our respective homes. Let me see, you said you don't remember the evacuation, right?" She looked at him and he nodded. "But do you remember all that came after that? The refugee relocation program, the founding of the city and the establishment of the orphanages?" He nodded again so she continued. "Well, you know how they split us up and the boys all went to a separate orphanage from the girls?" She looked over at him again and he nodded once more.

Apparently that was all he was going to contribute to this part of the conversation. She smiled at the thought and continued.

"Well I don't know much about the boy's orphanage but the girls got lucky. We were adopted by a group of nun's. They were also refugees. I found out later, that when they got to the city they had petitioned for help reestablishing the church. But that they had been told that while establishing a new church wasn't high on the priority list, orphanages were. So the Sister's decided that the quickest way to get their church and the best way to serve God besides would be to establish an orphanage that could help to care for the many children left orphaned by the shift.

The Sister's church had been all but destroyed by the terrible twister's that ravaged the northeast when the shift hit. Not knowing what else to do, they stayed close to their demolished home. They lived there as best they could, for months once the weather had settled. They had sheltered in the basements of the old stone abbey. They felt protected by the ruins of their erstwhile home.

Sister Mary was the cloister's gardener. In her exploration of what was left of the garden, she found that while many of the plants had been damaged beyond repair, a few had survived. The survivors had bolted from the extreme temperatures and lack of water and care. So she decided to nurture them as best she could." Looking over, she saw he looked confused.

"What is it?" She asked him, wanting to make sure she didn't lose him in her long winded reply.

He started, seemingly surprised that she'd noticed his confusion, he looked embarrassed.

"Actually, well, uh." He flushed a little and she wondered what he was so confused about. "Well, I-I just don't know what bolted means." He muttered, as though he didn't want to admit it.

She laughed, relieved that it was something so simple. She patted his arm reassuringly since he seemed even more embarrassed that she'd laughed. Taking pity on him tried to explain it in simple terms.

"It just means that they went to seed prematurely." She said with what she hoped was a reassuring smile. "Which brings us around to the answer to your question." She smiled at him again and he nodded, obviously wanting to show that he was with her this time. "Mary convinced the other Sister's that they should stay until the seeds were ready. They agreed that they would wait before they went in search of other survivors, which they had begun to discuss.

So when they arrived here, having finally connected with one of the search parties organized to round up survivors, Mary had all the seeds from their old garden. And she couldn't wait to get them in the ground again. As soon as the orphanage was established, she made herself a spot for a garden and began growing as many vegetables as the land there would support." She sighed happily at the memories of the many days that she'd spent in that garden, and forgot for a moment that she was in the middle of telling a story.

"So you got your seeds from her then?" Matt guessed, reminding her that she'd left him hanging. Now she was embarrassed and she smiled shyly in apology. He just smiled back though, obviously not bothered at all that she'd gone silent mid story.

"Yes." She said, "To make a long story short. I did." She was worried suddenly that maybe she'd rambled on for too long and lost his interest. He had asked a fairly straight forward question after all. When she glanced at him from the corner of her eye, he didn't look bored or irritated though.

"So, is that all there is to it then?" He asked with a smile. He was obviously trying to bait the rest of the story past her embarrassment. "Hm?" He bumped her shoulder playfully with his own as though trying to jump start her, bringing a laugh to her lips.

"Well, yes and no." She smiled at him. She was glad that she could keep talking about the garden and that he wouldn't mind. It was a really nice way to get her mind off the heat and their current desperate situation. Not to mention the possible plight of her poor plants in the other room. Just thinking about the good times that she'd had in that beautiful garden was very reassuring. "Hmmm. Where was I?" Now she'd lost what she'd been about to say.

"You were saying that Sister Mary grew as many veggies' as she could." He kept it simple but she was impressed that he'd picked up Sister Mary's name so easily. She had been such a central figure in Ashley's life growing up that it was lovely to talk about her and it was nice to hear him say her name.

She smiled at him again. *'I always seem to smile and laugh when he's around. I really like that.'*

"Yep." She said trying to get started again. "She did. She grew everything that would grow, which wasn't a whole lot at first either." She told him. "The soil there wasn't very good when they first arrived. Luckily Sister Mary knew a little bit about making her own fertilizer. Having grown up on a farm she had learned how to compost the kitchen scraps and turn them into fresh nutrient rich soils. She's been composting in that garden for over ten years now and the dirt there is like a little miracle. All that and she had never even heard of permaculture!" She said that with a little laugh. As she looked over at Matt, she could tell by his expression that he wasn't in on the inside joke. She cleared her throat, embarrassed again.

"So, what is permaculture?" He asked her tentatively. It seemed he'd decided it was best to admit his ignorance. That way he could learn from it instead of hiding what he didn't know and staying in the dark. "I think I've heard you talk about it before."

"Yes. Well, that's kind of a big question really." She took a deep breath, trying to decide where to begin. "It's a good question though! I am glad you asked." She reassured him, as he looked worried at her response. "It's a term used to cover a lot of topics, including organic farming and sustainable agriculture. In and of itself it is an ideal of completely self-sustainable, even abundant agriculture. It's a matter of harnessing your resources. The art of creating a close looped system where things that would have been wastes feed the needs of other parts of the system, in a self-sustaining organization. It's what nature does naturally, when it's in balance. In permaculture we're trying to engineer that balance intentionally. And trying to do so in the most practical, efficient, and mutually beneficial way for all involved. It's a great system, whether you're able to work with whole tracts of land or you just want to have a few veggies' in pots on the porch, like me."

He laughed at that.

"Right, a few." He winked at her when she looked over at him sharply. Though, she had to admit that they did currently fill her apartment. She laughed as well.

"So I take it that composting is part of permaculture then?" He said, apparently interested in getting the conversation back on track.

She was amazed and grateful that he was actually interested in this stuff. She was very passionate about it. She spent a lot of time studying and implementing it but she never had anyone to talk to about it, except for Sister Mary.

"Yes, it's a big part." She smiled broadly at him, happy for his interested questions. "The concept of permaculture encompasses a holistic approach to agriculture. The idea behind composting is to reuse any organic matter coming from the garden or the kitchen that would otherwise be garbage. To harness the nutrients stored in it, by feeding them back into the garden's soil. The soil then feeds the plants you grow and nothing goes to waste."

"So even though Sister Mary wasn't aware of permaculture, because she was making her own compost she was successful with her garden?" He asked her, smiling sideways at her. "Am I following you so far?" He seemed to be waiting for her to respond, so she nodded.

"All right. So now that I'm familiar with Sister Mary, and permaculture, and composting, where do you fit into it all? And where did you get your seeds? Are they the ones that Sister Mary brought with her? Or are they something else?"

Ashley shook her head, deciding to answer the last question first.

"Sister Mary has kept collecting seeds from all her plants each season for the almost ten years that she's been growing the garden here. She has a huge stockpile of them now and she shared some with me." She smiled at him and saw that once again he looked uncertain.

"Just how many do you mean when you say 'a stockpile'? Don't plants just make a couple of seeds each?" He seemed genuinely confused about it and she had to remind herself that he had grown up here in Newcity. And without the benefit of someone like Sister Mary to introduce him to plants.

She was almost surprised that he even knew that plants made seeds; given how limited his exposure must have been to them here. She smiled to herself at his curiosity as it reminded her of herself when she'd first discovered the garden. She would take him there, she decided all of a sudden, if the garden survived the heat storm that is.

'If we survive the heat storm.' She reminded herself pointedly. To take her mind off that thought, she tried to think of the best way to answer his question.

"Hmmm. Well, I guess the truth is that each kind of plant makes a different amount of seeds. They all make a different kind of seed as well. Some just make hundreds while some make thousands. Some seeds are big, like squash or sunflower seeds, and some are small, like most wildflower seeds. Their so tiny, that their like grains of sand. In general, the smaller the seeds are, the more that plant will make. Fruit on the other hand often have only a handful of seeds each, sometimes just one or two per fruit. Sometimes ten or twelve, but each fruit tree usually makes a lot of fruit. So if you're collecting the seeds from all of them, even they will add up fast." She smiled at him. She was happy to see him so interested and he raised a hand to pause her.

"Alright. Then why does she want to collect so many seeds? You say that she has a huge stockpile? Why? Isn't it more trouble than it's worth to collect so many? Where does she keep them all?" She looked at him sharply to see if he was serious. He did look curious. Just curious she decided. It seemed he was just trying to understand.

"Well, in answer to your first question, think about the state of the world right now. Have you been outside the city at all?" She looked at him for an answer and he shook his head. She supposed that she shouldn't be surprised. She doubted very much that many people went beyond the city's edge these days. It was very dangerous to do so. What with unexpected heat and wind storms and every other kind of dangerous weather imaginable only a moment's notice away.

"Well, I have." She sighed. "And you know what's out there?" She didn't wait for him to respond, although she saw him shake his head. "Nothing, wastelands, deserts. Vast tracks of desolate destruction left by the disasters brought on by the shift and the changes wrought by weather ever since. It will take millennia to correct it. To heal. As humans though, we can't wait that long, we'll die. The only hope that we have of survival as a species is to learn to heal that damage ourselves, one little piece at a time. That's why I'm so interested in permaculture, that's why I read so much about what caused the shift and what its effects were. Because if we don't fix it, just who do you think will?" Again she didn't wait for him to respond. Although she felt his shoulder shrug a bit against hers as he expressed his ignorance.

"Now think about your life. Think about all the people that you know. Now out of all those people, how many of them know how to grow their own food? And out of those, how many actually do it? In fact, out of all the people you've ever met in your entire life, how many people are even interested in the topic?

Even after all that we've been through as a species, all that we've been through as a people, so many of us are still content to do nothing! Nothing but sit around on our butts and wait for it all to come to us! Many are even more content to make the problem worse! For whatever reason might be playing out in their minds, they are somehow willing to do things that they know not only don't help our chances of survival, but actually actively disrupt it!"

She knew that she was getting overbearing now, but she was really angry. She was thinking of Jen. Thinking of how she was content to just sit on her butt and drink and smoke cigarettes and go to party's where she drank illegal alcohol. Yet doing nothing to help counteract all the problems that had landed them here living like hermit crabs in the broken and tattered shell of the old city.

She took a deep breath to regain her composure. She sighed deeply before continuing.

"So, if Sister Mary doesn't save the seeds to feed the world, who will?" She looked at him sadly, fighting back the tears in her eyes. They had begun in anger but the whole situation also made her desperately sad. He saw the tears. He saw the anger and frustration and the sorrow as well. Although he was only beginning to understand its causes, he understood exactly how it felt.

He lifted his arm and putting it around her shoulders, pulled her close against his chest. She had been trying hard to suppress the tears. To save them for later when she was alone but the warmth of his arm, strong around her trembling shoulders, was just too much.

With a choked sob she turned and buried her face in his chest. Her mind's eye was filled with the vast wastelands that she'd ridden though. The broken towns, the twisted corpses of trees, and the deep scars of rivers long gone dry. The horrible truth of what her species had done to their planet tore at her heart with every breath.

The human warmth of him against her, even in the terrible heat, was enough to pull soft sobs from her lips. Her desperate plea, to take it all back, went unanswered by the world. For what was done was done and there was no going back. The only path left was forward. Through the wastes of what was left. To a future that she hoped to help make green again.

Once she had cried herself out, she stayed leaning against him for a long time. She didn't want to move yet. She decided after a while that maybe it was time for a change of subject though. She searched her mind for a safer topic, one that might not lead to more crying. She thought she had a good one. So when she felt him move against her restlessly she asked him in quiet voice that was still rough with tears.

"So, um. You like music?"

# 11

Michael and Greg huddled together in the basement of the shop, crouched over a crate in the crowded little storage room. It was piled high and rather precariously with innumerable cases of supplies and all of the temperature sensitive instruments that they had wagged down here at the first hint of heat this morning. The room was cramped and the low watt lanterns Greg had hung above them made a confused pile of angles and curves from the shadows and light on the jumbled pile of instruments.

Michael scratched his head frowning at the cards in his hand but no matter how he looked at them, they remained stubbornly unhelpful. Sighing he tossed the hand face down on the little crate.

"I got nothin' I fold..." He sighed. It was always so boring down here, during the heat storms. Although it certainly beat being crammed into one of the city shelters, with all the sobbing terrified people and their whining kids. He sipped at the water by his elbow and wished he had enough light to work by. He had tried several times over the years to work down here during the storms. He had never been content with what he'd managed down here though, not once he had it in decent light again. It was hopeless.

"Aww come one, you're not even trying!" Greg complained as he gathered up the cards and shuffled them again but it was half-hearted at best.

"I might actually just take a nap, if you don't mind Greg." He finished with a yawn. "We'll either make it or we won't and I'd rather rest in the meantime I think. I just can't concentrate on cards right now, sorry." Greg waved a freeing hand at him as Michael half rose, questioningly. He wondered if it would offend his guardian, to be left to himself for a bit.

"Do as you like you stubborn cub. I can't force you to enjoy playing." He chuckled a bit. "Kind of defeats the purpose." He muttered to himself.

Michael saw him fish around for a book. As Michael himself crawled up to stretch out across crates and cases against the far wall. There wasn't enough floor space clear to stretch out on, so he had found this spot to be priceless over the years. He always tried to keep an area level, even as cases came and went. It wasn't perfect but since he'd stuffed one of his shirts in the crack to soften a sharp corner and rolled another into an impromptu pillow he found he was quite comfortable. So he settled in, to take a long hot nap.

His thoughts whirled a little in the heat, as he tried to relax enough to sleep. He took a deep breath to still his mind and pretended not to notice the sudden pungent whiff of bourbon and pipe tobacco from the lantern lit area. He smiled as he drifted into a hot smoky slumber. The thrumming of his pulse in his ears and the slow crackle of Greg, turning crisp old pages, became the hissing roar of burning gasses in the swirling flames, of the world of his dreams.

———

Matt was going numb. After sitting in one position in the cold water for so long he could hardly feel his butt anymore. He didn't really want to move either though. He tightened his arm around Ashley's shoulders. It felt great to hold her, even if it was because she'd been crying. He didn't want to be the one to break the mood. He rubbed her shoulder reassuringly and tried to get a little circulation going to his legs without moving too much. She noticed though, he felt her lift her head from his chest.

'*Damn it!*' He thought. He didn't want to have to let her go.

"So, you like music?" She asked him suddenly, settling herself more comfortably against him. He took the opportunity to stretch his legs and laid them hanging over the edge of the tub. The air felt hot on his cold clammy feet but he got some pins and needles in his butt and legs.

Sighing with relief he went ahead and kept his arm around her while he did so, hoping that she wouldn't mind. She snuggled closer, apparently quite comfortable. He smiled at her question. She was obviously trying to come up with a safer subject. Well, if saving the world was her passion, she'd managed to sum his up in one guess.

He chuckled as he answered.

"I think that's safe to say." He grinned down at her, though she didn't look up. Thinking that she was probably still self-conscious about crying, he figured rambling about music was just the thing to distract her. In trying to think of how to begin he decided to start where it had all begun for him, with Michael.

"When we were first getting settled into the orphanage, there was a boy who befriended me. We had come from the same area and he had been friendly on the bus ride out here. He had helped me, kind of keeping an eye on me. Sherrie asked him to since I was still really out of it back then, from the head injury."

He paused a moment, as she readjusted herself and wet her towel again. He decided that that was a good idea and did the same. He waited until they were both settled, wrapped once again in their heavy wet cloths before continuing.

"Once we were all settled here in Newcity, it was the FEMA members who ran our orphanage. When it came time, they let us choose our roommates if we had a preference." He sighed happily, remembering. "I got really lucky and Michael was willing to room with me. I didn't know it then but he's an incredible musician. He's the one that runs the shop downtown I've talked about. I keep meaning to take you there." She twisted her head to smile up at him as he said it.

"I've wanted to show you Sister Mary's garden too! We'll go, for sure! If it makes it through this heat, that is." He nodded as she settled herself against him again.

"I would really like that." He said to the top of her head and he found that it was true. He wanted to see the place that had inspired such a love of plants in her.

"Greg took a real shine to Michael." He continued. "From the time he first showed up to see the kid who could play the violin. Then he actually gave Michael a guitar not long later, so he could play it, too. Michael already knew how though. I guess he was some kind of prodigy or something before the shift. He doesn't talk about the past much. It's hard for him you know, to talk about his parents. But even back then he knew how to play the guitar and the violin, as well as anyone I've ever heard." He scratched his head absently, lost for a moment in his memories of that time.

"He's really amazing you know? But he's so humble that you'd never know it unless you heard him play. The day that Greg gave him the guitar, he came home in tears he was so happy. He just locked himself in our room for hours, playing the guitar and crying. I was so grateful that it was my room too and that I got to stay there and listen."

He remembered poignantly, Michael's smiling tear stained face as he lost himself in the music. Matt had crouched on his bed listening. He was endlessly fascinated and spent hours trying not to make a sound, so as not to distract him.

"It was the first time in my memory that I'd heard anyone play music, live and in person. To me, the sound of the harmonies was like the singing of angles, it made my heart swell with joy."

He could feel it now, his heart swelling with the sound as though it were food for his soul. He had never wanted it to stop and he'd never wanted to be apart from it. The sounds of harmonies working together were like the family he'd never known. While Michael, the person closest to a brother to him, had given him that.

He smiled despite the clinging heat of the little room. His fingers were itching just talking about it, he wished now that he had brought his guitar with him. In fact he was suddenly worried that it might warp in the heat. He sent a little prayer to the music Gods to please protect his instrument. Michael had given it to him years ago and it was more precious to him then water.

He sighed a little, realizing there was nothing he could do now, either way. So he decided to continue with his story.

"Michael could see how enthralled I was with the music. I begged him every night to play for me again. He did for the most part, since he loves to play but after a while, I guess it got old. One day he set the guitar down and glared at me. He said something like, if you like it so much, why don't you just learn to play yourself? I was shocked!" Matt laughed out loud at the memory of it.

"I'd had no idea that other people could play instruments back then. I thought it was just a magical gift that only Michael possessed!" He laughed again at his own ignorance.

"So that night he began by teaching me some cords. We handed the guitar patiently back and forth. I practiced and practiced, and whenever it sounded horrible he would reassure me that, it always sounded like that when you were starting out." Matt sighed again at the memory. "It seemed like I worked on it forever but eventually I could play the same songs that he could. It was amazing." He laughed again. He remembered his overwhelming joy, when he finished playing his first song through without messing up. Michael had applauded out loud like he was an audience, rather than his teacher.

Matt smiled lazily. The heat was starting to make his eyelids heavy again. He hugged Ashley close to him despite the grueling temperature. He heard her yawn again too and then she seemed to catch herself, she sat up a little and shook her head.

"I think we need more water, it must be getting hotter out there." She sent a worried glance in the direction of the other room and he realized that she must be worried about her plants. She leaned up and turned the cold water back on, reaching down with her other hand and pulling the little plug again.

The shock of the cold water made him jump, awakening him to how sleepy he had become. He was still dripping with sweat even up to his waist in water and he wondered just how hot it was in here. Taking the towel from his shoulders he held it into the cold stream of water while she drank and then wrapped the sopping cloth around himself again. The cold towel felt so good against his skin that he peeled off his sodden shirt and flung it clumsily into the water with a splash.

As Ashley continued to fill her cup and drink, he again wrapped the sodden towel around himself. He gasped in shock at how cold it felt.

"I feel like I have a sunburn I'm so hot." He said as she finished drinking and handed him the cup. He took it gratefully and rising to kneel he filled the glass and drank it dry several times, then stuck his face in the cold stream of water and gasped again at the shock.

As he settled himself back into their watery shelter Ashley slipped the plug back in and wrapped herself in her towel. She wiped her face with a corner of it and he could see how good it must feel by her expression, so he copied her. She sighed at the pleasure just as he was enjoying the sensation himself. He couldn't believe how hot his face was. The towel felt like rough ice on his hot skin. He tried not to wonder how much longer the storm would last.

———

As Ashley wiped her face with a corner of her newly cooled towel, she settled herself back against Matt's shoulder. She was hoping that he wouldn't mind the familiar gesture.

'*Obviously not.*' She thought to herself with a smile as he lifted his arm once more to pull her closer to him. His skin was almost painfully hot against hers but it felt so good not to be alone. At least if she did die here, she would not have died alone.

'*And, if he weren't here to lean against, I'd probably have drowned as soon as I passed out from the heat anyway.*' She snuggled a little closer against him and decided to mention it.

"You know. I'm really grateful that you came, despite what I said earlier." She felt him look down at her and she tilted her head to smile at him. "If you hadn't come, I don't know what would have happened but at the very least I would be very lonely right now." He smiled back at her. Though the strain in his face from the discomfort of the hot air and the cold water was clear, she could tell that he meant the smile.

"Are you sure? Even though I'm drinking all your water and taking up all your space in here?" He asked her, only half-jokingly. He raised one eyebrow questioningly.

She shook her head.

"It wouldn't have mattered. I'd have given all the water to my plants if I could have. Besides if I wasn't leaning against you, then I'd be trying to hold myself up, just to keep from drowning right now!" She saw his smile grow wider and she leaned into him again.

"You can lean against me anytime Ashley." He stroked her arm a little with his thumb and held her close. The warmth in his voice brought a flush to her cheeks but she didn't move away. She was really grateful to have someone to be close to right now.

It was a wonderful distraction from the danger of their situation. As well as from her concern over the welfare of her plants in the other room. She thought about kissing him, just in case they did die here today. She smiled at the thought but decided that it was probably best not to complicate things any further at the moment. So instead she just leaned into him, relishing in the sensation of being held.

---

Matt gazed down at the top of Ashley's head where she leaned against his shoulder, unconscious of the grin that split his face. Despite the severity of their situation, he was feeling incredibly lucky. He had wanted for so long to really get to know her and it seemed that this heat storm and the unexpected way that things had turned out was giving him the perfect opportunity.

He wanted to continue to ask her questions but the heat was making it hard for him to concentrate. He couldn't think of anything to ask. Instead he just leaned his cheek against the top of her head. Taking a deep breath he settled in, only half of him hoping that the storm ended soon, since it would mean that they would have to leave their tiny haven.

He had no idea how long they sat there that way, neither of

them saying anything. Since neither of them had the energy to speak. He allowed his eyes to close. He wasn't aware of the moment when his fuzzy thoughts turned to fuzzy dreams but soon he was flying.

———

*Ashley was flying, it was incredible. She curved her wings to catch the air, her tail whipping behind her as she looked down at the glowing surface of the earth far below. The hot air rising from its molten surface smelled lovely in her snout and she tucked her wings tight to plummet towards it. She fell faster and faster, like a shooting star.*

*She reveled in the sensation of the hot air rubbing against her skin as she fell and as she came closer and closer to the surface, she tucked her wings and dove into its molten surface. Leagues later she surfaced in an eruption of molten fire and spiraled skywards again pumping her wings. As the beauty of the glittering stars far above caught and held her attention, she let herself begin to fall backwards once more. Her wings limp, she plummeted back towards the earth, her eyes and mind lost in the beauty of the stars.*

Ashley awoke with a start.

'*Another dream of flying...*' She thought. She was breathing heavily and she realized that the heat from her dream was real. There was an immense weight on her, pushing her over. As she struggled against it, she woke up enough to realize that it was Matt.

'*That's right.*' She thought, looking around and realizing that they were in her shower. '*The heat storm! I must have passed out.*' She turned to look at Matt, propping him up with her hands. It was obvious that he had passed out as well.

"Matt! Matt!!" She called out, slapping his face as gently as she could manage, trying to wake him up. "Matt wake up! I need you to wake up, now!" He stirred a little and then suddenly took his weight off of her as he straightened up.

"Ashley?" He asked groggily. "I was flying..." He mumbled yawning as he rubbed his face. She looked at him sharply, surprised.

'*Did we somehow share our dreams because we were sleeping next to each other?*' She wondered. '*Or does he just have similar dreams to my own?*' She shook her head deciding that it really didn't matter right now. What was important was surviving this heat storm. She shook his shoulder trying to get his attention.

"I'm gonna turn the water on again. Alright Matt?" She didn't want the water to scare him if he was still half asleep but he nodded and she hoped that he really understood. She prayed that the storm was almost over, since this was probably going to be the last of her water. She got the cup ready with one hand. Standing she tried to catch as much of the water in the cup as she could. She drank it all and filled it again, handing the cup to him. Apparently the cool spray that got past her had brought him more fully awake and he took the glass from her with a grateful smile.

"Thank you Ashley." He said aloud before downing the contents of the glass. He handed it back and she filled it for herself again, and then filled it again for him. They took turns drinking until with a squeal and a clunk the valve shut off and the water coming from her showerhead slowed to a trickle.

"Damn." She said, trying to catch the rest in the glass, tapping the showerhead to try to gather the last few drops before she sat down again in the lukewarm water of their little tub. She decided that they should probably save the last glass for a while and so she set it on the floor right outside the curtain. When she turned back towards Matt she found that he was looking at her in concern.

"I'm sorry to have used so much of your water Ashley. I guess it was a really bad idea for me to come here after all." He seemed really depressed about it, she thought. She shook her head hard, trying to reassure him.

"No, not at all Matt! I'm really glad that you're here. I really am." She grabbed his hand in hers and squeezed hoping to make him realize how much she meant it. She smiled at him trying to coax one of his beautiful smiles back to his face. It kind of worked. He gave her a half-hearted grin and leaned back against the far wall of the little tub with a sigh.

"I'm sorry that I fell asleep. Do you know how long I was out?" He asked her with his eyes still closed, leaning hard into the wall. She shook her head. Then realizing that he still had his eyes closed, she cleared her throat.

"No, I don't." She said with a sigh. "I fell asleep too, so I have no idea how long we slept for." He opened his eyes at that. He smiled at her for real this time, obviously feeling less guilty knowing they had both passed out. She smiled back at him, glad to see his spark back and said. "I think it's a little cooler in here, don't you?"

She was just trying to be optimistic. She hadn't actually noticed any difference in the temperature but he nodded, apparently not willing to burst her bubble. She smiled, appreciating it. She leaned back against the opposite side of the shower stall herself. She didn't want to fall asleep again but the heat of the muggy little room was exhausting, the air heavy in her lungs and she soon found herself drifting off again.

Her last thought, was that if they were going to die here, at least they would be together.

# 12

Jen huddled as far from the mob of sweaty people as she could get. She had shoved herself partially behind the water storage, against the far wall. The water tank was cool against her side. She really hoped that no one else would figure out how good it felt and want to share her hidey-hole.

She had her flask in one hand, hidden only by her long sleeve but she hadn't had a cigarette since they hurried her in here. She'd snubbed it out just as the doors were shutting on the last of the panicked crowd. She'd gotten one in anyway, just outside the doors but it was mid-afternoon now and that had been well before dawn. She felt like she could pound her way to the center of the earth with the throbbing in her head, which she knew a cigarette would help with.

She surreptitiously sipped her flask, trying to make it look like she was scratching her nose as she watched the crowd to make sure no one noticed. The older woman in the blue dress had finally gotten the baby to stop fussing but it had been wailing for hours.

*'I can't blame the tike really. Given the sweltering heat in here and the stinking press of bodies. Who could be happy?'* Her roving eyes fell on the other scattered handful of children present in the shelter. Most were also asleep in the heat, in the arms of their family. There was not enough room for them to lie down.

*'There aren't very many kids being allowed these days. I'm surprised to see one so young.'* Her eyes went again to the now sleeping infant. *'He's actually kind of cute, now that he's sleeping. Fussy little bastard.'* She smiled just before she caught his yawn. When she again opened her eyes she found his mother watching her, apparently having noticed her scrutiny.

Jen smiled quickly. She thought really loud, just as Ashley had taught her, about how cute he was now that he was sleeping. The woman's eyes cleared and she smiled at Jen across the crowded room. As the woman turned back to her sleeping child, Jen heaved a quiet sigh of gratitude for having learned this kind of silent communication. She wedged herself even more firmly between the tank and the wall. Hugging her knees to her chest as a pillow, she tried her best to fall asleep.

––––––––––

Ashley woke groggy and shivering. If she'd had any dreams this time, she didn't remember them. She rubbed her damp arms and shivered harder as she realized suddenly, that she was cold. As she looked around herself straitening up she found that she was still sitting in her shower stall up to her waist in water and Matt was still curled in a ball against the opposite side of the stall. As she looked at him she saw him shivering as well. The realization struck her then, that the heat storm must have finally past and that they had survived!

In her excitement, she raised herself clumsily to her knees. She reached across the stall and shook Matt by the shoulders.

"Matt! Matt! Wake up! The storms over! The storms over!" The excitement in her voice and her gentle shaking seemed to bring him back to himself. Matt shuddered suddenly, as he realized that he was cold. He looked at her in wonder, as he sat up. She was so excited to be alive that she threw herself at him, hugging him fiercely.

"We made it! We're alive, Matt! We made it!" She repeated into his shoulder. "It's over Matt! The storm is over!"

She felt his arms circle round her and hold her tight. It felt wonderful, cold as she was and she buried her face into his shoulder. She was just happy to be with him and happy to be alive.

"Thank you Ashley!" He whispered into her hair, as he held her. "Thank you so much. You saved my life." He tucked his face into her neck and it sent little shivers down her back. She couldn't help it, she laughed out loud.

"I think you saved me just as much you know!" She said with a laugh. She felt him start to shake his head and she pulled back far enough for him to see the humor in her face. He stopped mid shake to stare into her eyes, obviously dazzled. She couldn't help it. She kissed him before she could think not to and once she had, she decided that she didn't want to stop.

One of his hands came up to hold her hair and he kissed her back, over and over. She felt more laughter welling up inside her. She pulled back only to let it release, laughing loudly before letting him kiss her again.

He kissed her mouth, her cheeks, her eyes, every part that he could reach. While she reveled in it. She was glad now, that she had gone ahead and kissed him like she'd wanted to. When his affections finally slowed she hugged him tightly, burying her face into his shoulder again. She laughed under her breath. She could feel his own laughter begin deep in his chest, long before it issued from his lips.

The rumble of it tickled her chest, pressed against him as she was.

"Ashley, Ashley." He said over and over, rocking her slightly in his arms. Apparently unable to express everything that he was feeling.

"Ashley, I Love you." He murmured into her shoulder and she gasped a little at his quiet declaration. She felt herself grinning widely, even as her mind was still trying to take in what she'd heard.

"I Love you too, Matt!" She pulled back to look him in the eyes as she repeated it. As much to taste the words on her tongue, as to hear herself say it. "I Love you." She started to say more. To thank him for thinking of her when the storm hit. To thank him for coming to check on her. And for being here with her now but he cut the words off with another kiss and she let him. She kissed him back, grateful for the feel of his arms around her and grateful for the love that she could feel pouring from him. It warmed her, even though she was cold.

That thought made her realize that they were still in her shower and still up to their wastes in water. She thought that it was definitely time to get out. When the kiss ended and they broke apart again she smiled asking him about it.

"Why don't we get out of here? I think it's cooled enough outside for us to leave the shower now." She grinned at him and he just smiled back but he released her and she stood up.

She swayed a little as she gained her feet. Catching herself on the wall of the shower stall, she realized that she was still incredibly lightheaded. She felt him grab her leg to try to support her and she patted his hand with a smile, grateful.

"Be careful when you get up, too. Do it slowly." She said as she pulled back the curtain to enter the rest of the bathroom.

The air outside of the little tub was a little warmer and it felt nice against her cold damp skin. She stepped gingerly out of the tub, a hand on each wall to steady herself and she heard the water splashing as it dripped and drained from him as he stood behind her. She felt her towel slipping from her shoulders and she let it fall to the floor hoping that it would help keep them from slipping in the wet little room.

"Careful." She called over her shoulder again as she made her way cautiously to the sink. She could feel the slightly cooled air of her tiny fridge still valiantly working it's hardest and she smiled as she shut its little door. She gave it a grateful little pat as she passed. She was glad all over again that she'd spent so much credit with Old Tom to have him fix it when she found it. The little guy had certainly proven its worth today.

She steadied herself on the sink for a few moments breathing deeply hoping that her head would stop spinning. When she again looked back at Matt she found that he too was clinging to the wall of the shower opening, obviously just as unsteady on his feet.

She cautiously touched the handle of the bathroom door and finding it only a little warm to the touch she cracked the door to her apartment just a bit hoping that she was right about the heat finally retreating.

The hot air struck her like a blow to the face as she looked out making her eyes water. As she opened the door further however, she found that while the air was still hot it was not scorching and it seemed safe to exit their tiny hideaway. She heard Matt following behind her and she cautiously made her way towards her kitchen counter hoping to prop herself up on it while she got her bearings in the darkened room, the only illumination being the streaks of sunset orange light streaming in around her protective reflectors.

When she looked behind her she found Matt had paused in the doorway to the bathroom and she assumed that he too had been struck by the heat. When she met his eyes however, he grinned sheepishly at her.

"Do you think I could use the bathroom? I really have to pee." She couldn't help the laugh that escaped, before she answered.

"Of course you can! You don't have to ask!" He grinned at her and gently shut the door. Looking around the crowded little room she decided that as much as she wanted to, she just didn't have the strength yet to take care of her plants. Instead she gingerly made her way over to collapse on the futon. She wiggled as much as she had the energy to and eventually worked the blanket free to pull it over her shivering shoulders.

*'It's nice and warm in here now, at least.'* She thought, the warmth of the blanket seeping over her. But she was still chilled from being in her wet clothes. The thought made her realize that she was going to

get the bed all wet. She forced herself upright to pull off her sodden shirt and to work her way out of her sticky wet pants.

She started to lie down again but the sound of the toilet flushing, reminded her of her guest. So she forced herself to stand again and tottered over to her clothes chest. There she pulled out a long shirt to sleep in and as the thought struck her, she pulled one out for Matt as well. She had just pulled it over her head, when she heard the bathroom door open again behind her.

As she turned to face him she had another dizzy spell and sat quickly and clumsily on the end of the bed. He was leaning heavily against the door frame. As he looked blearily at her sitting on the bed in what were obviously her sleep clothes, he shook his head once and blinked at her.

Then he forced himself to stand without support.

"I should probably try to get home. It seems to have cooled down enough to be safe now." He wavered a little on his feet, as he took a step away from the door. Ashley smiled at his attempt at chivalry, even as she threw the other shirt at him and collapsed back onto the futon with a sigh.

"Don't be stupid." She said as he struggled to catch the shirt she'd thrown at him. It had almost knocked him over when it hit him, more from surprise then force, she thought. "You'd probably fall down the stairs and kill yourself if you tried to leave now." She said yawning, as she crawled up towards her pillow and rolled over to make room for him on the tiny futon.

Through her bleary eyes she could see that the light leaking in around her foil was deepening in color now to a luscious dark amber. Apparently they had spent most of the day in the shower, hiding from the heat. She sighed. She knew she should be hungry but she was just too tired. After a moment she heard him sigh but she was already beginning to fade into sleep. She was vaguely aware of the rustle of him undressing, as though from far away. When the futon sunk behind her, as he crawled onto the bed, it startled her back to consciousness for a moment.

She gasped a little as his weight caused her to roll back against him and his hand was warm on her shoulder as he caught her. He rolled her back to where she'd been and she giggled, as he settled onto the mattress behind her.

Once he was settled in she snuggled herself back against him hoping that he would hold her. Without the need for further encouragement he did in fact, put his arm around her, hugging her to him.

"I Love you Ashley." He murmured into her hair. She felt him give her a soft kiss on the back of her head. She smiled slowly, as she faded back into an exhausted sleep.

---

Matt held Ashley against him gently, relishing in the warm closeness of her. He had never expected the day to end this way, when he'd sprinted towards her apartment to check on her this morning. He could tell by her deep and even breathing that she was already asleep in his arms and he was honored by her trust.

He smiled into her hair, the sweet smell of her filling his mouth and his mind. He was exhausted by the heat of the day as well but he was still riding the wave of excitement from their mutual declarations of love. He had never been this close to someone before. He snuggled against her, appreciating the closeness. She murmured in her sleep leaning more firmly against him, obviously enjoying the contact.

He didn't want to wake her but he was amazed to be so close to her. He lifted himself to look down at her, awed. He gently raised one hand and stroked her cheek softly.

He felt her smile under his fingers and it made his lips twitch too. He kissed the back of her shoulder as he settled himself once more. Tightening his hold on her, he took a deep breath and released it with a sigh. The room was dark but for the streaks of light shining through the cracks left exposed by her reflective window coverings.

One band of amber light lanced across them where they lay, slicing through the cloud of Ashley's curls beside him. Letting his vision blur he enjoyed the sparks created by the streaks of the bright orange sunset glowing through her hair. He let the color fill his vision as his mind began to wander and his eyes closed.

As he slipped into an exhausted sleep, the orange of the setting sun morphed into the familiar red orange glow of the molten stone and burning gasses of his dream world. *Waking fully to it, he snapped his wings open. Bugling his joy, he took flight on a surge of hot air.*

---

Jimi came awake all at once, his dad shaking his shoulders.

"Get up. It's time." He said gruffly as soon as he saw that Jimi was moving on his own. "The storm seems to have passed us by. It either dissipated or it's gone a different direction. So let's head out, it's after dark."

That did startle Jimi. He hadn't meant to sleep so long. He forced himself to sit up looking around the dark little room for the dog.

"She's in the other room waiting to go out." His dad seemed to know what he was thinking. "She woke me up; I guess she has to pee." Jimi could hear the grin in his dad's voice. It made him feel better to realize that his dad had fallen asleep too. He didn't feel like such a slacker then.

Getting to his feet they made their way to the outer room and the big sod door. He found the dog waiting there, whining by the entrance.

'*Apparently she did have to pee.*' He thought with a grin. He and his dad each grabbed two of the handles on the sod door and hauled it to one side, the fresh air that came pouring in was fantastic, and smelled cool and clean. It made him very conscious suddenly or the smell of earth that hung on the air in their makeshift cavern.

As he and his dad shoved the door to one side and the dog darted out. He turned back into the room to get his bike and his gear. At last they'd be starting their delivery trips. They would take their time making trades in the city, before beginning the trek back to base camp. He looked forward to making the rounds. They always met interesting people here in Newcity.

---

*Ashley was deep in her dream of flying through the fiery night sky, when she heard it in the distance. A bugling sound. She stopped, hovering for a moment, head cocked to listen. Then she heard it again, a loud keen, followed by a low bugling. Curious she swerved to head towards the sound. She was having the strangest sensation, a curious tingling sensation deep inside, and it had to do with that keening. She followed the sound more swiftly now, flying as quickly as she could. She could hear other sounds now, over the sound of the wind. It was a voice, almost a melody but she could only catch about every third note.*

*The song was getting louder and she was paying more attention to trying to catch each note then to where the sound might be coming from. So she was as surprised as the other was, when she flew right into him, following the alluring sound of the song. Wings entangled they began to fall together, she didn't know how to speak, she'd never met another before. She was shocked and he was beautiful. He seemed to recover faster than she did from the surprise of the collision. Rather than getting clear of her and righting himself however, he cocked his head and his eyes met hers. He looked at her as though he to, had never seen another before.*

*Moving swiftly he twined his neck and his tail with hers and opening his great wings he slowed both their decent towards the fiery planet below. They were a slowly lowering tangle of draconic limbs and tails. She was looking up at the sky above them but thoroughly aware of how much they were touching. And of the weight of her body hanging from his. The tingling the song had begun was stronger than ever and it was making her swoon. She felt dizzy and hot and she wasn't sure she was still dreaming.*

*At last he lowered her gently to the surface of the planet, safe in its fiery warmth. He slowly untwined their necks, but he kept hold of her tail with his. He lifted himself up over her, curving his long neck to look down at her with deep curiosity. He sang, softly, then a little louder. The same melody that had led her to him. She could hear it all now, the whole song. She felt that she could almost make out what he was saying.*

Ashley woke slowly, startled to find that the weight on her was real. As was the tingling. Now that she was awake she was much more aware of what it meant and she gasped at its intensity. Her first realization was that the weight upon her was Matt. The second was that they had apparently been acting out her dream. Distracted by his proximity and by that tenacious tingling, she didn't think to wonder how he had known what she was dreaming of, or whether they'd been dreaming together again. He seemed to be asleep, so she shook his shoulders, calling his name.

"Matt, Matt!" She called breathlessly squirming against him, trying to get enough distance between them to think clearly but he held her firmly to him, obviously still caught up in the midst of whatever dream he was having. His hands caressed her and his mouth sought hers, kissing her deeply.

"Oh, Matt…" She moved with him, unsure if she still had the heart to try to wake him. They moved in rhythm and she realized even amidst her distraction that it was the rhythm of the dream's song. She wanted him but she wanted him awake. So she shook his shoulders again, calling his name even as he pressed against her.

"Matt!" She gasped, biting his shoulder as hard as she could.

He came instantly alert gasping in pain as he jerked away from her. She lay there panting, almost sorry.

"Matt? Are -Are you awake now?" She asked him, as he shook his head and held his shoulder and seemed to try to make sense of it all. He seemed completely confused for a moment. Then with dawning realization, he looked at her in horror.

"Oh no, Ashley, what did- what did I do?" He looked so worried, that she pulled him to her reassuringly.

"You didn't do anything! We were both caught up in a dream, is all." She sighed settling herself more comfortably against him, now that he was awake.

"A dream?" He asked wonderingly, apparently blown away at how calm she was. "A dream of fire? And flying? And of music?"

She looked at him in surprise.

"You dream about it too? For real? How about before we met?" He nodded and she couldn't help herself. She threw herself at him again, pressing against him in joy.

"Oh, Matt." He gasped, as instinct tried to guide his response.

"Ashley, I love you…" He started to say, but she cut him off with a kiss.

They moved together to the rhythm of their dream song. Exploring each other and the new connections they'd wrought, until dawn just pinked the sky.

# 13

Jim and his son Jimi had arrived at Newcity just after full dark, so they decided to make the supply runs tomorrow. They would start by dropping off deliveries to the Underground and the Smoke shop and their other distribution points here in Newcity proper.

They settled in for the night in the empty husk of a building. They had chosen an old factory building today, right on the edge of the desert. They'd be up with the sun since they had to finish their deliveries before they could even begin their trading in the morning. Trading took much longer than simply dropping off stock, because of the time it took to haggle over debatable values. So they always saved the trading for last.

One of their last stops the next day was a little restaurant not far from the Library. Jim had no idea what kind of food they served but it smelled unlike anything he'd ever had. The last time he had come by offering canned vegetables and mushrooms, they had accepted a few of the mushrooms. Then the woman had gone to get them several types of empty cans by way of example of what they really wanted.

"This is what we really need." She had said, showing it to him and explaining. "It's the hardest for us to find and the most important." She had sent several empty cans with them as examples of what they were to look for. Luckily they had managed to find several cases and had taken them back to the storage caves. Since his people had no use for it, he'd brought half what he'd found and left some behind for the next trade.

Having brought a case and a half of them along with their more usual trade goods, Jim felt he had a pretty good place to bargain from. He was enjoying the barter more than usual, as he haggled with Sam over the value of the oil, now that it had been spoiled by the heatstorm.

While Jim was busy arguing with Sam in the kitchen, over how much oil he should get for the case and a half of coconut milk he'd brought. Nat snagged Jimi and they disappeared through the little curtain to the other room.

Eventually she came back into the kitchen and interrupted them.

"Oh be quiet Samyan, leave him alone and go get them some rice. The oil is bad. We would have had to throw it out anyway." Catching the surprised Jim by the shoulder, she steered him none to gently through the kitchen curtain and out into the restaurant. Finally turning him forcibly towards the booth where his son was already happily slurping up the soup she'd given him.

"Jimi!" He called sharply. "What are you doing? We're not here as customers!" He began to step angrily towards his son. Instead he found himself once again propelled against his will by Nat's firm hand on his shoulder. He found himself sitting down at the table across from his son instead.

"Now sit." She commanded firmly depositing a ridiculously tiny bowl in front of him. One that matched the bowl Jimi was already refilling from the large hotpot between them.

"Eat." She said, just as firmly, pushing a spoon into his hand. Turning on her heel, she vanished again through the kitchen curtain. Where her wise but whipped husband had stayed behind, when his wife had first gotten involved.

———

Jimi had never had a more delicious soup in his life. He was slurping down his third helping by the time his dad was ready to taste his and the look on his dad's face at the flavor, made Jimi laugh out loud, snorting into his spoon. They were both used to soups being mostly watery broth with some diced jerky or a can opened into it.

He had hid his grin behind his spoon, as his dad was neatly bullied and maneuvered by the woman who owned the restaurant. It was fun to watch. He imagined that this was probably how his mom had managed Jim, when she was still alive.

He took advantage of his dad's distraction, to help himself to a fourth tiny bowl of the delicious soup just as Sam appeared, carrying a huge pile of steaming rice. Jimi found his mouth watering just looking at it. Sam made two plates appear as if by magic, apparently by holding the rice plate on top of them. Jimi pounced on the delicacy before his dad could react.

He chopped the rice neatly in half with the sticks they'd given him and pushing half onto the plate he designated his by crouching over it. There he sat, shoveling the rice into his mouth between bites of soup. He was in complete bliss to have fresh cooked food instead of the dry packs, old granola bars and canned food that were their field rations. They might do the thing to get you through the day but there was no substitute for fresh cooked food. He couldn't help but make a pig of himself.

Just as his dad couldn't help but point it out. As Jim looked up from his renewed debate with Nat over not being willing to accept her generosity and saw his son shoveling food into his face as fast as he could go. He couldn't help the laugh that burst out, interrupting the argument he was losing.

"You act like I never feed you boy! Are you a starveling? Never seen food before in your life?" Jim laughed out loud again at the chagrined embarrassment on Jimi's face. Jimi straightened self-consciously from the protective crouch over his plate.

He swallowed what he had in his mouth, setting down the sticks for a moment before daring to look at the proprietor. He was embarrassed at having been eating like a wild animal in front of her but when he dared to look her in the face, he saw that she was smiling broadly.

"Well, that's settled then." She said in reference to the now seemingly forgotten argument and walked away as Jimi's dad spluttered at being outmaneuvered by his distraction. She patted Jimi's shoulder, giving him an affectionate squeeze and a warm smile as she passed him. It seemed that she had not been offended by his somewhat enthusiastic enjoyment of her food. Jimi was still flushed hotly though from his father's criticisms, so he went back to the soup. Which he took great care not to slurp this time.

His dad just chuckled, muttering something about women and shaking his head. He again lifted his soup bowl, now gone cold. Looking at the ridiculously tiny bowl with a grimace, he downed it in a gulp and refilled it from the hot pot.

"Good soup." He said sounding surprised as he tasted it hot. Then he set to, enjoying the meal as much as Jimi had been, if a little less enthusiastically.

———

Matt was sitting on the edge of the bed looking at her sketchbook when Ashley came out of the bathroom. He waved one hand at her, gesturing towards it.

"So what's the story with this picture? It looks…" He cleared his throat his cheeks flushing. "It, um, looks like you did. In the dream last night…"

Ashley chuckled sitting down next to him. She thought his shyness was cute but she didn't want him feeling awkward. Nodding, she took the drawing from his lap, looking closely at it.

"I saw it in a vision. Only…" She faded off, trailing her fingers over the eyes of the drawing. She shivered, remembering the intelligence she had seen in those eyes, the moment they had locked with hers. They had been so beautiful, glittering rainbow, every color at once.

"Only what?" Matt's question startled her out of her revere. "Only what, Ashley?" He shook her a little. "So you saw it in a vision, and then what?" He mock frowned at her as though thoroughly impatient but then grinned.

"Only, as I was drawing it, I felt myself move closer to the face. Once I was near to it, well. It, she, looked at me…" She shivered again and he put an arm around her shoulders.

"Was it scary? Did it seem menacing to you?" He seemed really concerned and she leaned into his shoulder with a sigh. It was such a relief, to finally be able to talk to someone about the dreams. She shook her head.

"No. It wasn't at all but it did startle me." She smiled up at him. "I may see things but I'm not used to my visions looking back at me." She chuckled a little under her breath. "It was a bit unnerving is what I'd say but not threatening or malicious at all. Curious maybe, sad…" Her voice trailed off again as her thoughts wandered back to those eyes. They'd been vague at first, then suddenly focused and questing as they sought and found hers. "Jen said it reminds her of a dragon. I described it to her over lunch and that's pretty spot on."

She shuddered once again and Matt tightened his arm around her. Deciding to change the subject she snuggled closer to him and tilting her head up began nibbling on his ear. He jerked back in surprise but upon seeing the playful quirk to her mouth, he quickly gave in to her. Leaning down to kiss her, he was surprised at her aggressiveness. He saw no further reason to argue the change of subject though and quite willingly let her press him against the bed.

---

They spent as much time together as their schedules allowed. Matt hardly ever saw Michael anymore and he really hoped that his friend would understand. In fact, he kept reminding himself that he had wanted them to meet. Ashley kept mentioning a friend of hers that she wanted to introduce him to as well. They had yet to go see her friend Sister Mary or her garden.

Instead they usually met at the library and talked or watched films together and pleasantly, the time slipped by. Occasionally they would spend time at her apartment talking about things, getting to know one another better. She had even mentioned wanting to take him out to the wastes, so that he could see them for himself. Somehow though that too, kept getting postponed. It seemed that there was just always so much to talk about. It was sometimes hard to drum up the motivation to do more than just hold onto each other and be grateful.

He wondered how their visit today would go, as he climbed the stairs to her apartment. He couldn't wait to see her, but he also wondered what they would talk about today. He usually left the topic of conversation up to her, since she had a much broader area of interest. If it was left up to him they would have little to talk about aside from music.

He smiled at the thought.

*'Maybe I should bring my guitar next time.'* He thought to himself. *'I'd like to play something for her.'* He couldn't help the broad smile that split his cheeks as he thought of playing for her. He wondered if it would make her feel as good as it did him. He hoped so.

When he got to the landing and knocked lightly on the door, Ashley opened it with a smile.

"Come in! Come in!" She said giving him a kiss on the cheek, before she'd even shut the door.

He grinned and swept her into a hug as soon as she turned around. He nuzzled her hair, drinking in the smell of her. He loved the way she smelled. She laughed and held him just as close, before pulling back to look him in the eyes. She tiptoed briefly and kissed him firmly, on the mouth this time. He shut his eyes, giving her his undivided attention. They kissed for several minutes, just happy to be together and when they parted, she laughed as she turned away.

When she turned back, she handed him a book. He could tell by her expression that she expected him to look at it.

"The Very Last Harvest." He read out loud, mostly for her benefit. "The genetic gamble that threatens to destroy American culture." He flipped it open to see when it had been published. "1995?" He said it questioningly, looking at her. He wondered what such an old book could have to do with them now, in their current situation. He trusted her though, she always had a point. No matter how obscure the reference she handed him seemed at first to be. He wondered how she found these old books. There were so many books in the library but every time he came over, she had new books and new information that he never would have come to on his own.

"I wanted to share this with you. Can you believe that they had this knowledge since the early 1900's and they still did what they did?" She asked. Rhetorically, since he hadn't read it yet. "Here look on pg 13." She said taking the book from his hands and flipping it open to the specified page and began reading it aloud to him.

"A few farsighted biologist anticipated this threat, that of genetic mono-cropping and lack of genetic diversity." She paused to interject. "At the turn of the century, that's meaning 1900's." She emphasized. "They began sending collecting expeditions around the world in search of seeds of potentially valuable wild and traditional crop varieties. The largest collection of these seeds is run by the US Department of Agriculture and housed in dozens of cavernous refrigerated vaults across the country." She flashed him a smile; this was obviously her point in reading this to him.

"The flagship of the U.S. 'seed banks,' as they are called, is in the National Seed Storage Laboratory (NSSL) in Fort Collins, Colorado. More than a quarter of a million packets of seeds are stored there! In 1991, a panel assembled by the National Academy of Sciences called the U.S. collections "a strategic resource essential to national and global agricultural security."

She was so excited that he saw her eyes skip ahead a bit and read. "Refrigerated vaults hold hundreds of thousands of seeds as different from one another as the multicolored kernels on an ear of Indian corn!" Can you believe it? All those seeds! All that genetic diversity and all in one place!" She was obviously really excited, and he smiled to show that he was trying to follow her. Then she frowned down at the book saying.

"And they still grew the same damn strain of corn all over the U.S! Even with all that diversity at their disposal! Shortsighted bastards!" She'd completely lost him with her sudden switch and he decided to try to get things clarified.

"So is it a good thing or a bad thing? I don't get it. I thought you were happy that they were saving seeds." She could switch so fast between being really happy and really mad that sometimes it was hard for him to follow what exactly she was mad about. He was just glad that she wasn't mad at him. And that she was usually patient enough to explain her train of thought. This time however, she pushed on ahead, flipping back a few pages and pointing at another section.

"Look, right here it says, "In 1991 American Farmers grew 66% of the world's export of corn, 32% of its export of wheat, and 66% of its export of soybeans!" You can imagine what this large amount of mono-cropping and mass agriculture did to the state of the soil right? All that tilling and over fertilization combined with growing the same thing year after year has robbed the soil of nutrients! Not to mention scraping off all the life that would have protected the soil from the elements and leaving it exposed to the wind and the baking sun. Once the rains stopped coming, everything just dried up and blew away. That's why all we have out there now are deserts." Ashley said frowning again.

"Why?" Matt asked. "I guess that I don't really get it." He admitted hoping that she'd explain.

"It's because in the natural order of things, each type of plant has a place in the ecological chain of the land. For example corn takes nitrogen from the soil, while beans and legumes deposit nitrogen into the soil. In a naturally balanced ecosystem, like you'd find in an undisturbed natural area, the plants all grow together taking turns as it were. Some of them create nitrogen, some of them eat nitrogen, some of them make phosphorous, and some of them consume it. In a balanced ecosystem, the plants support each other. Even when they die, their body's decay and give back the nutrients that they've taken from the soil to replenish it for the next generation." She responded with a smile for his patience.

"Like composting!" He interjected, excited to have recognized the concept.

———

"Exactly!" She smiled at him encouragingly. "But in the typical mono-cropping agricultural system, not only do they not compost, but they plant acres and acres of the same plant, plants that all eat the same thing. Then they must intentionally 'feed' them, often using chemically derived fertilizers of nitrogen or phosphorous or whatever they deem necessary for that particular crop. Then to make matters worse, when the crop is done and they harvest it they cut the plants down and drag them off to burn them or throw them away rather than letting them decompose where they grew to revitalize the soil.

That's one of the reasons that we have the vast wastelands that we do now. They raped the soil without offering anything back to it for so many years, that now it can't even support the plants that our ancestors thought of as weeds!" She sighed. She was angry again, but she couldn't help it. The shortsighted greed of her forefather's had created the depleted and desolate world in which she lived. It made her blood boil, that they had simply cared more about the state of their own wealth and well-being, than that of the future generations that they knew would inherit this mess.

She fell silent thinking about it all. She brooded about what could be done at this late date, to try to revitalize the poor depleted soils. Dropping down, she sat on the futon in defeat. Matt put a gentle hand on her shoulder, startling her from her thoughts. She jumped, even as he smiled down at her reassuringly. She smiled back, grateful. This was the first time that she really had someone to talk to about this stuff.

Even though he didn't understand all of it, he was so willing to listen and to learn. She was so grateful for that willingness and for his friendship. It made her love him all the more. She smiled back at him taking his hand in hers and leaning her cheek against it softly.

"Thanks for listening." Was all she said out loud, but she could tell by his deepening smile that he understood what she didn't say as well.

Dropping a soft kiss on the top of her head, he sat down on the futon beside her and wrapping her in his arms and asked over her shoulder.

"So what can we do about it? There must be something. I can't imagine that we're just screwed, just because of the actions of a few idiots that lived so long ago. Isn't there an answer in the permaculture books that you've read? Some way to revitalize the soil and correct what's been done?" She sighed at how simple he made it sound. Like they could just wave a magic wand and poof! everything would go back to the fertile green land that their planet had once been. She sighed, shaking her head, her hair brushing against his face.

"Short of burying the whole planet in mulch for a few generations, I really can't think of anything that could even begin to help! And without rain even that would likely not be enough. Not to mention that with the threat of heat storms and wind storms and ice storms and all the rest of it, who's going to be willing to go out and do even that?" She asked him over her shoulder, raising one hand to his arm across her chest.

It was so good to be held. It was reassuring. When he held her she felt that even though life here in Newcity was often desperate, somehow everything was going to be alright. She leaned back against him letting her eyes close. She simply relished in the sensation of being together for the moment, releasing her worries.

She couldn't blank her mind for long though because he didn't let it go.

"Well what's wrong with that idea?"

"Huh?" She had completely lost her train of thought now. She wasn't sure what he was talking about. "What idea?" She asked him, twisting her head to one side to try to get a look at him. She gave up a moment later though and was simply glad that he was there.

"Covering the planet in mulch I mean. At least as much as we can. It's worth a try isn't it? So what's stopping us? Let's look at it reasonably, one step at a time." He rocked her a little back and forth, trying to get her energy back she thought. She took a deep breath deciding to humor him and gave it some thought.

"Well first of all. To compost or mulch anything you need organic matter and lots of it. There's nothing growing at all out there anymore though."

"So the first step then is to find something stubborn enough to grow in the soil that we have left right? There must be something, what about the grasses that have survived?" He asked her but she was already shaking her head.

"No we can't use the grasses. They take a lot of nitrogen to break down and the soil just doesn't have it. They would do more damage than good."

"Hmmm. Well, that's our first step though, right? I'm sure that if we think about it long enough that we can come up with something. So what's step two? How does something living and organic turn into mulch?"

She sighed again. He wasn't going to let this go, she could tell. Besides, he was probably right, she reminded herself. If they could just get something growing it would be better than the dusty dead desert plains that surrounded the city now. She thought about it and tried to answer him clearly but truthfully.

"Well." She sighed, trying to think past the depression she'd sunk into, thinking about the wastelands all around them. "The next step would be to kill it." She smiled a little at the irony of the process. First nurture life back to health, then kill it for its nutrients. "That way we can use the plant bodies to add those nutrients back into the soil and begin the revitalization process."

"Really?" He asked. He seemed a little put off by her language. "We raise it and then we kill it?" She laughed a little at the incredulity in his voice.

"Yep." She reassured him, deciding to take pity on him and explain. "In a natural setting soil is never exposed to the elements, it is always covered by a densely layered system of decomposing plant bodies, generations of them. These not only nourish the soil with their decomposition but they act as a barrier to the wind and the rain that will otherwise wash the valuable topsoil away.

That's what happened here, in the old form of monolistic agriculture, they stripped the soil of nutrients by growing all one type of plant and they also stripped it of that protective layer. That way no weeds, as they called them, could sneak up through that top layer of protective mulch. That and it was easier for them to use their huge machines to do their farming for them with the soil exposed for them to drive on."

"I see." Matt said, and he did sound as though he understood. "So then, step one. We find something that can grow in our current soil, and conditions. Then step two. We kill it off and allow it to become the first layer in this protective layer that you're suggesting. Then what?"

"Well, basically we just keep on doing it. We find other plants, with nutritional needs that fit the spectrum left by the first crop. That will leave different nutrient spectrums that we can then layer onto the slightly replenished soil. We can grow them up and let them die, until we have a decently thick layer of protection for the soil beneath. It's all just a matter of time really." She sighed snuggling against him. She wanted to burrow into him. "And I suppose, maybe we can find the seeds we'd need in the old seed banks. Some may yet have survived." This talk had her feeling more hopeful but at the same time the sheer size of the project they were talking about was overwhelming.

It made her tired just thinking about it. She sighed, leaning harder into his arms. He obligingly tightened his arms around her, humming thoughtfully to himself, although he did let the subject drop.

A few days later, Ashley suggested that they go out on a treasure hunt. It had caught him completely by surprise. At first he had no idea what she had even meant. He'd followed her down the hill into the outskirts trepidatiously, unsure what to expect.

After spending most of the day with her though, scuttling and scrounging through the broken buildings that made up the outskirts of Newcity, he had a new understanding of this woman he was with. And a new found respect for her capabilities, especially when it came to turning anything and everything into a flowerpot.

Matt found that after exploring the ruins left of the lives lived by those before the shift, he had a profound new understanding of both the present and the past. Ashley called out softly to him where he stood with his dust laden goggles pushed up so he could see more clearly the tiny music box he held. It was dusty and dented but when he had opened it, it had still played true. He had stood for a long time looking around the room he had found it in.

Part of the floor had collapsed beneath the weight of the collapsing floors above in the earthquakes that had shaken this area. The earth's tremors hadn't stopped with the storms during the climactic weeks following the shift. He could feel the slight breeze through the gap where the other end of the room should have been. Shuddering a little at the wreckage, he wondered if the child who had lived here had survived the devastation.

'*Had they already fled to a shelter when the quake hit?*' He wondered. '*Or was it after the storms had passed and they had thought they were finally safe, that the earthquakes began?*' He didn't know the answer. He had been a child himself then. One of the lucky ones. One of those that made it to a shelter in time. Even if he was hurt on the way, he was still one of the lucky ones. Even more, he realized looking around at the wreckage, then anyone else. Since he at least, had no memories of what he'd lost to torment him.

He had always taken life at face value. He enjoyed things as they came and tried not to dwell on anything negative for very long. That's where music had become integral in his life. It had filled the voids left by family and security. He could always count on the music.

Striking even a single note on his guitar or on Michael's violin, even just humming to himself would instantly banish any dark mood that might take him.

No loneliness, no despair, no sense of loss or lack could not be banished by the music. Even the smallest humming would inspire melody after melody until soon he was singing and swaying without meaning to. And as the music bore him up and out of all his problems, he'd find that his sadness had dissolved before the endless joy of song.

He sighed, coming back to the tiny jeweled music box in his hand. Its song had taken him back to that happy place for a moment. Now he was here again, in the wreckage of this child's room, Ashley calling softly from the doorway behind him. Turning he found she had her hands full to and her backpack was bulging over her shoulder.

"Can I put some of these in your backpack?" She asked with a sheepish grin. "I'm out of room in mine. I need to remember to put my saddle-buckets back on my bike." She'd muttered to herself, as he wordlessly held out the empty backpack she'd given him with the goggles, at the outset. When they had both filled their packs for the day, Ashley called a halt to their explorations. She said that she'd like to head over to the Salvage yard to see her friend Old Tom.

"It's where I got your watch, remember? Don't let me forget, we need to get you a bicycle basket too!" She said over her shoulder as they rode towards the salvage yard. Turning back to the ride, she muttered further about compasses and maps.

She explained over her shoulder on the way, that she had known Old Tom since she was a child. She told him about how she and Jen had been making these salvage runs for him since they were little girls, and he found his already enormous respect for her increasing.

She didn't seem to notice his reaction though. She was caught up in telling him over her shoulder about some of her favorite spots in the outskirts, ones that she'd like to take him to. She mentioned that she couldn't wait to introduce him to Old Tom. Since he was almost as much an adopted father figure to her, as Sam was to him.

———

Jo raised his snout, sniffing in the way that meant someone was coming. With a sigh Tom put down his book and pushed himself up out of his chair. He limped over to look out the window facing the street. The most street facing window, of the many windows that is. This room that he called his study, being made mostly of windows, was oddly shaped and was the highest part of his irregular ramshackle home.

This room was an isolated tower perched high above the rest of his home at the top of two sets of stairs and a ladder. Its irregularly spaced walls were covered floor to ceiling with shelves of books except for the space removed by the innumerable windows.

His whole home was mostly windows, of all different shapes and sizes, giving the house its curious irregularity, as the walls had been haphazardly pieced together to fill in the gaps. He'd used whatever had come to hand, mostly bits and pieces of other buildings and all at often unexpected angles. It gave his home the overall appearance of a three legged multi-eyed patchwork lizard sprawling through the junkyard, head held high like a proud turret.

What would be the left haunch of the lizard and closest to the gate was the pawnshop, the heart of his little business. This was the only part of his home that anyone but his very close friends ever saw.

He kept the curtains drawn on the side of the house towards the public. He preferred the option of whisking a curtain aside if he wanted to see out, then to letting all the world see in. The many colored squares and oblongs of cloth showing through the windows of the string of rooms that was his first floor gave the lizard its patchwork effect, looking like large multicolored scales in the long irregular wall of the building.

The lizardly effect had not been his goal when he began his construction, he just didn't have a lot of tools or supplies. The biggest pieces of wood and sheet metal had gone to build the pawn shop. He had lived in the pawnshop the first few years while he scraped together more supplies to add on. Once he had enough windows he would frame them into a room with his best boards at the time and then fill in the rest of each space with anything that he could.

He'd collected pieces of scrap both on his own and in trade at the yard and each year he had built one more room. He'd expanded his house into one long trunk that splayed out on one corner into what was now his bedroom or the lizard's right haunch. It being the farthest from the street and the closest to the Pawnshop, so he could keep an ear on the place at night without even trying.

Just this year he had added the study and he loved it. Not only was it a bright place to read, even in the winter but he could see a goodly distance around from up here. So between Jo's keen nose and the tower Old Tom always knew who was coming to see him before they knew he knew. Which was more than just convenient, when you slipped as much by the law as he did.

Jo himself for example was an illegal animal, unnecessary pets being deemed as a waste of resources, they were not allowed within the City limits. As far as Tom was concerned however, he should be allowed to share his own water allotment any way he wanted. His tower allowed him the leisure of knowing when the enforcers were stopping in to, check on things. That moment's notice allowed him to make sure that Jo was well hidden in the back room and that there were no chew toys or telltale bowls of water in the pawnshop. Long before the enforcers sauntered in the gate to, check on things. As they were wont to do.

So it was with growing trepidation that he waited, with one hand on the head of his wolf-mastiff friend. Jo had butted his head against Tom's hip to help support him and together they watched to see who was coming. A moment before anyone came into view however Jo gave one of his rare woofs. A soft gruff puff of air and turned to amble to the slide that Tom had put in just for Jo.

He had salvaged it from a couple of the abandoned kiddy parks in the outskirts. It had taken several of them pieced together to make the slide long enough to accommodate his tower, but he had made it work by taking them apart piecemeal and then reassembling them here in the shape he had wanted.

Since the dog was too big to use the ladder and since Tom didn't want to have to do without his friend, he had built an addition of a dog ladder up the outside that looked a little like a precarious pile of brick-a-brac but allowed his friend to ascend at a rate that accommodated his shorter legs and doggy knees. Tom had put in the slide for Jo to get down again.

Convincing Jo to ride down a slide voluntarily had not been as easy however. It had involved weeks of first begging and cajoling, then riding down with Jo between his legs and finally a whole handful of snacks tossed into the slide which had finally led to an ecstatic leap onto the slippery surface. Now Jo had become quite accustomed to his new mode of transportation. If he was heading for the slide, then it meant that whoever Jo smelled coming was a friend and one that Jo liked well enough to go down for a visit.

Old Tom himself turned back to the window, truly curious now. Jo's excited reaction narrowed the possibilities to only a handful of people and he would be happy to see any of them. He was curious to see who it was though, before he went down to greet them himself.

When Ashley hove into view on her bike the next moment he knew immediately from her expression and the set of her shoulders that she was happy. Even more than happy she was proud, feeling good about something and couldn't wait to show it off to him. That had been a common enough occurrence over the last ten or so years of their friendship. He wondered what it was, beginning to rub his hands greedily, thinking of some of the amazing treasures she had found for him over the years.

Before he could get too far into his daydream of priceless objects however, the obvious object of her affection came around the corner behind her and Tom let out his excited breath in a gruff huff not unlike Jo's. He could see it in her expression when she looked back at the young man that she was leading, that he was what she was so proud of.

"Hrmh.." He grumped to himself.

*'So she's finally gone and grown up, has she?'* He wondered to himself. *'I guess it was only a matter of time.'*

He tried to pretend that to see her looking so happy and mature meant nothing to him. Or the fact that she was leading this young man to him, as though for her father's approval but he couldn't help the moisture that he pressed from his eyes before turning from the window to greet her.

Deciding to screw decorum he limped to the slide himself, determined to look as though he'd never left the shop since the last time she had been by to see him. It was a running joke with them whenever she visited. That he was always sitting on the same stool, working on the same peyote stitch pendant, every time she came.

She swore sometimes that there was a time loop and swore that he didn't seem to age either, which he knew to be a lie. It was one that made him smile though. Thinking of it made him smile now, as carefully taking the weight on his good foot, he landed on the old couch cushions at the base of the slide. It ended near his backdoor.

He slipped inside and fishing his peyote stitch project out of the drawer where he left it in between her visits, he settled himself onto the stool. He didn't think he would ever finish it now. It had come to represent so much more than the simple pendant he had sat down to mend, all those years ago, now it held years and years of their shared laughter.

Counting down under his breath, he was taking a deep new breath for "two, one," when the door opened and Ashley and Jo came tumbling in. The big dog all but shoved her inside in his enthusiasm, his tail knocking into the doorpost loudly and his tongue lolling in an uncharacteristic display of doggishness. Jo was usually a very reserved and calm dog. Being an old man himself he was born just before the shift he had stiff joints and all the rest that goes with being an old dog but ever since she was a girl, whenever Ashley came over Jo was a puppy again. Maybe it was partially because she called him puppy or my Jo, with her voice full of love. Either way the dog adored her.

"Oh Jo! I Love you! My Jo!" She was saying even now, having gone to her knees to embrace Jo's huge chest and his excited twitches ceased as he leaned into the contact. They hugged a long time while Ashley stroked his soft thick fur. Tom smiled at them both from the stool as she pet Jo's head with her hands and he leaned into the hug, bliss on his huge furry face.

---

It was into this oddly touching scene that Matt tentatively walked. He didn't want to disturb her or the huge dog but he didn't want to hover outside the door all night either. So, edging in just enough to close the door behind him, Matt stood patiently observing what to him was a rather odd and slightly frightening scene.

He had never seen any real animals in person. Other than those in films and those films had not led him to believe that dogs were quite this big! Sitting on her knees as she was, the dog was a full head taller than Ashley herself as she hugged him. The dog had lowered his head to her shoulder however and was obviously not aggressive.

Still he couldn't help the atavistic chill that ran through him looking at the sheer power of the animal.

'*And here she was calling it a puppy!*' He thought in amazement as he tore his eyes off the huge animal, to look for the man they had come to see.

Sure enough, just as she had described on their way over here, there was Old Tom, hunched over his microscopic beadwork. Matt wondered a little why it was the man always worked on the same thing. Shrugging he wondered more whether Ashley was likely to hug the dog all night and if maybe he should introduce himself. As if his thought had broken whatever spell of communion she and the dog had been locked into, she released the hug. The dog whined like he didn't want her to let go and she patted his head as they both stood.

"Hi Tom!" She said, turning to him at last. "Still hard at work I see." She grinned as she said it and Tom chuckled as well, as he set aside his beading.

Once the introductions were made Old Tom, who obviously loved Ashley as much as his dog did, invited them into his home. He offered to play an old record player for Matt when Ashley mentioned he liked music and Matt wasn't quite sure what to expect as the old man led them through the door in the far wall.

The room they entered was strange to say the least. The room that he took them to, which he called the drawing room was floored in black and white checkered tiles that where some unidentifiable material, slightly peeling and curling inwards at each edge giving the room a strange spongy quality. The curtains crowding the windows seemed to be red velvet or something like it, thick and heavy. Matt wondered how a simple pawn and junk shop operator got such plush things as velvet curtains and antique record players.

Other than the curtains and the strange spongy tile the room was mostly windows, none quite symmetrical and no two alike. Looking up Matt saw that there were even more windows in the ceiling, hung at such unlikely angles that it made him rather worried about the likelihood of them staying there. Keeping one wary eye on the ceiling and his other warily watching the huge animal that had refused to leave Ashley's side he followed her and Old Tom deeper into Tom's home.

Matt had been expecting a 20th century record player when Ashley had mentioned it, but as Tom pulled out tubes and boxes from the cabinet he seemed to store them in Matt realized that his assumption had been wrong. Looking at the ever growing pile of unfamiliar objects he felt his jaw sag as Old Tom produced from the back of the cupboard a beautifully preserved gramophone horn.

"Where did you- ?" Matt didn't manage more than that as Old Tom looked up at him and seeing his expression threw back his head and laughed. Matt shook his head a little trying to settle his thoughts, as Old Tom settled the gramophone gently into Matt's reverent hands.

The wood was light and smooth beneath his hands and yet it had a surprising weight to it. He gently cupped the funnel end to support most of its weight in one hand so he could stroke the wood of the rim softly with his free hand.

"Wow." Was all he managed. He felt the supple well balanced weight of it in his hands, as the weight of centuries. He sighed as he bent to return it gently to the pile of things Old Tom had hauled from the cupboard.

*'Michael would love this.'* He thought to himself giving the horn a final loving pat. He wondered if Old Tom would ever be willing to show it to him. Matt watched in awe as Old Tom reassembled the gramophone with the swift skill of an expert and soon he was neck deep in the cupboard again fishing for a box of records.

His voice was muffled by the cabinet as he answered Matt's unfinished question. "It just so happens that someone who lived here in Newcity before the shift was an avid collector of antiques. I was lucky enough to come across his stash on one of my spelunking runs through the ruins and I gleaned quite a few nifty trinkets from his treasure trove." He grinned over his shoulder at Matt as he pulled forth the surprisingly clean box of records and stood to place them very carefully on the coffee table.

"This is just one but from what Ashley was saying I thought you might enjoy it."

His grin was wide and took in both of them, welcoming Matt into their impromptu little family. Ashley was sprawled on the couch beside the coffee table, this area apparently set up for just such small gatherings of friends. As Old Tom began shuffling through the records Ashley leaned forward to help, pulling a couple from the box without even reading them, apparently familiar with its contents. The rest of the evening passed pleasantly as they listened to records and exchanged stories and in the case of Ashley and Old Tom memories.

Matt was quiet much of the time, eyes closed just drinking in the sound of the rumbling notes echoing from the gramophone. He listened to Old Tom's stories about tough scrapes he'd found himself in while out spelunking the ruins with only half an ear, although the stories themselves were quite interesting.

But whenever Old Tom started a tale about Ashley as a girl, Matt would open his eyes and give the old man his full attention. Especially the couple of times that Ashley exclaimed at the beginning of a tale 'No! Don't tell him that!'

This immediately captured Matt's attention and brought a smile to his lips. Old Tom invariable matched his smile at her exclamations and proceeded to tell his story with relish, as Ashley grew red with anger or embarrassment by turns. All told it was a musically miraculous night and it was well after curfew by the time he and Ashley were on their way home.

# 14

After their repeated excursions of late Matt was beginning to feel more at home in the outskirts and more confident of himself in his explorations. Although he had yet to find any of the musical instruments that Ashley had claimed for him. Other than the little music box.

He began to wonder if maybe he wasn't looking at things in the right way. Ashley would find an old shoe or a bucket, anything that could hold soil. Then she'd put an upside down ashtray in the bottom to give it some water storage and exclaim that she'd found an incredibly unique planter, meant just for her.

On their way home today, with one such find strapped to the outside of her bicycle basket, it being far too big to fit inside it, Ashley had given him an odd and thoughtful look when it was time for him to go to work. After a moment she'd asked if he could get away for a couple of days in a row.

Since tonight was his last work shift for this week he agreed that he could and she told him to pack an overnight bag and to be ready to go when they met at her place the next day. Not really knowing what to expect Matt didn't bring much with him, some clean socks and his toothbrush and a change of clothes. He arrived at her place the next day with his small pack, sorely puzzled by her ambiguity.

"Alright, so I'm here. I have a couple of days, what's this all about Ashley?" Matt stood in the doorway of her apartment with his pack over one shoulder and a puzzled look on his face.

"I wanna show you something." She bit her lip, glancing around to see if she had everything. She grabbed the bags she'd packed before he arrived. "Common! Don't ask question's it's a surprise, just come!" Shoving a large bundle into his arms she snagged the last pouch off the kitchen counter and loaded down like a bag lady headed for the door.

"Ashley!" Matt back peddled onto the landing trying to get out of the way. "How far are you planning on going with all this stuff? It's not going to fit on our bicycles!" She smiled as she shut the door behind her and swinging around bumped and jiggled down the stairs with Matt trailing along behind her. When they got to the bottom of the stairs she set down her stuff with a sigh. She was glad now that she'd already put her bucket's on before Matt came over, it would save time.

They were still going to have to try the one's she made for his bike and hope that they fit. Setting everything down on the landing she fished in one of the bags she had been carrying to dig out the screwdriver. Reaching into her back pocket, where she put all things important, she pulled out the brace she'd picked up on their last visit to Old Tom. Reaching into the stairwell behind the bike rack she pulled out the two five gallon buckets that she had pre-drilled and stashed there earlier.

"Bring your bike over here and hold it up, alright?" She turned to find him still standing with his arms full and looking confused. "Please?" She smiled to encourage him. She was being intentionally obscure because she wanted him to be surprised.

Sighing he set down the things he was carrying. Pulling his bike from the rack, he wheeled it over to where she knelt with the two bucket's.

"What are you doing with those anyway? What are the buckets for?" He seemed really puzzled and she couldn't help but laugh.

"To carry all that stuff for us of course, it'd be pretty hard to steer carrying it all, don't you think?" She winked at him and held the first bucket in place matched the brace to the bucket on the other side and tightened down the screw. "There, instant saddlebags." She tested one, tugging and jerking at it, then straitened it and tightened the screw further. Pulling the lid off she gestured grandly into it as she stepped back.

"Voilà! Go ahead and load your stuff! Just make sure you keep the weight balanced." She winked at him again, and turned to pack her own buckets.

Jiggling and wriggling the bundles she was able to stow all of her bags and containers between the two five gallon buckets and her front basket, and shrugging on her backpack she turned to see how Matt was doing at loading his own. She found him ready and waiting, already straddling his bike apparently having decided that he was excited after all.

"These are great!" He said gesturing to his loaded buckets.

"Thanks so much Ashley! I don't know why I didn't think to make something like them before! If I'd realized that you were serious about taking a couple of days I would have brought my guitar! Since I can put my stuff in these instead of in my backpack I could bring it on my shoulder strap." He grinned at her obviously well pleased with the idea.

"Do you want to go get it? I can wait here if you want. It might be nice to have it." She smiled at him encouragingly. She hoped he would go get it if he really wanted to.

"No, I shouldn't take the time. Let's just go, I really want to see this place that has you so excited." He grinned at her leaning towards her and she had the feeling that he was trying to tempt her into describing it.

It had almost worked too! She had been about to say that it was a wonderful magical place. The most magical place that she had ever been! When she'd suddenly remembered that she was trying to surprise him. So instead she smiled enigmatically and pushing off she wheeled her bike out and onto the street. She could hear him following her so she went ahead and stepped up into a hard peddle as soon as she was in the street. She glanced behind her to make sure he was following and he was already standing on his peddles as well.

———

Matt was really excited about this now that he'd had a minute to take in the fact that she was serious. He had been taken by surprise when she'd asked him if he could go away with her. He had been unsure what she'd meant.

'*Where could we possibly go?*' He had thought. It wasn't safe to leave the city anymore after all. Not with heat storms coming without warning. They had all been taught not to get too far from a shelter, just in case the temperature or winds started to rise.

'*Then again we're also taught that you can't survive a heat storm outside the shelter, and we proved otherwise didn't we?*'

Not that he wanted to repeat that particular process if he could help it. He could certainly see the intelligence in making the shelters. The whole experience had shaken his faith in some of the things that he had taken for granted though. He was beginning to question some of the things that he had always just taken at face value before.

When he'd brought up the fear of a heat storm coming while they were out, Ashley had shrugged.

She had said. "There are basements all over town Matt, the only difference is whether or not the CCC has stocked them with supplies or not. That's all the shelters are really." She had shrugged so nonchalantly. As though it should be obvious. Yet somehow it had never occurred to him before.

She had a lot of questions that had never occurred to him before and she had a lot of answers too. He had seen himself in those years of noticing her at the library just how much she read and how wide her range of interests were. Until he really got to know her though, he'd had no idea just how broad her scope truly was. Or how determined she was about her path.

He had never really thought much beyond the edges of Newcity. In fact, as she'd pointed out the first time she led him into the Outskirts, he hadn't even been thinking about the edges *of* the city itself. There was a whole no-man's-land surrounding him in every direction and he had always just taken for granted that it was there, without ever wondering what else might be in it.

Not having any memories from what life was like before the shift, it had been very easy for him to just let life wash over him. He took things as they came and made the best of whatever he had without questioning why things were the way they were. That was one way that he and Ashley were completely different. She never stopped questioning. She had an insatiable curiosity to know. Who, why, when, & how.

She had to know and that inexhaustible quest had led her primarily to research climate change and the possibility of sustainability. In her never ending campaign to understand just how we went so far off course and how we could possibly set it right again. He sighed heavily and tried to let the thought go. She even had him worrying about it now.

He intentionally quieted his thoughts. Letting the passage of the wind on his face pull them from his mind, he was soon crystal clear. Breathing deeply of the winds Matt noticed a change in the taste of the air. It was stale, dusty and dirty tasting.

Opening his eyes he realized that he had been riding along with them closed for quite a while. He pumped his pedals to catch up with Ashley embarrassed by his distraction. As he did, he realized that they had passed beyond the boundaries of Newcity and they were well into the Outskirts now. The changes were subtle but obvious at the same time. The most obvious being the refuse. Blown around, torn, broken or burdened by dirt, everything around them were examples of the degenerating shell of a once thriving metropolis.

He shuddered a little at the thought. It creeped him out to think that the empty and often broken buildings all around him had once held teeming masses of people. He couldn't help but wonder where they had all gone or rather, just how they had died. He knew that many people died in the first heat storms.

It had been speculated by his teachers at the orphanage that when the ice melted and cooled the sea, the winds of the world stopped blowing. For without hot spots and cold spots in the ocean, there was nothing to cause global air circulation.

Without any wind to circulate the globes humidity the clouds dried up and the cities were left to bake in the heat of the sun. Thousands died in those first heat storms. Before anyone realized how severe they actually were. There were too many people to be taken care of. Many were too weak to leave their homes by the time they realized that they needed help. So by then, it was too late.

Lost in thought as he was Matt was hardly paying attention to where they had been headed. He almost rolled into Ashley as she slowed to a stop in front of him.

"Well, we're here." She smiled at him over her shoulder and dismounted her bike. He looked around them to try to see where, here, was.

They seemed to be just inside an alley behind a store front, the wall was brick with peeling pain. He squinted at it. There seemed to have once been a huge arrow painted on it. Following the arrow with his eyes led him to a little door that was partially obscured by more of the blown about refuse littering the streets in the Outskirts.

"This little door? This is what we came out here for?" His eyebrows rose with his incredulity. He could not imagine that there could be anything worth dragging themselves all the way out here for, behind that grubby little door. As he turned to Ashley to ask what was so special about this place, he saw the wary look in her eyes and shut his mouth. He remembered suddenly that she had said that she'd never shown this place to anyone but Jen. Realizing his mistake in reacting the way he had, he quickly modulated his tone. Sighing out his impatience, he said in a much lighter voice.

"It must be pretty amazing to be hiding behind such a little door, right?" He winked at her and saw that she relaxed a little.

Rolling his bike up to hers he put one hand over hers on her handlebars.

"You ready? I can't wait to see it!" He found that as he said it, it was true. He was starting to remember how excited he had been before the gloom of the Outskirts had brought him down. Grinning he squeezed her hand again and slowly walked his bike towards the little door.

"Do we take our bikes inside or leave them out here?" He asked her over one shoulder as he reached for the handle.

She was smiling at him again. "Oh you should take your bike in with you, and I'll be right behind you." She looked awfully mischievous. He wondered for a moment if this was some kind of practical joke on him. What could possibly be so shocking on the other side of this plain little door that she could be so sure he'd be blown away?

He sighed again.

'Nothing for it. Guess I'll just have to look.' Turning the handle he pushed in the door slowly, waiting for a surprise. The only surprise however was that the space beyond was not completely dark. At first he could not tell where the light was coming from. Stepping in, he glanced around. His eyes had still not adjusted to the lower light level. But he pressed ever deeper into the room as he sought the source of the light.

He heard Ashley giggle behind him and the click as she latched the door behind her. As the light lessened even further with the shutting door, his eyes finally began to adjust. He could see now that the light was beaming down from above. As he moved closer, he saw that there were windows in the roof that were letting in the light. Looking closer he saw that the roof must be a long way up, because the windows were more like long tunnels. As he came into the first shaft of light he turned, skirting around what he had taken to be a display of some kind. Now that he was closer, it seemed to be a giant stone carving.

"Hey Ashley, what is this?" He asked her as he set his bike on its stand at the edge of the light and stepped closer to the intimidating sculpture. It was about as tall as he was and upon closer inspection, it looked like it might have formed on its own, like some kind of plant.

"Was it alive once?" He asked as he gently reached out to touch it. It was smooth and cold like glass, with sharp edges. As his eyes were adjusting to the light, he could see it had points like blades, and as reflective as mirrors.

"It's a crystal. Have you ever heard of them?" Matt shook his head and she sighed. "So much was lost in the shift. Crystals are one way that minerals grow here on earth. Just as plants grow, and coral grows and we grow, so to do crystals grow. Only they grow under the earth, the way coral grows under water." She looked at him, only to see that he was thoroughly confused.

"What's coral?" He asked a bit chagrined.

"Oh. Never mind about the coral then. Here let me show you." She went to one of the bookshelves that she had familiarized herself with, in her long hours of reading and exploring here. She pulled out one of the thinner books on minerals.

"Let's start with this." Coming back into the light she handed him the book and kissed him lightly. "You read up here, in the light. I'm going to set up our camp. Come find me if you get bored, lonely or if you have any questions, alright?" She smiled at him as he sighed and made a face at the book.

She had started doing this to him as soon as they started hanging out. If they reached an impasse in the conversation because he didn't know what she was talking about, she'd often pull a book off her shelf, flip it open and hand it to him. Then she'd go pick them a snack from her garden or something while he read the section she'd shown him.

It was no substitute for actually studying the stuff in depth but they could at least talk about things with a little bit of understanding. He had taken the hint and had put together a book of his favorite songs on the guitar for her in exchange. He was hoping that if she learned them, then they could sing them together while he played. Settling himself at the base of the crystal he leaned back against it and opened the book. He could hear Ashley rustling about in the darkness beyond the pool of light he sat in but he couldn't see into the darkness beyond its edge, so instead he focused on the book.

———

Ashley moved slowly as she unpacked their things. She was still only half adjusted to the dark herself and she was trying to be quiet, since she didn't want to distract him from the book. Books on minerals could be really boring in the beginning, she knew but she didn't know how to explain it all to him. The geological processes of the earth were complex beyond her ability to understand.

Since he didn't remember any of the education he may have received before the shift, he really had no clue about how the planet was formed or the various elements that made up the earth's crust. Unfortunately education had come in second to survival after the shift and most of what they'd learned in the orphanages had to do with either how to survive or how to cope in these troubled times.

She sighed heavily and leaned against her bike. She was tired, although not physically. She was fatigued mentally and emotionally. She really just needed a break from her own questing mind. To be still for a time.

'That's why I'm here now.' She smiled at the thought. 'That's why I brought him here, so we can both just relax for a few days and not think about anything heavy.'

Sighing again, she smiled as she gathered an armload of her things. She wound her way through the maze of rooms that made up the crystal shop, until she found her favorite room. It was a little cubby off the main hall between two of the largest rooms, it was almost round and she had discovered before that it was just the perfect size for her camp.

She had brought the blankets and their backpacks first, dropping them off in the little room, she went to the very back room in the shop to what she had dubbed 'the storage room' since it was the only one without crystal displays in it and pulled out the blankets and pillows that she had secreted there. She tried to bring a little more each time she came, and slowly this place had become her home away from home.

If she didn't have all of her plants to take care of, there had been a number of times that she'd been tempted to just stay here forever and never go back. But of course out here there was no water, and without water there could be no life. She pulled out the mattress she had made by stitching together the thickest blankets she could find. She had dragged them out here one or two at a time over the years and once she had enough she'd tack stitched them into a wide bundle. It was amazingly comfortable, although it could also just be the freedom of being out here that made it seem so.

Smiling to herself she made her way back to her chosen cubby and laying down the mattress, she took all the blankets in hand and began to make up a big squishy bed. She layered in the blankets and pillows. Once she was done, she flopped right onto the pile and burrowed in with a sigh. She relished in the quiet stillness for a few moments before flipping over and scratching her nose. Yawning hugely she decided to check on Matt.

She got up slowly and with great care to the many crystals displayed on the shelves surrounding the little room, she headed back towards the entrance. She could see as she rounded the curving hall into the second room that Matt was fully engrossed in the book. She grinned to herself and managed to sneak by in the shadows, hopefully without distracting him.

She pulled the last of their stuff from the bottom of her saddle-buckets. Seeing that it was the food and water she decided to go ahead and prepare them some salad for dinner, while the greens were still fresh. She carried their goods back to her chosen grotto and found that munching a leaf along the way changed her mind. Instead she decided to enjoy the moment and explore the place anew.

It had been a while since she'd had time to come here. She loved it, especially as no matter how many times she came, there was always more to see. She decided to begin her explorations in the little room across the hall. A few of her very favorite things were in there. Some statues and some really large crystal specimens. She was excited to once again revisit her favorite childhood retreat.

---

Matt was shocked at how much had been going on beneath his feet without him ever having realized it. Once again, by simply handing him a book Ashley had transformed the way he thought about something as simple as a rock and as monumental as the world.

In the last few moments stone had gone from an inert indescribable substance in his mind to a multifaceted, conglomeration of many different minerals. Each one with its own characteristics and qualities. It was amazing and it boggled his mind to think that some human had taken the time to qualify and name each one and to write them down in this book.

He took a moment to lift his eyes from the page and gaze into the darkness. Somewhere in the gloom he'd seen Ashley pull this book from a shadow shrouded shelf. He wondered what other books might be on those shelves. He wondered what else they might say or might be able to teach him. He looked back to the book he was currently holding and flipped ahead looking for pictures. He flipped past several before he saw something that looked like the one he was leaning against.

*'Quarts huh? Are they all this big? It seems so odd that people could have forgotten something so incredible in only ten years.'* He sighed to himself looking down at the small picture of a crystal similar to the giant one he leaned against. *'Perhaps it isn't that people have forgotten at all, maybe it's just that no one feels that they have the time to care anymore. I guess everyone's just too busy trying to survive.'*

He started flipping idly through the book again looking at the pictures, trying to make out the different colors in the distorted light but more often relying on the written descriptions. He was so interested in trying to pry the details of fluorite out of the half light of the setting sun that at first he didn't notice the sound.

It began in his stomach like a deep ache, swelling to a rough vibration that traveled up his spine and into his head. He put his tongue between his teeth to still their rattling and about that time his ears finally heard it. A low hum but growing louder and coming from deep within the building behind him.

"Ashley?" He tried to ask the darkness but it came out as a squeak. The vibration was so strong now he felt it was shaking his bones. He forced himself to stand, holding onto the crystal beside him for support, he could feel it too was pulsing to the rhythm of the sound. He realized that it had a rhythm. It was no longer continuous. The rise and fall of the humming, the pulsing rhythm of it made it sound alive. He was suddenly convinced that it was alive! That there was something in this shop of crystals with him and Ashley and it was humming really loud!

"Ashley?" He tried again but he still couldn't seem to raise his voice against that sound.

He decided to seek it out. He set off in the direction that the sound was strongest. The vibration led him through yet another long room leading to a twisting hallway with more rooms beyond it. One of which was issuing forth this glorious sound. As he came nearer to the source of the resonance he could feel the vibration in every cell of his body pounding through his chest, his heart and he felt that whatever it was, it was changing him on a deep level. The tone had clarified to a pure crisp note, it was absolute and it was perfect. He also felt clarified, as though the ringing singing sound had somehow harmonized every vibration in his body bringing them into perfect resonance with one another.

He took a deep breath relishing in the sound, convinced once again that this sound had a conscious cause, it was alive and it was powerful. He slowed as he came down the hall and realized that the sound was coming from the room just in front of him. He waited a moment on the threshold, hesitant to interrupt or frighten whatever was making that glorious music. As he hesitated however the rise to the pulse stopped and the sounds began to fade, the vibration moving slowly out towards and through him as he stood mesmerized by the sensation of the fading hum.

He hadn't even realized that he'd shut his eye's to better experience the sensation until he was startled by Ashley's exclamation.

"Oh!" She had come around the doorframe and almost walked into him. He caught her by the shoulders gently, to steady himself as well as her as they unexpectedly collided. "I didn't know you were standing there. You startled me!"

She grinned at him in surprise and leaned into his arms. He let his arms slide around her as he pulled her to him, relishing in how relaxed she felt. She was as limp as he was.

*It must have been that sound, it's melted both our cares away.'*

He sighed, holding her gently and then asked her hair.

"Did you make that sound? What was it? It was amazing!" He felt her sigh into his chest and tightened his hold on her a little, as she melted even further into him.

"It was amazing wasn't it? It's called a singing bowl. I should have known you'd like it." She smiled up at him, "I should have guessed you'd be drawn to it, since it's an instrument." She laughed a little and he laughed with her. The vibration had left him feeling peaceful and lighthearted. *What an amazing sound!* He thought.

"I can't believe that came from a bowl! You have to show me, please?" He begged her swaying her back and forth a little.

"Of course!" She laughed. Drawing away from him, she took his hand to lead him into the room that she'd just left. There was no light from the sky in this room and it took his eyes a long time to adjust. When he finally felt that he could see enough to move he saw that Ashley was crouched beside a giant white bowl. It was at least two feet around and it seemed almost translucent. She had a small stick in her hand and she was watching him expectantly. Waiting until he acknowledged that he could see her.

He sat down near the bowl and looked at her questioningly. Smiling, she nodded and placed the stick delicately against the edge of the bowl. She began to run it around the outermost edge, pressing gently so that the stick rubbed the bowls lip. Slowly at first she moved and he didn't hear anything. By the time she was beginning the third pass with the wand he was beginning to feel the vibration.

Again it began in his stomach but this time he shut his eyes and simply took stock of the sensation, of how it made him dizzy and lightheaded and happy all at once. How the feeling in his stomach almost made him feel sick or like he just fell from a step that he wasn't expecting. As it began to pulse through him it seemed to pass through every molecule of his body, like his own pulse, only endlessly more powerful.

He opened his eyes to see just what was causing the pulsing in the sound and found that it was the beat on which Ashley brought the stick around. She hesitated slightly, whether consciously or not, to catch the sound as it vibrated around the rim of the bowl. He could almost see it in the dim light, a shimmer traveling around and around the bowls rim, keeping just ahead of the wand in her hand.

*Just beautiful!'* He thought, letting the smile stretch his face that he just couldn't keep back anymore. He watched as she carefully allowed the sound to slow a bit before removing the wand entirely and allowing the sound to fade. Round and round the rim of the bowl it went, before settling back into quiet. Sitting this close to it, Matt had felt like the sound had gone right through him, right back to that place in his belly where the vibration had begun.

'*Going back to the beginning.'*

He shook his head, grinning at Ashley as she looked at him.

"How did you learn to play that? Did someone teach you? Is it hard to learn?" He cocked his head, hoping that he'd get to try it himself. '*I wonder if the sound would be the same if someone else played it or if it would be different for every person that did it?'* Ashley smiled at him and said.

"The first time I came here I found this bowl and it fascinated me. I had to know what it was. It was too fragile to try to move so I started looking all over the store hoping to find an explanation. Eventually I found their brochure's behind the counter, in the other room. It's called a singing bowl and this was one of a set that was apparently specially commissioned out of quartz. They were traditionally much smaller and made from brass, bronze or copper-"

"You mean this bowl is made out of quartz?" Matt was so surprised he completely interrupted her. "How is that possible if that huge thing you showed me in the other room is quartz? How did they make something like that into a bowl?" He was looking again at the massive bowl and rethinking how translucent it was. He reached out to touch it gently, feeling in it the tiniest tremor that was all that was left of the sound it had made. It was cool and smooth to his touch, much like glass or like the statue in the other room. It had something else in common with the other piece of quartz that he had touched tonight. Although he couldn't quite pinpoint what, there was a definite similarity in the way they felt.

"It is quartz isn't it?" He said it quietly to himself, talking to that part of himself that could feel the similarity.

"Yep." Ashley said quietly. She smiled when he started a little, guiltily realizing that he'd interrupted her in his excitement. "Once I knew what they were called I looked it up at the library. That's how I learned to play it. Trial and error." She smiled self-deprecatingly and shrugged.

Matt shook his head and smiled at her. "I'd say that it's pretty amazing Ashley. Will you teach me tomorrow? Can I learn do you think?" He didn't want to be pushy but he was having a hard time not touching it even now. The whole instrument was so fascinating he wanted to go get Michael and drag him down here immediately to see it. He didn't want to mention that yet but he was hoping he could convince her eventually since he knew that Michael would flip over getting to see an instrument that was new to him.

Right at the moment though, he was pretty grateful that they were alone. The vibrations had not entirely subsided in him.

"It's really amazing that you were able to figure that out on your own Ashley. That's really impressive." He wondered if the bowl's song had left her feeling as peculiar as it had him. "Did you say something earlier about setting up camp?" He asked her with a smile, hoping that he had heard her right at the time. "I'm actually kind of worn out from all that humming." He grinned as she matched his smile, standing.

"Common, you passed right by it to get here." Smiling she took his hand as she rounded the singing bowl and led him from the little room and back into the long hallway. "I put us in the little room. I always stay there, I hope you don't mind. It's my favorite spot." She smiled over her shoulder at him as she led the way. He could tell by the set of her shoulders that she was feeling a little shy.

He wasn't sure if she was shy about sharing her secret place with him or about them being alone together. Either way he decided to take things slowly for now.

"I don't know why I would mind you setting up camp in your favorite place. You must think it's the best spot for a reason." She smiled over her shoulder at him in the silvery twilight from the skylights. He pulled her gently back towards him and kissed her softly. She leaned into the kiss, returning it with interest.

*'Maybe it's not being alone together that she's shy about, after all.'* He thought to himself with a chuckle.

# 15

They settled pretty quickly into a routine of exploring the crystal shop, whenever there was light to see by. They nibbled on the provisions they had brought with them whenever they got hungry. Slept when they were tired and made love whenever they felt like it. They managed to pass several days under these pleasant conditions before Ashley found the dragon. She was exploring the storage room by the bright morning light. The sun was high and the skylight in this room was huge, so she had been organizing so she could find her things more easily.

She was pulling the blankets and sheets off one of the back tables when she heard something fall. She realized there was something beneath the cloth that she'd knocked down. Moving much more carefully she pulled back the sheet slowly, revealing a display.

*'This must have been a practice display of some kind? I wonder why it's set up in this back room?'* She wondered as she carefully peeled back the last of the sheets she had tossed her blankets onto. She was so intent on not moving too fast or knocking anything else off the table that she didn't really look closely at what the display was of until she had set the blankets down on the table behind her and turned to face the newly exposed surface.

*'It's a dragon!'*

She gasped at the beauty of the image before her, it was a framed painting of a purple dragon leaned awkwardly against the wall behind the table and it had been draped with a cloth. At the base of the painting on its side was a carved wooden statue of a more traditional Chinese dragon, which seemed to be what had fallen but it was the painting that had taken her breath away.

*'It looks like her! It has the same type of face as the dragon in my dreams!'*

More softly angled then the ferocious reptilian faces of the Chinese or European dragon's that she had looked up. The dragon she had seen in her dreams had a softer look to it, not so ferocious or reptilian, although always bathed in seas of fire.

Her hand suddenly itched to draw. She needed to paint, to create the image that thought had brought into her mind. Dashing around she gathered up one of the largest drawing pads she had stashed here and some coal. She had secreted many art supplies here over the years, since she found the crystals and the atmosphere here to be so inspiring. She flipped through the book trying to find a clean page. Many were still blank but had gotten smudged over the years. For this piece she wanted a clean canvass. Finding a few good pages she pulled them out and spread them before her. She fiddled for a moment with her charcoal and after a moment's hesitation; she discarded it and grabbed instead her fine point pencils.

Taking a deep breath and closing her eyes she let her hands run over the page. As she opened her mind's eye wide so she could see the image she wished to draw, she realized that it had changed since the initial spark of inspiration. Where there had been at first only one dragon flying towards the light of the sun, there were now two dragons curled together in the burning belly of the earth. Sketching quickly she put in the major lines of the first image in place and then quickly switched to a second page and drew the second image while it was still fresh in her mind.

She lovingly drew the detail of both draconic faces, each one unique, she knew them both intimately after all. She paused momentarily in her sketching of the flames surrounding them as she caught her breath with realization. She scrutinized the faces of the dragons once more and gasped in recognition.

'*That dragon is Matt!*'

Then she laughed at herself for not seeing it sooner, of course it was them. She finished out the details of the drawing. Then turned her attention to the broad gestures she'd roughed in on the one of the dragon flying toward the sky.

She couldn't remember at first. '*Was the image facing forward or was it from the side?*' She could clearly see both versions of the image in her mind but looking at the gestures she guessed that she'd been drawing it from the side.

So filling in the wings and tail she drew flames licking at its heals from the planet it was leaving and of beams of white gold light shining towards it from the direction it was going. Somehow she just knew that the dragon was trying to fly to the sun, to finally reunite with the perfection of creation. She slowed her movement's lingering on the elegant curve of the neck as it came to meet the charmingly angular head in profile.

Sighing she sat back and looked at it, then over at the other of the two dragons entwined within the fire. She looked at the third blank page, wondering if she saw something for a moment.

*'Was that another dragon? A different dragon?'* She shook her head as her stomach growled. It reminded her that she hadn't had anything to eat yet today.

"All right, all right, we'll go eat something." She smiled at herself for talking to her stomach. She got up to go forage for some snacks from their supplies and to check in on Matt.

───────

Matt was reading more about the crystals in the shop. He had gone from reading books randomly, to picking one with good pictures and looking up each crystal in the shop that caught his eye. One by one he was learning more about each one. Where they were from and what they were made of. With so many books and specimens in here and all the time in the world, it was endlessly fascinating to him.

*'I never knew that the world was so incredibly complex or that nature was so creative. There are so many different kinds of minerals and each type can take on so many different shapes! It's really unbelievable. I don't know why I never realized it. Even water crystallizes when it gets cold.'* He breathed out heavily, thinking of the water vapor in his breath.

"I wonder what my breath looks like when it's frozen? What kind of crystals do I make?" He mused aloud.

"Hm. That's an interesting thing to wonder." Ashley said from behind him. Turning he found her standing in the doorway with a huge carving under one arm, and nibbling on a carrot. "I'll bet that their beautiful crystals."

She smiled at him and came to join him at the base of the stone he was currently lounging against. He had just finished reading about it and had found out that it was feldspar, also known as labradorite. It was huge almost as tall as he was and three or four feet wide, and if you walked from side to side it winked at you with a big rainbow tinted turquoise shine on its surface.

"What have you got there?" He asked as she sat down beside him and placed the carving before them both in the light, handing him the half eaten carrot.

"I just found it in the storage room, along with a beautiful painting that you've got to see! It's of a purple dragon!" Her eyes were shining with excitement as she displayed her find and he laughed. He ate the last bite and set the carrot greens aside. Ashley had explained that she made broth from them sometimes so he saved them.

"This is a beautiful dragon all right." He said now able to focus on the statue. "Too bad it doesn't really look like our dragons, huh?" He stroked its head between the eyes. "Good dragon."

Grinning at her, he was a little surprised when she suddenly bounced to her knees, obviously too excited to keep still.

"But the painting does! That's why you have to see it! It really does look like our dragons!" He felt his jaw sag as he took in what she'd said.

"Really? How can it? How is that possible?" He wondered out loud.

*'How could anyone else possibly know what our dragon's look like? Especially someone from before the shift?'* He didn't want to admit it but he had been a little bit reassured that their dragons hadn't been exactly the same as legendary dragons. It had let him believe that they might only be dreams after all and of no more significance then that they had helped to bring him and Ashley closer together. He shook his head a little at the chill that ran up his spine.

"Can we go see it now? I want to see it." He stood and held a hand down to help her up.

She took it and led him through the maze of rooms and hallways to the very back of the building and into the storage room. Before he noticed the painting however he saw her drawings on the floor and as she turned to stop by the painting he let go of her hand to head instead towards her drawings.

"Ashley, were these here too? Or did you do these?" He looked over his shoulder as she turned to see what he was talking about. He pulled one towards him, the one of the dragon striving for the light.

"I know this." He ran one hand gently over the drawing. "I remember this, somehow." He suddenly felt a bit dizzy, like he did sometimes after playing the song from his dream all the way through. Like there was too much in his head to fit and he just might burst if he tried to remember it all.

Closing his eyes he took a deep breath. Ashley had come over and she put a hand on his shoulder, she rubbed his back and he smiled his thanks.

"So what do you think?"

She gestured to the drawings and he lifted the first one to look at the second. It took him a moment to recognize the dragons or the position they were in, twined together in the flaming heart of the world but when he did he felt his face flush a bit. He heard Ashley chuckle a little behind him and bending to put her arms around him she whispered in his ear.

"It'll have to be our little secret. I didn't realize what I was drawing until I was done." She smiled at him apologetically and he growled at her with his best dragon imitation. Pulling her into his lap, he kissed her deeply.

———

Michael had been having a hard time sleeping, haunted by fitful restless dreams. He couldn't remember most of them, but the ones he could remember were all too often haunted by Matt's dreamsong. The song he had played in the shop that day. It had triggered all those suppressed memories and emotions that Michael had been trying to pretend didn't exist. They were just dreams after all. He couldn't take time off over dreams. He couldn't expect sympathy when morning the loss of dream loved ones. He couldn't afford to waste time crying over such simple and inexplicable things, as dreams.

So he tossed and turned night after night, struggling with his unspent grief. As he observed countless lives and watched them die, as the world itself was turned from magma, to lava, to stone and then to ice, to oceans, mountains and back again.

*He shuddered with the spasms of volcanic eruptions and convulsed in time with the earth when she quaked. It was terrifying and it was devastating and at the same time it was gratifying, for there were long eons of peace, between the spasms. He as the earth floated contented, like a fetus in the womb, floating in the vast dark sea of star spangled space.*

*He floated for an eternity, slowly turning. His eyeless view ever changing ever sparkling and twinkling but for when the sun drove all others from his sight. As the earth, he noticed his crust, his exterior prickling with warmth on the side closest to the sun. He felt it.*

*He felt the attention of the small life forms thriving on his crust. Of the plants that had their roots sunk deep into him, it tickled. The revolutions of his spin were all that showed the passage of time but after a while his attention was drawn once more towards the sunside plants of his surface. Only this time his consciousness was taken within their own.*

*He was the trees, the vines and the underbrush. He was even the fungal mat beneath the surface of the soil. He held everything together, transferring moisture and nutrients about. The sun drew him like no other thing could, even water. For the sun drew the water as well. Drawing it up and up and up, from the deepest reaches of the roots within the earth where the water lay, up to the tiniest tips of his branches.*

*He stretched his leaves toward the sun, willing them to be wider, deeper and more full of water every moment, in order to take in more delicious delirious sun. The water tickled as he felt it trickling and surging in little spurts through each and every vein, each and every leaf and into each and every cell of his myriad thriving growing plant bodies.*

*He was life itself, the rich resilient life that coursed through and covered the planet. He could feel all things, and through them, the unity of all things within the universe. He found as he focused his eyeless attention upon the distant stars, he could even feel their warmth upon his surface. He could feel his own plants responding to those far distant energies. His consciousness focused on the vastness of space and the myriad consciousness he sensed within it. He came to realize deeply, the truth of universal oneness.*

Just as Michael felt his personal consciousness beginning to expand beyond that of the planet and the plants, reaching towards the nearest stars of heaven, he found the dream changing once again. They changed into more normal dreams, about working in the shop and talking with Greg about why he didn't want to go to college.

When Michael awakened he remembered nothing but the sense that he had learned something important. He woke with a weight of knowledge that he could not define.

Yet it stayed with him, a feeling of portent that followed him that day, all the way into the shop. Although the mundane tasks of running the shop and the near mindless state he entered when he carved only served as a partial distraction. Part of his mind continued to dwell on the unrest triggered by his half remembered dreams, long into the day.

———

Matt had been waking up early since staying at crystal shop. The skylights caused a gradual brightening that was hard to resist. Especially when the room around him was filled with as many amazing sights as the shop was. Ashley was currently a warm and slightly snoring ball beside him, where she was huddled beneath most of the blankets. It looked like he'd thrown them off again, as he often did, suddenly too hot to bear them.

This morning was no exception. He woke to find himself hot and parched. He reached for the jar of water Ashley kept by the bed but found it empty. He got up to go fill it from the big jugs she kept stored in the back room. When he'd asked about them she said she'd brought them from home a long time ago, one at a time, so she could camp out here for days when she wanted.

As he turned to head left down the hall however, he distinctly heard the sound of a drip of water, to his right. He looked to his right and noticed a small door at the end of an aborted hallway that ran along their bed nook. Somehow he'd overlooked it till now. It looked like it led deeper into the building. He was curious, they had not yet explored that way. Shrugging at his own curiosity, Matt managed to get it open shoving against the rubble partially blocking it on the other side.

When he stepped into the darkness of the hallway beyond, it was definitely damper in there. He could smell it on the air, a moistness that was not altogether pleasant. Still thirsty however and curious about the sound of that drip, he followed it.

The hallway was dark after the Crystal shop, as there were no skylights here. So he felt his way cautiously so as not to stub his bare feet or turn an ankle on rubble. The further he followed this unexplored hall the more rubble he came across. Apparently not all of the Crystal shop's building had fared so well. It seemed that the whole other end of the massive block long building had collapsed in one of the earthquakes of the shift. He realized he could go no further when the rubble, which he had been increasingly forced to climb rather than stepping over or around, suddenly became a wall of rubble that abruptly ended his explorations.

Tapping his lip thoughtfully Matt eyed the tumble of broken concrete wondering if the source of the water was beyond it. Sighing at the inevitability of the situation, he turned and went back towards the Crystal shop, to see if Ashley was awake yet. Just as he came in sight of the glow from the glass door to the crystal shop, a darker shadow drew his attention to the left hand wall. He reached out, putting one hand against the wall in the twilight. Squinting to try to keep the distant light from ruining his night vision, he walked toward the shadow curiously his hand trailing along the wall.

When he reached it his hand disappeared within, leaving him

unexpectedly off balance and as he pin wheeled his other arm to right himself he realized his mistake. What he had taken for a stain on the wall that he was hoping might be wet, turned out to be a gap. A gaping crack had opened in the wall here, just before things started getting really messy down the hall. Turning sideways he found that he could just duck into it, passing through to the room beyond. His night sight not yet recovered fully from seeing the doorway in the distance he kicked a stone stepping into the room beyond. Cursing and jumping on his good foot, injured toes in hand, he listened to the skittering plunk of the stone as it sped on its way.

The plunk however caught his attention. Turning back in the direction he thought he'd kicked it he crept forward, testing the ground before him carefully as he went. When his questing toe felt nothing, no floor, no water, just air, he caught his breath. He was grateful that he hadn't blundered around sightlessly, as he might have if he hadn't kicked that rock.

He crept forward, on hands and knees now until he could dangle his legs over the apparent rim of the room. His eyes were adjusting by the moment now that he was out of the hallway and he could just make out the edges of the room. He realized that this was definitely the source of the moisture. It smelled wet here in a way that he couldn't really explain to himself, not having much experience with abundances of water.

Shaking his head he berated himself for not having taken the time to bring some light. Ashley had a few light sticks that she'd gotten from Old Tom down at the Salvage yard. They hadn't used them yet thanks to the skylights, so he'd almost forgotten about them. He felt around and found another chunk of rubble near him. Apparently the floor wasn't the only part of the darkened room to have collapsed, and dropped it off the edge of the floor where he sat. On the count of three it plunked with a great splash that licked the bottom of his bare foot.

*I guess I found the source of the smell of water. Now I wonder what happened to the drip?* He thought to himself.

He decided that was all he could really accomplish here without light. Starting to stand in order to head back, he heard it, the distinctive sound that had drawn him here in the first place. It wasn't as steady as it had been, he heard it once and again, then nothing for a time, then once more. He was convinced though; this was what he had been looking for. Without light, he couldn't climb down to access the water though. He'd have to come back with Ashley.

*'We'll need a bucket and some rope.'* He thought to himself. *'We'll have to bring some light down with us too.'*

Sighing he headed back towards the crystal shop. He wondered if Ashley was awake yet. He wanted to ask her about the water down here. He wondered if she'd already known. When he returned however he not only found her awake but so excited by her dreams that he was completely distracted. Before he could mention what he'd found however, he found himself completely swept up in her exuberance.

————

Ashley woke suddenly, alone in their bed. She was startled and disturbed by the clarity of the dream from which she'd awakened. There had not been a dragon in sight but she had definitely tasted dragon on the dream. Chaffing her frozen hands together she tried to calm her racing heart.

*'It was just a dream, just a dream.'* She tried to convince herself. Somehow though, she wasn't so sure. Before she'd gone to sleep last night she had framed a question in her mind. She had addressed it towards that dragon flavored essence that seemed to be the source of her dreams.

"Why do you want to help us?" She had asked it. She had hoped to trick it into revealing its motives. Whether it meant to help them or harm them. The images of the dream from which she'd just woken had certainly been horrifying enough to think that consciousness could mean them harm. Except for the completely impersonal feeling she had felt while she was watching it all play out. It had been as if she were an observer. It was as though she were a star watching life on earth as a play, aware of but unable to affect that life.

That and the fact that all the horrific deaths she had watched in succession had been wrought by nature, not by some fierce winged predator. All night she had dreamed of natural disasters and natural deaths. Of privation, starvation, thirst and exposure in the deepeningly desperate lands that had become the wastes.

She saw replayed in gruesome detail the results of raging fires and relentless floods, of hurricanes and waterspouts, tsunamis and earthquakes. And not all from the perspective of humans alone.

She was now aware of the level of utter devastation such fierce weather and unfortunate circumstance could play on all forms of life. Down to the tiniest insect. As she was now as intimately aware of such devastation's effects upon the form of the planet's crust itself. Just as she'd been about to cry mercy, overwhelmed by the bombardment of devastating images, the dream had changed again. This time for the worse.

The scene she saw had changed to depict the world as it was now. Hanging before her in space, it was a solid mass of swirling cloud cover. Thin spots but no real break in the clouds shrouding the earth. She realized that something was happening, below the surface that she could not see. She could feel it though, as a rising tension in the air. She realized that she was feeling warmer, which was odd since she didn't seem to have a body to feel such things with. She was just her consciousness floating here in space, as she became aware of the growing changes beneath the ever present clouds. In the end it was mostly a matter of perception. Though she could not explain how she perceived.

She was first hot and then cold, and then hot and then cold, in varying and increasing degrees. Soon when she was hot she was burning up and when she was cold she felt still as stone. Just before she thought that the next flux might destroy her, it stopped. In a cold so deep that she didn't feel she could ever move again. She stayed there, seemingly for eternity, still and cold. Alone without even the sun to keep her company. She was sad and desperately lonely and she wanted to cry, but since she lacked a body in this dream she could not even do that.

Waking was a relief that she thought would never come, feeling as she did that time had stopped millennium ago. When the small globe below her had frozen. Her eyes opened with a start as with a jolt she returned to her body. She took a deep breath as she sat up slowly. She chaffed her cold hands together, in an attempt to warm them. Her heart beat as though she had been running. Spurred on by her desperate despair as she had floated grief stricken and alone, with the little frozen world.

"It was like an ice age." She whispered slowly to herself in horror. She'd learned of them in school even before the shift. How the mammoths and the cavemen had been frozen alive. Some of them had just been sitting around going about their business, when the world suddenly decided to do a flying leap, and she shook with horror. Now that she was awake, the dreams made a sick kind of sense to her. Especially if she thought about the question that she'd asked the intelligence behind her dreams, she realized.

"Why do you want to help us?" She repeated to herself aloud, before slowly piecing the answer together from the dream.

"Because you're going to die." That's what it was saying. "Everything, all things will die. You're all going to die, and then I'll be all alone..." The sadness in the response still tore at her heart. This then was the answer to her supposedly trick question. It was lonely, whatever this consciousness was. It had existed for eternity, observing everything and yet apart from everything. Observing, but alone, somehow unable to take part all this time.

Maybe it was the remaining vestige of the dream but she felt a harmonious resonance with the unknown being, which cared so much about distant creatures it would never even meet. She sent a quick pulse of gratitude and affection towards the source of that wisdom and for just a moment, she thought that she heard or maybe felt a startled response. Deciding that this was all too important to forget she went to the gift shop half of the front room to find a blank journal, she needed to start keeping track of these dreams.

After telling Matt about the dream, she had encouraged him to grab a journal as well and to try to make some direct communication with the dreams himself. So with dream communication in mind he took a few of the blankets and made himself a makeshift bed in the room across the hall. She was secretly glad, since it meant that there was no chance of accidentally waking one another, during an important dream this way. He said he had not had any dreams at all the night before though, which might have encouraged his cooperation.

Ashley decided to begin by framing a questioning in her mind, then writing it in the journal and saying it once aloud to herself before she fell asleep. She would then write down as much of her dreams as she could remember and when she was done summarize what she thought the answer to her question had been in words.

"Who are you? Where did you come from?" Ashley framed the words carefully in her mind. Then staring at them where she'd scribbled them hastily into her new dream book, she read them aloud. She tried to project their essence to that consciousness she was communicating with.

"Who are you? Where did you come from?" She repeated, making sure that her emphasis for the word *from* was on origin, not current location. She was trying to be as specific and clear as possible and was surprised at how quickly sleep took her. As soon as she had closed her eyes, even before she remembered setting down the pencil she was drifting away, fading into nothingness.

*For a time, she knew nothing. Nothing at all. Then she became aware, the first stirring of consciousness on the planet. Once the planet had cooled and condensed enough to finally form a burning molten ball of light, burning gases, fluid rock and molten fire. A glowing golden red sea of flame as the planet burned and spun and spluttered, as it hung in the bespeckled glory of the darkest depths of space.*

*As its molten form moved and was moved by the flow of heat and fire within, it slowly became aware, in a peripheral kind of way, of the presence of a larger and much warmer ball of burning light. It was not that far, it was first perceived as a slight massing of the molten little ball to one side, on the warmer side of its, body. As it unconsciously leaned towards the greater source of heat, unconsciously reaching for the loving warmth.*

*She didn't know how long, how many millennia passed, as that little ball of burning light swayed through the universe. Always reaching for the greater light held just beyond her reach, but eventually the pull became an emotion.*

*Need.*

*She was love and she needed that greater love, she had a need. She wondered what she was. That she might have something like a need. Was she somehow something separate? Was she apart from the greater love that shone down on her? Or was she a part of that greater glowing love light?*

*Just what was she?*

*As the soft consciousness that had developed, began to radiate into every cell of the little ball of burning light she became aware that she did indeed have a limit. As far as she could tell she was in no way physically connected to the greater ball of light that she was yearning towards.*

*A moment of concern flooded her every single cell and she felt truly desperately separate. For a moment it was as though every cell was separate from every other. She was no larger than herself now, for herself was no larger than a single cell. A single consciousness, she was she.*

*She was.*

*She wondered…*

*Clinging to that simple thought, she was.*

*She held to her consciousness like it was something precious. Like it was something special, something irreplaceable, and she began to realize. It was.*

*She was. She was something. I am something.*

*I am something!*

*I am!*

*Flinging this declaration into the face of the vast emptiness surrounding her, it seemed to resonate with the energy of her declaration. In her awe, in her fear of being alone, she fled contemplating, herself...*

*What was she?*

*Was she real?*

*What was she?*

*As her curiosity turned back inward she slowly felt herself expanding, one cell at a time as she took back her full form. That of a burning ball of light, slowly orbiting a larger ball of light.*

*'I AM.'*

*She spent millennia developing and exploring this awareness. She eventually become aware that she and the larger light where not alone. She'd first noted that as she spun in place in her orbit. She'd seen that the world about her was not all dark, not universally so. She noticed that there were actually many tiny balls of light for as far as she could perceive.*

*She wondered if they, like her, where conscious to. If they were looking back at her somehow. She longed to know, to be aware of another presence but as her orbit swept her round she saw a much larger ball of light, much closer and between herself and the greater ball of light she yearned towards. She stretched a thought of herself towards the other ball, tentatively calling.*

*"I Am. Are you?"*

*But there was no apparent response. Eventually they were pulled apart again by their orbits and she was alone once more, with the largest light of all as her only inconstant companion.*

*She paid more and more attention to her surroundings though, wondering if she'd ever see that ball of light again. Or if there might be others and eventually she did see others. Most were farther from the largest light then she was, some huge some small and every time she would send a questing thought.*

*"I Am. Are you?"*

*She didn't seem to get an answer. She wondered if they couldn't hear her or if they simply had no consciousness at all. She eventually got bored and went back to sleep. Her consciousness only occasionally resurfaced to watch the stars go by but she found herself often falling back into an unconscious slumber.*

*In her resting form the many cells that had once held her consciousness where dormant and held no consciousness within. But they did hold the possibility of consciousness. The memory of consciousness. They had each held consciousness, before.*

*One by one, the cells began to awaken on their own. They would rise to consciousness, only to find there was nothing to observe and fall into unconsciousness once again. One of the cells on the surface of the ball of fire awakened however and upon regaining consciousness was amazed by the glittering beauty of the stars. It remained conscious, held in awe by the sparkling lights of the universe that it could perceive.*

*Its consciousness moved and flowed on the molten surface of the ball of fire. Slipping, sliding and occasionally bubbling as it leaned in yearning towards the most beautiful of the stars that it could see. The pleasure of observing the glittering lights above was so immeasurable that the consciousness spread. A few cells at a time. As nearby consciousness also awoke and felt the resonant joy.*

———

At Ashley's suggestion, Matt had decided to try the dream journaling too. So he had set up a separate bed for the night, in the singing bowl room. He was interested in trying this dream-learning like Ashley seemed to be. He wasn't sure what to expect though, so he just followed her formula. He'd picked out a blank book from the cards and gifts section of the crystal shop and begun framing his question. Last night he hadn't remembered any dreams at all. So tonight he'd decided that this was important enough they should sleep separately, in order to sleep more soundly.

With the door open they were still only a few feet apart but it was enough distance that there was no chance of startling each other awake with an accidental touch. Settling onto his blankets he opened the book and tried to frame his question.

"Who are you and how did you get here?" He asked out loud. He was glad that he had at least a little distance from Ashley when he did this, as he felt decidedly awkward doing it. Even if it was her idea. Then he closed the book and laid himself down wondering if this would be another night of dreamless sleep.

*Slowly out of the molten ball of light arose consciousness. Becoming aware of the glittering stars at night and the glowing light of day. Beginning through consciousness to move.*

*To become. Separate.*

*To take on form, made from the same molten fire that created the heat and light to begin with. But alone, within that light. Able to look back and see itself. Thus were born, the first individually conscious beings on the planet's surface.*

*The firewyrms.*

*The dream faded into something new. It began leading him to the stories of the development of individuals. He started to think of them, in the dream, as dragons. They were now taking on individual thought and eventually, form. Taking on different types of form based on their individual personalities. While the star was still so hot and molten that they could easily shift and manipulate their form at will, they too were molten.*

*As the millennia passed however, the star began to cool. The firewyrms found themselves getting stiff and crusty. They found ways to change their exteriors again to protect themselves from the cold as the star began to cool. Millennia later when the star had cooled to a crust itself however, they were forced to spend their time down the only tunnels left to the molten core of the planet.*

*There they warmed themselves eating and bathing in the scorching molten fire to keep molten enough to move. Eventually they had no choice but to retreat below the surface completely.*

*When the first of the Old Ones laid down to rest and did not get up again, some of the Elder's began to panic. They had seen now the terrible sleep that the cold was bringing and they wanted no part of it. They decided amongst them, the oldest all, that they were not going to sit here and wait for the cold to come.*

*They argued that to become stiff and crusty this way was unnatural. For they had always been molten to the core! It was the only way and in the end they admitted enviously to one another that they wanted to be raw and molten again! Like when the world was young! Oh if only they could turn back time on their star! One of the oldest proposed trying to get enough momentum up to fly towards the sun, to return to the source of all heat, all light. To eternal youth and molten flexibility. To a loving reunion with the source of all life.*

*But the journey was deemed perilous. For once out of the radiant heat of the planet's atmosphere they would be destined to freeze into solid rock once in space. They would have to trust that the sun would eventually pull them to its surface and that they would then reawaken in the heat of the Sun and be able to once again swim and fly through space with intention, in order to live forever in the molten embrace of the creator.*

*The Elder's decided to go. They thought it was worth the risk. But some of the younger dragons wanted to stay on earth. They didn't want to leave and elected to stay and make whatever life they could for themselves in the cooling world.*

*He watched as their story continued after the launching of the elders and as those that remained behind multiplied and spread, forming pairs and families and communities, continuing to thrive for several millennia more. They lived just below the surface making their constant pilgrimages to the deepest reaches of the earth to warm up as often as possible. Some were able to stand the cold longer and longer, but always they had to return or they began to seize up.*

*As other forms of life also began to evolve on the surface of the planet, the now dormant star, the dragons observed passively the evolution of cognizant and then sentient life upon the surface of the world. They found they rather enjoyed the company once they became accustomed to the constraints of their increasingly limited movements.*

*Eventually however, it became too cold to go to the surface at all as the first ice age descended, freezing everything in its path. Everything on the surface of the planet froze. All the life there halted and the dragons, cold and restless each lay down to sleep. Having nothing left to keep them awake they rested. Hidden within the crust of the world, deep beneath the mountains.*

*There they slumbered. Long millennia past, awaiting the rebirth, renewal, and reactivation of their star. Somehow they knew he gathered that they would be taken care of. That they were here for a reason and that they would all be able to reunite with source energy and with one another somehow in the end.*

Matt woke suddenly, drenched in sweat and reverberating with the conviction of his dream.

"I guess, I got an answer…" He muttered to himself as he absently wiped the sweat from his face, rubbing his eyes to clear the sleep from them. As soon as he could see he gathered up his book and pencil to begin writing. He translated the experience into words as best he could, so that he could share it with Ashley. He couldn't wait to see what her reaction was.

When they talked the next morning, she had also had a dream. They exchanged books and read each other's. There were many similarities but also some obvious differences. Talking it out, they determined that although the intelligence's behind their two dreams were similar, they were probably not the same singular intelligence. Matt had seen more of the history of the Dragons themselves. Their race's prime and history. Their decline and the flight towards the sun that the elders had made. Flying round and round the earth to gain the momentum they needed to leave earth's gravity.

While Ashley had been shown the beginning of consciousness. The awakening of life on this planet, in the form of the firewyrms. The first thing she scribbled into her notebook when she woke up was.

*'We are the beginning. We are the end. We are the bridge that spans the two. We are living memory…'*

———

She may still not be sure of just who or what these creatures were but she no longer had any doubt that these beings were trying to help them. And that they had every reason to do so.

They spent the last two days before Ashley had to be back to work, talking about their dreams. They also read through some of the books about dragons that Ashley had found in the bookstore section of the shop. None of it seemed to pertain to the dragons of their dreams but still they read. The next two nights although they rephrased their questions, they each only remembered repetitive abbreviated fragments of their previous dreams.

They dutifully wrote down even those fragments, in what Ashley had started calling their dragon dream journals. Ashley sketched in hers as well, describing past dreams that she remembered from this draconic source.

Once they went back to Newcity they spent all their time together. They separated only to go to work or to go home to sleep and rarely then. They had decided to bring some of the books on dragon and fairy lore that they had found home with them. Matt was quickly reading through them trying to puzzle out the meaning of their dreams. He had a feeling of rising urgency that he could not explain. Neither of them had mentioned it out loud yet but he could see that Ashley felt it too.

# 16

"Matt, I think I'm pregnant…" She looked sideways at him through her lashes, afraid to see his face. She hadn't wanted to tell him this way. She hadn't wanted it to come to this. Of course she hadn't wanted to get pregnant at all! She honestly hadn't thought about it though, since sex hadn't been part of her life, before Matt.

She had expected an, oh shit, reaction from him. Instead he didn't react at all. It was like the meaning of her words just went right over his head. Instead his look said, huh?

---

Matt was utterly stunned. He had gotten to Ashley's apartment to hang out as usual. He hadn't been anticipating anything out of the ordinary. She'd been tense when he'd gotten here a few minutes ago but he'd never expected this.

'Pregnant…' He thought. 'As in going to have a baby?' The look on his face didn't seem to reassure her any. Ashley took a deep breath and began an obviously rehearsed speech, with the air of someone determined to have her say.

'Wait, she's going to have my baby! Oh my God!'

His mind was reeling. He'd never really thought about the possibility before. For some reason although they'd been sleeping together, it just hadn't occurred to him that she could get pregnant. It was as though he'd thought it simply couldn't happen to them. It didn't seem real. But the anger in Ashley's eyes, as she ranted about the City's policies against unlawful pregnancies, brought him quickly back to the conversation at hand. Her argument brought home the realities, of how this really might affect them both, on a very deep level.

"I am not going to let them touch my body Matt! That is much bigger than any written law, any City law!" She spat. "If it comes between their laws and my freedom to choose what happens to my body, what do you think I'm gonna choose Matt?" She had worked herself into a frenzy. Her eyes gone fierce and hot with anger at the perceived threat.

"Look Ashley, it's not their law, it's our law too. By choosing to live within the City we choose to live with the City's laws. We grew

197

up that way." He sounded a little uncertain though, even to himself. He tried to think about it from her point of view. If someone had wanted to cut him open just to appease a law, he might fight it to. He sighed heavily, thinking to himself.

*'Of course I'd fight it. And I can fight her on this and likely lose her completely. Or I can hear her out and weigh out our options.'* Matt sighed again, thinking quickly.

"Look Ashley, the most important thing right now is, what do *you* want to do?" As his eyes sought hers, the ferocity left them like a flame, extinguished by the tears that took its place. He pulled her to him, as her breath caught in a sob. He held her tightly as she cried. Her muffled sobs mixed with the murmurings of her hiccupped exclamations.

"I don't know, Matt. I just don't know…" So he just held her, rocking her a little and rubbing her back to sooth her.

Some while later, her sobs having quieted to hiccups, they simply sat together. Matt was thinking, Ashley in a stupor. He began to stroke her hair softly.

"Hey, how you doing?" He rocked her a bit, trying to bring her back to her body. "Anybody home?" He asked after a moment more, the smile plain in his voice. "Earth to Ashley. Earth to Ashley!" He felt her starting to respond, wriggling a little in his arms.

He decided to try to cheer her up before asking her opinion again. So he began pestering her with voice and with kisses. He kissed her head, her face and her hands when she tried to fend him off.

"Earth to Ashley! Anybody home?" He asked her laughingly, while she struggled to push away his relentless kisses.

"All right, all right, I'm here! I'm here!" She said, chuckling as she tried in vain to keep his face at a distance. Laughing out loud, she stopped trying to push him away and instead pulled him close. Kissing him back.

When he eventually pulled loose to breath, she tucked her head to his shoulder with a sigh. She still seemed to be trying hard not to think. Matt was determined to talk about it though. He started again as soon as she had caught her breath.

"So then, what are our options? Do we have any?" He pulled her against him as he said it and he saw the impact of his words in the pallor of her skin.

"We? *Our* options?" She looked at him, almost incredulous. "You mean, you…"

"Ashley. You wouldn't be in this position if it weren't for me. And frankly you're more important to me than anything in this City. Except maybe Michael and he's not the one who's in danger right now."

"Oh, Matt!" Her smile was thanks enough, even as he wondered at the decision he seemed to have made. Sometime in the silence, as he'd held her after she'd been crying, he had come to a decision. "What are you thinking?" She frowned at him, looking concerned. "You've thought of something haven't you?"

"Well, first, how will they know? How long do we have?" He looked to her, hoping she'd know. His education beyond the basic law was pretty hazy.

"Well, I think we might have a month or two before it will really start to show. I don't have any mandatory checkups due or anything. But what if they can tell somehow? What if they find out? What if they c-come and try to t-take m-me aw-way like those other w-women?" Her lip quavered at the thought.

"I won't let that happen." His voice was grim. Matt knew the stories she was talking about all too well. It was in the first few years after the founding of Newcity. Before the contraceptive distribution began in earnest. When it was still a person's personal responsibility, to make sure there were no unauthorized pregnancies. Every new mouth was seen as further stretching already tight resources.

He'd heard about how, when several women got pregnant without first suing for permission and getting the proper tests done, the CCC's enforcer's had forcibly taken them. Some of them had become pregnant despite the law and there were others for whom it was accidental but all had been forcibly sterilized. The procedure not only aborted the unformed children. It prevented any future pregnancies as well, as a form of deterrent to defying the law. Although there were also a few women who simply disappeared altogether and were never accounted for. He shuddered to think of that happening to Ashley. His Ashley. He held her to him tightly, at the thought.

He wondered about those vanished women though. One who had gone missing was his friend Sherrie. She had cared for him, the first two years he was at the orphanage. He'd thought of her like a mom. One night though, she didn't come back to the orphanage. With no warning and no goodbye. He had never seen her again and had often wondered if she had been taken or if somehow she had simply, escaped. Ashley hugged him back, obviously glad for the reassurance.

"How far have you explored beyond the City's edge Ashley?" The change of subject seemed to take her by surprise. She coughed a moment, clearing her teary throat.

"Well, back when I was too young to know better or maybe I just didn't care about the danger, Jen and I would ride our bikes out for days at a time in the summer. We only went a couple of times and we'd only go about a day's ride but they were some of the most beautiful times that I remember. It was the only time since the shift, that I think I actually saw a star in the sky. I swear I wasn't dreaming. Jen said she saw it too! So I'm sure it was there! For a moment and then it was gone. Why did you ask about that? What brought that up anyway?" She looked a little confused. He figured she'd probably forgotten his question.

"I had asked how far you've been from the City. I'm thinking of a couple of options. Other than going to the authorities, I think they're all we've really got. Firstly and this is best done sooner than later, I think we should move into the Outskirts, permanently. And only come back here for supplies. If we can keep anyone who might say something from seeing you, then we might just be able to avoid them ever knowing." She started to shake her head and he held a finger to her lips, smiling.

"It's so simple it's funny my love! You'll tell your neighbors that you're moving in with me and leave without a fuss. I'll tell my neighbors I'm moving in with you. While we'll both move into the crystal shop and no one will be the wiser! We can explore the wastes from there bit by bit and see if we have any other options." He thought it was genius but again she was shaking her head.

"There's no water out there Matt! I've thought often that I'd like to live at the crystal shop but there's no water." She seemed likely to continue but he interrupted her, in his excitement.

"There is! I found water dripping down the hall behind the crystal shop, when we were there last. I never got the chance to show you, but it did get me thinking. All of the city was once serviced by the aquifer beneath us, not just Newcity. So it makes sense that the pipes that survived are still plumbed, we just have to tap them! Maybe Old Tom has the tools and parts we need. Once we get you safely out of sight, I'll go and ask him-" Ashley was shaking her head furiously and finally broke into his thoughts, to share her own

"My plants, Matt! There's not enough water for them there and transporting them would not be subtle. It just won't work." She shook her head, looking down.

He reached out to take her hands in his.

"Ashley." He repeated softly, trying to catch her eye. Gently he said. "Ashley, I Love you. I don't ever want to see you hurt. There must be some way, that we can leave the plants here?" Her hands jerked in his as though he'd stung her and he hurried on. "You can bring all your seeds with you and if we can find somewhere hospitable beyond this place, you can grow more! Maybe you can have a real garden! Where our kids can play, Ashley! Free!" He kept a firm grip on her hands, his eyes pleading with her to understand, to see his point. Pleading with her to think, instead of simply reacting. But as he watched for her reaction he saw her eyes glaze over and he braced himself for a furious response.

What she said however surprised him.

"I had a dream last night..."

She sounded vague and far away. He held his breath, trying not to disturb her.

"I was flying out over the wastelands. I could see the City far behind me, just visible on the horizon. Suddenly before me, all of Paradise opened up! It was lush and green and even the air smelled sweet and tangy. Like you could almost eat the air and survive on it alone. I drank it in, it was delicious! I wondered. 'Is this my garden?' Then I woke up, with the taste of the air still on my tongue." Matt was still trying not to move. She had talked several times about visions and visualizations but this was the first time he'd seen her apparently drop into a trance.

She shook herself a little and turned, eyeing him curiously. Almost as though she was weighing him or perhaps his idea, against her own inclinations. She turned slightly to look out at her porch, obviously thinking about her plants. She was quiet and thoughtful for a long time. He simply held his peace. Her not rejecting the idea out of hand was a good sign and he didn't want to confuse or delay her deliberation.

Instead he concentrated on thinking about what they'd need, once they were living in the Outskirts full time and how he could most easily get it without raising suspicions. He couldn't exactly go to the local hardware store and buy the place out. No one in Newcity went camping or remodeled their homes. Most spent their time just trying to survive, too afraid of the storms to think outside their own basic comforts, their most immediate needs.

As he was making his mental lists, Ashley slowly began nodding. He turned to see if she was ready to talk, just as she turned to him.

"New plan. I'll tell my landlord I'm subletting to Jen and spending most of my time with you. While you tell your landlord that you're moving in with me. My apartment is covered automatically by my City Credit fund so I don't have to even be here to keep my apartment active and my water coming. At least till the first of the year when I won't show up for my physical." Matt nodded hard in surprise. Agreeing on all points but she continued, obviously thinking out loud.

"I'll ask Jen to take care of my plants, in exchange for all the water she wants. They have their own reservoirs. I built them to be self-sustainable units. Each pot has its own little water catchments in the bottom so she'd only have to water them once a week or so if she gives them enough. I've certainly explained the system to her often enough, that she should know how it works."

She might have continued like that for a long time but Matt interrupted her, urgently shaking his head.

"No one can know Ashley! It's not safe! No one can know!"

"But, what do you mean no one? You mean we can't even say goodbye?" Now she looked really distressed. "Even to Michael?" She pressed, obviously hoping that he would capitulate. Matt shook his head sadly though. He was thinking of his own initial reaction and the time it would take to convince each person, that this was the best course. The arguments and the denials. Especially Jen. He still hadn't met her in person but he could tell from Ashley's descriptions and comments. It was clear that she was no less fiery then Ashley herself and with a much darker bent to her as well. He didn't want to begin to imagine what arguing with her about something this important might be like.

He sighed sadly hoping his friend would forgive him.

"Even Michael." He agreed.

Ashley burst into tears again. He drew her to him, feeling his own eyes moisten and his own lips curl at thinking of leaving his friend without even a proper goodbye. But how could he possibly expect Michael to come with him, since he had the shop and Greg and everything? For something within him had solidified. He had made his decision. His gut knew as Ashley seemed to as well, that this was the right choice. It was their only choice.

"We'll write to them. We'll explain, but silently. After we're safely gone." He held her. His mouth was tight with suppressed tears of his own, wishing that there could be another way. Part of him wished that this hadn't happened at all. While another part of him knew, his gut told him, that this was the way it was meant to be.

He growled at his gut.

The next night, as they were finalizing their packing, he eyed the ever growing pile of books beside her.

"Are you sure you want to bring *all* of your books?" He asked her again. "If we're really setting off to explore the world, it's an awful lot to carry." He said it lightly but he'd already asked her several times. Sighing she turned to look at him, then set down her task, to come look again at the books still on her shelves.

"I just don't want them to go to waste. If we don't make it back here before year's end and they close up the apartment... I would hate to think that they'd be thrown away." She gave him a pained look, caressing the spine of one of her books. Sighing he tried to imagine how it might feel to leave his instrument behind. It helped him to sympathize with how she must be feeling. Especially since he was sure as hell bringing his guitar, even awkward as it was.

"Why not ask Jen to take care of it? Do you think that she'd mind? I guess it might be a lot to ask. What with caring for your plants and everything, but if she's gonna be over here to water them anyway..." He let the thought trail off, and left her looking thoughtful. He quietly returned to packing up small things that he thought she'd want to bring. It was the most useful thing he could do at this point, since he'd packed his stuff up the night before and given away what he didn't want.

He owned very little in the first place. Not much besides his clothes and his guitar. He just wasn't a very acquisitive person.

Ashley nodded hard, once. Apparently having made up her mind and returned to the papers she had set down in favor of the books a moment before. She had been working diligently on the note to Jen, explaining her disappearance.

'Note!' He thought, suppressing a chuckle. *'That book is over five pages long already, and she keeps adding more!'*

Even as he had the thought, she grabbed yet another piece of paper to begin scribbling on. Since she hadn't made a clear decision about the books yet, he avoided them for now. Grabbing only a couple that he was interested in reading himself. He figured that she'd do the same with her favorites.

He snagged pictures and trinkets that he thought might be important to her. Anything small enough not to take up room but that might make her feel at home once they arrived wherever they were going. He made sure to secure every crystal or rock that he came across. Although he secreted the very smallest of the stones into the nearby potted plant's pots. He rather felt that the little violet thanked him in its way. Or so Ashley would have said. Smiling at the thought he gave its fuzzy leaf an affectionate little pat.

———

Ashley was deep in thought, as she explained in detail what she was hoping Jen could store for her and what she was asking her to donate to the orphanage. She had decided. She'd been inspired by Matt's passionate speech about their children playing in the garden. As well as the vision that she'd had of Paradise. So she'd realized that she had to willingly release all that she left behind. Aware that she may never come back here again.

She must embrace the future and all its untold possibilities, and trust. She had faith that it would be her beautiful vision, lush and filled with plenty. She would hold that vision in her heart, breath it in, believe in it. She would make it real. Smiling to herself she doodled a bit in the sidebar. She drew first some beautiful swirling patterns while she thought. As her mind wandered the swirls became flames and when she was done, she saw the doodle itself looked like the profile of her dragon.

The dragons of her dreams were a whole other piece of the puzzle. The dragons wanted them to leave the City. From the moment that the option was mentioned, she had known deep in her soul that the dragons of her dreams greatly desired this. She had known somehow that the dragons wanted her and Matt to get out of the City as fast as they could. She hoped that perhaps in staying at the crystal shop, more would be revealed through their dreams. Sighing, she paused in her doodling to contemplate the dragon dreams.

She was unsure just what they were dealing with. They didn't seem to be spirits as she knew them and yet as far as she knew they had no corporeal form. At times it seemed that they knew everything, even things that they should have had no business knowing. All transmitted in images, experiences. Only rarely in words. Yet at other times their responses seemed slow and unfocused. Or like in the beginning, she would simply be a dragon. No longer conscious of herself as separate, as Ashley.

She thought for a moment, wondering exactly when the dreams had begun to change. It seemed to her that it was after they had spent that week camping in the crystal shop. The dreams had gotten progressively more complex since then. As well as increasingly intense. Ever since she had sent that question toward the feeling of those dreams.

That was when the dragon dreams had turned into different visions. They still had the taste of dragon on them but there were no dragons to be seen. Only the answer to her question played out as from above, like some of the documentaries she had seen. It took her a while that first time, to realize what the dream had meant. To recognized its significance in relation to her question. It took even longer to recognize the significance of the fact that she gotten an answer at all.

Whatever these dreams were, they were a separate consciousness from her own. They had responded to her questions independently. She was reminded of the first time that one of these separate entities had responded to her presence. When the eyes in her vision had looked at her. Not through her but at her. Shuddering a little, she pulled herself away from such unsettling thoughts, just as Matt dropped a kiss on her head.

"You looked serious enough to scare a fish." He said with a straight face. Then he winked at her, putting one hand on her shoulder. She patted his hand and smiled at him, giving herself another little shake to bring her back.

"Thank you." She leaned into his hand, smiling up at him. He took the invitation and wrapped his arms around her and giving her a squeeze. "I've decided that you're right about the books. I'm gonna leave most of them for the orphanage library. Hopefully I remember more then I think I do of all I've read." She smiled sideways up at him and laughed when he made a face at her, chuckling.

"You should bring the ones that are most important to you though. We'll find a way to carry them." Once again he was thinking of his guitar and what it would feel like to have to give it away. "At least bring the ones on permaculture, alright? Maybe some of the spiritual books? Or art?" She snuggled into him turning to face him within his arms. As he looked down at her she tilted her head up towards him and smiled a slow sweet smile.

"I Love you, Matt." She rose from her stool to kiss him, returning his embrace. "Now, no more packing tonight." She winked and pulled him towards the futon. "No more packing. Time to rest." Dropping his hand she skipped the extra step to the light switch and still managed to meet him at the futon.

———

After dropping off their goodbye notes early the next morning they moved into the crystal shop, with the intent of living there until they could think of something else to do. They spent the afternoon settling in and had an early dinner before settling down in their little nest. Matt pulled out his guitar. Its voice seemed to resonate with the crystals all around him as he played. Ashley hummed along from where she lay in the blankets beside him, obviously enjoying the music. Before long he felt as though his hands were buzzing from the resounding resonance of the larger crystals in the outer rooms and he had to take a break.

Now he knew why the singing bowl had affected him so deeply that day. The crystals seemed to enhance the resonance of sounds. The short break turned into a prolonged one when Ashley began stroking and petting the bits of him that she could reach from her prone position, seeming to suggest a completely different type of playing. Relishing in the comfort of contact after such an emotionally trying day, they were quickly worn out and fell into a deep undisturbed sleep.

———

Ashley woke with a start from dreams that had screamed with desperation. The message in her dreams was unclear but the urgency still filled her body. She turned in time to see Matt too, coming to awareness with a start. When she asked about his dreams his were even vaguer then hers had been. However he also felt impelled by the same sense of increasing urgency. So much so that with unspoken consent they repacked the little they had undone last night. Still confused by their mutually inexplicable restlessness and mussed by sleep, they left the City. Heading out into the wastes searching for they knew not what.

They set out southeast, vaguely trying to go around the deepest part of the old riverbed, while still following that inner knowing that they needed to go east. The urgency had not abated since they left the crystal shop that morning. Instead it was simply spurring them on, near thoughtlessly. Their packs high on their back and their saddle-buckets full, they rode out into the wastes on their street bikes. They didn't get more than a few miles from the city however, when the horizon seemed to darken as if it were already dusk.

Ashley looked up, alarmed since it was still early afternoon, and there was something about the angle of the darkness that was wrong. It took her a minute to realize that the darkness was on the northern horizon just beyond the City, not to the East as it would be if it were true dark.

A distant sound, like a high keening or humming gave her the clue she needed to identify the monstrosity. It was a huge dust storm, the kind that drove through the Newcity sometimes. It would scour the streets and buildings before it with any sand or loose rock it could gather. As this one was about to do, on its way to them. In the City, people would be fleeing for the shelters in panic. Since there was even less warning of this kind of wind storm, then there was of the heat storms. Out here though, they were completely exposed.

Thinking quickly, Ashley weighed their options.

*'The City isn't one.'* She realized. *'It will be in the midst of the storm long before we could reach it and then the storm would be between us and the only shelter!'* She scanned the distance all around looking for any options for cover at all. Even a crease or a gully would give them something to work with. Finally she realized, that what she'd at first taken for a bright spot in the distance, seemed on closer look to be a small mound.

Taping Matt's arm to get his attention, Ashley gestured her message. There was no way to talk in the growing shriek of the now not so distant winds. So she pointed towards it in the distance, blessedly away from the looming storm. He nodded, also not bothering to fight the quickly increasing sounds of the rising storm. It was coming fast. The storm was already beginning to pummel them, even now. So they wasted no time in rising on their stirrups, to pedal as fast as they could for the distant hill. The wind was beating them with sharp thrusts of force, driving sand and small pebbles as they reached the small hill. Desperately they circled it at the base seeking any kind of crevasse or dip that could offer them some protection from the increasing debris.

Finding in one side a small depression, they sheltered there huddled in each other's arms. They piled all their belongings, on top of themselves between their bodies and the wind. They huddled under everything they had brought with them, their bikes and the guitar included. They then covered the whole bundle with their blankets. Desperately clinging to the blankets edges, to hold it all together.

Matt was grateful for the goggles and mask Ashley had given him when they first began exploring the ruins of the Outskirts together. The mask was just enough to keep most of the dust out. Buried beneath their belongings and partially protected by the blankets, they eventually fell asleep once more. Wrapped in each other's arms, they slept on. Exhausted by the journey and the hypnotically monotonous winds, they were oblivious to both the raging of the windstorm all around them and to any dreams that they may have had.

# 17

Matt was roused by the strangest feeling that he was riding something. It was as though he was on a huge bucking animal that was trying to throw him off. His own yell and Ashley's startled scream as they both went tumbling brought him fully awake. Struggling to work out which way was up, Matt rubbed his eyes with one hand and groped for Ashley with the other.

"What th-?" He stopped, as he opened his eyes to look up as two of the beefiest and dirtiest men he'd ever seen, loomed over him.

'*Oh shit...*' His first thought was of the faeries they'd been reading so much about. Gnomes and hobbits flooded his mind and people from Underhill.

'*But aren't they supposed to be small?*' His mind gibbered. Only half awake and still muddled by sleep he was unsure how to react to their sudden appearance. His reaching hand found Ashley and gathered her to him. Encircling her protectively in one arm, he watched them.

———

Looking down at their frightened faces, the older man couldn't seem to help the laugh that burst out, at the sight of them.

"And we thought it was debris blocking the door. Ha ha ha!" He roared with laughter as he turned and went back inside the hill. The younger man gave them a puzzled look before turning to start clearing their stuff away from the doorway that had appeared behind him. When Matt looked closer he saw boards driven into a huge chunk of turf. It had been set to one side of the depression they had slept in the night before.

'*That must be the door. I guess we slept on it.*' He looked again at the perfectly mundane seeming chunk of sod set to one side. '*I guess they're not elves after all. Hmm.*'

"Excuse me. I'm sorry if we slept on your door last night. We didn't know it was there. We were just trying to take shelter from the wind, you know?" Patting Ashley's hand Matt climbed to his feet and started forward, to help move their things. Ashley stood slowly behind him and watched the stranger warily from where she was.

"Who are you? Why were you in that hill? Do you live here?" She cocked her head at them, almost accusing in her earnest curiosity.

The younger man looked at her, he sighed.

"Who are you to ask who I am? What were you doing sleeping on our doorstep, anyway? And what kind of idiot tries to sleep outside in that kind of storm?" He glared at her, waiting for an answer but she just stared back.

Matt looked from one to another of them. Sighing heavily he reached for the first thing that came to hand, beginning to move it out of the doorway.

He pulled the blanket loose to a reign of storm flung debris, when the other man came out rolling what looked like an antique combustion vehicle. Following close to his side was one of the burliest animals Matt had ever seen. It was smaller than Old Tom's Jo, in the shoulder but it was dense and its short fur showed off its incredibly muscular form. It must be another type of dog, he decided after looking at it closely. The dog seemed to have glued itself to the older man's leg. The animal watched him warily and he watched it just as warily back.

"Get your bike lad, we need to make daylight." The man said gruffly over his shoulder as he wheeled his great machine out and set it to stand at an angle. He turned to take in Matt and Ashley. They were standing in front of their small pile of belongings. Their street bikes, and their homemade saddle buckets and backpacks.

His weather beaten face split in a wide grin and he asked.

"And what's the story with you then? Where'd you two lovebirds come from? " He chuckled as he said it. Ashley seemed unsure whether to smile back or get mad at him. "It's obvious you two haven't been out here long. So where are you coming from? And where are you going?" This time the humor was gone from his voice. It wasn't quite menacing but it was obvious that he expected them to answer him.

Ashley raised her chin defiantly but she apparently decided to answer him. Maybe she thought he could help them find their way.

"We've just left Newcity looking for a better world. We plan to go east." Matt met her eyes and nodded.

"East." The man seemed thoughtful, rubbing his chin. "What's east for you? What are you looking for?" The older man's eyes were intent now. Matt could sense the younger man listening from the shadowed mouth of the hill cave behind him. Matt wanted to tell her to be careful what she said but he knew there was no way to do so subtly. So he held his breath and hoped that they weren't offended by whatever she did say.

"Arable land, that's my dream." She said with a sweet smile. "I want to help the land grow green again. To sow seeds and to see them grow. To make the land healthy again. Wherever I manage to go. To help return balance to the world, where balance has been lost."

Her eyes were shining with her vision of a green future and all the possibilities therein. When Matt looked to see what the two men thought of her passion he saw that the older man was smiling outright and the younger man was trying not to. He chuckled to himself and pulled her to him for a hug. He was grateful all over again, that it was her that his life's adventure had turned out to be with. Smiling, she hugged him back.

"Well, my dear." The older man said. "Seeing as how you two are but pioneering your freedom. I think we are but messengers of that freedom. Would you like a ride?" He smiled, gesturing broadly at the bikes. "Call me Jim my dear." He said lightly shaking her hand. "And this is my son Jimi." He waved roughly towards the younger man. Who upon closer inspection Matt suspected was around his own age, beneath the film of dirt.

*'Though I'd be dirty too, if I'd spent the night in the hill instead of on top of it.'* He smiled to himself and stepping forward, held out his hand.

"I'm Matt and this is Ashley. It's nice to meet you both." The older man, Jim, stepped forward and shook his hand with a smile.

"Alright. Great. Introductions over, we'd better hit the road. Who knows when something else will kick up out here after all? I hate to be all business but out here you have to be. We can chat more once we make it back to camp. We're still a few days ride away, so let's get going."

Jimi had disappeared back inside and he came out with his own bike, balanced between his hands. Matt looked again at the bike, this time with the thought in mind that he was supposed to be catching a ride on it. He tried to imagine all of their stuff on those two bikes, along with himself and Ashley and the strangers. He shook his head.

*'It was just too much. How could they possibly do it?'*

Seeing his puzzlement the younger man gestured to the pod like protrusion attached to his bike. Without a wasted work Matt watched helplessly as their own street bikes were summarily disassembled, into pieces that he hadn't known came apart. Their stuff was neatly strapped in bundles onto the outside of each bikes pod and he and Ashley were instructed to each get into a pod. At a whistle and a gesture the dog hopped into Jim's pod with Ashley and she wrapped her arms around it, getting the dog settled in her lap.

Within moments of having settled himself, Matt felt the bikes engine start up. Unaccustomed to combustion engines as he was, it seemed deafeningly loud and momentarily it was also noticeably hot.

"Let's go!" He heard Jim shout and both bikes and pods jerked into motion. Roaring with dizzying speed across the rugged landscape they rode off into the wastes surrounding Newcity, heading to the south and east.

They had three days of dawn to dusk riding, each night spent in another strategically placed mound. The shelters were spaced roughly a day's ride apart but now Matt could finally see their destination in the distance. He was riding with Jim this time. Who he found to be a taciturn but less antagonistic partner to ride with then his son, Jimi. Matt spared a glance from the dark blot rising on the horizon, to glare over at Jimi, who was carrying Ashley in his pod today.

'The sidecar.' He reminded himself firmly.

He'd had enough of Jimi's mocking snorts of laughter every time he didn't know the right name for something. He was sick of it. But not half so sick as he was of the way Jimi treated Ashley. He positively fawned over her sometimes, only to turn a cold stare at Matt a moment later. Jimi was also constantly soliciting her opinion when they stopped at night. *What do you think of the wastes? What would you have done out here on your bicycles? Where did you think you'd get water from?'* He made it abundantly clear that he only wanted Ashley's opinion, glaring at Matt if he opened his mouth to say anything.

Matt had a very hard time keeping his temper and his fists, in check. He had never so much wanted to punch someone in his life. Ashley seemed to know instinctively whenever he was about to burst. She always managed to catch his eye, to make a restraining gesture or to pat his knee in a soothing manner. He was finding it harder and harder, to let Jimi jerk him around this way though. Ashley putting up with him being just a little too solicitous didn't help any. It was only serving to make it even harder for Matt to keep his temper.

The fact that they were literally on the move the whole time, with no chance at all to speak privately, only aggravated the situation.

There was no time in the day that they weren't either riding the exhaustingly loud machines or in the little two room caves. The caves were only a single sleeping chamber, with an antechamber for mitigating the deadly heat from the storms. Or so he'd been told.

*'Well, hopefully that will change when we get to the camp today.'* He thought to himself. He was hoping they might be able to get some time alone together, when they arrived. So they could figure out their next move. They had been swept along so far, with no control over where they went or how fast. In some ways he was really grateful for the nomad's assistance.

'The trader's.' He corrected himself. *'That's what they call themselves.'*

He was determined to learn their terms, so he could stand on equal footing with Jimi on that point at least. For on the other hand, he was also nettled by their highhanded assumption that he and Ashley had needed their help in the first place. He was particularly sick of Jimi's condescending attitude. His attitude said clearly, you'd have died within days if we hadn't found you. Matt's mouth twisted at the thought.

*'Even if it might be true.'* He admitted quietly to himself. Sighing at his own ignorance, as his gaze swept the vast desert. They still had so far to go to reach the timid shelter of the nomad's tents.

*'I simply had no idea that anything could be this vast!'* He thought to himself for the hundredth time. Having grown up surrounded by the close in, crumbling walls of the heart of Newcity, he had never before seen such an expanse of open space as when they had first entered the wastes. The deeper in they had ridden, the worse it had gotten. Until eventually even the tallest spires of the city was lost to the horizon behind them. He had never known that all that endless openness could make him feel so claustrophobic.

All that horizon, meeting the featureless gray of the ever present cloud cover, made him feel as though he was going to spin right off into the sky. There were no convenient walls to hold him down. He shuddered to himself, releasing his tension as best he could. He focused instead on the comfortingly approaching smudge in the distance, which he knew were tents. He focused on taking in the slowly rising foothills just beyond, rather than looking back at the open expanse of uninterrupted horizon, slowly retreating behind them.

Upon finally arriving at the nomad's main camp, Jim left his bike in their care and took off as quick as they arrived. Ashley came over to help Matt beat the worst of the desert dust from his shoulders and he was enjoying having a moment together with her, when Jimi walked up.

"I'd like to offer you both the hospitality of my tent." Jimi said, as though offering a traditional invitation. He said it formally, without any of his usual sarcasm or innuendo. He gestured roughly towards one of the round tents along the western perimeter of the camp. When they hesitated to follow, he explained, showing far more patience then he had in their journey so far. "We are a fairly small group here and we don't have any extra tents set up. So, since I live alone right now, I have rooms to spare."

He must have seen something in Matt's expression that he took exception to though, for the uncharacteristic patience was gone as suddenly as it had come. "But if you'd rather. You're welcome to intrude on one of the other families. The living space, that is. That being the only room most of them have that's unoccupied at night."

With that he stomped off towards the indicated tent, leaving them to follow or not as they chose. He didn't look back to see if they followed. He just ducked inside, disappearing into the dark depths of the tent.

Ashley had hung back with Matt. Though when he looked at her, he could see it was out of a desire to talk to him, rather than out of fear of, or pique towards Jimi.

"Matt please! We have to try to get along with these people! They might be the only people out here! We can't afford to be making enemies right now. Especially not over simple things like just being polite!" She exclaimed in frustration.

She glanced nervously towards the tent but there was no further sign of Jimi. Apparently he really didn't care whether they followed him in or not.

'Not that we really have any other options right at that moment.' Matt thought sighing to himself. 'As he well knows.' Even through his irritation, he saw the inevitability of Ashley's argument and of their current circumstances.

"All right, I'll do my best, but I'm sick of him fawning over you! Tell him to back off when he leans in on you like that!" He growled back. "He's not gonna stop, unless you tell him you don't like it!"

Then he took a deep breath. He was starting to get angry again just thinking about the way Jimi had been flirting with her. Instead of answering Ashley took his hand. When he met her eye, some of the fight went out of him.

"I Love you Ashley. I guess, I'm jealous. It drives me crazy when I see him getting so close to you!" He tried to look away but she held his eyes. Eventually her calm amusement translated itself to him and he started to answer her small smile, still not seeing the joke.

"I'm carrying your baby, Matt." She reminded him, again with that small smile. "I'm gonna have your child! That didn't go away just because we didn't talk about it for a few days!" She smiled at him and leaning forward she kissed him lightly, curing the last of his foul mood. "Although, speaking of which. I don't think we should mention it for now, all right?" She looked a little nervous saying this.

"You don't think that they have similar laws to the City about pregnancy, do you?" He asked her, suddenly equally nervous. He looked around quickly. So far, they were being studiously ignored by the other members of the camp.

"I don't know. Of course." She said with a grimace. "But I'd still rather just keep it between us for now, alright? If they ask where we're going, we can say that we're heading for the old seed banks, to see if the seeds are still viable. The nearest one is to the east of here, if I remember right. Although it's still a good distance away, so that should make sense. I really would like to see it anyway, baby or not, so it's not a complete lie." She smiled a little at that and he put his arms around her. He was feeling very protective of her and their unborn child. He decided that for both their sake, he would try to make peace.

As they entered the tent, Ashley asked Jimi about the toilet and he directed her towards the outhouse. Once Ashley had left to follow his directions, Matt stood awkwardly in the doorway unsure how to begin. When his eyes adjusted to the dimmer light he realized that Jimi was balanced on a chair. It was an oddly shaped little room that had small carpets making up the floor.

They were a colorful overlapping mass that covered the floor from wall to wall. He seemed to be hanging a huge curtain from hooks in the ceiling. Matt realized that the hooks must be there for that purpose. Taking a closer look around the tent, he realized that the hooks divided the single round room into wedges. This was what Jimi had meant when he said that he had an extra room.

Now that his eyes had adjusted, he saw that the reason the room seemed so oddly shaped was because of another sectioned off area to his left, which must be Jimi's room.

As Matt was thinking this and wondering what to do, Jimi jerked hard on the curtain he was currently hanging, trying to free the end. He almost knocked himself off the chair in the process. As the cloth burst forth from the chair's leg that had pinned it, Jimi lost his balance. Acting on instinct Matt lunged forward, catching Jimi's elbow with one hand and righting the chair with the other. With that minor assistance and a firm grip on the now stationary chair, Jimi was able to resume his perch. Giving Matt an odd look, Jimi silently held out his hand for the end of the curtain. Matt handed it to him without a word, suddenly embarrassed by the situation.

"Is there any way that I can help?" He asked, not quite looking at Jimi while he did so. From the corner of his eye he saw Jimi's eyebrows shoot up in surprise before he could control his expression. Jimi turned slowly to look at him, his expression once again carefully neutral.

"Other than catching me if I fall, you mean?" He growled sarcastically, then laughed out loud when Matt blushed.

"I didn't do it on purpose…" Matt muttered scratching his head to hide his embarrassment. "I just reacted, that's all." He wasn't sure why he was so embarrassed about averting the potential fall but he was. He was so caught up in his own embarrassment that he was completely caught off guard, when Jimi slapped him on the back.

"You're an all right guy Matt." Jimi said, as Matt staggered under the unexpected blow. "You're all right." He repeated catching Matt's shoulder in his hand and shaking him in what Matt took to be a friendly way. "I don't know that I could accidentally save someone as rude as I've been recently." He said snickering. "You're a decent sort of guy at heart, aren't you?" He asked again chuckling. Matt wondered just what he was insinuating.

"Look." Jimi said, abruptly dropping the curtain and shoving his hand towards Matt. "Let's call a truce, alright? Obviously you're not the chump I took you for and just as obviously your girlfriend isn't interested in me." He said with a wink and a wistful look. "More's the pity." He finished with a sigh. He grinned at Matt as though inviting him in on the joke but Matt didn't find it particularly funny.

He thought about knocking Jimi's hand away, but then

remembered his promise to Ashley. He reluctantly took Jimi's hand instead. Matt sighed out his frustration as Jimi pumped his hand melodramatically and let go with a caw of laughter. Turning back to his curtain he bent to retrieve it before Matt could think to hand it up to him. Once he had it in one hand Jimi pointed with the other to a second curtain folded in a neat pile against the wall.

"That's the other wall if you want to get started. It explains itself once you're high enough to see the hooks. Just grab a chair." He went back to affixing the curtain to the ceiling even as he spoke and Matt gathered the other curtain to him looking up, uncertain where to start attaching it. He saw that the hooks where laid out in patterns of strait lines forming the wedges, like a star. He wondered how much space Jimi was planning on giving them. Jimi glanced at him looking irritated with his lack of movement but seeing where his gaze had gone, Jimi explained with more of that surprising patience.

"Third one over, count from the one I've started on, that a way." He gestured towards the door. Hooking a chair in one hand from beside the small table against the back wall of the tent, Matt counted three rows of hooks over against that outer wall from where Jimi was currently working. Stepping up onto the chair, he fumbled with the edges, until he found the right one and set to work. Jimi was right about the self-explanatory nature of the hooks themselves and he was soon pinning the curtain in place with ease.

Although he had seriously underestimated how unsteady the rugs over sand were as a floor, it made the chair he was standing on unsteady at the slightest shift in weight. He found himself unwillingly impressed with Jimi's steadiness on the mound of little carpets. Except for that first incident with the curtain, he saw Jimi didn't wobble at all. While Matt himself looked like a man just getting his sea legs as he struggled to keep from over-correcting and overbalancing in any particular direction.

He got frustrated with having to get down and move the chair for every other hook. And soon his arms were starting to go numb, from having to work with his hands above his head for so long. By the time he finished hanging his curtain, his hands were tingling with pins and needles. He stopped with the last hook hanging free as Jimi had done and looked at him curiously where he stood, watching Matt work. He noticed that Jimi was shaking out his own hands, flexing them to return the circulation. Proving that this part at least, got no better with practice.

Jimi lifted the curtain free to let Matt out of the newly created cubby, before he folded one to the other and hooked the ends of each curtain to the opposite row, squaring off the end of the room and leaving a short narrow hallway between the new room and the old. Seeing Matt's puzzlement he wordlessly showed him the door slit in the curtain that Matt himself had hung. Then turning on his heal, without a word, he left the tent. For a moment Matt was at a complete loss.

*'Did I say something wrong?'* He wondered. Then he went over and poked his head out the door to see Jimi was most of the way back to where they had left the bikes.

"Now what..." He wondered aloud before it dawned on him.

*'Oh! Our gear! The pods- I mean sidecars! Our stuff!'* Matt took off at a quick trot, trying to catch up to Jimi before he got to the bikes. He was embarrassed at not having thought of it before and irritated with Jimi for not just saying as much.

He didn't quite manage to catch up, but he did arrive while Jimi was still loosening straps and undoing clips, in order to free the baggage from the sidecars themselves. After watching Jimi and his dad adjusting the straps on their trip across the desert, Matt felt fairly competent at doing so himself. So he began on the sidecar that Jimi wasn't working on yet. As he worked, he thought that he saw Jimi smiling at his hands as he untied a knotted strap but Matt told himself that it could have been a smirk.

———

Ashley entered the tent again only to find it dark and different. The unfamiliar dusty smell of the heavy fabric made her nose itch. She paused in the darkened doorway, just inside the flap, as her hand brushed a felt wall that hadn't been there when she'd gotten directions to the restroom. She waited, trying to be patient as her eye's adjusted from the glare of the desert outside, to the muffled darkness of the tent.

"Matt?" She called softly into the shadowed tent.

She was beginning to wonder if she had counted wrong and wound up in the wrong tent. When her eyes finally adjusted to the darker interior and she could see that it was clearly not the same shape and that there was also no sign of Jimi or Matt. Now she was sure of it. She had turned to begin retracing her steps and counting tents all over again, when the tent flap opened before she could reach it. She stumbled back, startled by the sheer mass of the dark silhouette coming through the glaring doorway.

"Yeah, you'd better back up missy." Growled Jimi's now familiar voice, from the unfamiliar shadow. "I don't want to accidentally drop all this on you after all."

He sounded surprisingly friendly. Rather than fawning or flirtatious, just friendly. She decided it was a definite improvement, but wondered what had caused his change of heart. There was a second massive shape entering behind him, which resolved itself into Matt. He was carrying both of their backpacks, with the bundle that she recognized as his guitar on top. Their other various bundles and bags of gear were dangling from his arms.

The neck of the guitar bundle got fouled up in the top of the tent flap. Matt stopped, stuck and struggling, half in and half out of the tent. Without a word Jimi jerked the cloth free, leaving Matt reeling but fully inside the tent again. Then they each turned and began unloading their burdens into several piles, one of which she recognized as some of her own things.

*Did they manage to bring everything in one trip?* She wondered incredulously. It certainly looked that way as she took note of what she did and didn't see. As they each unloaded what they carried, she counted up everything belonging to her and Matt but their bedroll. It was a huge unwieldy thing because they had combined theirs into one.

Slipping past the bundle shedding men, she peered out the front flap. She squinted, her eyes tearing up in the blinding light outside, until she could make out the bikes in the distance. She could just see their bedroll and a few scattered items beside it and set off without another thought to collect what was left.

She did have a little trouble, similar to Matt's with getting the bedroll through the door flap. Carrying it strapped along her back, and with her hands and arms full with the rest of the gear, she didn't have a hand free to address it. She stumbled on the rug pile and was jerked around by the cloth of the tent door tangled with the bedroll. She squeaked and squawked in surprise.

Matt popped out of the tent wall beside her at the sound and helped to untangle her. Chuckling, he began removing dangling bags and bits of Jimi's gear from her arms as she squirmed and wriggled trying to get free of the bedroll.

Jimi, having also appeared at her involuntary cry, simply watched the scene with folded arms and a bemused expression on his rugged face. Matt assisted her in dragging all that was theirs through what she now saw was a split in the new curtain. Which explained how he'd appeared so quick.

"When we're settled in but before dinner, you'll be meeting with the elders. It's about half the people here." He added cracking a smile. "Most folks above ten anyway. Even I get to go." He said, with a self-depreciating grin. "So I thought I'd suggest that you eat something. Just in case the meeting goes long." His smile didn't leave her with a feeling of comfort. She decided to do as he suggested.

---

The meeting hadn't turned out to be the ordeal that Matt had feared it would be. They had talked it over while they ate and decided that Ashley would answer most of the questions. Once the initial questions made it clear that they weren't hoping to join the trader's camp, everyone lightened up and it turned into an impromptu welcome party.

The fire they had gathered around was stoked up higher and flasks and bottles began making the rounds. As well as bowls of some kind of thin soup and what he assumed was supposed to be some kind of thin brittle bread. As they ate and drank together, people continued to vent their curiosity, calling questions to Ashley one at a time.

"But why do you think these seeds would still grow? It's been ten years! Who knows if the building is even still standing?" The older woman waved her hand dismissively, as she spoke. Obviously she was convinced they were on a wild goose chase.

"Viability varies." Ashley answered, as though the question had not been meant sarcastically. "But if the people building the facility knew a lot about how to store seeds and the containers there in are still intact, then I'm sure that a percentage of them are still alive! Seeds can last for thousands of years, in their dormant state, if their stored correctly. Just think about all the ice ages and other major planetary changes the world has faced. Even before the latest climate shift. If seeds only lasted for a year or two, there wouldn't be anything green growing anywhere on the whole planet!" She finished triumphantly, sure in her own reasoning.

The group of trader's however just laughed.

"What's so funny about it?" She asked, hurt plain in her voice.

"Look around and you'll get the joke." Jim said, waving a broad hand at the night. "You said 'there would be nothing green in the whole world,' and well I'd have to say, that's pretty much the case at the moment, wouldn't you?" He smiled at her, trying to invite her in on the joke. Ashley frowned though and shook her head.

"Plenty of seeds are still alive and plenty of things still grow." Ashley's jaw was set and she looked determined to turn this into an argument. Matt decided to chime in and see if it helped or made things worse.

"She's right you know. Maybe out here it is a barren wasteland but if you'd ever seen her place, you would know she means what she says." Ashley shot him a grateful look and he grinned, winking at her. Jim was stroking his chin thoughtfully, looking form one to the other of them.

Seeming to make up his mind, he suddenly sat up straighter, looking Ashley in the eyes across the fire.

"Alright so tell me about this, place, of yours. Where you say, that you've grown plants in today's climate." He crossed his arms challengingly, his eyes on hers. His expression unwontedly serious.

Sighing Ashley shrugged, twiddling her fingers a little now that she was being focused on so intently.

"Actually, my garden isn't half as impressive as Sister Mary's garden is." She muttered. "In fact..." She said, suddenly gaining animation in her excitement. "You should go see it! You're in and out of the city regularly and I know she'd be open to trade! You should trade her something for some of her seeds! That's where I got all of the seeds for my garden." She smiled, obviously well thrilled with the idea.

Jim was frowning again though, and started to shake his head.

"Seeds don't help when there's no rain and seeds don't help when we can't make them grow." He growled as he said it obviously frustrated by the situation. "It's taken all our skills just to keep the few tobacco and other herbs and medicinal plants we've got going. Anything more sensitive doesn't even get past the sprout phase and believe me, we have tried." He sighed. He suddenly looked as old as the mountains behind them and just as tired.

"Then let me help you! I have to repay you somehow for all of your help and hospitality! Let me get some of your seeds started and I can show you how to build self-watering containers."

She would have continued but Jim's gesture cut her off.

"What? Self-watering what? We don't have any seeds, at least not food. We don't even have real soil here." He said shaking his head sadly.

Ashley stood, rounding the fire to take the older man's hand.

"I can help you Jim, if you'll let me. I can show you how to make your own soil, richer than anything the world has seen this last decade. With seeds from Mary and my techniques, you can grow enough food for all of you." He was still shaking his head, unable to believe in any claim so wild. "I'm not saying it's all easy, and you do have to baby them when their young. Don't worry, I'll show you. You keep them moist and protected from the weather. It is a process, but its worth it believe me."

"For what it's worth, her tomatoes are to die for!" Matt piped in with a smile. He almost drooled just thinking of them now. Sighing he said quietly. "I can't wait to find our own new home and plant our real garden." He smiled at Ashley in the firelight.

Leaving Jim's side of the fire she rejoined him, where he lay lounging against another mound of the tiny multicolored rugs. Settling herself beside him, Ashley turned her attention back to Jim and the conversation.

"I'll get started in the morning. You show me what you're growing already and what supplies you have. I'll show you some of the books I brought on self-watering pots and container gardening and we can go over some of the basic principles." She interrupted herself with a deep yawn. "Right now though, I'm beat." She admitted leaning lazily into Matt's shoulder, as he put his arm around her.

"Yes, you're right. Enough talk for now. We have guests!" That last was addressed to the listening crowd of elders.

"Let's celebrate! Sam where's your fiddle? Doc, get your drum! Let's party!"

The tempo and excitement only increased as the night went on. The soft glow of the fire and the warm closeness created by the music however, lulled him and before long both Matt and Ashley had fallen quietly asleep.

Sometime later, Jim noticed the two, over on the edge of the firelight. He smiled, although they were sleeping though the festivities in their honor. Chuckling to himself, he grinned with approval at the impetuousness of youth. He fetched a few blankets from amongst his spares and draped them across the young couple, before turning back to the music and the fire himself.

# 18

Bright and early the next morning Ashley set to, with a vengeance. She rigorously toured the tents, where they grew their herbs and the sad spindly plants they showed her, left her feeling sorry for the poor little things. Even if many of them were tobacco. She spared a moment's thought for Jen back in Newcity, smoking tobacco grown right here. For a moment it made her feel closer to her friend.

'*She would love to see this.*' She thought sadly. '*If only I'd known where we were going when we left.*' Shaking her head she released that train of thought, as being fruitless. '*We still don't know where we're going and we haven't gotten there yet.*' She reminded herself sharply, before bringing her attention back to the conversation at hand.

"What I need first is an empty pot or container that you want to grow a plant in. Then show me to your machine shop next. We'll need to create a few pieces if we want to do this on a food production scale." She frowned again, looking more closely at the spindly plants surrounding her.

'*Not enough nitrogen or iron, and this soil doesn't look like anything but clay.*' She thought, poking a finger at the dense soil in the pot at the base of one of the plants. She shook her head. '*Bare soil too, no wonder.*' She sighed heavily, wondering where to begin in explaining the process of bio-regeneration and the importance of mulching, to the traders people.

"First things first." She said briskly to herself and turning back to her guide, she said. "Please take me out to your mechanics now. I need to see what kind of tools you have at your disposal." Neil shrugged, flushing a little. The younger man was still a little star struck by her it seemed. Ducking his head to hide his flush, he did lead the way to their next tented destination.

She had found Neil on her way back from the outhouse that morning. He had been the first person she saw from the camp once she woke, still curled up beside Matt near where the bonfire had been last night. She'd been itching to get started on their food system although Matt was still sound asleep. When she saw the young man, she had latched onto him figuratively speaking, as a guide to achieve her goals.

She had asked if he could lead her to the things and people that she needed to see. Blushing furiously, while fighting to keep from bobbing his head at her, he had agreed. They had spent a pleasant morning so far touring the tents behind the living quarters, a little more sheltered from the rigors of the desert. This was where they grew the few plants that they had coaxed to life.

*Their almost all derivatives of weed species. Pioneer plants, no wonder they'll grow in even these conditions.'*

She thought it over as they walked the distance to the next cluster of tents that made up the mech yard, as Neil was explaining. She listened with half her mind, as another part of her tallied the conditions the Trader's currently had to deal with. Then what plants she knew of, off the top of her head, that would do tolerably well in these conditions. Then she mentally compared that list, to what seeds she knew Sister Mary had on hand.

"I need paper." She muttered to herself. She hadn't meant to say so aloud, but Neil answered her as though she had meant it as a question.

"We have reams and reams of paper in the storage caves. How much did you need?" He sounded so nonchalant that Ashley was momentarily taken aback.

*'Reams and reams?'* She wondered.

"I only meant something to write a list on, it could be a scrap even, not necessarily new." He was already shaking his head, a smile having finally chased away his blushes.

"Don't worry there's plenty. We certainly don't use it. Or well, other than for the kids to draw on." He added thoughtfully.

Smiling, Ashley shook her head. Although his comment sent her thoughts in a totally different direction.

*'Hmm, right, kids. Hmmm.'* She put one hand to her belly unconsciously. She pulled herself free of her thoughts, with a shake of her head as Ashley saw that they were approaching the mech tents at last. She realized suddenly just how huge they actually were.

Her jaw dropped and she wondered for a moment just why anyone would want a tent so big. Neil grinned at her expression and pushed her inside. She found herself not in a tent, but in a long rectangular room, filled with people and machinery. The sounds of screeching metal on metal, of sanders and scrapers and saws was deafening. She noticed that Neil had his hands over his ears and everyone else was wearing earmuffs.

Stuffing her fingers in her ears as far as they would go helped to take the edge off, but she could still hear every sound. She followed Neil towards an old man, who was at the very back of the long rectangular room. The old man seemed to be taking a nap. Amazingly enough given the noise, he was also tilted onto two legs of his chair. He balanced precariously, as he seemingly snoozed through the cacophony of shrieking metal. He slept on, balanced on his perch, seemingly unaffected by the echoing noises throughout the room. She wondered if perhaps he was deaf. Something about the way the sounds echoed made her realize that the ceiling was metal. Looking more closely at the walls and scuffing the toe of her shoe through the sand on the floor showed it was metal beneath the thin layer of sand and dust covering the floor as well.

'*Curiouser and curiouser. Now why would anyone want to work in a metal room, in the middle of the desert?*' She wondered. It was early enough, still being just after dawn that the room was still only tolerably hot, but she knew that it would be an oven in a couple of hours, tents to shade it or no.

The old man, although apparently asleep and obviously deaf, looked up at them with a faint smile as they approached. His smile widened perceptible when Ashley met his eye. His chair dropped noiselessly to the sandy floor, as he resumed a four footed posture, sitting up with interest.

"Now how can I help you today, my young lady?" He asked with a wiggle of his salt and peppered eyebrows. The longest hairs of which curled most intriguingly in all directions but the expected ones. She couldn't help but giggle, although she knew it could not be heard in the ruckus made by the competing machinery all around them. She contemplated whether it was worth trying to talk over the noise, or whether she could try sign language.

He seemed to perceive her dilemma, from her also inaudible sigh. With a grin he stepped up onto his now quite firmly four footed chair and cupping his hands around his mouth he shouted.

"Hey guys!"

The sudden silence was deafening. As all hands stopped what they were doing, turned off their machinery and all eyes turned towards him.

"Why don't you guys take a twenty minute break, huh? It's hot as Hades in this tin box! Why not go drink some water? Grab a bite to eat and bring me some while you're at it, eh?" He finished with a grin, as surprised smiles turned to chagrined laughter. Taking the less then delicate hint, the men filed out. Many cast curious glances at Ashley over their shoulders as they went. She smiled at them and waited for the older man to speak. He turned back to her as he resumed his seat.

"So. I'm Howard and I run this popsicle stand." He said, introducing himself before repeating his earlier question. "So what can I do for you?" He seemed a little more serious with his question this time. So she decided to get strait to the point.

"Well Howard, I need to talk to you about machining some parts. Do you have drills here?" She cocked her head to one side, hoping the answer would be yes. If so it would save a considerable amount of time.

"Drills, huh?" He said scratching his salt and pepper stubbled chin. "We have most things you could think of actually. It's been over ten years since we started raiding what was left of the world, after all. We've collected quite a haul." He looked very thoughtfully at her as he asked. "Why is it you ask? What is it that you want to drill exactly?" Head cocked to one side, his smile had faded and he seemed merely puzzled by her question.

"Actually the substance in question is less important than the ability to shape it. It could be metal or plastic, although wood would rot before long." She was thinking out loud and might have continued had he not held up a hand interrupting her.

"Just what is it that you're trying to make missy? Perhaps I can direct you to the ah, substance, you're looking for." He made a face, using the word as she had and waited for her to respond.

"Were you at the bonfire last night?" She asked instead of responding directly. She figured he had been. Given the elders comment Jimi had made and the amount of salt in Howard's once dark stubble.

She wanted to make sure though, before she assumed that he'd been party to that conversation. When he nodded though, she continued. "Well if you were there and if you heard what Jim and I were talking about at the end there, just before the music broke out." She smiled at the memory of the music. She wished that she'd had the energy to enjoy it. She hoped for a repetition of the celebration tonight, now that she was rested. "Then you may realize that I want to help you guys get some food growing before I move on. It's really not that hard to do, if you have a little insight. I would love to share what I've learned, with as many people as are interested." His scoffing laugh interrupted her, startling her into silence. She raised her eyebrows questioningly.

"My dear, if you can grow anything here better then we can, you will have all of our undivided attention, believe me." He looked very serious as he said it. She thought back to the spindly struggling plants that she'd seen so far.

"I can definitely help you." She said with a smile. "And with your help, we can make this whole adventure self-sustaining as well." His excited grin said more than words could have about the hardships of the life they led here at the trader's camp. She wondered just what it is they ate out here, since she'd seen no food crops growing in with the commercial crops she'd visited thus far. "First things first, where do you get your water? And I need containers of some kind to plant in. Old bins, buckets or boxes, anything that's water tight can be made to work. Oh, and where exactly did you get the soil that you're using now?" Although it wasn't ideal, the clay was still better than the sand dunes surrounding the camp. She could always deal with improving it, if they had to, once she knew what organic matter might be on hand to improve upon it with.

As Howard answered her questions, Neil stood by looking alternately enamored and confused. Howard explained that there were extensive cave systems in the hills just beyond the camp. It turned out this was where they got their water. From an underground river they had found access to. Somewhere in this same cave system, was where they stored anything the traders brought back to camp, which did not seem immediately useful or tradable.

Howard offered to take her out there to see what they might find for containers. Reasoning that he needed to know what she was trying to drill, in order to know what tools they might be able to use. As the cave system was quite a distance from here, she asked Neil if he would mind taking a message back to Matt, explaining where she'd gone and why. So that he wouldn't worry. She thought he might be awake by now. She didn't want him to get concerned, if he couldn't find her around camp just because she was spelunking with the old man.

Howard pulled the quad they'd ridden right inside the cave mouth, before turning off the engine to park it. The sudden quiet was deafening after the echoes of the engine off the cavern. Those echoes were still chasing themselves further in as she climbed off the quad and began looking around. It was noticeably cooler here, even just inside the mouth. She wondered why the trader's insisted on living out in the desert, when the caves were so much cooler. She asked Howard's as much and scratching his head and looking sheepish he admitted.

"You know, I just don't think it ever occurred to us…" He seemed embarrassed that they'd overlooked something so obvious.

"Well if you show me where you got that clay we might be able to do even more here than I thought to improve your current living conditions. Here I thought it was just the plants that I could help with." That last was she hoped under her breath but everything they said in here seemed to echo and amplify, as the sound bounced around the cave.

He led her into the storage caverns first. She gasped at the amount of things crammed into them. She saw all sorts of things that she would not have expected. It seemed that for some reason the trader's had collected everything that they came across, rather indiscriminately. She asked Howard why. He actually flushed a little, apparently embarrassed by this as well. She was getting the impression that he was less than impressed with the intelligence of his fellow traders. He explained that in the panic of the first few years they had simply taken anything and everything they came across, rather than sorting through to find the things of value.

"We wasted a whole lotta gas and time and energy." He said, again shaking his head at their folly. "But I guess we were still pretty spooked back then. We had no idea when the storms and earthquakes would renew. Most often we didn't want to take the time to sort through things at the salvage sites, so we just loaded up the trucks with anything and everything, emptying every building that we came across. We stuffed the trucks till they were fit to bursting, but if we'd taken the time to organize we could have brought a lot more functional stuff with us." He finished, sighing rather sadly at the foolishness of the past. Ashley started to nod agreement, when she reviewed that last statement mentally. Then asked him, incredulous.

"Trucks? You have trucks?" She felt her eyebrows crawling up in surprise as she put two and two together. "Wait a minute, so the mech room, is a truck?" She asked more surprised still when he nodded. Well that explained the metal walls and floor then.

"Yep, some old Mac's. Several of the boys used to drive and they were on the road when the shit hit the fan, so they kept their last loads. They each wound up wandering and got swept up by the rest of us when we were still travelin' around looking for other survivors. Their cargo was some of the first things we packed into the caves once we found the hidden river here. That's when we decided to stay close, making this our base camp." He said gesturing into the retreating darkness and she wondered just how far this cave system went, and just how much stuff they had in here.

"Most of the boy's though, Jim and Pat and Doc and Billy to name a few, they were all Hells Angels before everything went down. We were all the lucky ones. We found each other, in the mess of what was left behind by those storms. If it hadn't been for Nick and his tracking skills, who knows how many of us would have wandered alone until we died. But he and a few of the boys made trips out every week, once the founders had set up camp. They collected anyone they found by following tracks out there and bringing them back here. Much the same as the CCC's enforcers did around Newcity." He shuddered to himself, obviously remembering the experience vividly. Even though the memories were now over a decade old.

Ashley nodded quietly, as she herself knew, some experiences even time couldn't heal. Although even as she thought it, she realized her own memories and the pain that they usually brought, were currently overshadowed by excitement. She was beginning to feel really optimistic about the project, that of getting the traders sustainable. Her eyes flowed over the piles of stored goods here and she felt a little thrill at just how doable this project had suddenly become.

---

Matt woke to a toe in his ribs. He sat up, startled and was surprised to see it wasn't Jimi, kicking him awake. It wasn't a hard kick, but it still wasn't a pleasant way to wake up. As he sat up groggily, reluctant to rise from his surprisingly comfortable nest of rugs and blankets, he wondered what he'd done to irritate the young stranger.

"Ashley asked me to tell you that she went to the caves with Howard. So don't worry about her." His duty apparently discharged, the young man turned on his heel. Whistling tunelessly through his teeth, he walked off before Matt could wake up enough to ask who Howard was. Or what caves he was talking about.

Yawning, Matt rubbed the sleep from his eyes. Looking around he could tell it wasn't long after sun up. He wondered how long Ashley had been up and why she had left him sleeping here alone, to wander off with this Howard person. Curious, yet unsure where else to get answers, he trepidatiously headed for Jimi's tent. He still didn't really know anyone else well enough to ask. Halfway there however, he realized that he really had to pee and headed instead for the outhouse.

A little later, when he did tap tentatively on the flap of Jimi's tent, he was unsure that such a soft sound could be heard. After a moment however, Jimi pulled the flap aside, looking puzzled. His confusion cleared, when he saw Matt standing there, looking equally unsure. He smiled a little. Pulling the flap back a little further he pointed to the support pole to one side of the opening.

"We usually knock on this." He tapped it lightly with his knuckles as an example. "I wasn't quite sure I had heard anything. If it hadn't been rhythmic, well." He trailed off shrugging. "Come on in." He said turning back inside and Matt followed him gingerly into the tent. Jimi was waiting inside, arms folded and he snorted at Matt's insecure attitude.

"Look." He said over his shoulder.

Turning Jimi headed back down the short hallway, left by the two rooms. He led Matt to the tiny cubby left in the back with the table and chairs.

"I told you yesterday, I offered you the hospitality of my tent. Your stuff is here, so you accepted. Just because you slept by the fire last night, doesn't change that. So quit walking on eggshells and relax won't you? This is your tent too. Until you guys choose otherwise, so don't knock, alright? Just come in when you need to." He sat down in one of the chairs to eat what was apparently his breakfast. It looked like some kind of slimy gruel. Matt wondered swallowing, if he would be expected to eat it to. It didn't look appetizing. Jimi saw the direction of his gaze. He waved a hand at the pot on the table.

"It's not quite as disgusting as it looks, and it's loaded with protein. Help yourself." He followed his own advice, continuing his obviously interrupted breakfast. Matt hesitated a moment, then decided to accept the gesture in the name of peace. Especially since he'd come here to pick Jimi's brain about this Howard guy. And why he might have taken Ashley off to some cave. So he ducked into his own cubby to snag one of the cups he and Ashley had brought from home and trying to keep his skepticism from showing he scooped some of the glop into his cup.

It was worse than Jimi had said, but better then it looked, in that it had very little flavor at all. He forced himself to finish his first serving and finding that it did indeed fill his middle, he reached for seconds, raising a questioning eyebrow at Jimi for permission. Jimi just snorted and waved his spoon in a gesture of have at it, finishing his own bowl while Matt refilled his cup. Yawning he tilted his chair back onto two legs, one foot on the tables leg to help him balance and watched as Matt inhaled his second serving as quickly as the first. He chuckled at the expression on Matt's face as he ate. He seemed to be in a very good mood today.

"So where's Ashley at? I made enough for her too." Jimi asked gesturing towards the remaining contents of the pot, as Matt finally set his own cup on the table. He tried to push his chair back a bit. It caught in the rugs though and he saw the wisdom of Jimi's idea and copied him. He leaned back in the chair until he had a comfortable space between himself and the table. Jimi made it look easy but Matt found that he had to set all four of the chairs legs on the ground again to concentrate on asking his questions, so instead he leaned forward onto the table.

"Well that's actually why I came. I was hoping that you could tell me." At Jimi's surprised and questioning look he continued. "The kid who woke me said that she'd gone to a cave with someone named Howard?" He let the question hang there, trying not to show his irritation. Jimi answered by laughing out loud.

"You're jealous of Howard!" He crowed, slapping one leg and laughing so hard he rocked on his precariously balanced chair. "Oh that's rich! I'll have to tell him, he'll love that!" He chuckled to himself until he had to wipe his eyes. Matt was quite put out, wondering just what was so funny about being jealous to find his girlfriend gone off with some guy he didn't know. Matt's glare only set Jimi off again though and it was obvious that he'd have no breath to answer the question, until he'd had his laugh.

Matt sighed, telling himself to be patient.

"So are you going to explain why this is so funny or should I go ask someone else?" It was an empty threat. Since the only other person he knew was Jimi's dad. He had no idea which tent was Jim's anyway, but he was irritated and it did seem to bring Jimi back to the moment. Although he was still grinning to himself as he answered.

"Howard's our lead mechanic. He's in charge of all things mechanical that happen here in the camp. And if he's gone to the caves with your lady love at this time of day then I assure you it was her idea. He's usually hard at work bossing the other mechanics around in the mech tent right about now. So she had to have sweet talked him to get him to leave his post." He grinned again as Matt ground his teeth at the inference that Ashley would sweet talk anyone into taking her off to some cave but he didn't say anything. He didn't want to give Jimi the satisfaction of knowing how much the comment irritated him.

Jimi laughed again to himself. Apparently Matt had not been so successful at hiding his irritation as he thought. At least it was clear now that Jimi was just screwing with him. Finally taking pity on him Jimi wiped his eyes once more. Having laughed himself to tears at Matt's expense, he settled his own chair firmly on the ground and gave Matt a more serious look. Although his lips still twitched and Matt was sure that he hadn't heard the end of it.

"Howard is older than my dad if that makes you feel any better. I don't think it's very likely that anything, um improper, is going on out there." He couldn't help a snicker, before he continued.

"Given the way the conversation ended last night she's probably out there trying to find things to plant in. If I judge your lady right she's as stubborn as they come. So impossible or not she's going to try to grow us some vegetables out here in this mess." His gesture took in the wastes beyond the tent walls, only barely visible through the small window flap that was tied open above the table.

"It's not as impossible as it seems." Matt muttered. He was still irritated with Jimi for laughing at him so uproariously. Although he was grateful that Jimi was finally answering his questions. That made a lot of sense actually. It sounded exactly like what Ashley would do.

He was very reassured to hear that this Howard she was out

there with was not actually competition as he'd feared. Despite her reassurances when they arrived, he was feeling very insecure here amongst all of these unknown traders. He'd never been particularly sociable, preferring to spend most of his time with Michael and Greg or at the Library. He just wasn't used to being around so many people at once and he was unsure about how the social dynamics of such a group would play out.

Growing quite serious at his comment Jimi asked him.

"Really? Are you sure? Because, if what she was saying is true it would really change the way we live out here and for the better." He looked like he meant it and Matt reminded himself of the unidentified gruel he'd just eaten.

"Yep." He said, even managing a small smile, remembering his own surprise when he'd first seen her garden. "I'm not sure how all she does it yet. I'm still just starting to learn but she was growing almost all of her own food back in Newcity and that was just in pots on her balcony. So I'm sure that she can help you guys to get something going. If you have the container's and can get the seeds from Sister Mary. No reason at all." He shrugged at Jimi's incredulous look when he described her balcony.

"I ate from it myself, when we first met." His small smile broadened considerably when he thought back to that first lunch date at her place and all that they'd talked about.

*'That seems like a lifetime ago now. Like it was on another world.'* He thought, looking out the small window at the waves of sand blowing gently off the dunes surrounding the camp. In the face of that endless desert, he could see why Jimi and his dad doubted so strongly.

# 19

Having found plenty of containers to use to plant in, Ashley had explained to Howard what else she needed and why. She left him to it, as he began the loud but fairly quick process, of machining the interior parts for the self-watering containers. She left her book on it with him, so he could use the diagrams like schematics and left him to work. While he did so, she went to see if she could work out a good source of soil.

She found Matt and Jimi in their tent, seemingly just finishing up breakfast and realized how hungry she was herself. She explained what she needed from Jimi, in between bites of tasteless gruel. He said that he could take her out to where they got the clay. He warned her that it was all the way over in the foothills though, and it would take most of the day to get there and back.

She shrugged.

"I have nothing better to do, are you able to take me or should I ask someone else?" She cocked her head to one side questioningly. She wondered if he maybe had other things he needed to do but he shook his head emphatically.

"I think that this is the most important thing going on in the camp today. Anything else can wait for now." He started to get up immediately, apparently ready to go. Bolting the last of her food, Ashley jumped up as well. Jimi smiled at her but shook his head.

"This may be a day trip but it's still the wastes, we're not going anywhere without a full kit. Just in case. So you stay here and finish that off, while I gather what we'll need."

Matt gave an exaggerated sigh and she noted the slight pout to his mouth. She wondered what was wrong. Jimi turned back to look at him over his shoulder.

"You wanna go too, don't you?" He asked. His mouth quirking into a crooked grin that Ashley didn't understand. Matt nodded.

"I know the bikes only hold two though, so I'm just gonna have to deal with it." He sounded far more irritated then she thought the comment called for. Jimi laughed though and she gathered that she was missing something. Shrugging it off for now, she helped herself to what was left of breakfast, scraping the contents of the pot into her cup.

"Tell you what." Jimi said, turning to face Matt more fully and looking him up and down where he was lounging in the chair across from Ashley. "I've been thinking and I think it would be a good idea for you to learn to drive a bike." He held up a hand as Matt began to protest. "I mean the motorbikes dummy. Their nothing like riding your street bike on pavement, this is the wastes and the sand is unforgiving of fools."

He sounded very serious all of a sudden.

"This will be a good opportunity for you to practice. While I'm still here to hold your hand." He smirked at Matt's irritated frown. "I'll have to head out of here sooner or later and there's no telling if the other guys will think of it or not. So why don't we start today? I'll get gear for three together and two bikes ready while you two eat up and do the dishes." The seriousness gone he grinned and headed for the door flap before either of them could respond. Not that Ashley was going to argue about the dishes, after all he'd made them breakfast.

Shaking her head at his odd behavior, she turned back to Matt and asked around the mush in her mouth.

"What's up with him?" Matt just shook his head and took her free hand in his.

"I'm glad that your back." He said instead. "I missed you this morning."

Snorting through her breakfast, she laughed.

"I was only gone a couple of hours." She smiled at him. "I'm sorry I left you so suddenly. I didn't plan it that way. I just got caught up, one thing led to another and-"

She broke off as he shook his head, giving her hand a soft squeeze.

"Don't worry about it Ashley. I'm just glad your back." He smiled at her with such warmth that she flushed. She was suddenly glad that they had a moment alone.

---

*'Well, he was right.'* Matt thought, much to his chagrin. *'This is nothing like riding on the street.'* Jimi had run Matt through the basics of starting up and controlling the antique combustion vehicle. Giving him what at the time had seemed like a lengthy explanation but now seemed a short overview. Since he was now riding that vehicle across

the wastes. It was both easier and more difficult than he had thought it would be. It was easier then riding his street bike in some ways, since he didn't have to pedal but he found he still had to muscle the wheel in the direction he wanted it to go. The sand had a tendency to push the wide off road tires around and his nervousness made him cling fiercely to the seat with his legs.

He had never thought that he would look back on riding in the sidecar with longing, but compared to this it had been a breeze. It was much easier to just sit there and hold on. He was just keeping up with Jimi and Ashley, who was riding in Jimi's sidecar. Jimi had said Matt would have his hands full just learning to drive. Matt had been resentful at the time, thinking it would have been nice to have Ashley by his side, but now that he was out here he was infinitely grateful for Jimi's wisdom. He was having a hard time controlling the bike and it was taking all of his concentration to keep it going in the direction that he wanted it to. It would have been terribly distracting, if he were worrying about Ashley being on the vehicle too.

When he next dared look up from the dune just before his tire, he saw that they were almost to their first stop. They were headed for the next finger of hills over from the one that stretched down to the edge of the trader's camp. Jimi had explained that there was a dry streambed here. It was where they had found the clay that they were currently using to grow those plants they had gotten growing.

When they reached the firmer soil at the base of the hill, Jimi looked back at Matt, signaling that he should continue to follow. Although Matt couldn't see more then the goggles and mask covering Jimi's face to keep the dust and sand out, he thought that Jimi was smiling beneath his mask. Matt hoped it was just because he was still keeping up.

When Jimi pulled to one side and parked his bike, turning off the engine, Matt followed. Pushing up his goggles and pulling down his mask he took a deep breath, grateful to have made it at last. Ashley spent some time poking around the clay of the streambed Jimi took her to. After a little while though, she insisted that they walk up into the hills, to see if anything was growing and to look for better soil.

After wandering up and down what Ashley called the watersheds, but what looked like the clefts between the hills to Matt, she found an area of less compacted soil. Following the watershed further she found much to Jimi's surprise, a few plants growing.

Some sparse wild grasses and succulents were growing along the ground up the watershed, implying some subsurface moisture in the area.

Encouraged and excited she followed the cleft until she came to a place where the soil was soft and moist. It was soft enough that she could dig into with her bare hands.

"This is perfect! We can make some great soil now, no problem! Especially if you can get Sister Mary to give you a few worms when you trade seeds from her. That will really do the trick." She dug into the soil with her hands a bit. Looking for those worms, he assumed.

She seemed very pleased with herself. Happily off in her daydreams of healthy soil and growing things, she didn't see Jimi's puzzled look, until he asked.

"Worms, Ashley? Are you serious? What do worms have to do with anything?" He seemed really puzzled. Just as Matt had been the first time it came up and Matt smiled to himself, waiting for her response.

"Worms make soil, duh. Didn't you know that?" She looked at him a little incredulously. "Where did you think soil came from?" She seemed to be waiting for a response and after a few minutes Jimi shrugged.

"I guess I never thought about it before. So you claim, worms make soil? Then why do you want more? If you've got soil right here?" He gestured to the upturned earth she'd been digging in and she shook her head.

"It's not the same at all. This soil has been through hell, just like the rest of us. It's been exposed to such ferocious weather and sun that most of its nutrients have been baked out or washed away. The worms if you can get some will make fresh nutrient rich soil which will make your crops thrive! Believe me my friend. It's well worth the small effort of growing the worms for all the benefits that you gain from them."

"Grow the worms?" This time it was Jimi's turn to look incredulous. "Like a worm farm? What the hell are you talking about Ashley? We can barely sustain ourselves and you want me to waste my time growing worms?" He almost spluttered with indignation at the thought and Ashley sighed. Matt could see though that if they could convince Jimi, then it would be that much easier to convince everyone else. "Worms." Jimi muttered to himself and Matt couldn't help but grin at his tone.

He decided to put in his two cents. He based it on what Ashley had explained to him when they'd talked about how to re-green the barren earth.

"Look. If you take the time to do it, to grow worms like she'll teach you, then you'll have healthy crops and vegetables for life. If you try to grow the same crops in your containers of soil without replenishing that soil, your crops will get weaker and weaker. Right?" The last was directed towards Ashley and she nodded. "You see, I didn't know this until I met Ashley but plants eat to." He nodded at Jimi's startled look. "And the things that plants eat from the soil, what Ashley calls nutrients, have to be replenished in the same quantity that they've been used. Otherwise you wind up starving your soil and your plants."

Matt could see that Jimi was thoughtful now. He thought maybe Jimi was thinking of the plants that they'd been struggling to grow for the last few years.

"Have your crops been a little weaker, a little less resilient every year?" He asked, and at Jimi's unwilling nod he gestured triumphantly. He hoped this proved his point in the other man's mind. "So have you been replacing the soil in your containers or have you just been dumping the same type of plants in the same soil, year after year and expecting them to do alright?" Jimi's chagrined expression was all the answer Matt needed and he gentled his tone to try to bring the deal to a close.

"So listen to Ashley. She's done this, we haven't. If she says you should grow worms, then you should grow worms. It's really not hard. From what I understand anyway. You didn't do much to tend to them when I was over anyway. Does it take much?" He turned to Ashley to find her smiling broadly at him. She seemed quite pleased to have heard her own arguments poor from his lips. She shook her head in answer to his question though.

"They take almost no maintenance once their established and they'll keep making babies. They reproduce like mad, so all you have to do is find stuff to feed to them."

"We have a hard enough time feeding ourselves." Jimi muttered, but he didn't argue further. Ashley looked thoughtful at his comment though and after a moment she said.

"Actually your right." Jimi looked startled and then momentarily smug before she continued. "Hmm, they usually eat vegetables scraps and you don't have any yet." She tapped one finger thoughtfully on her lip thinking hard. "I know!" Her eyes lit in realization and she turned towards Jimi excitedly. "You can gather scraps in the city, from the restaurants and even from Sister Mary, if you ask her to save you some. That will get you going until you have your own first season of crops. From then on the cycle should be able to repeat itself. You'll feed the scraps of your crops to the worms and feed the worm castings to the plants and one will feed into each other and before you know it you'll have a continuous food supply!" She was grinning from ear to ear with excitement, seemingly inviting Jimi to join in her enthusiasm but he still looked skeptical.

"Castings? What's that?" He asked, instead of jumping on her band wagon.

"Worm poop." Matt translated succinctly, before Ashley could begin to wax eloquent on the topic. He himself had heard more than enough about worm digestion and bio-regeneration. He didn't think Jimi was quite up for learning that many new words today. He thought maybe nutrients and castings were enough of a vocab quiz for one day. Ashley seemed to agree. Since after a moment's thought, she nodded but didn't add anything.

"Hrmph." Jimi grumbled. "So I wag worms, seeds and rotting veggie bits back here from the City. I feed one to the other and then collect its poop to feed to the new veggies?" He actually looked a bit less puzzled as he said it. "It's gross, but I guess it might work."

"I'll teach you to build a house for them so that you're not sifting through rotting veggies looking for worm poop." She grinned at his grimace, laughing. "It's actually much easier than that. You have to water the worms once in a while anyway and the water that comes out of the bottom of their house is the liquid fertilizer you feed to your veggies. It contains their soluble cast-uh, poop. As well as worm eggs, which will grow even more worms in your potted crops. I'll make it as simple as I can for you." She smiled again and Jimi answered it. His own smile was crooked and doubting but he said no more.

As they worked their way back to where they had left the bikes however, Matt heard him muttering to himself.

"Worm houses, worm poop! Trading for veggie scraps, it all sounds so ridiculous!" Matt chuckled at his tone but seeing as Jimi didn't make any of these complaints within Ashley's range of hearing. He saved himself from further worm poop lecturing. Matt laughed softly to himself at the thought.

———————

With Jimi's help, Ashley told the other traders why they needed worms. She explained why they needed to gather better soil and why they should cover the soil with mulch in the form of dead leaves or rocks, anything to try to retain moisture. An expedition was made to collect more soil, led by Jimi who showed them to the soft earth that Ashley had found.

Howard had finished building her small army of self-watering containers within forty eight hours of receiving the assignment. Ashley was both surprised and gratified at his obvious enthusiasm.

"You've brought the camp to life, little lady." He said, as she tried to thank him for his efforts and he waved her thanks aside. "We had become too complacent, stagnant. We were content to wither away, our resources slowly eroding. And none of us knew the first thing about what to do about it. Then you and your young man showed up and zoom! No more complacency! Just mentioning that things could be done to improve our lot here, has given everyone a second wind as it were. I haven't seen Jim this fired up about anything since Laura died. It's good to see the light back in his eyes again. It's been pretty gloomy around here the last few years. Thanks for cheering us up!" His dark eyes twinkled as he spoke and she smiled back. She really liked Howard and she was glad that he and Matt had seemingly struck up a friendship as well.

With their army of containers ready and waiting, all that remained was to go get the seeds. Ashley had assisted Howard in building the worm bin that would become their home. She had also insisted that instead of the super-heated tents in the desert, the new plants were to be kept in the mouth of the storage caves. That way they could be pulled inside, in case of inclement weather. The water was easy to access to this way. Instead of having to haul it all the way back to camp.

Matt just shook his head at how quickly she had taken control and completely reorganized their lives. There was even talk of moving the whole encampment, trucks and all, closer to the caves for ease of access. Some said that they might even move right into the caves, as she had suggested. Especially during the hottest part of the season. Some of the caves were already set up as shelters for descending heat storms. Although the storms were much less common out here, then they were in the depths of the desert, where the City lay.

The encampment worked tirelessly to create the resources that would hopefully become their new food supply. Ashley also enlisted a few of those too young to help with the heavy work but old enough to read and write legibly, to help her hand copy some of her books. They made two or three of each of her books on how to grow in containers. She had them copy books on companion planting and how to harvest and store seeds. They would likely have done more, given the time.

She had already made up her lists of plants that would do well here. She had written up a list of seeds that Jim and Jimi were to try to get in trade from Sister Mary. It included how many they were to ask for of each kind. She had included another note explaining to Sister Mary that she had built them a worm bin and that the worms had a safe home waiting for them. If only she would send some of them with the men.

She knew that Sister Mary would never send her little worms off, unless convinced that they were going to a good home. She just hoped that Sister Mary considered her note convincing. She prayed that Sister Mary forgave her for the quick exit she had made from Newcity. Without so much as a by your leave, from her old guardian. Looking around at the diligence with which everyone was working, Ashley felt her mouth stretch into an involuntary smile.

'*Well.*' She thought. '*It's certainly not what I expected to be doing when we left Newcity last week, but...*' She looked around again, at the kids, carefully copying were she had set them. Then she looked over at the flurry of activity around the adults. Some were mixing soil and sand as she'd shown them and some were assembling containers.

'*I am very content to be able to help them. This is so much more rewarding then just growing a little food for myself. I should have been teaching people back in the city too.*' She sighed, shaking her head. '*Don't should on yourself.*' The thought made her smile again, it had been one of Jen's favorite sayings whenever she caught Ashley saying such things. Her smile faded, thinking of her friend. Her eyes wandered to the ever shifting horizon in the general direction of Newcity, as she wondered just how everyone was doing back home.

Jen sat at her usual table in the back of the Underground, crouched over her notepad. She scribbled furiously. She was just drawing little illegible diagrams representing her thoughts. She was mentally reviewing the last few weeks. The squiggles and arrows representing what she knew Ashley's life recently. Her new boyfriend and little things Jen remembered her saying. She was trying to figure out what had led her friend to leave.

Pausing for a breath in her furious thinking, Jen sipped at her drink. It was a malt whiskey, her second of the day, after a breakfast of a more calorie dense Guinness. She savored its bitterness across her tongue and pressed the cool glass to her sweaty brow. The muskiness of the drink filled her senses, seeping into her overburdened mind. It melted away a little of the stress and not so little of her intense focus; finally bringing her to a point of blessed mindlessness, if only for a moment.

Taking a deep breath, she gazed blearily down at her newly drawn map of the past. Her diagram of thoughts, those squiggles and arrows, dates and times represented when she'd met with Ashley. With what little she knew of Matt scribbled into bubbles within her sketch. The arrows connected the rough times on her time line. Where she thought the two had met and when they had left. The two points connected only by a gaping question mark in between.

She looked once more at the date she'd hastily scribbled on the top of the note Ashley had left her.

She snorted at the thought.

*'It's more like a book then a note.'* She flipped idly through it, scanning the pages just as mindlessly as she'd stared at her own doodles. She had read it so often she had it memorized. From the books Ashley had wanted her to donate, to her friend's careful instructions on how to care for and tend to each plant on the balcony. Sighing Jen scrubbed a hand across her face and glared at the note as though it were Ashley herself.

"And where do you get off shoving all that on me?" She asked the note, not so silently. "What gives you the right? To just abandon me and dump all your baggage on me to boot?" She was crying now and the soft sound of the tears hitting Ashley's note brought her to herself sharply. She brushed ineffectively at the spreading stains of water on ink and tried blotting it off on her shirt.

Rubbing her face again, she took a deep breath to steady herself and matched it with a sip from her drink. The whiskey's acrid tang once again cut through the sticky sorrow of her unshed tears. She took a deep breath, not wanting Jack to decide that she was too wasted to be trusted tonight. She wanted him to sell her more than a few bottles after all. She needed to be able to drink at home if she was going to be able to sleep.

That's why she'd been buying expensive drinks all day. She had started with a rare Guinness and a big tip for Jack. She always tried to make sure to sweeten the deal when she was buying for the road. He could always refuse her and she knew it. Selling bottles rather than drinks was a risky business and it was only done for certain customers. She wasn't sure what had gained her that status. Perhaps it was her somewhat shallow friendship with Jack himself but the prolific abundance of liquor that resulted, was truly a godsend.

"Hrmph, a godsend!" She mumbled to herself, snorting with laughter. "Sister Mary would just love that! Hawah!" She laughed out loud thinking of the Sister's likely reaction to Jen's fervent prayer. When her slightly drunken laughter had faded she flipped to the page in Ashley's note about Sister Mary. Ashley had asked Jen to give most of her books and her worms and as many of her plants as Jen herself didn't want to Sister Mary.

Jen reread the words once more, her eye's blurring with tears. Their meaning was clear. Wherever Ashley had gone to, she wasn't planning to come back, ever. She would never have asked Jen to dismantle and distribute her books or her garden if she had been planning on coming back. Jen knew how much that garden had meant to Ashley. It had been her little haven in a broken world. If she had left it this way, it could only mean that she was never planning to come back to Newcity again.

Her breath caught in her throat as Jen fought a burst of fresh tears at the thought that she'd never see Ashley again. After several steadying breaths, she realized that this was as recovered as she was likely to get. She really just needed to go home and cry out her abandonment.

Surging unsteadily to her feet, she apprehensively approached the bar. The look Jack gave her was a jaundiced one and it didn't leave her with high hopes for her return haul. In the end though, with a sigh and a shake of his head, he did sell her the bottles she asked for. Their cold clinking weight in her backpack was comforting against her back. Perhaps tonight, she'd be able to drink enough, to get some sleep.

———————

Matt found himself feeling rather redundant amongst the flurry of activity. So he sought refuge with the mechanics who were not currently working on the food project. Although he had never before found an opportunity to explore his own mechanical aptitude. He found that all his training in music had left him with nimble fingers and a strong grip that served him well. The older men seemed to take pleasure in taking turns teaching him about the bikes.

He was fascinated by the different types they had. Some were summer bikes and some were winter bikes, they had explained to him. The fuel they derived from the cooking oil they gathered in trade ran their summer bikes. They called it bio-fuel and the distillation process made his head spin but he couldn't argue with the results.

They had raided an old military base for the experimental heavy duty diesel dirt bikes that they had adapted into their waste mobiles, as they jokingly called them. Howard had served on that base as a mechanic back before the shift. Knowing where it was and roughly what was available there, he and Chuck had made the argument for the raid to their peers.

"The oil goes solid on us in the winter though." Jack explained, taping one knuckle on the gas tank. He was the one who'd taken Matt under his wing today. "So rather than messing about with trying to keep them warm or preheating the tank and risking getting stuck somewhere you don't want to be in a cold snap. Instead we pack 'em away for the season and we use these baby's in the winter." He lovingly patted the bike he was working on. "It runs on the alcohol we make from grains we've salvaged from the old silos." Seeing Matt's aha expression, Jack laughed. "Did you think we brewed it just to drink?"

He laughed again, at Matt's guilty flush and smacked his shoulder in a friendly way.

"Oh believe you me, we drink a good share of it too!" He winked, making Matt smile. The wink reminded him of Sam. "But the real impetus that got the stills built in the first place was the impending winter. We were lucky enough to have Chuck with us who

245

knew about making the bio-fuel and how to adapt the engines. He warned us right away though, that we had to come up with another fuel for winter. We spent that first summer scrambling, burning the remains of our fossil fuel trying to find the parts and pieces we needed to build the stills."

Matt had found in the last few days, that he had far more in common with the other men of the camp then he ever would have imagined. He shared in the music making at night around the fire. Sometimes playing solo the songs that they didn't know or improvising around the songs that everyone knew but him. He really enjoyed that time of night, especially the improvising. He'd never had such a diverse group of musicians to play with before. He had played mainly by himself at home, baring the very occasional jam with Michael and Greg. Those had been really great too. But with Greg's teaching schedule and since Michael was more interested in making instruments then playing them most of the time. Well, he had more often than not found himself playing alone.

He was really enjoying this chance to experience camaraderie and the sense of community that he felt when they were all playing together. He felt the same way when he was helping on a bike or laughing together over a tasteless but filling meal. He found that he enjoyed the company of the traders immensely.

He found himself thinking that if he and Ashley did not find the paradise they were looking for, it might not be such a bad thing to settle here with the traders, after all. He was learning so much every day. Both new music and more about how these combustion vehicles worked. He'd even poked his nose into the still works to see how the fuel was made. It all fascinated him and the days ran by swiftly, while they all did what they could to prepare for the inevitable coming of fall.

Soon all the preparations that could be made, were. It was time for Jim and Jimi to head back to Newcity for their next trading mission.

Where hopefully, they would meet Sister Mary and trade for seeds as well. Matt raised one hand to wave at the retreating dust plume that was Jimi and his dad. They were just beginning the three day trek back towards Newcity, with canned goods and other packaged foods. All to trade for oil to the people of the city. And with reams of paper for Sister Mary, at Ashley's insistence. He thought about the message he and Ashley had asked them to share.

It had turned out that Jim and Jimi actually knew Nat and Sam, from trading with them. They had proven more than willing to share a word of mouth message to their friends, letting them know that the couple was alright.

Jim bore the list of plant seeds that Ashley had suggested, including the side note about the worm bin that she'd built. Matt was sorry that he had never gotten the chance to meet Sister Mary. When he and Ashley had first met, the idea of seeing Sister Mary's garden had truly excited him, but somehow it had never turned into the visit that they had often talked about.

Just as he had never gotten to introduce Ashley to Michael. He sighed sadly, thinking of his friend.

He thought of him constantly. Especially every time he learned a new piece of music from one of the many musicians among the traders. He thought of him most especially when he was adapting one of the fiddler's songs to play it on his guitar. He missed his friend. He could hear a hole in the music at night. The harmony his friend would have filled. When he took the time to think about the future and that Michael would not be there with him. He had to find something else to take his mind from it, or the prospect brought him close to tears.

He was feeling that way now, as he watched his new friends drive off, to go see his old friends. Knowing that he himself wouldn't likely see his old friends again. He turned to head back to the mech tent. At least he could lose himself in work on the bikes until dinner. He could fill his mind and still be doing something productive. He headed for the far tents, hoping that Jet or Jack would be up to talking. Since he didn't feel much like talking himself.

———

Ashley was exhausted, but the excitement was still coursing through her veins. Her heart was pounding, and her limbs tingled with delicious overexertion. Until moments before she had been dancing on the rugs in the firelight to the whirling gyrations of the fiddlers reel, overlaid by the hauntingly draconic counter melody that Matt coaxed from his guitar.

With Doc's battered bodrahn and Nick's tired jembe offering a grounding rhythm to her hips and feet with their drum beats, she had flown and flapped about. Eyes closed, trusting in her intuition to keep her from leaping blindly into the fire, she danced. She'd leapt and twirled in her feverish rhythm in response to the melodies Matt was coaxing from his strings.

Her dance had been a wild and unconstrained expression of her pent up feelings. Her emotions about her unborn child and the dragon dreams as well. As well as her inability to express how helpless she felt. Out here in the wastes, with such an uncertain future. Led by her body's need to move, her kicks and thrusts in time to the song, expressed the tingles and aches of muscles needing to be stretched and moved. In the end, she had worn herself out long before the musicians needed a break. She had danced till she dropped.

She lay panting on the edge of the rugs she'd been dancing on. She sprawled, with her hair in the sand at the rug's edge. Her limbs outstretched, she delighted in how cool the evening air felt against her flushed skin. Relishing in the delicious sensation, she slowly stretched her overused muscles against the warm rug covered sand. Taking a deep breath she sighed it out, just as the song came to a close.

———

Matt quietly excused himself from the other musicians, to check on Ashley where she lay. They just chuckled and waved him away as he made his way to where she lay panting in the sand. As he neared, he could see the huge smile despite her gasping breath and his half formed worries eased. Carefully setting down his guitar by the strap Nick had made him he bent to kiss her, obviously catching her by surprise.

Her startled exclamation was muffled, as was his answering chuckle as she belatedly embraced him. She allowed him to pull her into a sitting position as she resisted ending the kiss. Chuckling again at her enthusiasm, he pulled away to ask if she was really alright. Nodding she snuggled against him. Laughing out loud he gave up on going back to the music for the moment and settled in to rest a bit with her. He found that he enjoyed it here, on the edge of the firelight. As his friends continued to dance and sing and play a host of wonderful songs he didn't know.

Holding and hugging her to him in the dim light of the distant fire, he surreptitiously stroked her still flat belly with his thumb. Leaning back against him, she opened her eyes at last and brought his attention to the sky, with her gasp of surprise. Seeing a ghostly golden green glow in the clouds outlining the tents between them and the open desert, reminded him poignantly of the urban silhouette he was accustomed to. Matt found his breath caught in his throat, arrested by the surprising beauty of the unexpected spectacle.

"Look Matt! I think that's an Aurora! Remember the film? It's radiation impacting our atmosphere. Probably from solar flares from our sun. I guess its true Matt! The magnetosphere that protected our planet is gone! Or it's much weaker than it was. We shouldn't be able to see that here, it must have happened like they predicted in that 21st century film we watched."

"Hey look Ashley. It's changing color!" He said, drawing her attention again to the sky. "It's even more golden on that end now." He was excited to see this example of all that they'd been talking about. Even as he watched it shaded into pinkish red within the gold. He couldn't help but wonder what it would look like without the omnipresent cloud cover. In the film they had watched there had been dancing ribbons of light on the star spangled velvet of the sky beyond. All he could see were glowing clouds, slowly morphing their colors, but it was still beautiful.

Thinking of the rainbow ribbon streaked skies shown in the film. He couldn't help but think also, of the cities populated with happy people observing the natural light show. Which the film had portrayed.

He sighed for the optimism of that depiction. It would have been nice to experience such peace and beauty. As something other than a film of what people once thought the future would be, that is. As the lights in the sky grew rosier and the music back by the fire grew rowdier, Matt grew restless. The reels were too much for him to keep still through. Kissing Ashley awake where she'd fallen asleep in his arms, he told her he was going back to the music for a bit.

———

Murmuring a sleepy acknowledgment, she gave him a squeeze as he released her, and snuggled back into the warm rug covered sand. The desert was still radiating the heat of the day and it felt lovely, now that the night had cooled off a bit.

As Matt joined the music once more, Ashley smiled to herself, happy for his addition to the melody. It was always unique, since he had yet to learn many of the trader's songs. He usually improvised around whatever they played. Which she found delightful. Burrowing deeper into the carpets, she watched the sky, absently stoking her belly. She relaxed her eyes and tried to watch the whole sky at once, hoping for more auroras.

The sky however, remained stubbornly dark but for the radiant white glow of the moon setting to the west. Its ever inconstant glow as it waxed and waned each month was, with the sun, the only contact earth had left with the greater universe.

Stroking her belly again Ashley closed her eyes, releasing her thoughts to the music. She allowed her consciousness to ride the sound like waves. Soon she was seeing the waves of her inner sea, dancing in time to each melody played. The reels they played raising jagged spikes like chop in a storm; each rising or crashing in time to the music. Then as Matt pulled the next song into a somber waltz, it was the other musicians turn to scramble to improvise with the unfamiliar music. The waves grew calm and slow, rising elegantly against the night sky beyond.

The lumbering movements of the lazy waves were very soothing, after the noisy reels and jigs. She felt as though she was swaying gently upon the sound. Rising and falling with its rhythm, like a tiny boat upon the windswept sea.

The spikes of unexpectedly erratic waves tossed her about, as Nick filled the silence that had followed the waltz with a sudden ecstatic expression on his jembe. The rat-a-tat-tat of his lightning fingers on the tight skin of the drum brought her halfway to sitting in surprise. Nick broke off laughing, as everyone who was left around the fire looked at him in surprise. He rat-t-tatted once more with a grin before jumping up obviously filled of some mischievous energy. He ran for the outhouse as everyone laughed, at his unexpected display.

Ashley settled back to the sand, though now thoroughly awake. As the musicians chatted and tuned their instruments, in an impromptu break, over by the fire. She mused, thinking about her future and her options. She patted her belly once more, as she made up her mind. She would go talk to Carol tomorrow. She was one of the oldest women in the camp and she was at least somewhat knowledgeable. In fact she had been introduced to Ashley as being the one in charge of growing the medicinal herbs.

She would ask her some questions about childbirth tomorrow

and see if Carol mentioned any laws that the traders might have into the bargain. She sighed, depending on what Carol said, she might ask for her help. She really didn't want to face having this baby on her own. She knew that Matt would do anything for her, but she also knew that he knew even less about this then she did.

So having made her decision and content in the knowledge that Matt would support her no matter what she chose, she settled more firmly into the sand once more. One of the fiddlers struck up a long sad note to begin another round of music around the fire. Taking a deep breath she allowed her thoughts to drift, trying not to think any further, while the music played on around her.

———

As the last of the music drew to a close and the trader's slowly wandered back to their tents in ones or twos, Ashley came up and gently took his arm. Matt looked up from stowing his guitar, to see she had a small secretive smile on her lips. It was just barely visible in the glowing embers of the fire.

"What?" He asked, feeling an answering tug at his own lips. He wondered what had her in such a peculiar mood. "Well?" He coaxed when she didn't answer right away.

"Well." She responded, uncharacteristically shy. She ducked her head, bumping into his arm as she said. "I was just thinking that it's been a long time, since we've been alone together. And that we have the tent to ourselves, for a few nights at least." She smiled up at him in the soft orange light of the dying firelight and he finally caught on. He straightened quickly, as he felt a grin stretching his mouth without having consciously decided to smile.

"I see." He said, and he did. He hurriedly tied his guitar into the fabric case that Jet had made him to replace the blanket he'd wrapped it in for the trip out here. And swinging it onto his shoulder, he slipped his free arm around her waist. Pulling her close, he kissed her softly and the enthusiasm with which she returned his kiss in the warm twilight had him tingling from head to toe.

"Then let's get on and enjoy our tent tonight, shall we?" Hand in hand they walked back towards Jimi's tent.

'*Our tent, tonight.*" He corrected himself with a smile. He couldn't help but watch her silhouette against the dimly lit desert out of the corner of his eye, as she walked beside him. He admired the way her curls bounced with each step and he was grateful all over again to be here with her now.

Much later that night, Matt woke to Ashley shaking his shoulder. Softly at first but with growing urgency.

"Matt. Matt wake up." She said softly, and the desperation in her voice brought him awake faster than anything short of an earthquake could have.

"What?!? What is it?" He asked, groggily sitting up and hoping that his head was going to catch up with the rest of him. Since it vaguely felt like it was still on the pillow. Putting a hand to his face he made sure it was where it was supposed to be. Everything seemed to be attached, but he was still groggy with sleep and a yawn split his face involuntarily as he she answered.

"We have to go Matt! We have to go now!" She seemed really upset about something, and still half asleep he looked around for fire, sniffing for smoke. The only smoke he smelled was the stale smell of campfire smoke from last night's clothes where they lay crumpled a few feet away.

*'So there's no fire, what's the emergency?'*

Still trying to make sense of his thoughts, he put a hand on her shoulder where she crouched beside him.

"What is it Ashley? What's wrong? Are you feeling alright?" He had a flash of panic, that something might be wrong with the baby that brought him completely awake. He asked again, this time fully conscious.

"What is it? Is it-?" He couldn't bring himself to name his vague fears aloud, but it didn't matter since she was already shaking her head.

"I'm not sure why but we have to go! The dream was quite clear. We have to leave camp today! We have to go east, it's out there! I think that, we're almost there!" She was babbling a bit, obviously still caught up in the intensity of her dream.

Now that he was awake he could see that it wasn't yet dawn. There was no light at all seeping through the tent walls. Not even the gray light of dawn shining through cracks where walls and ceiling met. He remembered how they had been rushed from the Crystal shop by a similar feeling of portent and how following that feeling had helped them to connect with the traders just in time to catch a ride.

"All right Ashley. We'll go, but can it wait until dawn at least?

Our hosts deserve an explanation and a thank you. As well as a goodbye." He hoped that they could wait that long. He could think of no positive outcome to trying to hoof it off into the deserts in the dark with no provisions, as she seemed to be suggesting. In fact, he could think of no way for that to end, other than a lingering death by exposure when the sun rose.

"Please Ashley? We'll leave tomorrow, first thing but in the daylight." He begged, as he felt the brush of her hair on his bare shoulder as she began to shake her head. She paused mid motion.

"It stopped." She said, sounding both relieved and even further disconcerted. "The pressure, the need to go now, it just stopped. The moment you agreed to go." She sighed in relief, sagging between his hands and he echoed the sound. At least they wouldn't be taking off in the dark then.

"Alright, good. Then let's fill up on sleep while we can. It sounds like we have a long day ahead of us tomorrow." He settled back to the blankets and she nestled in beside him. Her breathing settled quickly back into the rhythm of sleep, but Matt lay awake a long time staring into the darkness of the tent. He was thinking. Wondering just what it was that was urging them onward, and whether it was guiding them to help them or for some unknown purpose of its own.

# 20

Not long after dawn the next morning he and Ashley stood ready to leave. Their stuff repacked and their bags beside them, they said their goodbyes.

"I'm so sorry that I can't stay to help you get the seeds started! That was my intent, but we have to go. I have a growing sense of urgency. We have to leave today." She had already verbally walked the women who had tended the tobacco through the process of nurturing the seedlings until they could survive on their own. She had reminded them which seeds they could plant together and how to space them, but obviously she still felt the need to apologize. It was clear that she felt like she was abandoning them, but the message of her dream last night had been implacable. They both knew it. They had to go now.

Howard just shook his head sadly. He had already tried to convince her to stay, at least until they got the seeds in. Apparently he had come to the conclusion that it was pointless to argue.

"Stubborn as a mule." Matt had heard him muttering, while Ashley had explained the seed raising process to the women in charge of it. Now he just stood, watching them sadly, waiting for their inevitable departure. He'd sent Jet and Chuck off with a motion and a few words. Matt assumed he'd sent them back to work. He was sorry about that. He would have liked the chance to say goodbye to his friends.  He understood that work had to get done though, and winter waits for no man. He sighed hard at the thought, looking up into the hills they were heading into themselves, in a few moments. Consciously, he knew what they were about to do was just as stupid, as riding out into the wastes on their bicycles in the first place.

The turn in the weather was only a month or so out. When it would change from the drastically hot summer to the drastically cold winter. Yet here they were, heading into the wilderness of the mountains without a clear destination or any shelter from the ice storms that would soon descend. He sighed, for there was no help for it. The dreams were implacable, allowing neither argument nor delay. Anytime he began to second guessing the wisdom of their choice, that same sense of urgency that had driven them from the city, would rise in his gut. He'd begin to fidget and pace with the need to move. Driven by the need to go east, as soon as possible, as fast as possible.

He felt it now, even as he wished that he could stay. The longing to stay was as sharp as his homesickness for Michael. Somehow he had come to think of many of the traders as his friends. Fighting the urge to pace with impatience, from the urgency pushing him on, he bent to lift his pack. He settled it in place upon his shoulders before reaching for his guitar. Just as he was lifting it to try getting it in place as well, he heard Jet shouting from some distance away. Looking up he saw his friend pushing a motorbike between his hands, complete with sidecar, and not far behind him, Chuck, pushing another.

"What?" He began cocking his head to one side puzzled, even as Howard stepped towards him, apparently just noticing that Matt was gearing up to go.

"They're for you guys." Howard said, answering his unfinished question. "One sidecar is full of fuel and water, and the other I thought you could get your gear in. Consider it a trade since you left your street bikes here." He gestured vaguely to where some of the kids were taking turns playing with his and Ashley's street bikes between the tents. They rode back and forth on the many layered carpets around the fire. The bikes had been completely impractical for the deserts but equally so for heading into the mountains. So they had decided to leave them here, instead of trying to carry them along in pieces. That was not a fair trade though and he opened his mouth to say as much, but Ashley beat him to it.

"You can't Howard! You know that's not even close to a fair trade! We can't possibly accept such generosity! You folks need all the resources that you have!" She would likely have said more but Howard's laugh interrupted her.

"Oh Ashley! You of all people have no room to say anything about being too generous! You've taught us all so much in a week that it's going to change the way we live for generations!" He held up a hand to stop her from arguing, as her brows drew together in preparation for a fresh spate of words. He said. "If you insist, let's consider it a loan then, alright? These babies will only help you for another month or so anyway, before the fuel hardens up. So if you can't find whatever it is that you're looking for by then, come back and winter over with us, alright? Actually the fuel won't hold out till then anyway, but it should get you a little further then your feet alone would." Seeing she still looked argumentative, he added.

"And if you aren't ready to give up your search just because of impending ice storms, then come back and you can trade these in for winter bikes, alright? We'll get you more fuel then and you can try again." She shook her head once more but she didn't argue further. Jet and Chuck rolled the huge mechanical monstrosities closer. Instead she flung her arms around Howard's neck, much to his obvious delight. Chuckling he patted her back a little awkwardly, obviously quite as overjoyed by her sudden hug, as she was by the unexpected gift of transportation.

"Thank you, Howard." Matt said with feeling. He wasn't about to argue the wisdom of having some mode of transport other than his own two feet. These may be foothills but they were still the steepest inclines he'd ever seen. He hadn't been looking forward to hiking up them with his backpack and all that he owned strapped to his back. Setting his guitar down again, he untied his belly strap to lower his backpack once more. Eyeing the approaching sidecars, he wondered just how full the one with fuel in it might be.

'*It's going to be an oftly tight fit.*' He thought as he tried to imagine all of their things in the single sidecar. '*Then again, we managed it before.*' He reminded himself. On the way out here in the first place, he had been riding in the sidecar himself after all. Yet Jim and Jimi had managed to strap all their stuff to the outside's with their nets and buckles.

"Don't mention it, it was actually Chuck's idea but we all agreed that you've both done so much for us. This is the least that we could do." Howard was smiling broadly as Ashley finally stepped away from the hug and straitened her hair a little.

"Thank you anyway, Howard. Please, thank Jim and Jimi for us when they get back! I'm sorry to have to leave without giving them a proper goodbye." She seemed subdued and Matt thought that she was trying not to cry. Taking her hand, he pulled her into a hug and she let him. Sure enough he felt wetness on his shirt and heard a small sniffle. So he held her gently until she had gotten control of her emotions again.

Once all their gear was redistributed onto the sidecars and Chuck had ran him through how to get the fuel from the tanks into the vehicles without spilling it, they settled onto the bikes ready to go. Ashley hadn't driven before so Jet walked her through the same instructions that Jimi had given Matt. Howard had a few last minute words with Matt under cover of their conversation.

"Look Matt." He said, unwontedly serious. "I don't know what it was that you two were running from when you left the city, and I don't want to know." He said quickly raising one hand to cut off Matt's half formed denial. "All I want is for you to know that you're both welcome here, anytime. No matter what we said at that first meeting. You would both be huge assets to our people and I wanted you to know that you will always, be one of us. If you ever need an *us* to belong to. Alright?" He held Matt's eyes until he nodded. Then seeming satisfied, he pulled Matt into a quick hug as well.

"Alright!" Howard repeated more loudly stepping back, as Ashley practiced the motion that started the bikes. "Last call for hugs goodbye y'all. I think these folks are heading out!" He stepped back grinning, as the kids came running to say goodbye and Matt also stood on his petal to start the bike.

Ashley copied him a little unsteadily. He was grateful, for her sake that they'd be onto firmer ground once they reached the foothills. It wasn't going to be easy for her to keep the wheel strait against the push of the sand. With the whole encampment waving a teary goodbye, they headed out. Matt took the lead and Ashley struggled to follow. When he glanced back he saw that she kept over correcting for the push of the sand and was weaving a bit. Thanks to the steadying addition of the sidecar however, she was in no danger of falling over. The determined set to her jaw reminded him of Howard's earlier comment and he repeated it to himself.

"Stubborn as a mule, indeed." Chuckling to himself he increased his speed a little. Checking to see that she was still following, it was clear that although she was struggling with the tide of the sand a bit, she was determined to make it work.

She was going to be fine.

———————

Jen was at Ashley's apartment again. She had come twice before, to water the plants. Each time though, she'd wound up getting mad at her friend and so upset at her disappearance that she'd only got the job half done before she'd quit. She'd finally finished today. Except for the two inside, she'd now watered every damn plant. Truthfully, she was still so bitter about Ashley's betrayal that she wanted to chuck the little bastards against the wall.

The only thing that stopped her was Ashley having made her watch The Sacred Life of Plants all those years ago. It had left her with the certainty, that if she followed through on her impulse, she would be murdering innocent creatures.

"Still." She eyed the African violet on the bookshelf beside her speculatively.

*'It's just the right size for chucking.'*

She sighed however, thinking again of the film. She wondered if the little plant quailed in fear at her threatening thoughts. She rather hoped so, the little stinker. She knew that it knew where Ashley had gone, and it wasn't telling. If only plants could talk, she was sure they knew where Ashley had gone and why.

She thumped to the futon and sat in front of the bookcase, half reclined and wondered if she should try to nap. She hadn't been able to sleep well since Ashley had vanished. She woke at every sound now, thinking it was Ashley returning. She was just starting to relax, when a new book on the shelf caught her eye. It wasn't one that she was familiar with and she had read most of Ashley's library over the years. It lay across the top of the other books as though it had been set down in a hurry, and as she lifted it to see what it was, she saw the title.

Dragons. She wasn't sure why she jumped at the sight.

The image on the cover was a beautiful fiery creature surrounded by purple patterning. It was lovely, but for some reason the sight sent a chill up her spine. Looking at the painting on the cover she found herself filled with both longing and dread. Sorrow and grief battled with a persistently glimmering hope within her heart, as she fought to keep from remembering. She was awash with inexplicable emotions and the terrible looming certainty that she did not want to know what frightened her. She knew that she did not want to remember whatever it was that she'd forgotten.

Reaching for her flask with one hand, she shoved the book back onto the shelf with the other, using far more force than necessary in her hurry to put it away. Her hand shook as she tipped back her flask. The fiery liquid helped to cut through her irrational fear and blunted the memories burgeoning in the back of her mind. Taking a steadying breath she dug out her cigarette case and leaned over to push the sliding door open wide.

She could revenge herself on Ashley in this small way at least.

When she got back Jen just knew that she'd complain that the apartment smelled like an ashtray.

"Serves you right." She muttered towards the little violet. She lay down lighting her cigarette, lazily blowing the smoke towards the open door. She took a perverse pleasure in knowing how mad Ashley was going to be when she got back.

Jen clung to the thought.

*'When she got back.'*

She no longer thought about the note. She kept it in her back pocket, but she did not read it. She had done nothing to follow Ashley's instructions other than watering, and she had no intention to. Instead she waited, impatient and insomniac, for her heartsister to return. As she dropped her cigarette butt into the mouth of an empty bottle, she pressed her salt dampened face into Ashley's pillow and refused to admit that she was sad.

---

After several false starts, following trails that dead ended in blind canyons, Matt and Ashley decided it might be best to hike after all. The second night they stopped they were lucky enough to find a shallow cave to overnight in. Ashley suggested that since they had more time than they had fuel, they should leave the bikes and most of their gear in the cave they'd found, and hike until they were sure of their route. Then they could return for the bikes and the rest of their gear and bring it all to their new camp.

It was in this leapfrogging pattern that they traveled, not making ground very fast, but not making as many false starts either. They traveled this way for a little more than a week, slowly getting used to the process of hiking with their day provisions, until they were sure they were going the right direction. Sometimes they would overnight before going back for the bikes, sometimes not.

Although she said nothing, Matt could see that Ashley was not always feeling well. She was starting to refuse breakfast in the mornings, drinking only water. On the twelfth day of their leapfrogging travels, he was concerned by how pale she was. By the time they'd found a cave to overnight in, he had decided it was time to change the plan.

"Look Ashley. I can tell you're not feeling well. I think we need to rethink this. We aren't making very good time this way and even though we're saving on fuel it's wearing the both of us out to hike twice the distance that we need to." It spoke to how weak she was that she didn't even argue, just nodded faintly and waited to see what else he would say.

"Now that we're out of the lowest part of the foothills there aren't as many of those gully's to get lost in, so let's rethink this. Alright? Why don't we rest here a few days? I'll head down to get my bike and our gear now, but I think I'll leave the other bike and half the fuel, in that last cave we stayed in, just in case we come back this way. It was deep enough to offer them some protection. Once we've gotten everything here, we'll reorganize and re-prioritize. I think we can get it down to one bike. All right? You can ride behind me or in the sidecar. How's that sound?" She started to shake her head but he could see that her heart wasn't in the argument.

"Look love." He said, taking her hand. He said as softly as he could. "I know that you're tough. I know that you're not used to being taken care of, but think about it as I'm taking care of our baby. If you get sick what's going to happen to the little one?" She looked stricken, and he took her hand, leaning forward to kiss her forehead gently. "I'm going to make you a bed and you are going to sleep until I get back with the bike, you got that?" His tone brooked no argument and with a sigh, she nodded. Once he had her settled in, he left to gather the remainder of their gear. He brought as much as he could with him, so he could begin reorganizing their things while she slept.

The day after next, they set out, with one backpack and one bike. They had left the majority of their non-essentials. Including all but a handful of the books in the cave, packed away as well as they could in the very back. Ashley was feeling much better for the rest, but she was still feeling ill in the mornings. He kept one eye on her where she sat straddling their water jug and hugging their backpack in the sidecar. They slowly made their way deeper into the mountains.

Another ten days travel showed no improvements in her condition but a decided difference in the amount of fuel that they had with them. They had now burned through a little more than half of what they'd had when they left the second bike and he was seriously beginning to wonder about the wisdom of pushing on.

Howard's parting words echoed in his mind and he found himself longing to take his advice and return and winter over with the traders. He kept one eye on the sky these days, nervously watching for signs of storms. He was very much aware of the lack of cover out here should the weather change suddenly. He knew it was only a matter of weeks now before the weather did change and for the worse. It was already much cooler than it had been back at the trader's camp. He had no idea if it was only because they were getting higher and higher into the mountains, or if it was the season that was about to change from hot to cold.

"Ashley. I think we should leave the bike here this time." He said as they shared some of their dwindling food supply. Before long, they'd be down to their emergency rations. Which were lighter weight, but he was concerned that they would not be enough to support Ashley's growing need for more. After all she was growing a whole other person in her still flat belly and he didn't think that the dried goods had been designed to provide for growing babies too. She still insisted that they press on however and he too was feeling the urgent message to go east every time he woke. Although not nearly so strongly as she seemed to. He wondered if maybe his skepticism about the source of the wordless wisdom, was perhaps buffering his emotional response to the summons.

"Because of the fuel?" She asked nodding. "I was thinking that too. If we coast part of the way we would have just enough to get back to the other bike from here, with what we have left. I still hope that there really is somewhere that we're going to, out here somewhere." She looked wistfully out the mouth of the cave as though their unknown destination might simply appear before her.

As it had, he supposed, in her dreams. He had yet to be graced with such a clear vision of their destination. So far he had received only the desperate urge to keep moving. He had to trust to what she said she had seen. A beautiful garden of verdant green. He sighed. It would have been so much easier to believe, if he had seen it too. Of course, if he had seen it then it wouldn't count as belief. Shaking his head at his own circuitous thoughts, he agreed with her assessment. So again, he opened their remaining backpack to try to lighten their load once more.

Leaving their dirtiest clothing behind didn't lighten the load any but he had a second incentive for doing so, scent. Two nights ago they had both been startled awake by the howl of dogs in the distance. Huddling closer together, eyes wide with fear in the darkness, he had realized that if those dogs were anywhere nearby, they would smell him and Ashley. Given how little wildlife he had actually seen out here in the mountains so far, he was betting that they were hungry.

So they scrubbed themselves down with as little of their dwindling water as they could and left their smelliest clothes behind with the bike, hoping that the dogs might find that instead of them, if they came this way. They traveled on foot, even deeper into the mountains. Hoping against hope, that they'd come to their destination before their food ran out. Or that they'd come to the conclusion that there was no destination, so that they could begin the long trek back to the traders camp in the foothills.

Just as the light of another day began to fade, and they were looking around for any kind of shelter for the night Matt heard a howl. He saw Ashley's head snap up, looking back the way they had come.

"That wasn't far away." Her voice shook a little as she said it and he found his hand was trembling as he reached to take hers. "I think they found our trail." She turned to look at him in the amber light of the setting sun. "Dog's run really fast Matt." She whispered, her mouth pinched with fear. "Really fast, especially hungry dogs."

She didn't elaborate, but then she didn't have to. As a second howl answered the first, sounding even closer yet.

"I think we'd better run." He whispered back, his eyes wide. He hadn't meant to whisper, but his throat had closed with fear.

"There's nowhere to run to!" She argued desperately, but tugging her hand he broke into a jog in the direction they were already heading. There had been a little bit of a path here and he prayed that it led to another cave.

'Or a hill.' He thought desperately. 'A stone cabin, anything defensible!' He didn't remember when his jog had become a trot but Ashley was keeping up with him without saying a word. On the third howl, sounding almost on their heels they both broke into a wild run following the narrow path blindly into another canyon. They both ran almost mindless with atavistic terror.

As they ran through the narrow canyon, his eyes scanned the walls of the gully, desperately looking for a rout to the top. Only then did he realize their mistake, the walls of the narrow cleft were growing taller and more rocky as they ran, not a sign of an exit in sight and he realized where he had seen this pattern before. In the other blind canyons they had gone down. Only this time they could not simply retrace their steps and try again. This time there were wild dogs all but nipping at their heels.

The triumph, clear in the howls he hard behind him, spurred his panic. He sprinted faster than he had ever run in his life. As he rounded a bend, he realized too late that they had reached the dead end of the blind canyon. He was going so fast that he was all but dragging Ashley forward by their joined hands, and in his haste, his momentum was such that he could not stop. Even when he saw the confusing maw, of some rectangular beast, loom from the dusk shrouded canyon before him. As he hit the bars on the back of the cage in his forward rush he heard a clang behind him. Turning he saw that he had dragged Ashley into a huge trap. They were penned in a huge structure now, tall enough to stand up in and maybe barley wide enough for him to lie down. He shook the bars he had crashed into in the fading light but they held steady, barely moving for all the force that he could throw at them.

Ashley's whimper of fear brought his attention back to the mouth of the canyon in time to see a huge wild dog stalk stiff legged around the corner that hid the end of the canyon. It was halfway between the size of Bella and Jo. Its brown speckled short black fur made it seem to vanish anytime it held still, in the fading light, of the long since retreated sun.

He could just make out shadows he thought were its ribs showing and its teeth flashed whitely in the gathering dusk as it growled. The sound made the hair rise on the back of his neck. Shuddering, he pulled Ashley into his arms. The two of them huddled together in the very center of the huge cage. As the dog advanced, legs stiff and hackles raised, its growl rolled over them like thunder before a storm. It wasn't until it threw itself at the cage, growling and clawing that Matt realized that perhaps those implacable bars would protect them from the beast. He held Ashley tightly against him as it clawed and growled, whining its frustration at being unable to reach them.

Suddenly it spun, facing back the way it had come, hackles rising again. Its growl grew threatening again rather than frustrated. As two more dogs both solid black in the darkness, visible only as separate pieces of moving shadow and glinting eyes, came around the bend and into the end of the blind canyon. Their growls rose in intensity, as the three dogs fought vocally for dominance, before the fighting began in earnest. Silent as the shadow it seemed a part of, one of them leapt upon the dog with the brown streaks.

The shrieking barks and ferocious growls of the fighting rose in intensity, as they wrestled and bit only a few feet away. It was almost deafening and Matt pressed Ashley's face hard against his chest trying to shelter her from the sound. He could feel her sobbing against him but whether in fear or in misguided sympathy for the dogs themselves, he did not know.

The fight seemed to continue forever. The cacophony of sounds continuing to rise in intensity, until one or another of the dogs got a bite in, on some tender bit of flesh. The wild yip of pain startled the attackers long enough, for the injured dog to break and run. Pelting back the way they had come, the other two gave chase a moment later, leaving Matt and Ashley suddenly the sole possessors of the tiny box canyon. The only sound now that of Ashley's muffled sobs.

After what seemed to be an eternity of waiting, when none of the dogs returned Matt slowly unlocked his knees. He slid to a half kneeling, half crouched position, perforce dragging Ashley's limp and sobbing form with him. They huddled there together in the center of the giant cage and he didn't have the energy to wonder how it had gotten here. He only barely registered his gratitude that it had somehow saved their lives.

He didn't remember sleeping. At some point he must have passed out however, because it was lightening to the east when he was awakened. By the sudden jab of a sharp stick.

Coming awake all at once, Matt flailed his arms, accidentally hitting Ashley were she lay huddled against him. She came awake with a cry, sitting up and backing away as though anticipating another attack. As they blinked at one another in confusion, Matt's attention was drawn outside the cage they were still in, by a repetition of what had woken him. Awake now he caught the stick in his hand, and his eyes followed its length in surprise. At its end he saw a battered old man. His white hair obscured by an equally battered white fedora. The lines around the old man's eyes deepened as he squinted down at his captives, in the dim light of dawn. They stared back at him. Apprehensive, and unsure of his motives.

'*Is he here to help us?*' Matt wondered. '*Or have we been caught, yet again?*'

"You're human." The old man said slowly, his voice rough. As though he had not spoken in a while. He coughed and tried again. "Haven't seen any other humans in, a long time." He spoke slowly, seeming to search for words. As though it had indeed been a long time since he'd had a conversation. "How did you get here? Where did you come from? Are there more of you?" He frowned as he asked. As though there being more of them would be some terrible crime.

He didn't seem friendly and Matt was unsure which question to answer first, let alone how much to tell him.

*'Then again. If we can't convince him to let us out of here, we're gonna starve to death pretty quick.'* They had somehow dropped all of their gear, in their erratic flight from the dogs and he was suddenly aware of how very thirsty he was. While the water, was in his backpack somewhere back on the side of the mountain. As he gathered his thoughts to decide which question to answer first, the old man studied them. He seemed ready to wait all day, for the answers he was looking for. He made no move to open the cage. No motion to release them and Matt sighed, trying to think of just what the old man might want to hear. Ashley, it seemed, had recovered from her fright however and stood up. Putting one hand on Matt's shoulder she took it upon herself to answer the man.

"We are traveling alone, if that's what you mean. We were chased by wild dogs, into this cage." She gestured with her free hand, Matt having covered her hand on his shoulder with his own. "It seems that it saved our lives last night. If it's your cage, then I would very much like to thank you." Matt scowled, finally releasing his grip on the stick. He saw no reason to thank the man, when he hadn't been here. He certainly hadn't put this cage here to help them. Then again, perhaps it would be best to be polite for now, at least until he let them out of the trap.

Sighing he nodded, agreeing with her.

"Yes. Thank you, if this is your trap. Which I guess it probably is, since you're here now. We would have been dog food without it." He shuddered, thinking of how close they had come to becoming part of the lower end of the food chain last night.

"In fact another few inches and we might have been dog food anyway." He shuddered again. He felt some of the tension finally drain from his shoulders as his overactive hindbrain, finally acknowledged that the predator was well and truly gone. He took another look at their current captor.

*'At least the obvious predator is gone. But just who is this guy who lives in the wilds and doesn't like humans?'* He wondered.

"And where did you come from? Are there more people there?" He asked, his frown deepening at having to repeat himself. Once again Ashley answered honestly before Matt could think of what to say.

"Well yes. We came most recently from the trader's camp at the foot of the mountains. They were kind enough to help us on our way, but we both come from Newcity. It's in the center of the wastes or as near as I can tell." She frowned a little, probably doubting her own description, but the old man's eyebrow's rose to nearly touch his hairline.

"The city you say?" He asked incredulously. "There are people, living in a city? Seriously?" He seemed completely shocked and Matt wondered just how long he had been out here in the mountains, not to know of the only human city around. He noticed the old man looked much less intimidating when he wasn't frowning and worked up the courage to ask his name.

"My name's MacArthur, but you can just call me Mac. Everybody... well, everybody used to." He finished lamely, his voice trailing off as his eyes got the faraway look that Matt associated with people looking into the past. He'd seen it a lot growing up in this day and age. Most people preferred to spend time with their memories, rather than the wreckage of the world they were faced with now.

Standing, he took Ashley's hand in his and said.

"I'm Matt, and this is Ashley. I'm sorry if we've inconvenienced you in any way, but could you possibly let us out now? I'm afraid it was a rather eventful night and I uh-" He tried cracking a smile to make a joke of it. "I have to admit I've really got to pee." He grinned crookedly, hoping that the old man was as friendly as he suddenly seemed. He was much less gruff now that they had answered his questions. Without the scowl, he actually had a very kind, if careworn face.

"Hrmph." Mac responded. Giving Matt an odd look. Then he worked his way to the side of the cage facing the canyon mouth he pulled a lever that Matt hadn't noticed. The whole side of the cage rose slowly. Grunting with effort as he held it high, Mac twisted another lever of wood to hold it up. Stepping back he swung one hand in a, be my guest, kind of gesture. He flushed a deep crimson when Ashley smiled at him her thanks obvious. Before she left the cage and scrambled around the bend, probably also to relieve herself. "So what are you two doing out here? Just where are you trying to get to in this wilderness and without so much as a stitch of extra clothes?" Mac raised one eyebrow, having taken in the lack of any visible supplies.

Matt explained that he'd dropped their gear in order to outrun the dogs last night, but that they had food and some water, if they retraced their steps to where it had fallen. Excusing himself, Matt went to the other side of the cage to pretend he had some privacy and relieved himself, while Mac pretended not to notice. About the time that Matt was heading around the bend of the canyon, to look for their supplies, Ashley came back that way carrying them. It looked as though the dogs had only lightly chewed their backpack, and not finding it tasty, had come after them instead.

She set it down to fish out their water, offering it first to Matt and then to Mac, before she drank some herself. Mac waved away the offer but he smiled at the gesture. Matt was sure now that the old man was not a threat to them, but just a grumpy old hermit. He asked Mac why he was out here, but Mac only shook his head refusing to explain. He insisted instead that they answer his questions first, as to what they were doing out here and where they were going. He grew very thoughtful, as Ashley explained that they were heading east, in the hopes of finding the old seed banks, and that they were planning on trying to rehabilitate the land with what they found there.

He seemed ever more kindly disposed towards them, the longer they talked and finally he smiled, as he took off his hat and wiped his face with his sleeve. They had been talking for quite a while, as Matt and Ashley shared out some of their rations. Ashley again offered some to Mac, but he waved it away with a smile. The sun had risen while they spoke, so it was growing quite warm. Although not as hot as it had been in the height of summer. By the time they had answered all of his questions to Mac's satisfaction, they were all hot and sweating. Ashley was waving one hand, to fan herself.

Mac had been particularly interested, as Ashley explained the self-watering containers she had built and those that she had helped the traders to build. His heavy white brows had risen again, as she explained about Sister Mary and her seed collection and how they had sent Jimi and his dad to trade for seeds and worms from her.

He'd actually smiled, as Ashley spoke about the worms, and of how they're essential to the long term production of good quality vegetables. He didn't interrupt. Even when she grew a little long winded espousing the benefits of worm castings and companion planting. He just smiled and listened, nodding once in a while as though he agreed.

Matt was just thinking that maybe he had been wrong about the man being a hermit, when Mac suddenly stood. Slapping his hands on his knees raised little clouds of dust from his pants as he said.

"I think I've heard enough." He gave them both a measuring look and said. "Alright, here's the deal, I still need to run my trap line and make sure nothing and no one, is caught in any of my other traps, before I head back. But once I'm done, you two are welcome to come home with me if you like. You can come by for a spot of tea, as it were." He grinned and Matt had to chuckle at the incongruity of talking about tea and trap lines in the same breath.

"This is actually the closest trap to my place so why don't you two wait here the day and I'll swing back by on my way home and lead you to it. I should be back around just about suppertime. If you're willing to wait, that is. Unless your quest is so pressing that you feel the need to move on?" He looked at them questioningly, apparently quite willing to let them leave if they wished. That last reassured Matt that Mac had no designs on them but was honestly just offering his hospitality.

"I don't know." Matt began as he looked at Ashley to see what she thought but she was already nodding. "All right then." He said with a smile. "We would be honored to accept your hospitality for the night Mac, again." He gestured vaguely back towards the trap and Mac laughed out loud. He had a good laugh, Matt was happy to hear and he was glad that Mac had gotten the joke.

"I can assure you that tonight's accommodations, while not the Ritz, will be a hundred times more comfortable then last nights." Still chuckling to himself, he gave them a jaunty wave and left, whistling a little tune. Apparently he was either glad to be running his trap lines or more likely, excited to have unexpected guests.

As soon as he was out of sight, Matt turned to Ashley to ask if this was really alright. He was glad for the break from travel, more for her sake then his own, but she had been so doggedly determined that they push on before now. He was surprised that she had agreed to wait the whole day just to stay the night with Mac.

When he asked her though she shook her head and said.

"Can't you feel it Matt?" Shaking his head to show he didn't understand, she took his hand. "The urgency is gone. I don't know why but the pressure to head east suddenly eased up as soon as Mac offered to let us stay the night." She smiled, as his he felt his eyes widen in surprise.

"Does that mean-?" She was already shaking her head.

"I don't know what it means Matt, but I think that it means we are supposed to stay the night with him. For whatever reason, we are supposed to be here right now." She looked east thoughtfully, as though wondering just what it was that was drawing them onward. He joined her in looking, although there was nothing to see but the convoluted folds of the mountain range they had been pressing steadily deeper into. He also wondered just what it was that they were being drawn towards, and what it could possibly mean that the urgent pressure had stopped.

After an afternoon of lazing about recovering from the night before, Mac had arrived for them at twilight. Matt had just begun getting nervous about the dogs coming back in the lowering light, when Mac had arrived and led them unceremoniously away. He led them up through a valley leading north and then a little west. Finally bringing them the not so short a distance to this cliff face, all without any explanation as to where he actually lived. Matt was totally turned around at his point, unsure where they were or what direction they faced. Mac had stopped at the base of the sheer rock cliff before them, waving a hand towards the stone.

"Welcome to Paradise." Mac gestured grandly towards a deep crevice in the otherwise sheer stone cliff, just a dark gash in the hillside in the gathering twilight. With a grin over his shoulder at them, he crawled over the rubble at the base of the crack and carefully stepping around the small ferns clinging to the rock he climbed into the narrow hole into what appeared to be a solid hill. As Matt stepped forward to follow, Ashley stopped him with a hand on his arm.

"What is it?" He asked her, turning to see her face. What he could see of her expression in the twilight looked excited but worried too. He cocked his head questioningly, wondering at her sudden hesitance.

She sighed and bit her lip a moment then said.

"Doesn't it remind you of the stories about Faerie? Randomly meeting the perfect person on the road and having them lead us off to a crack *into a hill*?" She giggled a little nervously, gesturing ahead of them in the twilight. "I'm warning you now Matt if its daylight in there or he starts flying around or something, don't eat anything! Or we can never go home!" She said it with such desperate panic that he couldn't help but laugh. She glared at him, obviously fighting to keep from giggling.

"I'm serious!" She said stepping over to him and poking him with one finger. "We could be stuck in Faerie forever…" She smiled up at him teasingly.

Wrapping his arms around her and pulling her close he kissed her lightly.

"Ashley." He said with a smile. "Stuck in Faerie with you sounds like heaven to me." He winked at her as she laughed at his cheesy line. Taking her hand, he led the way up the slippery rocks at the base of the crevasse, into which their guide had disappeared.

Matt kept Ashley's hand in one of his as he stepped into the crack. He stopped with one leg in and one leg out and grinned over his shoulder at her.

"See, I don't feel any different." Still grinning, Matt stepped fully into the dark cavernous crevasse. It was much wider within than it had looked like from outside. He reached out to try to touch a wall and had to take a step to find it. It was so dark within that he had no idea where the wall was until his hand encountered it so he decided not to let go. "Hold onto me Ashley, its dark in here, don't trip." After an intermittent time of stepping carefully one hand on each other and each with one hand on the cavern wall they traveled through the long dark tunnel.

"I think I see something!" Ashley was sure she'd seen a glimmer of light ahead. "Up there, on the right! There's light ahead!" She pulled a little at Matt's hand as she hurried down the tunnel. They had tried to call out to their guide, once they had gone within the hill but there had been no answer. So hoping that there was only one tunnel, they had followed the right hand wall of the cavern so far.

"Hello!" She tried again to hail the man they had been following.

Surly he would have waited at the entrance to whatever place they were going to. Straining her ears, she was startled to hear a definite reply from up ahead.

"So there you are! Hurry up you two! Or you're gonna miss the sunset!" His voice echoed back strangely through the tunnel, distorted and odd sounding. Ashley shuddered a little involuntarily.

She turned to Matt with a strained smile in the dark.

"Sunset? I thought it was almost night!" He put one arm around her and propelled her forward, laughing a little.

"I'm telling you Ashley I think it's alright. I have a good feeling about this." He did too. He wasn't sure why, but he just felt like it was right for them to be here. He couldn't wait to see what was waiting for them at the end of this tunnel, and not just because he was tired and hungry either. He grinned at his own pragmatism as his stomach growled.

"As I said." The voice of their guide floated down the tunnel to meet them just as Matt came close enough to see that the light on their right had been nothing but a reflection. The tunnel made a sharp left here, opening into a beautifully carved archway. It was carved of white stone, rounded and curving with green leaves dripping into the open mouth of the cavern they were about to leave.

"Welcome to Paradise!" Their guide stood grinning, arms crossed at the top of a set of stone stairs that were roughly head high. They lead from the archway that they stood in, to a golden sky and draping greenery beyond.

Smiling at Ashley, Matt took her hand and started up the steps. As they came eye level with the ground around them he could see that they were coming out onto the floor of a plateau, upon the ridge of an opening valley. As he looked up, to take it all in, his mind swam with all the green he was surrounded by.

Having grown up, isolated in a landscape of broken buildings and cracked concrete, to suddenly be surrounded by so many plants was mind boggling. Add in that Ashley had him more than half convinced that plants had thoughts and feelings too, so really he was surrounded by dozens, no thousands of other living organisms. Of conscious beings, plants, people.

"Wow."

The valley around them was breathtakingly green and overgrown with tangled vines of all varieties hanging from trees and cliffs alike.

Matt's mind couldn't quite take it all in. He'd never dreamed that so much greenery could grow in one place. It was like the jungles he had seen in some of the movies in the library. Only it was living, vibrant and all around him. He took a deep breath of the succulent air.

*'It even smells green!'* Sweet and savory at once, the air had a soft moistness, unlike he'd ever felt. Except maybe in that dank flooded basement back in the crystal shop.

"Welcome to my home." Mac said quietly, as they both craned their necks to take it all in. "Not many outsiders have gotten to see it actually. I'm really glad you're here." He smiled at them both, the lines around his eyes deepening in amusement at their reactions. Turning, he lead the way down a slight slope through the jungle of plants following a path that was obviously well worn, made up of large flattish stones with smaller stones between.

Matt noticed that small plants were growing in between the smaller rocks and sometimes up onto the big rocks as well. He wondered vaguely what kind of plants they were, but didn't think about it long. He was still straining his neck trying to see everything at once. He could smell the sweet tang of the plants bruised beneath their feet, and he tried to be more conscious of where he was stepping. He noticed that Ashley, ahead of him, was somehow managing to walk only on the rocks even while she gawked at the plants of the valley surrounding them.

Without warning the plants surrounding them so closely as to almost seem to be pressing in on them, were gone and the walls of the narrow valley palled apart opening up with every step they took. The valley, narrow though it had been around the entrance they had come in through, suddenly opened up into a huge valley spreading out below them. The walls receded to far cliffs covered in vegetation, and they found themselves standing on a densely vegetated bluff, over an abundant green valley.

The golden-orange light of the setting sun was beautiful, but blinding as it poured over the valley below them.

"Oh wow." Ashley said, shading her eyes so she could see better. "Oh, wow... Is this what is used to look like Mac?" She turned to look at him, an earnest look in her eye. "Is this how the world used to be? I want to believe it, but I need to hear it!" Her eyes pleaded with him to tell her it was true.

That the world really had been a green and fertile place once, and so possibly, could be again. Matt put his arm around her shoulders, squeezing her gently, and turning she buried her face in his chest. Matt was almost in tears himself at the sight of so much uninterrupted life. It was amazing and a little overwhelming. After traveling though the stark barren wastelands as they had been for the last few weeks.

"It's how the whole world used to be, at one point or another. Just as the whole world was under water once and the whole world has frozen solid more than once. You know the world even began its life as a molten ball of fire. Don't take it so hard Ashley, the world is made of change and made by change. Without change everything would grow stagnant and die. Don't morn for what we've lost, that's done now. Instead rejoice for what may yet be! Look around you! Hope is abundant and it is a vibrant green!" He patted her shoulder gently and she smiled at him through her tears.

"Oh! Thank you Mac! Thank you for sharing this with us. Did you make this place?" At his slight nod she said again. "Thank you! For proving that it can be done, even now!" Her grin was wide and seemed to encompass the world.

Mac laughed out loud, obviously equally amazed at having come across them the way he had. "The world works in mysterious ways." He muttered to himself.

The breeze picked up a little, bringing with it the sweet scents of the millions of lush green plants blanketing the valley that spread out below them. Matt smiled, listening to the hum of the wind through the trees. It keened softly, a sad but welcoming sound.

"Do you hear that Ashley?" He asked, pointing it out to her. "Green music! Like in that movie about the plants! They're singing!" He grinned down at her as she nodded. He couldn't help thinking out loud. "It is paradise, isn't it Ashley?"

His hand softly on Ashley's belly, where she stood wrapped in his arms, their eyes shone with matching excitement. Matt's smile was so bright it eclipsed the setting sun, as he repeated Mac's greeting out loud.

"Welcome to Paradise."


To be continued...
Look for book two of **DRAGON DREAMS** coming soon!

Excerpt from Book Two of **DRAGON DREAMS**
# DRAGON'S DAWN : DRAGON'S SONG

He'd gotten word from Matt! Michael couldn't wait to tell Jen.
When he reached the landing, he pounded the door as lightly as his
excitement would let him.

"Jen! Are you here? I need to talk to you! Anybody there?" He
pounded again, just as he herd grumbling and fussing on the other
side of the door. Once inside, his news burst forth all unbidden.

"They sent us a message Jen! They said that they're sorry for
leaving, but that they love us." His smile turned to a grimace at the
pittance of information. "But that's not good enough damn it! It's
just not! I want to know where they are! I want to know why they
left! And I sure as hell want the chance to wring his neck for not
taking me with him! Damn it!"

He stopped pacing to face her and continued.

"I don't know how you feel about it Jen. Maybe your content to
just stay here waiting forever and drink yourself to death but I'm not.
I'm gonna talk to Greg about leaving and I'm gonna find those
Traders. I'm gonna make them take me to him. Wherever he is! If
they have a message from him, then they must know where he is! I'm
not about to let the only clue we've had in all this time get away!"

———

Jen gave a little more thought to what he had said about leaving.
About going after them. Wanting to follow these trader fellows out
into the wastes, to try to hunt down their friends.

It was preposterous!

It was ludicrous!

It was, exactly what she'd been dreaming about when he
knocked. Taking a deep drag off her cigarette she thought seriously
for a moment about her dreams.

They had taken on a different quality since she had moved into
Ashley's apartment. Instead of dreaming of the dragons, she was
hovering over the world. Long before the shift. No humans yet. Just
animals, and birds and trees and plants. As she watched the story, of
how the world unfurled.

Her thirsty mind drank in the sight of the stars all around her,
the real stars! With swirling galaxies and nebulas. Things she'd only

read about with Ashley. Now it seemed that wherever she turned her attention, her vision would focus. She found that she could see in detail the images of galaxies that were very far away.

A sudden sense of urgency drew her attention back towards the beautiful jewel of a planet, hanging in the glistening space before her. Just in time to see catastrophic changes occurring across its surface. Her breath caught in horror at the sight of the entire sky filled with beautiful swirling spirals. She realized that each one was a ferocious storm. Like the one that she and Ashley had lived through as kids. From here and now, though, she could clearly see that everyone had suffered equally. The whole world, devastated. As the earth went into wild and turbulent movements before the clouds simply settled into a thin atmospheric fog.

*'This is how it is now.'* She thought. She turned, looking for someone with whom to share her thoughts. But she was alone in the Universe except for the little earth before her.

*'No rain, because there's no wind. No wind because there's no sunlight hot enough to warm the water. Nor any ice at the poles to cool it. Nothing but tepid water and tepid air. Nothing to cause convection and thus no circulation. It's like the planet has stopped breathing…'*

She sighed heavily wishing she could smoke a cigarette in a dream. Only to again feel her attention being pulled towards the little planet below. She looked closer, to try to see what was nagging at her now.

She found herself looking for Newcity and found it much faster then she would have thought. There she saw two men, both dusty and dirty, slowly walking their bikes out of the city. She knew that area of the Outskirts. It wasn't too far from where Ashley had discovered that crystal shop.

She wondered if this dream was accurate. Or if it was all just make believe. That last question seemed to send a ripple through the Universe she floated in. The world before her began to fade away.

*'No! Oh no! I didn't mean it!'* She thought frantically, but it was too late. The images faded around her, leaving her somewhere between waking and sleeping. Until she'd been startled fully awake by someone pounding on her door.

She eyed Michael speculatively where he was pacing restlessly around the tiny kitchen.

"How serious were you about what you said?" Jen asked him

suddenly. The change of subject seemed to catch him by surprise.

"What the hell are you talking about Jen?" Michael stared at her. He seemed to be unsure whether she had really woken up yet or not.

"Do you mean about Matt? About finding him?" His look turned far more serious as she nodded. "I'm dead serious. I'm gonna go find him. As soon as I possibly can. As soon as I know where to look. I'm going after him. What about you? Have you made up your mind?" He looked a little surprised at her apparent change of heart.

"Then get packed. Let's go!" She grinned, as his jaw sagged in surprise, shrugging. "We'd better go now if we want to catch them. The traders are already on the edge of the city."

She smiled again as he stared at her, and reaching over she grabbed her pack off the chair. She dumped the library books out of it to start packing.

"Now hold on just a minute! How do you know that?" He asked her incredulously. She just shrugged and finished packing. "You can't just say something like that and then just leave me hanging! How in the hell do you know where they are? And how do you even know *who* they are? Common Jen, spill it." He glared at her.

He was obviously unable to think of a single way, that she could know, what she claimed she knew.

She glared right back at him and said nothing.

*'Ashley would have told him'.* She knew.

Ashley would have proudly proclaimed that she'd had a vision and that they should all follow it. Jen wasn't that credulous though.

She didn't think Michael was either. Jen wrote a quick note to Sister Mary, pleading with her to find someone to water the plants once a week.

She worked on it while Michael wrote his own note to Greg, begging his forgiveness for leaving so suddenly.

---

"I don't mean to abandon you. You've given everything to me and I can never thank you enough. But my guide is leaving without me and I have to go now. I have to go, or I'll never know what happened to Matt. I'm so sorry."

As Michael wrote those final words, he realized what Matt had meant by his own note. As well as by the new message they had received. Matt was never coming back. He had planned a new course, and he didn't think it would bring him back here again.

The dreams had changed. Matt was no longer a dragon but himself. There was still that heavy feeling in the air though. That weight, which he associated with the past. He was in a huge cavern and there was a soft glow off to his left. It felt strange after so many dreams of flying or of sauntering on all fours, to be walking through these caverns in human form.

As he came to the last bend before the glow of the chamber below, he hesitated. He wondered just what he might find, and whether he was truly ready for such an encounter.

He was completely lucid. Conscious that he was dreaming, he remembered the long talks he'd had with Ashley about the dreams. He knew why he was here and he knew that he must go on, but still he hesitated.

*'What if we're wrong?'* He asked himself. *'What if these creatures are no friends of ours? Why would they want to help us?'*

**'More to the point would be, why would we want to harm you?'** The voice echoed strangely. It seemed to resound within his head. Matt took a moment to realize the implicit meaning, of receiving an answer to his thought.

*'Well, if it can read my thoughts, then there really is no use in hiding.'* He reasoned with himself.

**'My thoughts exactly. Get out here where I can get a look at you.'** Easing into the glow, Matt could just make out a huge silhouette, but the shape was momentarily meaningless. **'Do you really need to wonder as to my shape Mathew? Even after all that we have shared?'** Matt froze again.

"How would I know your shape then?" His voice cracked. He knew he was being deliberately dense, but despite having talked about the possibility with Ashley, he really had not been prepared for this to be real.

**'If you had not been prepared for it, it would not have happened. You may not understand it yet, Mathew but you are an important part of the future of this planet.'** The head of the creature before him, turned into the light a little so that he could make out some details of its shape and his breath caught.

"You're me! Or well, maybe I was you? How can that be?" Matt exclaimed as he recognized the features of the dragon that he had dreamed himself to be. Ashley had rendered them perfectly in her drawing of them in flight together.

The dragon before him laughed. A rumbling below and of a growl but the good humor pouring from its mind, had his lips twitching though he didn't get the joke.

*'I'm you! That's rich! Indeed! Although I have existed far longer than any of your race! You see me and exclaim, 'You're me!' That's hilarious!'* Laughing again the dragon reared back on its considerable haunches. *'You are an amusing creature Mathew. Although I must admit that I had not anticipated you being, so very small.'* The dragon cast a dubious eye on him. Matt squirmed. It was quite formidable having such a large and ferocious creature frown at you.

"You're an alarmingly large creature yourself, dragon. I had not expected you to be so large either." He took heart in its apparent intelligence and good humor. He did decide to be as honest as possible, especially considering that it apparently read his thoughts. "Um, not to be rude, but just how is it that you know my name anyhow, dragon?" The dragon cut short it's chortling to give him a sharp look.

*'Dragon this and dragon that. I find it rude that you don't know my name, human.'* The dragon glared at him lowering its head, coming far too close for comfort as it watched him. The hair came up on the back of his neck as its hot sulfurous breath washed over him.

*'How is it that you have shared my dreams? My thoughts, my very memories... and yet you do not know my name?'* He stopped with his head only feet from where Matt stood petrified, looking into the ever changing eyes of the dragon. Blue one moment, green the next its quicksilver eyes watched him, waiting for a response as he held his breath in fear.

Sighing, the dragon snaked his long neck back. It settled its head on its crossed forepaws.

*'I see. You don't understand our shared dreams, you had no idea it was going on. You don't even know how you got here. What a bother. Well until you can release your fear and hear my name, I am afraid that I have no further use for you. Goodbye.'*

Matt woke clinging to the blankets, slick with sweat. The voice of the dragon ringing in his ears. **_'Until you release your fears and hear my name I have no further use for you…'_**

'*What did he mean by release my fears? What did he mean by hear his name?*'

Excerpt from Book Two of **DRAGON DREAMS**
**DRAGON'S DAWN : DRAGON'S SONG**

Look for it soon!

# ABOUT THE AUTHOR

Chandelle Hazen is an avid permaculture advocate
as well as an artist and musician, who is very passionate about
sustainability practices. This is only the first installment of the
Dragon Dreams series, so look forward to more. Chandelle lives in
the beautiful Pacific Northwest, where she enjoys reading, gardening
and cuddling with her many cats.

Made in the USA
Middletown, DE
09 July 2017